Romantic Suspense

Danger. Passion. Drama.

Defending The Child
Sharon Dunn

Lethal Wilderness Trap
Susan Furlong

MILLS & BOON

DEFENDING THE CHILD
© 2025 by Sharon Dunn
Philippine Copyright 2025
Australian Copyright 2025
New Zealand Copyright 2025

First Published 2025
First Australian Paperback Edition 2025
ISBN 978 1 038 94059 9

LETHAL WILDERNESS TRAP
© 2025 by Susan Furlong
Philippine Copyright 2025
Australian Copyright 2025
New Zealand Copyright 2025

First Published 2025
First Australian Paperback Edition 2025
ISBN 978 1 038 94059 9

MIX
Paper | Supporting
responsible forestry
FSC® C001695
www.fsc.org

Published by
Harlequin Mills & Boon
An imprint of Harlequin Enterprises (Australia) Pty Limited
(ABN 47 001 180 918), a subsidiary of HarperCollins
Publishers Australia Pty Limited
(ABN 36 009 913 517)
Level 19, 201 Elizabeth Street
SYDNEY NSW 2000 AUSTRALIA

Cover art used by arrangement with Harlequin Books S.A.. All rights reserved.

Printed and bound in Australia by McPherson's Printing Group

Defending The Child

Sharon Dunn

MILLS & BOON

Ever since she found the Nancy Drew books with the pink covers in the country school library, **Sharon Dunn** has loved mystery and suspense. In 2014, she lost her beloved husband of nearly twenty-seven years to cancer. She has three grown children. When she is not writing, she enjoys reading, sewing and walks. She loves to hear from readers. You can contact her via her website at sharondunnbooks.net.

Books by Sharon Dunn

Wilderness Secrets
Mountain Captive
Undercover Threat
Alaskan Christmas Target
Undercover Mountain Pursuit
Crime Scene Cover-Up
Christmas Hostage
Montana Cold Case Conspiracy
Montana Witness Chase
Kidnapped in Montana
Defending the Child

Alaska K-9 Unit

Undercover Mission

Pacific Northwest K-9 Unit

Threat Detection

Mountain Country K-9 Unit

Tracing a Killer

Visit the Author Profile page at millsandboon.com.au for more titles.

To every thing there is a season,
and a time to every purpose under the heaven.
—*Ecclesiastes* 3:1

For my readers as always,
whose encouragement keeps me writing.

Chapter One

Marielle Coleman awoke to the sound of someone moving around in her house. The noises emanating from downstairs were muffled, and her first thought was that her four-year-old foster son, Ian, had crawled out of his bed and gone downstairs for a snack. Not something he had ever done before, but maybe he was starting to feel more comfortable here.

Her pounding heart told her something more sinister was taking place. Still listening, she sat up in bed and pulled back the covers.

Another noise reached her ears, a heavy boot tread on the floorboards, probably coming from downstairs. Her breath caught in her throat. She had not imagined an intruder. Someone was definitely in the house—and she had reason to be afraid. Ian was the only witness to a crime in which his mother, Kristen, had been killed and his father, David, had disappeared. Police believed that Ian had seen the man who killed his mother, but the boy had gone mute from the trauma. He could only nod or shake his head when asked questions. The police were not sure if the murderer knew Ian had witnessed the crime, but this home invasion confirmed that he had.

Her chest squeezed tight as she reached for her phone on the table by her bed and dialed 911.

The operator's crisp voice came across the line. "911. What is your emergency?"

"Someone's in my house, 1811 Maverick Lane. Hurry," she whispered and disconnected, not wanting any noise to cause the intruder to find her all the faster.

Still holding the phone, she bolted up from the bed. After stepping into her slippers and grabbing her robe, she put the phone in her bathrobe pocket and rushed down the hallway to Ian's room. The glow of the night-light revealed a blond head and tiny arms that held a well-worn stuffed giraffe.

She touched his shoulder and whispered, "Ian, wake up."

The child turned over on his side but remained asleep.

More footsteps. The intruder was on the stairs. Panic threaded through her making her heart race. The police wouldn't get here in time. She lived fifteen miles from the nearest town.

She picked up the boy, taking his giraffe and blanket with her. Ian drew the stuffed animal closer to his chest and let out a tiny moan.

They could not leave by the front door without encountering the intruder. Holding Ian close to her chest, she hurried back to her room. She transferred him to one arm so she could grab the go bag she'd prepared for this possibility and pushed open the sliding glass door that led to a balcony and stairs. Cold air enveloped her as snowflakes landed on her face. Ian stirred against her, and she sped down the stairs.

Snow soaked through her slippers when she ran around to the front of the house where her car was parked. After tossing the go bag in, she placed Ian in his car seat in back and clicked him in. He was still half asleep.

She patted his arm and pressed her hand on his cheek. "There you go, little guy. Snug as a bug."

She turned her attention to the dashboard as a whole new level of terror sank in, taking her breath away.

The car keys were inside the house.

She straightened up and glanced down the lonely road at lights in the distance. It was too far to run to the neighbors. In slippers, the trek would be close to impossible.

When she looked at the house, she saw a light flashing at a window on the second floor. The intruder was still searching up there. It would be only a matter of minutes before the culprit figured out how she and Ian had escaped. Her hands had been too full to close the balcony door, providing evidence of her escape route. All the intruder had to do was glance out a front window and see that she was by the car.

She had to get out of here and fast.

Rushing toward the front door, she tried to ignore how cold and wet her feet had become. Though she'd locked the door before going to bed, it opened when she twisted the knob. Her car keys were in a bowl on a table in the entryway. She grabbed the whole bowl. Her feet were frozen blocks by the time she made it back to the car. She swung the driver's door open, grabbed the keys and tossed the bowl on the passenger seat.

She shoved the key in the ignition and shifted into Reverse. Once she was turned around, Marielle switched on the headlights, revealing the long, snow-covered driveway and a sports car parked some distance from the house that must belong to the intruder. He or she must have walked the rest of the way to avoid detection.

Marielle pressed the gas and dared herself a look in the rearview mirror. A silhouetted figure, most likely male, stood in the downstairs doorway. The image sent chills down her spine, and she floored it. Five minutes later, the neighbor's house, shrouded in shadows, came into view. All the windows were dark. She remembered then that the Wallaces had gone on a two-week cruise. She wouldn't find refuge there. She headed toward the main road that would lead into the nearest town. Clarksville was fifteen miles away.

Snow flew across her field of vision, and she switched on the windshield wipers. She barely came to a stop at the crossroads before turning onto the paved road.

Shivering, she switched the heater on high, thankful for the warm blast that hit her face and feet. The snow was coming down hard enough to reduce visibility. She was grateful that her four-wheel drive could handle the slick roads.

She pressed her car through a series of curves. When the road straightened out, she saw a set of headlights behind her. Her grip on the steering wheel tightened.

That had to be the man who had invaded her home. No one else would be out at this hour in this kind of weather.

She could see Ian in her rearview mirror. He rubbed his eyes with a tight fist and looked around. She thought she read fear in his expression.

More than anything, she wanted to protect Ian's heart and mind. The child had been through enough. Both his parents had been drug users and low-level dealers, though his mother had gotten sober in the last months of her life.

She swallowed to try and erase the fear from her voice. "It's going to be all right, kiddo."

The other car loomed behind her, drawing closer.

She wasn't going to be able to shake him.

The snow cleared momentarily, and she saw the sign on the side of the road indicating that the next exit would take her to the Bridger Bible Camp. The pursuer's car fishtailed on the icy road, and a thought occurred to her. The man's car was a low clearance sports car. She might not be able to outrun him on the highway, but he'd most likely get stuck or not be able to traverse the mountain road that led to the camp. Her four-wheel drive would make it easily. She'd gone there as a kid and a teenager and then worked as a counselor when she was in college. It also happened to be where she'd met the man she thought she was going to marry. Instead, Graham had broken her heart and left the state for a job as a DEA agent. But that wasn't important now. What mattered was that she knew the back way to get to the camp, and as far as she could remember, it was unmarked. So even if he followed her where she turned off the main road, he wouldn't know where she'd gone.

She drove past the Bridger sign and the road that led directly to the camp and kept going, scanning for where the unmarked access road was.

Without signaling, she waited until the last second to make the turn. The other car whizzed by. It would take the driver time to get turned around, if he dared try to follow her.

When she checked the rearview mirror, Ian had fallen back asleep.

Her vehicle scaled up the curving road until she came to where it split off. She turned, knowing that this would connect her to the road that led to the camp and hopefully conceal where she'd gone. She raced up to the top of a hill and turned a tight corner. Down below, the camp, with its large main meeting hall surrounded by smaller sleeping cabins and other buildings, came into view. A single lamplight provided enough illumination to show the outlines of some of the buildings and a snow-covered parking lot.

Snow was still twirling around her car as she headed downhill. If memory served, Adrian, the man who managed the camp, often had a caretaker stay on the grounds in the offseason. Perhaps she'd find some help here.

When she was nearly to the camp, she glanced in the rearview mirror. No headlights were behind her as far as she could see, and none were coming up the main road either. She'd lost her pursuer. When she looked ahead, she saw lights in the building beside the meeting hall.

She took in a deep breath.

Someone was here.

Though she was pretty sure she'd shaken the man in the

car, this refuge would be temporary until the storm passed. If the intruder had been so bold as to break into her house, there was no telling what else he would do. No doubt, the culprit would come after Ian again.

When she pushed open the car door, a gust of wind and snow blasted her.

She trudged toward the warm glow of the light coming through the windows and pounded on the door.

Footsteps came from inside and then the door swung open.

"Please can you help me?" Her voice trembled as the wind whipped her long brown hair against her face. She hunched down against the cold. "I saw the light and hoped someone would be here."

"Sure, why don't you come in and get warmed up? This storm is only going to get worse."

She picked up on the note of suspicion in his words. Understandable. She'd shown up at this out-of-the-way place dressed in pajamas and a robe.

"Thank you." She lifted her head to look at the man who was her impromptu rescuer. Shock spread through her. "Graham?"

"Marielle?" Graham Flynn felt like he'd been punched in the gut. Running into the woman he'd left ten years ago was not on his itinerary, especially not here, in the place where they'd first met. It was here they'd been campers and then counselors together, where they'd fallen in love, even where they'd chosen which college they'd go to together. And where he'd asked her to marry him.

It was a plan he'd been happy with, until he'd been recruited by the DEA. He hadn't realized before then how much he craved excitement and escape from small-town life. The work would take him all over the world. He'd asked Marielle if she was open to postponing the wedding or having a long-distance marriage for a few years. She'd said no. Marielle had dreamed of a quiet life in Montana raising a bunch of children and being a part of a small, close-knit community. She deserved to be with someone who could give her that. Given that he had grown up without a father, he thought he could do a lot more good in the world by becoming a law enforcement officer than a parent.

The last ten years of undercover work had made him feel like he was making a difference in stopping the drug trade. He was in his element and had found a vocation that fit his skill set. He'd thought the job was what he was meant to do—until the death of his CI a few weeks ago. He'd come up to the camp as a respite after sixteen-year-old Cesar had been murdered in a cartel explosion.

Perhaps the same memories of the camp were running through her mind as she narrowed her eyes and pinned him with her gaze. "I have to say. You're the last person I thought I would ever see again." Her voice had grown stronger as she lifted her chin slightly.

The tinge of anger in her words didn't surprise him. Choosing to ignore her emotional state, he took a step to one side. "Come in. You must be freezing."

She turned back toward the car. "I have someone with me." She descended the first step.

Her exposed ankles were red from the cold. "Let me help you."

"It's better if I do it," she said. "Ian is slow to trust strangers. I don't want him to get scared."

He grabbed his coat, which hung by the door, and followed her. As he bent over to shield his face from the wind, snow stabbed his skin like a thousand tiny swords. He watched as she reached into the back seat. She held a bundle beneath a blanket.

Of course, there was a child. There was probably a husband too. Had he thought time would stand still after he'd left town? He wondered, though, why she'd shown up here in such a state, dressed like she was, as if she'd fled a violent situation in the middle of the night. The thought of anyone hurting Marielle made him grind his teeth. Even after all these years, he still felt protective of her.

He closed the car door behind her and then followed her inside. "Why don't you two sit by the woodstove?"

He ushered them over to a love seat that was situated perpendicular to the stove and across from an overstuffed chair. The fire had nearly died out. He opened the door, stirred the coals and then threw on another log from the pile in the wood box.

She settled on the love seat and pulled back the blanket, revealing a blond boy of maybe three or four years of age. His cheeks were rosy. He stared up at Marielle while he clutched a worn stuffed animal. She stroked his head and made a shushing sound. "It's going to be all right. We're safe and warm now."

The boy rested against her chest.

Graham stood. "Your feet must be frozen." He went to the bedroom to retrieve a pair of his heavy wool socks from the dresser. Without thinking, he sat on the floor and pulled her wet slippers off. His fingers grazed over her skin. "Very red but doesn't look like you have frostbite."

She lifted her foot so he could put the sock on. "Your fingers are warm."

He pulled the sock up her ankle. "There you go."

"Thank you," she whispered as she looked at him. Her gaze softened. She still had the same long, wavy brown hair that had always made her so pretty. Eyes the color of dark chocolate only added to her beauty.

The look of appreciation in her face made his heart beat a little faster. His face flushed. He cupped the other foot and slipped the sock on over her soft skin.

She stared at the fire through the glass window while he rose and grabbed a blanket from his bed to wrap around her.

"Thank you." She pulled the blanket tighter around her shoulders.

Clearly something bad had happened to her and he wondered if she'd share the details with him, but first he needed to get her warmed up. "How about I make you some hot tea?"

She continued to gaze at the fire. Her eyes were unfocused as she rocked the little boy in her arms. "That would be nice."

Her appearance suggested that she'd escaped some kind of violence. He only hoped that she hadn't brought trouble to his door. It wasn't just what she might be running from that worried him. Working undercover for the DEA meant he was always looking over his shoulder. The cartel had killed his informant with a car bomb. They could have just as easily figured out who Graham was and followed him up here.

The remoteness of the camp afforded a degree of protection to both of them because it was so hidden, but it also left them vulnerable if anyone knew where to find them. Cell phones did not work this high in the mountains, and the satellite phone was being repaired for when the camp was full of people. If danger found them, they were on their own.

He went to the kitchen and busied himself with the tea, trying to quell the rush of memories. Images of the time they'd spent together, of the kisses and the hikes and the long talks planning their life together, bombarded him, making him feel weak in the knees.

When he returned to where she sat, she'd laid the boy down on the love seat and covered him with the blanket.

He handed her the steaming mug. "What brings you to this camp on such a snowy night?"

Marielle stared at him with a piercing gaze as his question hung in the air.

Chapter Two

"I might ask you the same thing." Marielle looked at him over her cup of tea. "After all these years."

She was surprised by the sting in her words. Seeing Graham face-to-face after ten years brought back intense pain as if his rejection had happened yesterday. He'd chosen his job over a life with her.

Graham sat down in a chair that faced the love seat. "I needed some time off, and Adrian offered me time alone at the camp if I kept an eye on the place."

"Time off from what, exactly?" Her question sounded more like an accusation. Emotions that had been kept at bay for years assaulted her. At first after he left, she was devastated, but she'd gotten on with her life. She thought she'd healed. But now with Graham sitting only feet from her all the anger, hurt and confusion seemed to rise to the surface.

He averted his gaze. "You know, life, work, stress."

That sounded vague. There was probably more to the story. She shook her head. "After all this time. You came back and you didn't even get in touch with me?" Her words came out as if she were shooting them at him. Wasn't she at least owed that courtesy?

He leaned forward in his chair, pointing at the slippers on the floor. "You haven't told me what's going on with you and your son."

So that was his tactic, to change the subject. "Ian is my foster child."

His expression changed. The muscles in his face relaxed as though he was pleased by the news. "Oh, I thought…"

"I never married, and I don't have children of my own." After Graham's departure so close to their wedding, she'd poured herself into getting a master's in child psychology. She didn't want to date again and risk such unbearable pain. Her profession allowed her to help children if she was never going to have any of her own.

Graham rubbed his beard. "So why did you come here… tonight?"

He'd never been one to stop shaving. He looked different with facial hair. Still handsome but in a mountain man sort of way. His expression and especially his eyes held a tiredness that had not been there years ago.

She reached out to touch Ian's shoulder while the child slept. "This little guy witnessed a crime. Certain people may not want him to talk and identify them. Tonight, someone broke into my house, and I have to assume it's connected to Ian. When the intruder pursued me in his car, I had to shake him. That's why I came up here."

Graham jerked to his feet. "How do you know he didn't follow you here?" He seemed jumpy. Maybe it came with the territory when you were a DEA agent, but she doubted it.

Her eyes fell on the holster on his hip, which she hadn't noticed while he was seated. She gasped. "Graham, what is going on with you?" She pointed to the gun. "Surely you don't need that if you're taking time off?"

"Oh, it's just for protection, lot of wild animals out here." He was trying to make his voice sound casual, but she picked up on the tension underneath. He thought he needed protection even when he was hiding up here. Was she in some other kind of danger after escaping the intruder?

His explanation made no sense. He was carrying the gun on his person while he was inside. Besides, a rifle or shotgun would be better protection against wildlife. She had the feeling he was keeping something from her. Maybe his on-guard attitude wasn't just about her showing up here after being pursued.

Graham paced toward the window and looked out. "How do you know this is a safe place for you to bring Ian?"

She rose and stepped toward him. "I don't think the car the home invader was driving could make it up the back road. It was a low-clearance sporty-looking thing, probably rear-wheel drive. Plus, I took the unmarked road that leads up here."

"I remember that road." He ran his hands through his hair, something he always did when he was nervous. "What kind of crime are we talking about here?"

She glanced over to where the boy still lay asleep. Then she crossed her arms and turned to stare out the window before speaking in a low voice. "Ian witnessed someone kill his mother. He stopped speaking after it happened, but the police think he might be able to identify the murderer once he's able to talk. Both his parents were connected to the local drug trade."

"Why didn't you have a protection detail?" Graham asked, frowning in thought.

She sighed. This was a discussion she'd had with the police more than once. "Ian was probably hiding when it happened. Otherwise he might have been killed too. The police didn't think the killer had seen him and you know how small-town forces are. They couldn't extend the resources for protection unless they were sure it was necessary. I had a go bag just in case. Now I know that the killer knows. Whoever came after Ian tonight probably killed his mom."

Graham shook his head, clearly upset. "To go after a little

kid like that…unbelievable." He looked at her. "Why was the mom killed?"

"Who knows? Life is cheap in that world. Maybe Kristen had drugs someone wanted or somebody thought she'd ripped them off."

"Was there a husband or boyfriend in the picture?"

She frowned. "A husband, David. Ian's father. He's missing, but police don't think he did it."

He met her gaze, and she thought she saw admiration in his eyes. "And now you're in the middle of this, taking care of the boy."

"I just want to protect an innocent life." When she stared out the window, the blowing snow nearly camouflaged her car even though it was parked only feet from the door. "You asked why I came here. I think this place always seemed like the safest place in the world to me. Maybe that's why I made the choice to come up the mountain."

He offered her a faint smile. "I always thought of the camp that way too. A refuge from life's struggles." Some light came into his eyes, reminding her of the Graham she'd known, not the world-weary one she was seeing now.

The moment of connection made her smile too.

Her heart fluttered when she met his gaze. The attraction was still there after all this time. She studied him for a long moment. The warm feelings faded when she remembered the pain he'd caused her, and she took a step back.

She'd given up trying to get a clear explanation from him why he'd come back after all this time. She had the feeling if she asked, he'd just continue being evasive.

He turned sideways so he could stare out the window, as if her looking at him had made him uncomfortable. "The storm's getting worse. No one is coming in or out until this lets up."

That meant she was stuck here with Graham while all the questions and intense emotions dancing in her head.

She returned to the couch to sit beside Ian, who stirred but did not wake up. "I'm just glad somebody was here." Though she wished it would have been somebody other than the man who'd torn her world apart.

"Why don't you and the little guy get some sleep?" He pointed toward the bedroom.

"I don't want to move him. It's warm and cozy by the stove," she said. "I can rest in the chair."

"Suit yourself." He handed her the blanket he'd draped over her earlier.

She drew the blanket up to her shoulders, grateful for it and the heat from the woodstove.

Graham wandered through the small manager's house, and she watched him check that all the doors and windows were secure. When he retreated to the bedroom, she noticed his hand resting on the butt of his gun. Maybe his training made him never let his guard down.

She closed her eyes and drifted off.

She awoke when Ian stirred, making a sound of distress. Was he having a bad dream or remembering something? She rose and stroked his head, making shushing noises. He cried for several seconds, and she took him into her arms.

"I've gotcha," she whispered as she swayed back and forth and then sat on the love seat. In the days since he'd been in her care, she'd discovered that he was responsive to touch and being held.

Kids who have come from physically abusive situations often bristled when touched. Someone had loved and protected Ian enough so he could be soothed despite his life circumstances. There were no grandparents in the picture, so she assumed his parents, despite their struggles, had taken care of him.

The boy quieted as she held him. After a while, she laid him back down on the love seat, making sure his blanket covered him.

She returned to her chair to sleep. Maybe the storm would keep the man who broke into her house at bay, but that didn't mean they wouldn't come for Ian again. She'd have to see if the sheriff's department could provide some protection once they got out of here now that it was clear the killer was after Ian. She closed her eyes and prayed.

God, keep this little boy safe and give me the strength to do right by him.

As she drifted off, she could hear Graham in the next room tossing and turning and then pacing. Was he as stirred up by her presence as she was about his or was it something else? The fact that he claimed to be taking time off but carried a gun scared her. He must have been worried about some kind of danger long before she'd shown up, and she doubted it was a bear or wolf.

Despite all her fear, or perhaps because of it, the fog of sleep invaded her mind.

She awoke with a start in the darkness, not sure how much time had passed. She could just make out Ian, a blanketed lump on the love seat. Still caught between consciousness and dreaming, she thought she heard a sound like a doorknob being rattled.

Heart pounding, she listened, but no additional noise reached her ears. She rose and walked toward the door, her footsteps silent in her borrowed wool socks. She touched the doorknob, but it was unmoving. Maybe the sound had been the wind.

She retreated back to the chair. Perhaps her fear of being found had caused her to dream that someone was trying to break in. She and Ian were trapped here until the storm lifted, and that was increasing her worries.

The last thing she heard before falling asleep was Graham moving through the house as if on patrol.

Actions that indicated he too was concerned that they were not safe.

* * *

A gust of wind rattled the glass of the window Graham gazed out of. He saw nothing but darkness outside, yet he could not let go of his unease. Snow still fell as if dumped from buckets.

Though his training made him vigilant out of habit, his need to detect and eliminate potential threats seemed to have ramped up since his informant's death. Cesar had been a sixteen-year-old kid who wanted something better for himself and his family. Undercover work was tricky. Even though you weren't supposed to form attachments, he'd begun to think of Cesar as a little brother.

His thoughts turned again to the events in Mexico that had brought him here. His handler didn't think there was anything he could have done to prevent the explosion that had killed Cesar. Graham felt, though, that he should have gotten wind of what the cartel had planned. That he should have known that Cesar had been outed as a CI. Had he not been careful enough when setting up their meetings?

He turned away from the window to gaze at Marielle in the chair. She looked beautiful as she slept, her wavy brown hair falling across her cheek. Her showing up gave him even more reason for insomnia.

After all this time, she hadn't married. The thought made him sad. She'd always talked about having lots of kids. Being a mom had been her dream. By breaking up with her, he'd thought he had given her a chance at that dream.

The truth was, when the DEA recruited him, he'd thought he was doing her a favor. True, they were both Christians, but Marielle came from a stable family that had generations of faithful people. He'd grown up without a father and had only come to the Bible Camp as a teen to hide out before the police found out he'd stolen a motorcycle. The director of the camp that year had figured out what he was up to and had agreed not to call the police if Graham would stay at the camp all summer and commit to the activities.

He'd been well on his way to becoming a juvenile delinquent. Little did he know that his encounter with God at the camp would lead him to confess to the police and change the whole direction of his life.

Still thinking about the past, he returned to the bedroom. He sat down on the bed, resting his hands on his knees and running his palms over his head. The truth was, he'd thought Marielle deserved someone better than him, someone who could be a good husband and father. He feared he was not up to that task and that he could better serve God by chipping away at the drug trade.

He swung his legs onto the bed and pulled his covers up to his chin while he stared at the ceiling. Sleep came gradually.

Mindful of the need to stay on guard duty, he awoke hours later in the dark silence. He rose and peered out each window and checked that the door was locked. He looked out the front window where the snowfall had lightened up a bit.

He jerked his head back when he saw a flash of light. It was there and gone as though a curtain had been lifted and been pulled back down. He leaned toward the window.

Marielle appeared beside him. "What's going on?"

He hadn't even heard her padding across the floor, she walked so delicately. She stood close enough to him that her shoulder brushed against his.

"I thought I saw a light out there," he said.

She gasped. "Are you sure?"

He turned back toward the window, studying the area where he'd seen it before. "I'm not sure about what I saw." He moved to the other window and peered out, still searching.

Her voice feathered with fear. "Who would be out there?"

He wasn't about to tell her that the cartel may have found him. She had enough to worry about. "I heard someone built some vacation cabins a couple of hills over. I just can't imagine someone going out in this on purpose, unless they didn't realize the danger. Look, the darkness and the storm can play tricks on what you see."

Maybe he'd just imagined the light, a sort of winter mirage. His concern over intruders could make him see things that weren't there. He may have caused Marielle to be upset over nothing.

"I'm pretty sure that man's car couldn't make it all the way up the mountain. Even if he did, he would've had to guess at which way I turned." She rubbed her arms.

He put his hand on her shoulder, hoping his touch would help alleviate her fear. "We don't know anything for sure. Soon as this storm clears and the plows come, we can get out of here."

She studied him for a long moment. "But until then, we're stuck here, right?"

As he gazed into Marielle's brown eyes, he wanted more than anything to assure her that they were safe. But that would be a lie. He'd been fine when it had only been himself up here. If he was attacked by the forces that might be after him, he could take care of himself, but now he had a woman and child to think of.

"Tell you what. There isn't much of the night left. Why don't you and Ian go to the bedroom and get some sleep? I'll keep watch. This storm should let up by morning."

She nodded.

He watched her move to the couch and pick up the sleeping boy. At least he'd gotten a little rest. After the bedroom door clicked shut, he settled down into the chair that provided a view of the windows. He placed his gun on the side table.

For the next few hours, he stayed mostly alert, nodding off from time to time and then rousing himself. Light streaming through the windows woke him for the final time. Morning finally.

Graham rose to his feet and stepped closer to the window.

The sky was white. A milky film covered the sun, but the snowstorm had stopped.

Everywhere he looked he saw drifts. He was glad he'd parked his truck in the garage—Marielle's car was half covered in snow. He saw faint impressions in the snow that might have been footprints. The blowing and drifting made it hard to say. An animal could very well have wandered into the camp and made them. All the same, now that the storm had died down, he needed to do a search of the camp. In the calm daylight, they were more vulnerable. It would be easier for someone to make it up here before the plows came and allowed them to escape.

After grabbing his gun, he put on his boots and coat and stepped outside. His feet sank in the drifts, making it hard to move. He circled around several buildings and studied the road leading in, not seeing anything that indicated someone else had been in the camp. Satisfied, he returned to the manager's quarters.

Marielle was up and watching him from the window. The expression on her face, the raised eyebrows, communicated an unspoken question.

He hung his coat up. "I didn't see any evidence that anyone was out there."

She stared out the window. "It looks so calm." She pulled a strand of hair behind her ear. "At least the storm is over. Ian and I will be out of your hair soon. Can you help me dig my car out?"

"Actually, it could take all day for the county plows to make it up here. Maybe even not until tomorrow. Priority would be on the roads that have higher use. You'll just get stuck if you try to leave now."

Distressed, she shook her head and fiddled with the collar of her bathrobe. "Oh, I didn't realize."

Was she that anxious to get away from him?

She pulled a cell phone out of her bathrobe pocket.

"They don't work up here, remember?" he said.

She put the phone away. "I just thought maybe we could call and let the authorities know there are people stranded up here."

She acted like she couldn't tolerate spending much more time with him. "We just need to be patient and wait. I'll dig your car out so you can leave as soon as possible." He spoke softly, trying to hide the hurt her coldness toward him caused.

At the sound of small footsteps, they both turned. Ian stood at the open bedroom door.

"Hey, sleepyhead." Marielle rushed over to pick him up, talking in soothing tones and rubbing her nose against his.

The picture of the two of them together warmed his heart. Regardless of how Marielle felt about him, he could extend hospitality to both of them.

"Why don't I make the two of you some breakfast?" He wandered over to the kitchenette. "I have some shelf-stable milk left to make some pancakes. Got some canned apricots to go with that. Sorry, no meat or eggs."

"Food sounds good," she said.

When she tried to place Ian on one of the chairs, he shook his head and held on to the neckline of her pajama top. Ian remained in her arms as she took a chair at the table that seated four.

He opened another cupboard. "What does Ian like? I have some instant oatmeal."

"He'll eat the pancakes."

Graham turned on the grill and grabbed the pancake mix. After stirring the milk into the mix, he poured the batter out on the grill. He set plates and syrup on the table, then returned to the counter and waited for the pancakes to bubble so he could flip them.

"I see you've learned how to cook." There was a note of levity in her voice. When they were dating, they had a running joke about his various cooking disasters.

He managed a laugh but the reference to the past was like

a stab to his gut. Now seeing her all these years later, he wondered if he'd made the right choice. Cesar's death had shaken him and made him wonder if he still wanted to be an agent. What would his life have been like if he'd stayed here and married her? Maybe they would both be in a better place.

When he'd left, he'd assumed she would meet someone new, marry him and find a greater happiness than Graham could ever give her. Graham placed the pancakes on a plate and put it on the table. "Sorry, no butter."

He opened the can of apricots and poured them into a bowl. Marielle scooted an empty chair closer to her and encouraged Ian to sit in it. This time the boy complied.

Graham took the chair opposite Marielle. "You mind if I say grace?"

"Sure, that would be great."

Marielle bowed her head. Ian laced his chubby fingers together.

"Lord, we thank You for this meal. We pray for all those affected by the storm. Please bless this food to nourish our bodies."

"Amen." Marielle placed a pancake on Ian's plate along with some apricots. His head was barely above the table.

"Here." Graham jumped to his feet and retrieved a pillow from the love seat.

Marielle lifted Ian up so he could shove the pillow underneath the boy. "Better?" She brushed her fingers over the boy's cheek. Ian nodded and picked up a fork.

The kid had clearly been through trauma. Graham wanted more details but knew it would be wrong to ask while Ian was listening. He and Marielle would probably not have a chance to be alone. She'd made it clear she wanted to leave at the first opportunity. Seeing her stirred up old feelings. They would part ways as soon as possible. Though her anger was hard to take, he didn't blame her. A few hours together wasn't going to heal the wounds he'd caused.

After they finished, Graham gathered the plates and took them over to the sink. When he peered out the window, he saw smoke coming from the building where the washers and dryers were housed along with other supplies. The backup generator was also in there. Though the building was partly obscured by another cabin, he could see puffs of smoke rising into the air.

Graham ran toward the door. "Stay here. I've got to check something out." He raced toward the door, stepped into his boots and grabbed his coat.

She followed him. "What's going on?"

"Looks like there might be a fire." His first thought was that drifts on the roof might have blocked vents and caused some sort of combustion. He reached for his hat at the same time that his other hand was on the doorknob. The cold air hit him as he stepped outside.

As much as the deep snow would allow, he rushed toward the smoke. As he drew closer, he saw flames through an open window where the smoke had been escaping. He darted over to the cabin next to the one that was on fire where he grabbed a shovel propped against the door.

When he touched the doorknob, it was not hot. He pushed the door open. Though the room was filled with smoke, the fire was confined to a pile on the floor. He coughed and stepped outside, shoveling up a heap of snow and carrying it inside. He did this several more times. The fire persisted. He ran outside, coughing, to gather more snow on his shovel until he saw no more flames.

In the dim light, he studied the burned remains of the fire. He could just discern a fragment of an unburned sheet and a piece of a towel. He checked the shelf where the linens were kept in airtight containers. Several towels had fallen to the floor. He detected the faint scent of diesel fuel, which was used for the backup generator.

A terrible realization sank in. This fire was no accident. Someone had made a pile on the floor and poured fuel on it.

His heart pounded as he ran outside back toward the manager's quarters just in time to see a man in a black-and-red coat reach for the doorknob. The man must have been hiding somewhere in the camp waiting for his chance to get at Marielle and Ian once he'd lured Graham away to deal with the fire.

Marielle and Ian were in danger. He tried to run as his boots sank down into the snow. He prayed he could get to them in time. He didn't want to think about what would happen if he didn't.

Chapter Three

Marielle chose to focus her energy on Ian, trying not to think about what the fire meant. It could have been started by anything. Power lines could have gone down in the storm. Graham had searched the camp and not found any sign that anyone else was around. Still, the butterflies stirred in her stomach.

She'd taken Ian to the bathroom to wash his face when she heard the front door open. She breathed a sigh of relief. Graham must already be back. Crisis averted.

She stepped out of the bathroom with Ian toddling behind her. He held on to her bathrobe. "Hey—"

A muscular man with dark hair, not Graham, stood in the doorway. He smiled at her even as his voice held a note of menace. "Sorry about barging in. My car got stuck and I saw these buildings." His attention was drawn to the little boy behind her.

Her heart pounded as she reached a protective hand toward Ian. In his haste to take care of the fire, Graham had left the door unlocked. Marielle took a step back.

She felt a prickling at the back of her neck. "You were out driving in the deep snow all the way up here?" Her voice wavered, though she attempted to sound casual. Graham had said something about vacation rentals nearby. It could be the man was telling the truth. Still, she couldn't shake her feeling of unease. She continued the conversation to buy time.

He advanced toward her, his boots pounding on the hardwood floor. "I was hoping you could help me." The way the man lifted his chin and puffed out his chest struck her as aggressive. Plus, the man had just let himself in without knocking.

And he kept coming toward her.

Alarm bells went off as her heart rate skipped up a notch. She needed to get out of here with Ian fast. "I don't think that'll be possible. Why don't you wait outside until the manager gets back?"

"Oh, I think he's quite busy dealing with a fire." He turned back around, took a few steps and clicked the dead bolt on the door.

Fear raged through her even before he returned his attention to Marielle.

"Just hand the boy over to me."

So he *was* the man who had come after her in her home. She reached out for Ian, lifting him up and running to the bedroom. Heavy footsteps pounded behind her. She clicked the lock on the bedroom door. The man pounded on the door. "Let me in." The pounding grew more intense. He must be smashing against the door with his body.

Marielle slipped into a pair of boots she found at the foot of the bed and grabbed Graham's coat off the bedpost.

Ian let out a cry. She reached for his blanket and wrapped it around his shoulders, holding him close. "It's okay. I've got you." It wasn't just his physical safety she worried about. She'd do anything to keep him from experiencing more violence.

The assault on the door continued as she ran over to the window and flung it open. It was a short drop down. Ian lifted his head, round brown eyes watching her. This would be scary for him. She pressed her hand against his warm cheek. "We're going to have to go out this way. I'll let you down and then I'll come out right after you. Do you understand?"

Ian nodded.

"Thanks for being so brave."

A voice came from outside the window. "Hand him down to me." Graham. She thanked God he'd figured out what was going on.

The bedroom door had begun to splinter. She lifted Ian and helped him out feet first. Graham stepped back and held the boy while she put one leg through the window.

Her feet had just hit the snow when the door burst open and the man came to the window. Still holding Ian, Graham tried to navigate around the deeper drifts. She sought to step in the holes he'd made. The boots were too big for her, but at least they kept her feet warm.

A shot rang out behind them. The man had a gun.

Graham led her in a circuitous pattern through the camp around cabins. She thought she heard a noise behind her. Her heart pounded when she glanced over her shoulder fearing that a bullet would find its target. No sign of the other man.

She was not sure what Graham had in mind until he came to the back door of the main meeting house. He pushed it open and they stepped inside. "Get upstairs. There's a lost and found. You and Ian put on as many warm clothes as you can." He handed Ian over to her and pulled his gun.

Holding Ian, she headed past closed office doors, glancing into the main worship area before turning a corner where the staircase was. She had trod up these stairs hundreds of times and knew exactly where to find the lost and found boxes.

She ran by storage totes and shelves with books, binders and sheet music on them until she got to the lost and found boxes. This third story of the building had a slanted roof with windows at each end. Graham joined them, checking out each window and then positioning himself at the top of the stairs.

After putting Ian down, she sorted through the box, tossing aside swimming suits and shorts. "What is the plan here anyway?"

"There's a snowmobile in the garage."

She lifted up a child's coat. Too big for Ian but it would have to do. "But the roads are drifted over."

"I know, but the snowmobile will be more agile than a car." Graham stalked back toward the window. "He won't be able to keep up with us on foot."

She found a pair of canvas shoes and slipped them on Ian's feet over the socks he was already wearing. These would hardly keep him warm for long. Now she wished she'd had time to grab the go bag from her car.

She rooted through the box, retrieving a man's wool sock which she put over one of his feet. She wasn't sure about this plan. Without the proper equipment, they wouldn't stay warm for long on the snowmobile.

She looked over at Graham who lingered at the window. "Do you see him?"

He turned halfway toward her and shook his head. "On the pristine snow, he'll be able to follow our footprints. It's just a matter of time before he figures out where we are. Did you find what you needed?"

Once again, she wrapped the blanket around Ian. "Not really." She held up a blue knitted cap which she placed on Ian's head. "But we'll make do."

He looked at the both of them. "You won't stay warm for long on a snowmobile. Maybe there is some more gear in the garage."

"Graham, I'm not sure if this is going to work. Will we even be able to get very far on the snowmobile?"

He studied her for a long moment. "I'm hoping we can get off the mountain. Maybe find some help." He rubbed his scruffy jaw. "But if we can't, we just need to get far enough away so he thinks we've left the camp, and then we can hike back in and hide until help comes."

So, they would be playing cat and mouse with a killer until the plows pushed through. There were no good options. "Whatever you think is best."

"Let's get going." With his gun drawn, he led them back down the stairs. He stepped out of the back door first, signaling that they needed to hang back. He gestured that the coast was clear. Once again, he led them around buildings that didn't provide a direct path to the garage but kept them mostly concealed. Both she and Graham had an advantage over the assailant in that they knew the layout of the camp.

While she held Ian, they both rested their backs against a cabin to catch their breath. Graham rushed to peek around the corner to make sure it was safe to keep going.

She caught movement in her peripheral vision. The man had just slipped behind a cabin not too far from where they were. The assailant must have spotted them and sought to conceal himself for an ambush.

She sprinted toward Graham. "He's right behind us."

Even though Ian was small for his age, he'd grown heavy in her arms. But she had to keep carrying him. No way could he run and keep up. Plus, the canvas shoes he had on would get wet. She raced ahead as fast as she could while Graham took up the rear, still holding the gun and checking over his shoulder.

She reached the door leading into the garage and pushed it open. Nothing around here seemed to be locked. She supposed it made sense. Normally, there was very little risk of robbery or danger especially with a caretaker on the grounds. The garage had four bays filled with lawn equipment and tools. The snowmobile was on the opposite side of the building. The truck next to it must belong to Graham.

There was no time to put on the snowsuit she spotted, but she grabbed it and tossed it on the seat of the snowmobile. She hurried over with Ian, grabbing a child-size helmet for him as well as one for herself.

Graham stepped inside, twisting the knob to lock the door behind him. By the time he made it across the room, the door-knob was being shaken followed by pounding. Graham jumped on the front of the snowmobile without grabbing a helmet, but he'd picked up the garage door remote. In one swift motion he started the engine and opened the garage door.

A gunshot reverberated by the door. The attacker had shot the door open and stepped inside just as they zoomed out into the open, even before the garage door was completely up.

With Ian between them, she pressed close to Graham's back, praying that they would get away before another bullet hit its mark.

The echo of gunshots reached Graham's ears as he twisted the throttle of the snowmobile. Wind hit his face. His bare hands grew cold. There hadn't been time to put on his gloves. He veered away from a high drift and headed toward the road that led out of the camp. Though they traversed the smaller drifts and made it up the hill, it was obvious once they turned the corner that the snow was too deep even for a snowmobile to navigate through.

He chose a path closer to the tree line where the snow had not blown as much. He found an opening and drove into the trees, then killed the engine. Marielle scooted back so he could get off.

He stared down at the two people he was charged with pro-tecting. Marielle had wrapped her arms around Ian, drawing his back close to her chest. The boy looked up at him, brown eyes filled with uncertainty.

He leaned down and brushed his knuckles over the boy's cheek, making a funny noise, which produced a faint smile on Ian's part.

He straightened up. "I'm going to hike out to a high spot

ten minutes in one direction to see if there is any other road or way out or another dwelling close by. I'll come back in no more than twenty minutes. No way can that guy hike up here in that time and hopefully he'll think we escaped." Plus, they were hidden by the trees. His voice softened. "I know you two can't stay out here in the cold for long."

She nodded and rested her hand on Ian's head. "We'll be okay for a while."

As Graham stepped away, he heard her talking in a soothing tone to Ian.

He wasn't so sure about their situation. If they couldn't find a path of escape or some kind of help, the situation was dire. The temperature hung just above freezing at this time of day, but it would grow colder as the day wore on. As he'd speculated, their only choice would be to go back to the shelter of the camp, and the intruder might still be there.

Graham checked his watch before he stepped away from them. He pulled his gloves from his pockets and put them on. His boots sank down into the snow as he made his way to a high point. Once he reached the top of the hill, he had a view in three directions. A snow-covered hill blocked out much of Bridger, but he could see one of the buildings at the edge of the camp. He peered off in the other two directions, shielding his eyes from the sun glaring off the pristine white snow. No buildings, no foot tracks, no roads. He wasn't sure where those vacation homes had been built, but he saw no sign of them. They must be some distance away.

Following the depressions of his footsteps, he returned to where Marielle and Ian waited for him. Marielle had placed Ian inside of the adult-size snowsuit, and they both sat sideways on the snowmobile seat.

Her concern was for the child more so than herself. She had always been such a caretaker, and not only of other children. She had been perpetually adopting wounded animals too. It was a quality that he'd been drawn to.

She lifted her head when she saw him, a faint, hopeful smile gracing her soft features.

He stood several feet from the snowmobile, placing his hands on his hips and wondering how he was going to give her the bad news. Framed by the blue knitted hat Marielle had found for him, Ian's rosy cheeks and soft brown eyes were endearing. "Someone looks toasty warm."

She drew the boy into a sideways hug. "Yes." She pressed her nose close to his. "I figured he needed it more than me." She picked up one of the snowsuit arms and waved it around. "It's a little floppy on him."

"I can help you with that." He pulled a Swiss army knife from his pocket and proceeded to cut the excess fabric from the arms of the snowsuit. Ian watched him intently as he worked. Next he cut the pant legs, leaving them long enough so they covered Ian's feet.

"Much better." Marielle tossed the excess pant legs between some trees. "What did you find out on your walk?"

He stepped closer to the snowmobile, resting a hand on the windshield. "There's no way out where we won't risk being stranded in the snow and cold."

She lifted her chin to meet his gaze. Her mouth was drawn into a pensive line. "I guess we don't have a lot of choices."

He pointed in the direction of the camp. "I'm going to hike over and see if I can figure out what that man is up to. We can probably hide in one of the buildings at the edge of the camp if we can sneak in unnoticed."

She nodded.

What he didn't tell her about his plan was that if the man had chosen to remain at the camp, which would be the smart thing to do, Graham thought he might be able to take him into custody. He had to make sure, though, that Marielle and Ian wouldn't be in harm's way before he attempted something like that.

He needed to assess where in the camp the man was. Following the road that led back into the camp, he came to the place where the road looped around. He had a view of the buildings below as he perched at the top of the hill behind a drift. He could see the tracks that the snowmobile had made as well as footprints that followed at a short distance. Marielle's car had been dug out and brushed off. It may have been moved a few feet. The man had thought to follow them in the car but then realized the futility of trying to drive in the deep snow. He scanned the rest of the camp, not seeing the man anywhere.

Graham moved in for a better view of the whole area. Knowing that his dark clothes would be visible against the white snow, he remained low and moved quickly. Now he could see that smoke still curled out of the manager's quarters. Light glowed through the windows. Maybe the man was inside getting warmed up after trying to follow them in a car.

Graham returned back up the hill to where Marielle and Ian waited. Her face had grown red from the cold. She looked at him with expectation in her eyes. She'd found the pair of gloves he kept in the pocket of the coat she wore.

"I think he's inside the manager's headquarters. Let's take the snowmobile and circle around to the back of the camp."

If the assailant remained inside, he wouldn't hear the snowmobile. That was a big if. He could be patrolling the area looking for them and Graham had just not been able to spot him. Walking on foot would exhaust them, though, and they'd get colder faster. They needed to utilize this snowmobile as much as they could.

Still holding Ian, Marielle rose to her feet, giving Graham room to climb onto the seat. He turned the key in the ignition. Marielle placed Ian behind Graham and helped him with his helmet, then put on her own helmet and climbed on too.

The plan was fraught with risk, but they couldn't stay outside for long. Though it got dark early, around five o'clock, they could not wait for the protection that the cover of darkness provided. They'd be too cold by then, and night would only cause the temperature to drop faster.

Graham chose a path where the snow was less deep. He could not begin to know what was going on in the attacker's mind. Maybe he knew they'd be forced to return to the camp and was just waiting for the opportunity to come after them.

Graham would do everything he could to make sure that didn't happen. He intended to arrest the assailant no matter what it took.

In any case, he felt like they were walking into the lion's den.

Chapter Four

Marielle hunkered down behind Graham's back, grateful that she was shielded from most of the wind and cold. Ian wiggled in his seat. At least he would stay warm in the make-shift snowsuit.

Lifting her head to peer over Graham's shoulder provided her only a partial view of where they were headed. Graham wove in a serpentine pattern, probably to avoid the deeper snow, and then headed closer to the trees.

When she glanced off to the side, a hill blocked her view of all but the outermost buildings of the camp. She shivered. Though Graham's coat reached almost to her knees, her thin pajama bottoms provided very little protection from the cold.

He veered away from the trees and headed downhill before stopping and switching off the engine. He turned his head slightly to talk to her. "This is as close as we should get. I don't want him to hear or see the snowmobile. Edge of the camp is just over that hill. We'll walk the rest of the way."

She got off the snowmobile, took off her helmet and looked around. They'd come down into a small valley that created a sort of bowl. The high roof of the three-story main building was visible, and smoke rose up from one of the other buildings, probably the manager's quarters.

He reached his hands toward her. "Here, let me carry Ian."

Exposure had made her even more fatigued, and she was grateful for the help. Ian didn't seem to mind the handover, nestling against Graham before they headed up the hill. She sank into the snow several times. At least Graham's tall oversized boots kept her feet dry. When they came to the top of the hill, she saw the camp down below. The white blanket of snow would not conceal them. If the attacker came outside and gazed in this direction, they'd be spotted. When she looked behind her, she could see their footprints in the otherwise untouched snow. If only the wind would blow and cover their tracks.

Her stomach tied in a knot. Though she realized they had no choice, it felt like they were walking toward danger. She said a silent prayer for God's protection.

Her face grew numb as they made their way downhill and came to the first building at the edge of the camp.

Snow had drifted over the door, making it impossible to get inside. After trying to open the door, Graham shook his head and pointed.

She tensed up.

They would have to go deeper into the camp, probably closer to where the attacker was. They trudged through the snow. When they came to the next building, Marielle opened the door while Graham held Ian. The door eased open. It appeared to be a storage shed for outdoor equipment. In the dim light, she could discern bicycles and kayaks. The building had no windows.

Once inside, Graham led them toward the back of the large shed. Still shivering, she settled onto the floor. Graham positioned Ian close to her. The boy turned his face toward her as if asking a question.

"We're just going to stay here for a while to warm up," she explained. They had no heat source and no food but at least they weren't outside. In response, Ian nodded. The snowsuit made swishing noises as he turned to look at Graham.

"We'll huddle together for warmth." Graham sat down next to Ian. "Why don't you and Ian get some sleep?"

That meant that Graham was going to try to stay awake and keep watch. She leaned her head back against the wall and closed her eyes. Now that they were out of the elements, her shivering subsided. Her arms and legs were heavy with fatigue, but her mind was alert.

After about twenty minutes, she heard Ian's gentle snores. Her mind relaxing a little, she nodded off. She woke up when Ian stirred beside her. Graham was gone. The door was shut, and the shed seemed even darker than before. She wasn't sure how long she'd slept.

Ian touched his mouth to indicate that he was hungry. "Me too, kiddo." She knew that even lack of a regular mealtime could set Ian back emotionally. She ached over what he was being put through, but she had little power to change it other than to comfort and reassure him.

She stared at the shut door. Maybe Graham had gone to find food. She imagined there would be canned goods or other mouse-proof items stored in the cafeteria, but that was in the main building in the center of camp, where they'd have a greater chance of encountering the attacker.

The door burst open. Marielle startled and Ian jerked as well.

It was completely dark outside. She'd slept a long time.

Graham rushed toward them. "He knows we're here. We need to keep moving."

Fear shot through her like an arrow. They were on the run again.

Graham's heart pounded as he reached out a hand to help Marielle to her feet. She turned to pick Ian up, and then Graham guided them toward the open door, stopping at the threshold to peer out.

Moments before, he'd seen the attacker. From where he was concealed, Graham had watched the other man discover his footprints and follow them. The footprints would lead around a couple of buildings before arriving at the shed where Ian and Marielle were hiding. That meant they had only minutes to get out of harm's way.

Adrenaline surged through him as he pulled his gun and glanced side to side. A flash of light shone several buildings over and disappeared. The man had acquired a flashlight and was getting closer.

Graham led the other two around the back of the shed through the darkness. They hurried to the shelter of the next building. Light flashed off to the side, and both he and Marielle pressed their backs against the outside wall of the building.

The goal was to move in the direction opposite from the man's path. Graham racked his brain for a semi-secure place for them to hide as they made their way to the next building. If he could find a safe place for Marielle and Ian, he might be able to go after the attacker and take him down. That would end the siege they were under, but he wasn't about to put them in the line of fire.

Marielle moved slower than Graham with Ian in her arms. He stepped behind her, searching for the beam of light that would indicate where their pursuer was but not seeing it. Maybe the attacker was having a harder time seeing the footprints that led to the back of the storage shed or he might have taken time to search the shed seeing that the footprints led inside the shed as well. Whatever the reason, the assailant had not yet come around to the back of the shed.

Graham hurried toward the main building and opened a side door that led to the vestibule. The main building contained a sanctuary, the cafeteria and offices and third floor storage. Plenty of places to hide, plenty of entrances and exits.

Marielle collapsed on a bench.

"You stay here," he said. "I'm going to make it look like we kept running."

"Okay, if you think that's best." She was still trying to catch her breath.

He ran out the side door and toward the next building. Grabbing a branch to brush out his footprints, he backtracked a different way and created a second set of footprints alongside the ones he had just made. He found a set of footprints that indicated the pursuer had walked the camp earlier along with their own footprints from when they had initially escaped to the garage.

He was out of breath by the time he reentered the vestibule. Marielle and Ian were barely visible in the darkness.

"I'm going upstairs to look out a window and see if I can find him."

"Ian and I are both starving. Can I take him to the cafeteria?"

He stared out the nearest window, which faced the direction they'd just come, seeing only darkness. The assailant must be searching each of the buildings, and that would slow him down. With so many footprints at the center of camp, it wouldn't be that easy to figure out where they'd gone. They had a little time. "I suppose that would be okay. No lights," said Graham. "I'll join you as soon as I can."

"I understand," she responded.

Graham went into the sanctuary and then took the side stairs that led to the second-floor offices. He peered out two windows but didn't see the telltale flashlight beam.

He watched and waited for a long moment. Only part of the manager's quarters was visible from here. Lights were on inside, but he couldn't make out anyone moving around. He'd hoped the man would just give up and return to the warmth of the manager's quarters, but it didn't seem likely.

He traversed the hallway to the other side of the building

and stepped into another office. This window faced the direction where he'd created the misleading footprints. No flash of light there either. After running up the stairs, he checked the windows on the third floor, still seeing no sign of the other man. Wherever he was, he wasn't close to this building.

Graham hurried downstairs and stepped toward the back of the sanctuary and then through the door that led to the cafeteria. All the tables had been pushed against one wall and the chairs had been stacked.

He sped toward the kitchen. Just enough moonlight came in through one of the windows to let him see Marielle and Ian sitting on the floor. Both of them were munching on something.

Marielle half stood up. "Do we need to go?"

"No, I think we're okay for a little while." He sat down beside her and pressed his back against a cupboard. "He's not close."

"We found some breakfast bars and juice boxes in an airtight container. You want some?"

His stomach growled. He hadn't eaten since breakfast. "Sure."

She reached around Ian to pull the container toward her and dug into it. "Here." She touched the back of his hand in the dark and he turned it over. She placed something square in his palm, her fingers warm against his skin. Then she handed him a juice box and turned her attention to helping Ian with his juice.

She leaned toward the little boy, so her forehead was almost touching his. "Does that taste good?"

Ian made a positive sound and nodded his head. Marielle laughed.

It was the first sign of contentment he'd witnessed from the child.

Graham took a bite of the fruit-flavored breakfast bar. "Amazing what a full stomach will do for your mood."

"For sure," she said.

The brief moment of calm was interrupted by a noise from somewhere inside the building. Graham tensed. A door opening, maybe?

The kitchen had an exit that led directly outside. Graham bolted to his feet. "The garage is two buildings over. Go and find a hiding place. I'm going to see if I can take this guy down."

Marielle was already standing. "Oh, Graham. That's so risky."

"Do what I say. This will end if I catch him. Then we won't be running and hiding all night."

He was grateful that she didn't argue further with him. Instead, she picked Ian up. Graham opened the side door and checked that the coast was clear. The noise had come from the front of the building.

Marielle and Ian rushed down the steps and disappeared into the darkness. He said a prayer for their safety, pulled his gun and headed toward the sanctuary. Taking in a deep breath, he braced himself for a violent encounter.

Chapter Five

Marielle moved as fast as she could through the deep and drifted snow. Even in the darkness, she could see her breath as it came out in puffs. It was getting colder. Ian snuggled close to her chest. The silhouette of the garage came into view.

She kept trudging ahead, refusing to look back toward the main building. Tension knotted through her chest. She wasn't so sure about this plan. It was true that they would be safe if Graham was able to subdue the other man. But what if the assailant was able to overtake Graham? He would come looking for them, and she and Ian would be the next target.

The thought tumbled through her mind as she made her way past the building beside the garage. She couldn't put Ian at risk, but if Graham didn't have her help, they might all end up dead. There had to be something she could do to ensure that Graham was not harmed or killed.

She prayed that God would give her clarity.

Finally, she turned to check the main building, which was still completely dark. She could see the window of the sanctuary where Graham thought the noise had come from. Ian's hand clutched the collar of her coat. They had to press on.

She pushed open the door of the garage. There was enough

moonlight streaming through the windows for her to see that there were plenty of places to hide.

Setting Ian down, she glanced around. After taking a few steps, she pushed aside a rolling toolbox to reveal a dark corner, a good hiding place. For two? Or could she leave Ian here to go help Graham? She had only seconds to decide.

Ian made a pleading noise, and she turned back toward him.

The little boy lifted his hands toward her, opening and closing them, as he gazed up at her. The face of innocence. She kneeled down and wrapped her arms around him, holding him close.

She had her answer. Her job was to protect this little boy and trust that Graham would succeed in his mission.

She touched his warm cheek with her fingers. "You and I are going to play a game. Do you understand?"

He nodded.

"We're going to hide—" she pointed in the corner "—and be very quiet until we hear that nice man's voice, Graham's voice."

Again, Ian nodded.

Marielle led him to the corner and both of them squeezed in. Hooking her feet under the toolbox, she rolled it toward her. Once it was within her grasp, she reached out and pulled it even closer. As the darkness engulfed them, she positioned herself with her knees close to her chest. Ian squeezed into the tight space beside her. She wrapped her arms around him.

The metal roof of the garage creaked in the wind. She closed her eyes and prayed.

Oh, God, give Graham strength, keep him safe. Protect all of us. You are our refuge and our fortress.

She would have to trust that God would help Graham as he entered into what might be a fight for his life...and a fight for hers and Ian's.

* * *

With his gun drawn, Graham entered the sanctuary through a side door and pressed against the wall.

Though his ears were tuned into his surroundings, he heard no additional noise. His own breaths seemed unusually loud in the room, which was otherwise heavy with silence.

As his eyes adjusted to the darkness, he could make out the rows of pews and the platform where the worship team and pastor stood. He surveyed every inch of the room, not seeing any movement. The gun felt heavy in his hand.

He'd been in gunfights before, but this was different. The lives of Marielle and Ian were at stake.

Barely breathing, he waited, listening and watching. The minutes ticked by, and he came to a decision. Deliberately, he made a noise by patting his hand against the wall. Then he took a few steps and ducked behind a pew. Graham heard no other sounds. If the attacker was still here, he would've re-acted and moved toward the noise.

The man must have left the sanctuary. Was he still in this building as he searched for the people he meant to kill?

Graham edged back toward the door he'd come through and out into the hallway, still not hearing or seeing any sign of the other man. His feet padded softly on the linoleum. Had the pursuer already left the building?

A muffled noise reached his ears.

His heart pounded as he pressed against the wall and took a few cautious steps forward, trying to discern where the noise had come from. Another similar sound floated up the hallway. He moved a little faster. It sounded like someone was in the kitchen at the back of the cafeteria, but the noise had been so faint, he could only make an educated guess.

He hurried down the hallway and into the cafeteria, then through the eating area toward the kitchen. The attacker would see the juice boxes and wrappers and know that they had been there.

His heart pounded as he slipped through the open door frame into the kitchen. But before he was even across the threshold, a heavy weight smashed against his shoulder. A second blow to his back caused him to lose his grip on his gun. He heard it hit the floor as he swung his fist and sought to land a blow against the other man in the dark.

Graham made contact with flesh, but he could not see clearly where the man was. He heard heavy breathing and lunged toward the sound, landing another blow. This time the man grunted in pain.

Motion flashed in his peripheral vision just as a fist connected with his jaw. The pain reverberated through his head, but he righted himself and fought back, punching several times. The other man slammed against a wall, and Graham dove toward the noise. His hand gripped the man's shirt. The assailant's heavy breathing surrounded him. The man grabbed his arm and twisted expertly, hitting a nerve that caused Graham to lose his grip.

Graham heard several footsteps as the attacker retreated. Silence fell once again. No breathing, no movement. The attacker must have fled. Graham silently ran his fingers over the wall in search of the light switch. It was a risk, but he needed to find his gun.

The other man hadn't tried to shoot him, which made Graham think that either he hadn't had time to pull his gun or, hopefully, he was out of bullets.

Just as Graham flicked the switch, weight landed on his back, and he was thrown forward onto the floor.

He landed on his stomach, and the attacker pinned one arm at the shoulder and smashed Graham's head against the floor before he could react.

Sparkles traveled across his field of vision from the blows to his head and the sudden brightness after so long in the dark. Because his lower body was not restrained, he managed to turn enough so he could avoid another blow to his head. He could only see the other man in his peripheral vision as he fought to free his shoulder. He wrestled free and turned over, then rammed his fist into the attacker's solar plexus. The other man's face filled with rage as he wheezed. Graham had knocked the wind out of him.

Breathing heavily, Graham crawled on all fours until he reached the countertop, grabbing it to hoist himself to his feet. He was halfway to standing, scanning the bright room to assess the situation, when he saw the attacker reaching for something on the ground. Graham's gun. He couldn't get to it before the attacker did. He had to escape the line of fire.

He threw himself through the exit to the seating area a second before a bullet hit the door frame. The shot echoed in the empty space. He hurtled into the darkness outside the cafeteria and ran as quickly and quietly as he could. The other man's footsteps pounded behind him.

He'd taken Graham's gun. His own that he used earlier must be out of bullets or not operational.

Graham headed toward the sanctuary, plotting to use the side exit and ambush the attacker as he ran out after Graham. Maybe he could get his gun back. The sanctuary flooded with light. The attacker was already in the room. Graham ducked behind a pew, hoping he hadn't been was spotted.

The other man's footsteps padded over the carpet. "Come out, come out, wherever you are."

Graham clenched his teeth.

"What have you done with the boy?" The menace in the attacker's voice bounced off the walls of the sanctuary.

Graham crawled underneath the pew and then rolled to the next one. He could hear his pursuer walk past, working his way toward the outside door. Graham rolled and crawled under another pew, moving in the opposite direction.

When he came to the last pew, he stopped with his stomach pressed against the carpet. The footsteps had ceased. He heard no sound of a door opening and closing. The other man was not going outside to search. He must have figured out that Graham was still in the sanctuary.

"I know you're in here somewhere," said the attacker.

Graham held his breath and listened as the attacker opened and closed doors at the back of the room, checking the coat closet and storage areas. He needed to get out of here and fast. It was only a matter of seconds before the attacker searched the pews again and found him. He rolled out from under the last pew and kept crawling to stay out of sight. Footsteps plodded slowly up the rows on the other side of the pews.

Graham exploded to his feet. A shot shattered the silence around him as he raced back into the dark hallway.

He ran, pumping his arms and willing his feet to move faster. He sprinted past the cafeteria, seeking another escape route. The darkness would help keep him hidden. He pressed against a wall and moved slower.

He was nearly to the back of the building when he realized he no longer heard his pursuer.

Sweat trickled down his temple as he paused, leaning hard against a wall. He waited a few seconds, not hearing any evidence that the other man had followed him. Fear seized his throat as realization sank in.

The attacker must have gone looking for Marielle and Ian while Graham was occupied with his own escape. He knew that the woman and the boy were in the camp alone somewhere, vulnerable targets. Graham had to protect them.

He found a window, desperately searching for the other man. Outside, a light flickered by before disappearing into the building next door—next to the garage. Graham's worst fears were confirmed.

He raced toward the nearest door and burst outside into the dark and cold. Light shone in the building next to the garage as the attacker searched. Graham slipped into the shadows provided by eaves of the main building to avoid being seen. He crouched as he ran past the building where the assailant was and headed toward the garage. He prayed that he could get to Marielle and Ian before the attacker did.

Chapter Six

After she'd heard the second gunshot, Marielle had pushed the rolling toolbox out of the way and stood up with Ian in her arms. The boy had been wiggling from the moment they'd crouched in the corner.

She glanced around, searching for a better hiding place. Each gunshot had caused her to pray for Graham's safety. She had to believe that he was still okay. She knew she needed to stick with the plan despite her fears. Graham expected to find her in the garage so that was where she and Ian needed to be.

She set the boy down on the concrete floor and held his hand. "Let's see if we can find a hiding place with a little more room. How does that sound?"

Ian stuck two fingers in his mouth, tilted his head and nodded, staring at her with wide brown eyes. She glanced at a large plastic storage tote next to the empty spot where the snowmobile had been and then at the truck that must belong to Graham. As her gaze moved past the window, she thought she saw movement.

A moment later, Graham rushed through the door. Fear was written all over his face. He glanced in their direction for only a moment before nodding to the truck. "Get in, I'll get the garage door opener."

Scooping Ian up, she ran toward the driver's side of the truck. What was Graham's plan? The vehicle might be rugged, but it wouldn't get far on unplowed roads.

She sat Ian on the seat beside her and swept her gaze over the dash, grateful to find the key in the ignition. At the rumble of the garage door opening, she turned the key, and the truck engine hummed to life.

Graham yanked open the passenger side door and jumped into the cab just as she saw a bobbing light emerging from the building next to them. The attacker was no doubt drawn by the noise. She threw the truck into Drive before Graham had even closed the door and pressed the gas.

She saw the attacker just outside the nearest building, hindered by the deep snow. He held a gun. Her side of the truck was closest to him, and he only needed to get within range to make a fatal shot.

"He's got a gun," she barked, slipping down low behind the wheel as Graham bent his upper body over Ian, wrapping a protective arm around the boy. She sped up the road, or at least where she thought the road was, that led through the camp. A shot hit the front part of the truck.

She slammed the gas pedal to the floor. The buildings had provided enough shelter so that the snow wasn't as deep here as outside the camp. Still, it was only minutes before the truck slid to a stop, wheels spinning uselessly. She tried to reverse out of the rut the tires had created. The truck moved back a few inches and then the engine made a grinding noise.

Graham glanced over his shoulder. "No time. Get out," he yelled and gathered Ian into his arms.

Her heartbeat drummed in her ears as she jumped out of the truck, crouching low when she landed. She headed toward the front of the truck, which would provide a degree of cover.

Graham was already several yards ahead of her as he held Ian close to his chest.

She followed as Graham sought cover behind the first building they came to.

Another gunshot echoed through the nighttime silence.

Graham stood with his back pressed against the building. "That's my gun, and I know he's going to run out of bullets soon. He has one, maybe two left. Go to the manager's quarters." He handed Ian to her, and the boy wrapped his arms around her shoulders. "I'm going to provide a diversion. There is a second gun underneath the plastic bag liner in the kitchen garbage."

She knew there was no time to protest the plan or express surprise that he'd apparently stashed weapons in the camp. She didn't want to be separated again, but she hurried to the backside of the next building as Graham ran out in the opposite direction.

She cringed when she heard yet another gunshot, momentarily paralyzed by the thought of what might have happened to Graham.

Trust Graham, stick with the plan.

Her heart pounded as she pushed herself toward the next building. No more gunshots reached her ears when she edged closer to the manager's quarters. Finding the back door unlocked, she moved up the stairs bent over from exertion and gasping for air but still holding Ian tightly.

Once inside, she put Ian on the floor and tried to catch her breath. They were in a little mudroom where some boots sat on the floor beside a tinderbox and a stack of wood. After locking the door, she ushered Ian into the living room.

Ian made a happy sound when he saw his stuffed giraffe on the love seat.

Marielle rushed around the house making sure the windows and doors were locked. When she peered out the windows, she saw no sign of either of the two men.

She pushed the love seat around so that it created a barrier between the windows by the front door and inside. She placed Ian on the floor by the love seat with his blanket and his giraffe.

"You stay here. Do you understand?"

The boy nodded and hugged the giraffe to his chest. Such a small thing made him feel more secure. She touched his cheek with her palm and looked into his eyes, searching.

"You're a good boy, Ian." She kissed his forehead.

He rose and fell into her arms.

She brushed the top of his head with a kiss, sat back on her legs and closed her eyes as she held Ian and rocked, praying silently.

Dear Lord, heal him from all he has been through, now and before with his parents, as if You pulled a curtain across his eyes and heart.

She rubbed his back and held him for a long moment before releasing him.

Marielle rose and moved to the kitchen. Taking a deep breath as she opened the cupboard, she lifted the trash liner and reached in for the gun. Her hand touched cold metal.

A small revolver. Six shots. Easy to shoot even for someone like her who was out of practice.

She put the gun in her coat pocket. When she peered in at Ian, he was pacing sucking his fingers and holding the giraffe. He needed a distraction. She searched several more cupboards for something that might serve as a toy for Ian. She brought him several small pots, a pie tin and a wooden spoon and showed him how to make music.

With Ian's light rhythmic tapping as background noise, she moved from room to room staring out each window for any sign of Graham or the other man. The gun felt heavy in her pocket. She brushed her fingers over the metal, feeling her throat grow tight. Could she shoot a person to save herself? To save Graham or Ian? Would it come to that?

She looked out into the darkness as a knot of tension formed at the back of her neck. The way Graham had laid out the plan had made it sound like he might risk his life to try to save hers and Ian's. The power of the sacrifice he was willing to make floored her. Why else tell her about the gun unless he thought she might have to defend herself?

The percussive boom of what he was pretty sure was the final bullet being fired surrounded Graham as he dove for the snow, praying he wouldn't be hit.

After a long moment, he raised his head and surveyed the buildings. With the gun rendered useless, he and the attacker were on equal footing. Unable to see much in the dark, he stared in the direction he thought the shot had come from. The man must have moved to the shelter of a nearby building... or maybe he'd opted to go after his primary target, Ian and Marielle. Graham's muscles tensed as he watched and waited.

Satisfied the man wasn't going to come after him, Graham rose to his feet and headed across the snow-drifted road to the side of the camp where the manager's quarters were. Aware that he might be watched, he didn't want to take a direct path back to Marielle and Ian.

He rushed around to the back of one building, keeping alert as he moved to the cover of the next. Worry settled in as more time passed without a sign of the attacker. The man couldn't have seen which way Marielle had gone with Ian, but if he was systematically checking each building, he would end up at the manager's quarters sooner or later.

Graham quickened his pace as the backside of the manger's quarters came into view. He reached the back door and found it locked. He'd knocked twice when a force like a brick wall crashed against him from the side.

The attacker was on top of him. Graham had only a moment to turn sideways so his face wasn't planted in the snow. Closed-fisted blows came fast and hard against his body.

Suddenly, the attacker angled away, lifting his weight from Graham's body as if reaching for something. Graham took the opportunity to sit up and grab the other man's ankle. The attacker fell, twisting away from Graham's grip and sitting up, holding something in his hands. Graham was still prone, and before he could react, the man attacked again from his seated position, pummeling Graham's torso and legs with the object. Pain vibrated through Graham's whole body, but he scooted away and got to his feet, the other man pushing to stand as well. Before the attacker was fully upright, Graham landed a series of blows to his face and shoulders, driving him into a defensive position. Graham reached for the object he held, fingers grazing wood. A thick piece of dropped firewood, perhaps? Something that could do serious damage.

The attacker spun free, still holding his makeshift weapon, and lunged. He struck Graham several times on the head, and then an explosive blow crushed against Graham's chest. With the wind knocked out of him, the world seemed to whirl around him.

The attacker meant to kill him. When the man raised the wood again, Graham feinted and grabbed it from his hand.

The attacker swayed, clearly exhausted from the fight. Graham raised the piece of firewood himself, hoping to knock the other man to the ground. But his arm dropped. He too had been weakened by the fight. Dizzy and breathless, he bent at the waist.

He could feel himself losing consciousness even as he fought to stay upright.

God, help me.

The attacker saw the opportunity and dove toward him. Graham lifted the piece of firewood to defend himself but felt his strength draining.

A gunshot rang out from behind him. Graham watched the other man jerk at the sound. Another shot was fired, and the attacker scrambled away, running in the opposite direction until he faded into the darkness. Moments later, Marielle made her way along the side of the manager's quarters holding the revolver. She turned back toward Graham who had slumped to the ground.

"We need to get you inside."

He tried to push himself to his feet, but his knees buckled. Somehow, she got him up and into the mudroom. He must have blacked out for a moment. She had repositioned herself, so his arm was around her shoulder. She gripped his waist to support him.

His head bobbed and his vision went dark again. When he opened his eyes, he was slumped in the easy chair. Marielle had retreated to the kitchen. He heard running water.

Ian stared at him from the floor by the love seat. The boy looked afraid.

"It's going to be okay, little buddy." He tried to sound reassuring, but he tasted blood when he spoke.

Clutching his stuffed animal, Ian rose to his feet and moved toward Marielle as she returned from the kitchen.

She held a wet washcloth. "You're bleeding pretty bad." She leaned forward and touched his temple and then his mouth with the cloth. It felt warm against his skin.

Ian moved closer to Marielle and clung to her leg.

Graham's voice grew soft as he kept his eyes on the boy. "Is there some way we can make him feel less afraid."

Her free hand brushed over Ian's head and she let out a sigh. "Things could be going a lot better to help him heal, but we can't change what's happening."

She placed the washcloth on Graham's forehead. He winced. Ian moved toward him and patted his leg as if to offer comfort. The gesture touched Graham. Despite the pain he was in, he reached out and rubbed Ian's back. The boy leaned against the couch and stared up at him.

Graham rested his head against the back of the couch.

"We have to be prepared. He knows we're in here. I'm sure he'll return."

"I know." She straightened up. The white washcloth had turned pink. She gazed down at him, then shook her head. "You're in pain. I'll get you some aspirin." She retreated again to the kitchen and returned with a couple of pills and a glass of water, which he gratefully accepted.

She scrutinized him, the lines of worry in her face deepening. "Graham, what do we do? You're in no condition to keep running."

She was right. Even when he tried to sit up straight, he felt dizzy. He needed to rest in order to recover. He had no idea what time it was, but morning couldn't be that far off. Would the plows show up by daylight?

She pulled the gun from her pocket and handed it to him. "There are four more bullets left. You're the one who uses a gun for a living."

"You handled the gun just fine. You saved my life out there." He took the gun and put it in the pocket of his coat. Right now, it didn't feel like he would even have the strength to lift it, let alone shoot accurately.

Their situation was not good.

Marielle sat down on the floor with Ian. She'd moved the love seat to create a barrier for her and Ian to hide behind. She picked up the wooden spoon and tapped out a rhythm on the pie tin, singing softly.

He recognized the melody. A song they used to sing right here at camp, but a world away from the dire situation they were in now. Life had been so clear-cut and innocent back then.

His eyelids grew heavy. He could feel himself fading. Marielle's sweet voice grew more distant as the blackness engulfed him.

He came to when Marielle shook his shoulder. "He's out there. I saw him."

Pain radiated through his body, but he had to find the strength to protect Marielle and Ian.

Chapter Seven

Worry lanced through Marielle's gut as she watched Graham try to push himself out of the chair, grimacing with pain. He managed to get to his feet, but he was still weak from the beating he'd taken. If he was to recover, he needed rest. She wasn't sure that was possible.

She pointed toward the front window. "I saw him through there. He went behind the sleeping cabin directly across from us."

He must have been prowling around this whole time, assessing the situation and waiting for the right moment to attack.

"I'm sure he's not going to stay there. He's probably trying to figure out a way to get at us, but he has to be smart about it. He knows we're armed. He doesn't know we only have four bullets." He looked directly at her. "You locked the back door?"

She nodded. "The place is as secure as it can be." She sat down on the floor beside Ian, pressing her back against the love seat and closing her eyes, hoping the silent prayer she said would quell the fear rising up in her.

Graham remained quiet for a few moments, and she opened her eyes again when he said thoughtfully, "He's taking his time to come at us. Do you think one of those shots you fired at him might have injured him?"

She shook her head. "I doubt it." She'd been shaking with terror when she'd pulled the trigger, so her aim was far from accurate. The gunfire had been enough to frighten the attacker away, no more.

Graham looked again toward the front window. "I wonder what he has in mind."

Marielle sat holding Ian while Graham moved through the house, crouching as he went past windows. Her heart pounded, and she struggled to take a deep breath. The attacker knew they had a gun and he didn't anymore. He wouldn't just break down the door and come directly at them.

Graham returned to his chair and sat down. He was sweating. The patrol had exhausted him. The bruises on his face had grown more distinct in the last hour.

She listened to the sound of his breathing and Ian nuzzled close to her and nodded off. She placed Ian on the love seat and covered him with his blanket.

Then she sat on the floor once more with her back resting against the love seat, her own eyelids growing heavy. She could feel herself fading again.

She'd been asleep a short time when the sound of shattering glass caused her to jerk awake. Graham was not in his chair.

More breaking glass, a window in the kitchen.

Her heart pounded as she took in a shallow breath.

She turned and touched Ian who was still asleep, but probably wouldn't be for much longer.

The taint of smoke reached her nose.

Marielle bolted to her feet. A burning rag had been thrown through the broken window. Another rag burned close to the front door. She raced to the kitchen for water, where she found Graham trying to stomp out a fire in there as well.

Cold wind blew through the shattered kitchen window.

Another window shattered somewhere in the house. Maybe

the mudroom. The attacker was trying to smoke them out. Graham had already put a bucket beneath the kitchen faucet. Though it was only half-full, she grabbed it and rushed to the living room.

Ian was coughing. She was pouring the water on the first fire when she noticed a third burning object had been tossed into the living room.

Smoke filled the room. Graham emerged from the bedroom carrying a wool blanket that he threw on the second fire just as another burning rag landed in the room.

Ian sat up and coughed.

"Get him to the bathroom. There are no windows in there."

She hurried across the floor and picked the child up. The hallway leading to the bathroom was filled with smoke. She sat Ian down on the closed toilet and grabbed a towel.

"I need you to put this under the door for me after I close it."

He let out a cry of protest and reached for her. She held him close as tears rimmed her eyes. "I know this is scary. I'll come back and check on you." She kissed his forehead then handed him the towel. "I have to help put out the fire."

He was clutching the towel in one hand and his stuffed giraffe in the other when she closed the door.

The smoke had grown even thicker. She could hear Graham coughing in the living room. When she checked the mudroom, she found that one of the rags had landed in the box of kindling, where flames now rose.

She ran into the kitchen, grabbing several buckets from the cabinet underneath the sink. She put one bucket under the kitchen faucet and ran to the bathroom with the other. Ian was sitting on the toilet holding his toy and sucking his fingers when she stepped inside, turned on the bathtub faucet and placed a bucket underneath it.

She patted Ian's leg. "Thank you for being so good."

She closed the door behind her as she raced back to the

kitchen where the bucket was nearly full. She could hear Graham fumbling around in the bedroom, probably trying to put out another fire in there as well.

She lifted the bucket and ran to the mudroom, where the flames had grown even higher. She saw that the fire was eating up stacked firewood and newspapers too. Her bucket of water did little to subdue the flames that licked at the wall.

Her face grew hot from the intensity of the burning. She ran back to the bathroom and picked up the now full bucket out of the bathtub. She grabbed a washcloth and dipped it in the water.

"Ian, put this over your mouth and close the door behind me. Put the towel back in place."

She was out the door before she had time to witness his reaction. In the mudroom, the flames had intensified. She poured the second bucket of water and turned to see Graham.

"You need to get in the bathroom with Ian. The attacker is trying to break down the front door. He probably thinks we've passed out from the smoke."

Sweat glistened on his forehead.

She grabbed his arm. "Are you sure?"

"It's the only way. Go take care of Ian." Graham pulled the gun from his waistband.

She ran toward the bathroom through the hallway that was even more smoke filled. She found Ian sitting on the floor holding the washcloth over his mouth, his eyes watching her.

She touched the top of his head. "It's okay. I'm here."

After closing the door and putting the towel back in place, she wetted a washcloth for herself and then took him into her arms.

She could hear Graham coughing in the living room.

The burning smell seeped into the bathroom even with the barrier of the door and towel. They couldn't stay here much longer. The fire in the mudroom was going to get more and more out of control even if all the other fires had been put out. But if they ran outside, the attacker would be waiting for them.

The door flew open. Graham bent over and coughed before he could talk.

"Change of plans. There's too much smoke. We have to get out of here."

"Is he still trying to get in?" She rose, holding Ian.

"The noise has stopped. I saw him circle around the side of the house toward the back. He's probably assessing the damage the fires have done or trying to find another way in."

Graham reached for her, placing his hand on her back as he guided her down the hallway. The smoke stung her eyes.

"We'll go out the front door. The living room is the least smoky and I think he's still at the back of the house."

With Marielle in front holding Ian, they hurried through the living room. All of them were coughing as they reached the front door.

Her heart raged against her rib cage. She prayed they would find a hiding place before the attacker came around the side of the house and saw them escaping.

When he glanced over his shoulder, Graham caught a glimpse of the other man at the side of the house by the mudroom entrance, his back to them.

They had to hide before he saw them.

Adrenaline raged through his body. Despite his injuries, he felt a surge of energy.

He sped toward Marielle's car and swung the door open. "Get in the back. I'll keep watch."

Marielle and Ian crawled into the back seat and lay down as he closed the door silently. He slipped behind the back bumper just before the attacker reappeared around the side of the house. Hidden in shadows, Graham was fairly confident he couldn't be seen as he watched the man make his way to the front door. If he checked it, he'd find it unlocked now and re-alize they'd escaped. Graham pulled his gun and watched in-tently. Sure enough, the assailant opened the door and stepped inside. Smoke curled out from the back of the house. The man emerged a few seconds later glancing from side to side and coughing.

Graham ducked back behind the car, staying unseen but also losing sight of what the assailant was doing. He tuned his ears to his surroundings as the wind whipped around him. He held the gun close to his chest and pointed it at the sky while he listened.

He heard footsteps crunching in the snow, but they got softer as the seconds ticked by. When he scooted to the other side of the bumper and looked past it, he could just make out the backside of the other man as he stepped back into the main building.

The sky had already started to lighten. They would not have the cover of night to conceal them much longer.

It would take some time to search the main building and re-alize they weren't there. Now was their chance to find a more secure hiding place.

He rose and opened the car's back door.

"Let's move."

Marielle sat up, inched to the edge of the seat and got out before reaching for Ian.

"Where is he?" Holding Ian, she drew the blanket over his head. She must've taken off the snowsuit at some point.

"Inside the main building." He surveyed the camp and made a decision.

Still gripping his gun, he directed Marielle and the boy in the opposite direction from the main building. She followed his lead through the camp and uphill to the sleeping quarters. He hurried them inside one of the larger cabins. The room was only slightly warmer than the chill outdoors. Eight sets of metal bunkbeds with no bedding or mattresses on them filled the room. Marielle had a vague memory from her time as a counselor here that the mattresses were stored where the mice couldn't get at them.

She slumped down on the floor away from the windows while Graham moved toward the window that provided a view of the camp below. It had grown even lighter out in the few short minutes it had taken them to get to the sleeping cabin. He spotted the assailant headed up the snow-drifted lane back toward the manager's quarters.

Graham ducked out of view. Still crouching, he approached the door they'd come through. There was no way to lock it.

Fortunately, there was no other door into the long, narrow cabin. Climbing through one of the windows would be too slow.

Marielle brushed a long strand of hair out of her eyes. "Now what do we do?"

He was fatigued and out of breath from the little bit of running they'd done to get here. Trying to play offense and go out to take the man into custody was out of the question now. He was too weak.

"Why don't you and Ian go over there by that wall away from the door?"

While Marielle shifted positions, he got up and peered out the window by the door. His throat went dry. The assailant was methodically searching each building working his way toward where they were hidden.

Assuming he moved in a straight line, he had three more buildings to look through. One of them was a small storage shed that would take no time at all.

Marielle settled with Ian against the wall opposite of where the door was. "Where's he at?"

Graham pulled a storage locker away from the end of one of the bunkbeds and sat down on it, facing the door with the gun in his hand.

He could not go after the other man and hope to take him down, but he could wait and be ready for him.

"He's coming this way," he said. "We have only a few minutes."

When the man came through the cabin door, Graham's plan was to shoot him.

Chapter Eight

Tension threaded through the space as Marielle wrapped an arm around Ian when they sat side by side on the floor. Her stomach was tied up in knots.

Graham spoke to her without taking his eyes off the door where his gun was aimed. "Why don't you and Ian get even farther away from the door? Back in that far corner on the opposite wall."

When the attacker came through that door, it was clear that Graham's intent was to shoot him. While she realized that Graham had no choice, Ian would witness more violence. Maybe he was hoping she could shield the little boy at least from seeing if not hearing what was about to happen if she was some distance from the door.

A chill set into her. Though she still wore Graham's boots, she'd slipped out of the coat when she was fighting the fire. She wrapped the blanket tighter around Ian.

"Are you cold?" Graham took his coat off, tossing it in her direction. "Put that on," he whispered before drawing his attention back to the door. "This will be over soon."

The intensity of his words made her heartbeat kick up a notch.

Ian stood beside her. He still clung to his giraffe while

brushing hair out of his eyes. Not wanting to be spotted through the window, she crawled across the floor and reached for the coat. She rose to her knees and slipped into the coat which was still warm from Graham's body heat. "It seems like he should have gotten here by now." She lifted her chin but could not see anything through the window by the door from where she kneeled on the floor.

"Maybe he's moving through the buildings in a zigzag pattern instead of coming straight here. Checking more buildings that way." His arms, which had been straight holding the gun, bent slightly.

Marielle led Ian to the far side of the room and settled into a corner, wrapping the big coat around him after she pulled him into her lap. She could feel his torso expand and contract as she held him.

She peered at Graham through the labyrinth of the metal bunkbed frames. Ian slumped in her arms, resting but not asleep.

The seconds ticked by. More light streamed through the windows as the sun came up.

Graham let his hands relax. "Something's not right. He must be up to something." Staying low, he moved toward the window by the door to peer out. He shook his head and made his way toward another window.

Ian stirred in her lap and moaned softly. She made shushing noises, hoping it would calm him.

"I'm going to check outside," he said. "I won't go far."

She let out a fearful breath. "It's daylight." What if the assailant had figured out where they were and was waiting for Graham to step out?

"I have to assess what's going on. I'll be careful." He pulled the door open a few inches and stood watching for a long moment before stepping outside.

She steeled herself, waiting for the sound of bodies hitting the wall or gunshots. The silence settled around her. Even though he was weak from his injuries, Graham had a gun.

He had the training to keep both of them safe. In a way, his leaving her all those years ago was now the thing that could save her and Ian. Only God could have provided such perfect timing for her life.

She tried not to picture something bad happening to him. *Don't let your mind go there. You need to stay strong.*

Ian wiggled in her arms. Eyes wide open, he lifted his head and stared at her and then patted her cheek. He must have picked up on her anxiety and wanted to comfort her.

"Sweet boy," she said. For someone so young, he seemed to be tuned in to the emotions of the people around him.

The door of the cabin creaked open, blown by the wind. Not surprising. The cabin was old and in need of repair. She stared at the door, deciding that the smart thing would be to stay put.

A single gunshot exploded outside. Her whole body jerked in response to the noise as her heart raged against her rib cage.

It didn't sound like the shot was right outside the door.

Ian sat up straight and twisted around. He slid off her lap and stared at the door swinging on its hinges. By the time she stood up, Marielle's mouth had gone dry. Her heartbeat thrummed in her ears.

Her attention remained on the open door. Ian pushed himself to his feet and reached for Marielle's hand. "Stay here. I'll be right back."

She ran to the nearest window that faced the direction the attacker had been moving as he made his way toward the cabin. The wind kicked up a flurry of snow, but she saw no sign of either Graham or the other man.

The door blew shut and open again, banging against the frame. The noise made her jump.

She ran back toward Ian and swept him up. This place felt really unsafe. But this cabin was where Graham expected to find them.

She'd taken two steps toward the door when she heard another gunshot.

* * *

Graham took aim and pulled the trigger just as the other man dove behind a pile of firewood by the main building. Once he'd spotted the attacker emerging from a building, Graham had pursued the man through camp. He'd used up two of his four remaining bullets.

His drive to keep Ian and Marielle safe masked his pain and exhaustion.

The wind had intensified, blowing snow tornadoes through the camp.

With his finger still across the trigger guard and his arms straight, he stared at the woodpile. The shot he'd taken must be lodged in a piece of firewood. "Come out with your hands up." The chase had left him out of breath and a little shaky but the notion that he was close to taking this man in energized him.

His hair ruffled in the breeze. His head and neck grew cold. There'd been no time to grab a hat, and he'd given Marielle his coat.

A faint mechanical noise reached his ears. When he glanced toward the main road, he saw snow spraying into the air. Relief spread through him. The snowplow was here and working its way down the road toward camp. They would be able to get out of here in less than half an hour. Hopefully, the snowplow driver would not been put in harm's way.

He intended to leave with the attacker in custody.

He drew his attention back to the woodpile as he stalked toward it then swung around to the back of it ready to shoot if necessary. The man was not crouching behind it. Tracks indicated that the man had dragged himself along the ground to stay out of view. Graham glanced at the corner of the long building just as the attacker disappeared behind it with a piece of firewood in his hand.

He was probably pressed against the building waiting to ambush Graham and hit him with his new favorite weapon.

The noise of the plow grew even louder as the driver made his way down the main road into the camp.

Up the hill, Marielle poked her head out of the cabin and was staring down at him. She turned slightly, noticing the plow. He gestured for her to go back into the building. He didn't want the attacker to know where she was in case this didn't go as planned.

Graham stalked toward the man's hiding place. With his back pressed against the outside wall, he moved a little closer to the back of the building where he assumed the man still was. He took a few more steps so he'd be close enough to get an accurate shot if the man ran out this way.

After several minutes, he realized the man was either still waiting or had run out in the other direction. He held his breath as he edged toward the corner of the building. Before turning the corner, he listened. Not hearing any indication that the man was there, he leaned out with his gun aimed, using the corner of the building to shield himself.

His breath hitched when he saw that the attacker was three buildings away. He was running along the back of the buildings and focused on fleeing, but he was still getting closer to Marielle and Ian's hiding spot. Had he seen her stick her head out of the building?

Graham had to get to them first. The plow had just reached the road that led through camp when Graham got to the front side of the buildings.

There was no time to wave the driver down and ask him to call the authorities when he got to the base of the mountain. Besides, he didn't want to risk the man becoming a target too. Maybe he would notice the burned portion of the manager's quarters and know something was amiss.

Graham headed up the hill to Marielle and Ian's cabin. He kept checking for the attacker as he moved but couldn't see the man anywhere. Though it looked like the fire was no longer burning in the manager's quarters, the blackened windows indicated that much damage had been done. Graham quickened his pace, praying that the attacker hadn't reached Marielle and Ian.

When he arrived at the cabin, the door was flung open. Fearing that Marielle was in a fight with the attacker, or worse, he gripped his gun and approached the window by the door in a crouch. His chest grew tight as he peered over the sill and scanned the interior. He saw no sign of the attacker—or of Marielle or the boy.

It took some mental effort to push away thoughts of the bad things that might've happened to them. Keeping his gun drawn, he stepped into the cabin. They were not inside. There was no blood on the floor, no overturned furniture, no indication that a struggle had taken place.

But she must've been afraid and taken shelter elsewhere. He looked through one of the small windows opposite the door. Tracks in the snow indicated where to search first.

He hurried to the next building, another sleeping cabin. The door burst open when he was a few steps from it. Marielle stood there. Flooded with relief, he stepped into the building and wrapped her in his arms. "I was afraid something bad had happened to you two."

He held her close. Her long brown hair smelled like burned wood but was soft to the touch when his hand brushed over it.

She pulled away and gazed up at him with wide brown eyes, the color of dark chocolate. "I was afraid he'd spotted me when I stuck my head outside the cabin. I knew we had to hide somewhere else."

They were standing so close that he felt her breath on his face when she spoke. When he looked over her shoulder, he saw Ian standing close by, holding his blanket in one hand and his stuffed animal in the other. Something about seeing the little boy made his throat tight.

"I'm just glad you're both okay," he whispered.

She took a step back as her expression became sterner.

His show of emotion had made her uncomfortable. From the moment Marielle had shown up at his door, he had felt a responsibility to protect both of them. Maybe there were other feelings blossoming, but Marielle clearly didn't share them.

He cleared his throat and said, "The plows have gone through. We can get out of here now."

Graham stepped outside to check their surroundings. Down below, he saw the road through the camp had been plowed. When his gaze landed close to the manager's quarters, he saw that Marielle's four-wheel drive was no longer there. The attacker had chosen to escape in her car, probably fearing he might be stranded up here and caught now that the roads were clear. That explained why he hadn't come after them.

Marielle came to stand beside him. "The truck is stuck in the snow still. How are we going to get out of here?"

The plow had swerved around the truck as it plowed, creating a bank around it. Feeling a rising tension, he stared down at his truck still lodged in the deep snow.

The attacker had known which vehicle was usable, and which wasn't. He might have driven a short distance away and be looking down for the opportunity to come at them again knowing they didn't have a clear way to escape.

He prayed that they were not still trapped here, easy targets for their attacker.

Chapter Nine

Fighting off despair, Marielle looked at the tracks her missing four-wheel drive had left behind. "Maybe the snowmobile can get us out of here."

Graham stroked his beard before shaking his head. "That involves hiking beyond the edge of camp and a cold ride to the bottom of the mountain. Let's see if we can dig the truck out first."

She followed him down the hill. While Graham went to get another coat, she put Ian in the cab of the truck, turned on the heat and went to look for shovels in the garage.

By the time she'd found two shovels, Graham had returned. They worked together quickly to dig out the front tires, then shoveled out the bank the plow had made around the truck.

After about twenty minutes, she leaned on her shovel to catch her breath. Graham straightened and swiped his forehead with his gloved hand. He walked the length of the front bumper, staring at the base of the truck. "That should do it. You get behind the wheel and back it out, and I'll push from the front."

Marielle glanced toward the plowed road that led up and out of the camp. What was the attacker planning? He'd left them stranded here, but she didn't believe he'd given up so easily. Was he going to come back, or was he waiting for them somewhere on the road, knowing they could get out now?

She got into the cab and gave Ian's leg a pat before attempting to reverse out of the bank. The tires spun, the truck refusing to move. Shoulders slumping, she let up on the accelerator. Doing this was only getting them more stuck.

Graham stopped pushing and straightened to look through the windshield. She shook her head. He walked around to the driver's side window which she rolled down.

"I think there might be some kitty litter in the truck bed. After I spread that around the front tires, try putting it in Drive then Reverse, rocking back and forth to get out of the rut."

She nodded and rolled up the window. The truck bucked back and forth, finally getting out of the ruts the tires had created. Graham gave her the thumbs-up.

"All right." She let out a sigh of relief and smiled at Ian. "We did it."

Ian kicked his legs and hugged his giraffe tighter. Though it was faint, he smiled back at her. "It's good to have something go right, huh?" She ruffled his hair.

Graham came around to the driver's side, and she scooted over on the seat, lifting Ian into her lap and then setting him in the middle seat. While Graham climbed into the cab, she made sure Ian was buckled in. His car seat had been taken along with her car.

Graham continued to drive slowly, heading up the plowed road that would lead them back to civilization. "Once we get down the mountain and have cell service, we can call in a stolen car report. Highway patrol might be able to pick the guy up before he has a chance to ditch your car."

As they climbed up the mountain road, she craned her neck for one last look at the camp. "You'll have to tell Adrian about the damage to the manager's quarters."

"Yes, for sure." A note of sadness entered his voice. "It's

hard to see that kind of destruction. This place has a lot of special memories for me."

"Me too." A flood of emotions stabbed at her heart. Remembering how good they'd been together made her sad for what they had lost. Like a movie reel playing, the memories spun through her mind. Swimming in the lake, walking the trails together, sitting around the campfire laughing with the other campers while Graham wrapped his arm around her.

"I'm sure the place is insured." He shook his head. "Still bothers me."

Was he remembering that this was where they'd met and fallen in love?

She gazed at his profile as he focused on the road and making the turn that would lead them back down the mountain. "Are you coming back up here to watch the place after you get Ian and me to town?" She still didn't know why he'd come back to Montana or why he hadn't gotten in touch with her when he did. Certainly, it wasn't just to be a wintertime caretaker. She pressed her lips together, feeling that stab of pain in her heart again. Graham still had a lot of explaining to do, but that didn't mean he would.

"Not sure of the plan at this point," he responded. "That man was after you two. While he's still at large, I need to make sure you're both safe, for starters."

"I appreciate that you want to help, and I'm so grateful for all you've done for us, but the local police will provide protection now for sure. I've been working with them from the start. We don't want to trouble you." She sounded cool, but her voice no longer held the tone of hostility she'd initially directed toward him. If the last couple of days had shown her anything, it was that Graham would do everything in his power to keep her and Ian alive. If she was honest, she would be a little sad that they were parting ways.

"It's no trouble," he said.

She studied him for a moment while his focus was on the

road. Even though she felt herself softening toward him, the old feelings of hurt, confusion and anger were still there. When he'd hugged her with such affection back at the camp, she'd become afraid. The last thing she wanted to do was to open her heart to him so he could rip her world to pieces again. "You must have work that you need to do. Or are you on vacation while you're here in Montana?" The question was intended to probe for answers.

"Some bad things happened connected to my work." He glanced in her direction. "I came back up here to try to get my head in the right place." His words were clipped and filled with angst.

"I suppose the solitude of the camp is good for that."

"It always felt that way to me. I thought if I prayed and cross-country skied, that it would put me in a better place." He kept his eyes on the road.

"Did it?"

"Not really."

She wanted to know more, but the tone of his voice indicated that this was not the time to press.

Graham slowed down as a car-sized lump covered in snow at the edge of the road came into view.

He veered the truck toward the shoulder as they passed by it. The wind had blown some of the snow off a sporty-looking hood.

"That must be his car," she said. "He made it this far up the mountain before he got stuck."

"We'll have to look into getting it towed. Chances are it's a rental or stolen, but it might provide evidence as to who he is."

Marielle stared at the car as they eased by. That meant he must've hiked the rest of the way into the camp in cold, windy conditions. Actions of a man who was determined to complete his mission and was also in extremely good shape. The memory of the attacker coming after her and Ian caused a chill to run down her spine. "He must be the man who..." She glanced meaningfully down at Ian, not wanting to mention Kristen's murder now. "Clearly he knows Ian can identify him."

Graham shook his head. "I'm not sure that makes sense. This guy had some skills and wasn't emotionally involved. And he didn't hide his face, which means we can identify him. I think a larger organization is at work here." He was speaking in lightly coded language too, shielding Ian.

"I think his intent was to make sure you and I were out of the picture and then take—" she nodded down at Ian instead of saying his name "—with him. He seemed more interested in getting him from us than doing anything permanent, at least at first." She drew her borrowed coat a little closer to her neck as if that would keep the icy terror from invading her awareness as she relived what had transpired the last couple of days.

"Yeah, he made that pretty obvious, that we were collateral damage. Still, I think he might have been hired for this job. The guy had some skills for sure."

She hadn't thought of that possibility. If it was true that their attacker was simply a contract killer, then whoever killed Ian's mother wasn't just some addict who didn't want to pay his debt or was so messed up he'd lost control. And that made sense. After the killing, Ian's father had gone on the run rather than trying to stay with his boy. If the killer had resources, if he was part of a larger organization, as Graham said... Thinking about the home invasion and all that had transpired at the camp overwhelmed her.

"Course we won't know anything until we figure out who he is. I saw his face briefly," said Graham. "You did too, I assume?"

She nodded. Though it had been dark for much of the time, she did remember what he looked like. She'd seen him clearly when he'd first come into the manager's quarters. "I think if I saw a picture of him, I would recognize him."

"We'll give the description to the police. It'll make it that much harder for him to get at you two and easier to catch him."

"I hope that's true." She stared down at Ian who had fallen asleep. If the attacker was hired muscle, wouldn't the real killer just pay someone else to come after the boy once the attacker was caught? Would this ever end?

Graham got to the base of the mountain and turned onto the paved road that led into Clarksville. His gaze traveled from the road ahead to the rearview mirror several times.

She looked over her shoulder. "Do you think he's waiting for us along this road?"

"We have to consider every possibility," he said.

Though there was only a semitruck behind them, his hypervigilance made sense.

"Why don't you see if your cell phone works now? Call the police and let them know about your car. I have a feeling he'll ditch it at the first opportunity, so we need to be fast."

"I know who to call." She pulled her cell phone from her bathrobe pocket. After bringing up her contacts, she pressed the number for Detective Strickland, who was working on Ian's mother's murder investigation. He was her contact in the department. When he answered, she told him briefly what had happened and that they were on their way in for a fuller report. She wanted to talk about security for herself and Ian too. He promised to notify highway patrol to look for her stolen car. She gave him a description of the man who had tried to kill them. She realized her description was generic at best. Tall, muscular, dark hair.

"Sorry, I guess there was nothing overly distinct about him." She pressed the phone to her chest and spoke to Graham. "Do you have anything to add?"

He shook his head. "Nothing that stands out about his appearance. Only saw him in the daylight for a few seconds."

She talked into the phone. "Sorry the description is so vague."

The detective spoke up. "We might be able to produce a more precise description of him if we can get the two of you to look at the database of known criminals in the area or bring in a sketch artist."

"Okay. We'll get to the station as soon as we can. I just need to get changed and cleaned up. Ian and I could both use something to eat."

"As fast as you can," the detective agreed.

She thanked him and disconnected.

"Can we stop at a store? I need to get some different clothes." They were headed into town, not back to her house. She wondered if it was even safe to go home. Certainly not alone. Her world had been turned completely upside down.

"I get it, but I don't want to take too much of a chance with staying out in the open for long. Why don't we hit a drive-through so we can take it over to the police station and eat it there?"

She crossed her arms over her stomach. "I suppose you're right." Just a reminder that she could not take a deep breath until the man who was after Ian was taken in.

Graham rounded a curve and slowed down. "What have we here?"

Up ahead, the lights of several police cars flashed. Graham eased toward the line of stopped cars.

"Must be an accident," she said.

Graham brought his truck to a stop.

The line of cars was long enough that she could not see the accident.

"I don't like delays like this." His voice held a nervous edge as he glanced out the side windows.

She sat back in her seat, feeling the tension sink back into her bones. "He wouldn't come after us with all the police so close by, would he?"

Picking up on her nervousness, Ian stiffened as well. She stroked his hair.

Graham's attention was focused on the patrol vehicles up

ahead. "I don't know what he'll do. I just don't want to take any chances."

The line of cars began to roll forward. The car in front of them swerved a little. Graham shifted back into Drive and followed the other cars, keeping enough distance to prevent a collision if he did start to slide.

As they moved past the accident, she saw that neither of the cars involved was her stolen car. The attacker hadn't been behind them when they turned onto this road, and he wasn't in the line of cars ahead. "I don't see my car anywhere. Where do you think he went?"

Graham shrugged. "I don't think he'd just give up. Maybe he went ahead into town to wait by the police station since that's the most likely place we'd go."

They'd made it off the mountain, but that didn't mean they were at all safe. The relief she'd felt when Graham turned onto the paved road vaporized.

"Maybe it would be best if we just went directly to the police station. We'll figure out food later."

As long as that man was still out there, there was no safe place for them.

Graham drove past the accident. As the cars in front of him sped up, he did too but exercised a degree of caution. The roads were still icy, and it had begun to snow again. He was grateful for Marielle's suggestion that they go directly to the police station.

Though nothing bad had happened, sitting in traffic made him realize how vulnerable they still were. He vowed to work with the police to get the man into custody. He hoped that would end the danger for Marielle and Ian.

It seemed that Marielle preferred police protection over his anyway. There was still a chasm between them. He understood her anger over what had happened ten years ago. But still, it hurt to feel like she was pushing him away.

He glanced down at Ian. The boy's expression as he held his toy close to his cheek tugged at Graham's heart. To be so little and to have been through so much. Graham felt protective of him, just as he had felt protective of Cesar. It was just too easy to form attachments. Maybe he was no longer cut out for undercover work as he once was.

The snowfall intensified. Graham switched the wipers onto a higher speed. The road that led into town was winding. He pressed into a curve and focused his attention on his driving.

Once they got to the police station, he needed to get in touch with his handler. He still didn't feel like he was ready to go back to work. He'd asked for a week off and only used four days of it.

If there was nothing pressing to deal with, perhaps he would return to the camp to help with repairs of the manager's quarters once he was sure Ian and Marielle had protection. Time spent being around and praying with Adrian might help him work through the loss of Cesar in a way that being alone had not.

Graham let up on the gas. Visibility was down to a few feet even with his headlights turned on. The truck swerved slightly.

Ian made a noise that sounded like a gasp that got stuck in his throat.

Marielle glanced through the windshield, then took the stuffed giraffe from Ian. Singing a children's song, she made the giraffe dance. Ian clapped his hands. Graham appreciated that she was trying to distract Ian from being scared about the hazardous road conditions.

While the windshield wipers worked at a furious pace, Graham gripped the wheel and leaned forward.

Marielle turned sideways in her seat. "That car behind us is really close."

Graham glanced in the rearview mirror, seeing only the headlights of the other vehicle made murky by the falling snow.

"The guy must not be from around here. He doesn't understand about safe braking distance in hazardous conditions."

Though his attention was on the road in front of him, he could feel her gaze resting on him for a long moment.

"Yes, that must be it." Her voice came out in a monotone.

Neither of them wanted to say anything that would frighten Ian unnecessarily. But both of them were concerned about another assault.

Marielle's phone rang. She pressed the connect button. "Hello...yes...you found it already...where...thank you, Officer. We should be at the police station in fifteen minutes or so. It's kind of gnarly out here on the highway."

She pushed the disconnect button. "They found my car. Back up the road a ways. There's that café and bait shop that's right before the fishing access."

He had a vague memory of it. "Yeah."

"The owner reported his car stolen. They found my car up the road a piece, out of sight."

"Isn't that close to the camp road?"

"Yes, less than a mile," she said.

The man had not wasted any time in ditching Marielle's car.

When he glanced sideways, the other car had come up beside him. Passing in these conditions on a curving road was extremely risky. Graham lifted his foot off the gas.

Marielle let out a half scream that chilled him to the marrow. Ian stirred awake.

The other car was veering toward them.

Graham turned the wheel toward the narrow shoulder of the road and sped up. The other car slammed into the bed of his truck with its front end.

Ian gasped.

Graham clenched his teeth. His body stiffened in response to the impact. Pain from his previous injuries intensified. Marielle drew a protective arm around Ian.

His truck fishtailed as Graham fought to regain control. He

snaked along the road, praying that they would not meet on-coming traffic. In an effort to keep from wrecking, he lifted his foot from the gas. The erratic path the truck had been traveling in straightened out. He let out the breath he'd been holding.

Marielle peered over her shoulder. Terror lanced through her words. "He's getting closer."

He'd barely processed what she'd said when he heard and felt the jarring impact of metal crunching against metal. His teeth pressed together as his body was flung forward. The seat belt dug into his chest. His truck loomed toward the edge of the road as he sought to turn the wheel in the other direction.

A second collision to the back of the truck made it impos-sible to wrestle his vehicle under control. Snow swirled across the windshield while the wipers continued to work, creating a rhythmic and intense swishing noise at odds with the attack.

He pumped the brakes and tried to turn the wheel but to no avail. The tires left the road as they sailed through the air. The front of the truck impacted with a solid object.

He was flung forward and then back, pain from hitting the steering wheel roaring through him. The truck was too old to have airbags.

When the wipers stopped moving, the windshield filled with snow, blocking any view of the outside world.

He was breathless and light-headed. He turned to see if Marielle and Ian were okay, but his eyes would not focus. He saw blurred movement. Marielle wiggling in her seat.

His door opened suddenly. He was still restrained by his seat belt, so the attacker had the advantage, landing several blows to his head before Graham got in a single punch to the man's jaw. Black dots filled Graham's field of vision.

He heard the unbuckling of a seat belt and Marielle's pro-tests coming from very far away as if she was speaking through thick fabric.

"Don't you hurt him," Marielle repeated over and over,

her voice filled with panic and pain. She was close to his ear now even as he felt himself fading. "Graham, stay with me."

His world went black just as he heard the sound of glass being broken and Marielle screaming in protest.

Chapter Ten

The attacker smashed the window and reached in to unlock the passenger side door. She scooted across the seat to avoid the glass hitting her, though there was not much space with Ian between her and Graham. Her body shielded Ian.

"You can't have him." A maternal fierceness rose up in her.

The man grabbed Marielle by the collar. She shouted Graham's name, hoping to rouse him, but he was slumped over the steering wheel, blood dripping from his forehead. He did not move. Was he even still alive?

The attacker held on to her coat at the shoulders with both hands. When he sought to pull her out of the truck, she beat his arms.

The distressed and frightened noises that Ian made caused her to fight even harder. With her fingers spread, she clamped her palm over the man's face and pushed.

The man grabbed her neck and squeezed. In response, she clawed at him, wheezing for breath as she struggled to pry his hands off her, angling her body to try to break free in the restricted space of the truck cab.

The man's face was very close to hers. His eyes were filled

with rage. The fear it struck in her only fueled her need to survive.

He gripped her coat at the shoulder with his free hand and jerked her out of the truck, lifting her slightly and tossing her on the ground, where she landed on her stomach. The snow was still coming down. Icy cold surrounded her face. She brushed away the snow from her eyes and cheeks, then turned toward the truck. The attacker was reaching in toward Ian.

She shook herself free of the terror that threatened to paralyze her. She had to save the little boy.

Marielle flipped around, grabbed the man's foot and pulled. His attention wavered, gaze flicking back down to her. She tried to scramble to her feet, but he pushed her back into the snow and lifted his boot. She drew her arms up toward her head and her knees toward her stomach to protect herself from the kick.

The impact never came.

She pulled her hands away from her face. The man was running toward his stolen car, which he'd parked in front of their wrecked truck. With some effort, Marielle pushed herself to her feet.

The attacker jumped into his car and sped off.

Swaying, she stared up the road in the opposite direction the attacker had fled. The flashing lights that filled her field of vision explained why the attacker had retreated. The police must have been headed back to town after dealing with the accident.

She stumbled toward the police car as the officer got out. A deputy she knew by sight but not by name came toward her through the snow.

He reached and held out a hand to steady her. "Ma'am, are you okay?"

"We need an ambulance." She pointed up the road. "A man ran us off the road. He drove away."

"I'll radio it in. What was the man who ran you off the road driving?"

Everything had happened so fast, she couldn't remember. "It was a dark color. The car that was just stolen from the café and bait shop up the road."

"Got it." The officer headed back to his patrol vehicle.

The sound of the officer talking on his radio became background noise as she rushed over to the truck. She peered through the open door where Ian had clicked himself out of his seat belt and was leaning against Graham, patting his shoulder. Graham's face still rested against the steering wheel.

The boy turned his head toward Marielle and spoke a single word. "Owweee."

Marielle let out a breath. Even through her terror, her heart warmed and a sense a joy filled her. It was the first word he'd spoken since she'd taken custody of him. "Yes. He's hurt."

At least, she hoped that was all that was wrong with Graham.

She ran around to Graham's side of the truck, where the door was still open. He did not stir at all when she spoke his name. Ian seemed to have formed an attachment to Graham. She prayed that he was all right.

She reached in, putting her palm on his cheek. His skin was warm to the touch, and the cut on his head did not look severe. It was the internal damage she was more concerned about. He'd sustained several intense blows to the head, both here and at the camp. She touched his neck to find a pulse, grateful when she felt the rhythmic push against her fingers. Ian stared up at her. His expression held a question as he sucked on two fingers.

"We'll take Graham to a doctor. He's going to be okay." She prayed that what she said was not an empty assurance.

Ian's face brightened.

"You like him, don't you?"

Ian nodded.

The officer came up beside her. "Ambulance should be here any minute."

"Can we ride with you to the hospital? We're supposed to go to the police station, but I need to make sure he's going to be okay." She nodded toward Graham.

"Why the police station?"

"This little boy witnessed a crime. We need protection. If you talk to Detective Strickland, he will fill you in," she said.

"Sure, we can do that, but why don't you just fill me in right now? I'm Officer Zetler, by the way." He reached his hand toward her.

She shook his hand. "Marielle Coleman. This is Ian Roane."

"Roane, you say. I think I already know a little about this case." He looked at Ian. "I'm sure I can learn more when I read the police report."

She appreciated his sensitivity to not giving details in front of Ian. While they waited for the ambulance, she went to check on Graham.

She was grateful to hear the siren and see the flashing lights come into view.

Her stomach knotted as she watched the EMTs place Graham's still unconscious body on the stretcher, load him in the ambulance and close the door.

Ian held his arm out toward the ambulance, opening and closing his hand.

She snuggled him closer. "I know you're worried. I am too, baby."

The snow was still swirling down from the sky as they drove behind the ambulance in Officer Zetler's patrol car.

They came to the edge of town.

As they rolled down Main Street toward the hospital, she found herself checking the rearview mirror and glancing around at the parked cars. She had a strong intuition that the attacker would try again to get to Ian, that he was waiting and watching for a moment of vulnerability. It was just a matter of time.

* * *

Graham woke up in a dimly lit hospital room. When he tried to sit up, his head was throbbing. The rest of his body ached. Despite the pain, he pushed himself up on his elbows. How much time had passed?

The curtains were drawn. No way to tell what time of day it was.

Bigger questions loomed in his mind. Had Marielle and Ian been injured too? Were they even still alive?

He tensed. The idea that he may have lost them made his heart ache. Why had he not been ready when the attacker opened his truck door?

He reached for the call button, mind racing until, less than a minute later, he heard the padding of heavy-soled shoes. A nurse stepped into the room. She was a plump, fortysomething woman with brown hair, glasses and a kind smile.

She came around the side of his bed. "So good to see that you're awake, Mr. Flynn."

He touched his hand to his forehead, where he felt a bandage. "How long has it been?"

"It's nearly dinnertime."

He'd been out most of the day. "Was I given a sedative or something?"

"The doctor thought it would be best." She lifted a pitcher of water that rested on the rolling tray and poured some into a cup, which she handed to him.

The cool liquid soothed his parched throat as he drank. "That tastes good."

The nurse folded her hands over her stomach. "You must be getting hungry too."

His stomach was growling but he had more important things on his mind. "When can I get out of here?"

"The good news is that you don't have any broken bones. You're just very bruised and cut up and you have a concussion. Once the doctor gives the okay, you'll be free to go."

He handed her the cup. Trying to get a deep breath hurt his chest. He must have bruised it when he slammed into the steering wheel. The memory of the collision and the attack made him shudder.

He had to ask the question he'd been dreading. He had to know. "There was a woman and child with me in the truck."

The nurse patted his arm just above the elbow. "They're here. They've been waiting for you to wake up. Would you like to see them?"

"You mean they're okay?" He finally felt like he could fill his lungs with air as relief and joy spread through him.

"Yes, they're both just fine," said the nurse. "The doctor already checked them out."

"Yes, I'd like to see them." Marielle had cared about him enough to stay around. It was a risk for her not to go directly into police protection.

"I believe they went downstairs to the cafeteria," said the nurse. "But I'll let them know when they come back. They both were quite worried about you."

A sense of panic made him try to sit up again. "They shouldn't be wandering through this hospital alone."

She straightened his pillow, so it was propped against the wall and then helped him into a sitting position. "No need to worry. A police officer has been with them this whole time."

He relaxed a little, but his heart was still pounding. Though he was grateful that Marielle had gotten an officer to stay with her and Ian, they would remain in danger as long as the man who had come after them was at large. He had to do what he could to make sure he was brought to justice.

"Can I have my phone? It should be in the zippered pocket of my coat." He needed to call his handler to see if he could stay and help Marielle and Ian…if she would let him.

"Sure, I'll bring it to you. But I think we better also get some food in you. I'll see what the food services can bring up for you."

The nurse retrieved his phone for him and left the room, and he was relieved to see the battery still had a little charge.

His thumb hovered over his handler's number, and for the first time in hours, he thought of Cesar. The young man's death would continue to haunt him. But the time for retreat and refuge was over. He wasn't about to have someone else die on his watch.

He called his handler. Bruce picked up on the second ring.

"Agent Flynn, I was wondering when you were going to check in. We had an interesting development in your neck of the woods."

"Really?" He tried to sit up straighter, but his head throbbed.

"Do you remember that truck we were going to follow to try to identify key players in drug transport?"

"Yes, the one Cesar told me about." Though the truck was scheduled to haul produce from Mexico to the States, Cesar had learned that it would have drugs hidden in it too.

"It left Mexico January thirteenth and seems to have ended up not too far from where you are. We found the truck, empty of course, but K-9s detected drug residue. Are you in a better head space and ready to get back to work?"

What a loaded question. He wondered how much he even needed to share about what had happened. The man at the camp was after Ian and needed him and Marielle out of the way, but the murder of Ian's mother was a case for the local police. "I'm as good as I'm ever going to be. It's a long story, but I had some injuries that put me in the hospital."

"You going to be all right?"

"I'm fine." He wanted to focus on the case. "So you found the truck but nothing on the driver?"

"Actually, we found out quite a bit. We have a name for our truck driver. But we don't think it's a regular cartel guy. Our techs have been combing through surveillance footage at the border trying to figure out when this guy crossed down into

Mexico to get that truck. We got a positive ID on a car with a Montana plate registered to a Charlie Roane."

Marielle and Ian stepped into Graham's room, a police officer hovered just outside the door. Ian's eyes lit up when he saw Graham, and Graham waved his free hand at the child. Marielle was wearing clothes that looked like something she'd gotten in the hospital gift shop: leggings and long T-shirt with a Christmas image on it. She still wore his oversized coat. They exchanged smiles before Graham turned his attention back to the phone call.

"The car was found in Mexico?" he prompted Bruce.

"Yeah. The car is registered for Lane County in a town not too far from where you grew up, not reported as stolen so we can be reasonably sure it's Charlie Roane we're looking for. We found the car abandoned in Mexico. Mexican authorities have agreed to turn it over. Our forensics guys will go through it, but I don't think it's our strongest lead."

Graham shifted in his bed which caused pain to slice through his head. "So, the million-dollar question is: Was Charlie Roane working for the cartel or did he steal the shipment from the cartel?"

Marielle startled and gripped the bed railing, her expression darkening from the welcoming smile she'd worn a few seconds earlier. Ian drew his brows together and moved toward Marielle, grabbing the hem of her coat. He wondered what had caused the sudden mood change.

Bruce said, "We need to track down Charlie. Also, we'll probably need the support of local law enforcement. They've been briefed on the case and one of the officers already went to Charlie's last known residence. Of course, he'd cleared out."

There was more he wanted to talk to Bruce about, but he sensed that Marielle was upset about something. "Thanks for doing that. I'll call you back in a bit." He disconnected and looked up at her. "Everything okay?"

"What's going on with the man named Charlie Roane?"

Ian jerked his head up, his focus intently on Marielle.

"He's an important piece in an investigation I'm working on. Why?"

Marielle's face had drained of color. She scooted Ian toward the door. "Ian, why don't you go talk to the nice policeman?" She said something to the officer, turned and closed the door. "I didn't want him to hear this." She stepped closer to the front of Graham's bed. "Charlie Roane is the brother of Ian's missing father, David."

Graham was trying to process what she was saying. "David is the man who disappeared after Ian's mother was killed?"

She nodded. "The police don't think he killed Kristen, but they don't know why he's gone into hiding."

Graham spoke in a low voice. "Maybe he feared for his life." That would be the case if the cartel was somehow involved. He rubbed his beard, wondering what the connection might be. Maybe it was coincidence. Two brothers involved in separate crimes. "What was the exact date of Kristen's murder?"

"January sixteenth," she said.

The man they now knew was Charlie had been seen leaving Mexico in the truck on January thirteenth. It was approximately forty hours of driving to get from the middle of Mexico to southwest Montana.

Charlie had been out of state when Kristen was killed.

Marielle tugged on the open zipper of her coat, saying the words that he had been thinking. "What if these two cases are connected?"

"They could be." If the cases were linked, the implications were frightening. "If that's so, it would confirm that Kristen wasn't killed by some addict who thought he'd been slighted. This whole thing could link back to the cartel. The drugs hidden in that truck were most likely theirs. We don't know if Charlie was working for them or someone else. Maybe he was their regular pickup guy for northwest deliveries. We need to find out more about him."

"You think Kristen's death somehow connects to the cartels?" Her voice cracked.

He saw the fear in her face. He couldn't lie to her, even though the words caused a tightening in his gut. "It's a high probability at this point, which means we're dealing with some very dangerous people."

Chapter Eleven

Marielle drew Graham's open coat tighter around her body and crossed her arms, fighting off a chill that had nothing to do with the temperature of the room.

Her mind reeled. "That makes it all the more likely that the man who came after Ian and me was a hired killer."

"True." He reached out to rub her arm, which comforted her a little. "The only way we will know for sure will be for us to figure out who that man was and catch him."

She took a step back, shaking her head. "This is all too much."

Graham was using the word *we* a lot. So much had changed since the shock of seeing him only two nights ago at the camp. She appreciated that he wanted to protect her, and Ian seemed to have grown attached to him, but the wounds his departure had caused and the pain from the destruction of all her hopes and dreams were far from healed. Now that the immediate threat had receded, it was impossible to keep the hurt at bay. It would only worsen if she spent more time around him.

The realization of who was behind Kristen's death made her thoughts turn to Ian. "I have something encouraging to tell you. Ian spoke for the first time since the murder. He expressed concern about you when you were unconscious in the truck."

He sat up a little straighter. "Really? That's great."

"He...cares about you. He hasn't spoken a word since, but it's a good sign."

"I think it's wonderful." He shook his head. "Poor little guy. He deserves a chance at overcoming all that he has seen in his short life."

Graham had connected with the child as much as Ian was drawn toward Graham. She stared at him for a moment, relishing the warmth she saw in his eyes before looking toward the door.

Though she was still trying to process what all this meant, it felt like the conversation was over for now.

"I'll go check on him," she said instead. A sense of urgency to see Ian compelled her out of the room. He sat on a chair in the hallway with Officer Zetler beside him. He was eating a bag of chips that they must have gotten from a vending machine. Orange dust covered the area around his mouth.

She held her arms open to him. The boy slipped off the chair and ran to her. She lifted him and stood up, his smooth cheek brushing against hers as he shifted the bag of chips.

"I'll stay right here," said the officer.

She set Ian back down inside Graham's room, and the boy walked over to Graham, who was propped up in the bed. He pulled a chip out of his bag and held it up toward Graham.

"For me?" Graham reached down and took the chip. "Thanks, buddy."

A bond had definitely formed between the two of them. She wasn't sure if that was a good thing.

Ian handed Graham another chip.

Graham crunched on it loudly. "Yum yum. Mmmm good."

Ian lifted his chin and giggled.

It warmed her heart to see the boy's face so filled with life. At the same time, it made her afraid. She thought of how

Graham had left so abruptly ten years ago. He'd claimed it had been for his new career, or had that been an excuse to get away from her? Did commitment scare him? Would he just disappear again, and this time hurt a little boy too? So many unanswered questions.

The nurse stood in the open door holding a tray. "Supper-time."

Marielle took a step back from the bed and from the feelings and thoughts that threatened to overwhelm her.

While the nurse set up the meal on Graham's rolling table tray, Marielle pulled a chair closer to Graham's bed and sat down. Ian wandered over to her, and she pulled him onto her lap.

After the nurse left, Graham took a few bites of his meat loaf and potatoes. Ian munched on his last chip and then held the empty bag up for Marielle to see.

"Are you still hungry?"

Graham smiled at Ian. "Thanks for sharing with me. You can have my cookie if you like." He held the cookie out.

Ian slid out of Marielle's lap and walked over to get the cookie, swaying his body back and forth in delight as he nib-bled. Was it a good thing he was bonding to Graham? Her pri-mary job was to protect Ian not just from physical harm but emotional hurt as well.

"So are you working on the case that Charlie Roane is con-nected to?" She needed to know how soon he would exit from their lives.

He scooted food around on his plate with his fork, making a scraping noise. "Yes, I think so. I'm here. I know this part of the state pretty well."

Time to ask the question she was most concerned about. "After your case is wrapped up, will you be leaving Montana again? That is the nature of your work, right?"

"Yes, my job takes me all over North and South America," he said.

She laced her fingers together. "Do you enjoy what you do?"

Ian had come over and was standing by her chair while he ate the last bites of his cookie.

"I like that it feels like I make a difference." Graham took a bite of food and then rested his head against the propped-up pillows. "I used to feel that way, anyhow. I loved my job, but some things have changed so I don't know anymore."

"You mentioned something bad happened?"

He put his fork down and stared off into space. "A teenage boy I cared about who was helping me with a case was killed." His voice had become heavy with emotion. "His name was Cesar. Just a kid."

She shifted in her chair, not sure what to say. "I'm sorry. That sounds hard." When she looked at Ian, he was occupied feeding pretend bites of cookie to his giraffe. She was glad he wasn't tuned into their conversation.

"It's never okay to have someone die on my watch." He shook his head. "It's not right, and I can't fix it."

A heavy silence settled into the room. Graham was dealing with a great deal of pain and confusion connected with his job that she could not begin to fathom.

She rose and reached out to put her hand on his.

Ian had finished his cookie and was dancing from one foot to the other. His antics broke the intensity of the moment.

"He has to go to the bathroom." She stood up and took Ian's hand. "I'll be right back."

With Ian walking beside her, she hurried out the door and by Officer Zetler. "Potty run," she explained as they passed.

Officer Zetler nodded and followed them down the hall. She ushered Ian into the bathroom and opened a stall for him. "Do you need my help?"

Ian shook his head. She waited in the bathroom by the sinks until he was done and then lifted him up to the sink to help him wash his hands. She had just pulled out a paper towel for him when a shrill noise filled the air.

The fire alarm. Her heart raced.

Ian put his hands over his ears. His features crinkled up in agony and he bent over.

She swept him up into her arms. "It's okay." Her voice was barely audible over the auditory assault.

She entered the hallway, not seeing Officer Zetler anywhere. Several people rushed past. Her heart pounded as she caught the attention of a nurse. "Where is the nearest exit?"

The nurse pointed down an adjoining hallway as she ran by. "I have to go. We need to get the patients out."

Marielle moved to go up the hall. "I need to help my friend."

The nurse squeezed her arm. "No, you need to get out now. We'll take care of him."

She ran toward where the nurse had pointed.

Perhaps Officer Zetler had gone to help get the less mobile patients outside.

Still holding Ian in one arm, she pushed open the exit door.

She came out into a parking lot at the back of the hospital where a large group of people were milling around. Many of them were staring at the hospital, probably trying to figure out where the fire was. Some were dressed in medical uniforms and others must have been in the waiting room or were patients with minor injuries.

No flames furled out of any windows. She hadn't smelled smoke while inside. If there was a fire, it must be deep within the building.

Now that they were outside, the intensity of the alarm had lessened, but Ian still had his hands against his ears.

She pressed her face close to his as she walked away from the building. "It's not as loud now. You can put your hands down."

Ian gingerly pulled his hands away. She stood off from the group of people who had escaped to this parking lot. Several more people came out of the exit and joined the crowd.

A short, bald man with his arm in a sling came up to her. "Excuse me, are you Marielle?"

She blinked in surprise. "Yes. How did you know?"

"A man named Graham described you and the boy. He's not very mobile. He asked me to find you and let you know that he's looking for you."

"Oh, he must be worried about us," she said. If only she'd been in the room with him when the alarm had gone off. He would know she got out safe.

"He said you could meet him by the pocket park with the horse sculpture."

She was familiar enough with the hospital that she knew the area the man was talking about.

The hospital was shaped like an H with somewhat crooked arms, which created lots of nooks and crannies. The park was in one of those nooks. Carrying Ian, she hurried around the hospital grounds, compelled by the need to assure Graham that she and Ian were okay. She encountered another cluster of people outside an emergency exit. They too were looking at the hospital, where there still was no sign or smell of a fire.

She slowed down as she turned the last corner and neared the little park. Sheltered on three sides by the strangely shaped hospital walls, the park was quiet and peaceful, tucked out of sight of the crowd she'd just walked through.

She took a few more slow steps, and the horse sculpture at the edge of the park came into view. No people milled around the area. This section of the hospital was bordered by a grove of trees without connection to a parking lot. The wind made the bare branches creak.

The park appeared unoccupied.

Though she saw nothing suspicious, her heart beat a little faster. She had the sense that someone was close by, watching her.

She swallowed to get rid of the lump in her throat. "Graham?" Ian wiggled in her hold as she took another step toward the park. An empty bench came into view.

Something didn't feel right. Still holding Ian, she turned to go back to the crowd by the emergency exit.

She heard footsteps behind her. She looked over her shoulder and screamed. The attacker from the camp was running toward them.

She let out another scream, knowing she could not outrun him with Ian in her arms and praying someone would hear and come to help them.

The attacker caught up with her. He grabbed the hood of her coat and then tightened his hand around her upper arm, spinning her around as he sought to wrench Ian from her.

She screamed again.

People came running from several different directions. The attacker glanced around, assessing, then let go of Marielle and fled toward the trees.

Graham, dressed in a hospital gown and coat, burst out of the crowd and chased after the man. Officer Zetler was behind him.

Out of breath and shaking, she held Ian close.

The nurse who had been in Graham's room came toward her, wrapping her arm around Marielle's shoulder. "I saw what happened. That must've been very frightening." She ushered Marielle toward a bench.

The bald man with his arm in a sling had set her up. Maybe the attacker had given him money or just told a lie and said he was Graham.

Marielle's heart was still pounding as she sat down. Ian clung to her neck. She kissed the top of his blond head and hugged him tight. "I know that was scary for you."

She wanted to say that it would never happen again, that she would keep him safe no matter what. With every ounce of strength she had, she intended to protect him, but it was clear that whoever they were up against were determined to hurt Ian.

A few moments later, an administrator announced, "We can go back inside. Turns out there was no fire."

The kind nurse supported Marielle's elbow as she rose from the bench. "Do you think someone pulled it to raise a false alarm?" Marielle asked.

"Looks that way," said the nurse as she led them back toward the hospital.

The attacker must have done it to get Marielle outside and vulnerable where he could get at Ian.

Before entering the hospital, she gazed in the direction that Graham and the officer had gone, praying that they would capture the attacker.

As he ran, Graham struggled for air. His side hurt from the exertion. His injuries had weakened him. Determined to not let this man get away, he willed himself to keep going.

The attacker sprinted into the trees by the pocket park and Graham followed, with the officer close behind him. The row of trees bordered an empty parking lot by a disused building. Snow covered the sidewalks and the windows were boarded up.

Both men stopped abruptly, not seeing any sign of the attacker. Graham did not hear retreating footsteps. The guy had to be hiding somewhere. He surveyed the area until his eye caught movement.

"There." Graham pointed to a hedge on the other side of the parking lot.

Graham sprinted across the concrete while the officer stopped to call for backup on his radio.

When Graham got to the hedge, he spotted the man crouching behind it to conceal himself as he moved along it.

The attacker glanced over his shoulder. He straightened at the sight of Graham and broke into a run again, bursting across the street and running toward a residential area.

Pumping his legs, Graham fought to fill his lungs with air

and get beyond the pain and weakness that slowed him down. He closed the distance between himself and the other man.

The attacker darted behind a house. Graham followed, coming out into a back lane where he saw no sign of the man he was chasing.

Officer Zetler caught up with Graham. He spoke between breaths. "Backup is on the way."

"He's around here somewhere." Graham glanced up and down the lane. The attacker could have gone in one of two directions—deeper into the subdivision or out toward the street. "You go that way." Graham pointed toward the houses before choosing the second option for himself.

He ran through the edge of the subdivision and out onto the street. Across from him were houses that were under construction. Some had been framed, others were only concrete slabs. Everywhere there were stacks of construction materials and piles of dirt along with heavy equipment. There were no construction workers around. Of course, it was Sunday. He'd lost track of the days.

He caught movement in his peripheral vision by a stack of wooden pallets. Graham ducked behind a backhoe that was close to the pallets. He saw the attacker from behind as he peered out, clearly looking for Graham.

His gun had been taken off him, he assumed when he was admitted to the hospital, but he still had the element of surprise on his side if he acted fast.

Graham ducked under the arm of the backhoe and rushed toward the man.

The man turned just as Graham was about to jump him. Graham stepped out of the way as the attacker swung at him. No way was he letting this man get away again.

Graham punched the attacker in the stomach and followed it with a blow to his chest, which took the wind out of his assailant. The man tilted forward as he wheezed in air. Graham grabbed the man's arm and bent it behind his back while at the same time securing his free arm around the man's neck to restrain him.

The man fought to break free, shifting and angling his body. Graham tightened his hold on him. He was exhausted from the pursuit and his earlier injuries, and he wasn't sure how much longer he could keep the man under control. Despite the winter chill, sweat ran down his face.

Graham breathed a sigh of relief when he heard sirens in the distance. The suspect's struggle to break free had grown half-hearted and then stopped altogether.

"It's over," said Graham, and he marched the attacker around the pallets and out toward the street.

Officer Zetler had just emerged from the subdivision. When he saw Graham with the attacker in custody, he stopped to talk on his radio, probably to let the police know where to find them.

Within minutes, a police car showed up. After he'd been read his rights, the attacker was cuffed and taken away. Now they would find out who he was. Maybe knowing his identity would clarify if the two cases were connected and if the cartel was involved.

Graham and the officer walked back toward the hospital. As satisfied as he was with the capture, he wasn't sure if it meant that Marielle and Ian were any safer. If the man was a hired assassin, the forces behind these attacks might just send someone else.

Chapter Twelve

Marielle sat on the floor of the interview room in the police station with Ian. One of the officers had supplied her with a box filled with toys and books meant to help young children feel comfortable before they were questioned.

Ian took a drink from his juice box and leaned against her shoulder as she read a picture book to him.

There was a gentle knock on the slightly ajar door and Graham spoke up. "Can I come in?"

She cleared her throat. "Sure," she responded, feeling a tightening through her torso.

Graham entered holding a small laptop.

Once Graham had been released from the hospital, they'd gone to the police station and had agreed upon a plan for questioning Ian in a way that would cause him the least amount of stress. She explained that they needed to set up an environment where Ian felt safe, taking time to play with him and then casually introducing the questions they needed answered.

She hoped it worked. The second Ian showed any sign of distress, she would pull the plug on the interview.

Ian's face brightened when he saw Graham. A light came

into Graham's eyes as well. He sat down on the floor beside the boy.

It seemed that Ian trusted both her and Graham now. Rather than have a police officer be a part of the interview, having the two of them work together in a relaxed environment would create the best circumstances for getting answers from Ian. The interview room with only a table and chairs was less than ideal but the snacks, books and toys helped.

"We're almost done with this story," said Marielle. She finished the last couple of pages, locking gazes with Graham when she closed the book. She said a quick, silent prayer.

Please, God, protect this little one's heart and mind.

Graham gave her a slight nod and opened up the laptop. "Ian, can you look at some pictures for me?"

Ian put his juice box down and nodded, gazing up at Graham who was tapping on the keyboard of the laptop.

Marielle leaned closer to Ian. She and Graham had talked through this plan at length. Ian might be able to shed light on the nature of the relationship between his dad and uncle, David and Charlie. More importantly, they needed to find out if the man Graham had taken into custody, who they now knew was named Lee Masters, was the man who had killed Ian's mother.

The first photograph came up on the screen. It was of Charlie Roane.

"Do you know this man?" Graham put his finger on the screen.

Ian nodded.

As planned, Marielle asked the second question. "Was he ever at your house with your mommy and daddy?"

Again, Ian nodded. She wasn't picking up on any distress from the child. Every question had to be phrased for Ian to give a yes or no answer. Though he had uttered that one word over concern for Graham, she couldn't count on him speaking now.

The idea was to tag team easier warm-up questions until they got to the question about the killer's identity.

"Was he nice to you?"

Ian nodded.

"Was he nice to your mom and dad?" Graham's question.

Ian let out a little breath but then nodded. His forehead crinkled. Perhaps he wanted to give a more nuanced answer.

She had to try. "Is there anything else you want to tell us about this man?" Maybe he would talk.

Ian wiggled and then drew his knees up toward his chest before shaking his head. It wasn't clear from the question what the nature of the relationship between the brothers was. Charlie had been to David's house, so the brothers weren't estranged.

"Did you ever see this man fighting with or yelling at your mom or dad?" She was impressed. Graham had come up with a way to phrase the question so that Ian might be able to respond.

Ian shook his head.

Progress. It seemed the relationship between the brothers had not been antagonistic.

"Good job, Ian." Marielle ruffled his hair. "You still have some crackers left in this package. Would you like one?" She reached for the snack Ian had been munching on earlier.

They let Ian eat his snack for a few minutes before they moved onto the next photograph and the harder questions.

"I have another picture I want to show you. Is that okay?" After Ian gave the go-ahead, Graham brought up the picture of the man who had come after them at the camp. It had taken the police only a quick search to find out that Lee Masters was a local who had been arrested for drug use. Lee had returned to the area a few years ago after fifteen years in the army. Police had been unable to get any information out of Lee while he sat in a jail cell, though the drug history suggested a motive for why he might have killed Kristen.

The sight of the photograph of Lee caused Ian to stop chewing his cracker.

"We know this man was not nice to you or me when we were at the camp in the mountains." Marielle wrapped her arm around Ian. "But he's not going to hurt you anymore. The police locked him away because he was bad." Ian's body softened against her.

Graham piped up. "Ian, can you be brave and answer some questions for us about this man?"

Ian glanced at Graham and then nodded before taking another nibble of his snack.

Marielle tried to relax as she prepared to ask the next question. "Do you remember the night a bad thing happened in your house?"

Ian's body tensed but he managed a nod.

Graham pointed at the screen. "Was this man there that night?"

She flinched, concerned that Graham had asked the final question a little too fast.

Ian took the last bite of his cracker. She listened to the sound of his chewing as the seconds ticked by. Graham leaned closer to him as the little boy stuck his fingers in his mouth. Ian stared at the screen for a long moment before shaking his head.

She pointed to the screen. "You're sure this man was not at your house?"

Ian gazed up at Marielle and then nodded.

Graham closed the laptop. "You did good, buddy."

They had their answer. Lee had not killed Ian's mom.

Ian stood up and crawled into Marielle's lap, resting his head against her chest. She rocked back and forth and stroked his hair. "Thank you so much, Ian. I bet you're tired now, huh?"

She offered Graham a faint smile. She was pretty worn out as well. Graham still looked a little pale, probably because his injuries were still hurting him. Most likely the chase after Lee had set him back. Neither of them seemed to want to move.

Ian nodded off in her arms.

"That was helpful, huh?" she whispered.

"Yes, we learned quite a bit. Lee was probably hired by

whoever killed Kristen to kidnap Ian and hand him off to Kristen's killer."

She did not want to speculate what would have happened to Ian after that. The implications led to places she didn't want to think about. "So Lee was hired by someone who took a risk in killing Kristen and didn't want to pop up on the radar again. Someone with money and connections, like a cartel member?"

He nodded. "I need solid evidence, but I don't think the timing with what happened with the brothers and Ian's mom is a coincidence."

"A shipment of drugs belonging to the cartel leaves Mexico and disappears. A few days later, the sister-in-law of the driver is killed."

"I think the killer went to the Roanes' house looking for answers about the shipment knowing that David and Charlie were brothers and when he didn't get them, he got angry. The murder was impulsive."

She checked that Ian was completely asleep in her arms. "Kristen died. David feared for his life and went into hiding. We don't know what happened to Charlie."

Graham nodded. "We still have lots of dots to connect. In any case, I think we'll have to work more closely with the local police to try to make the connections we need to make."

"Thank you for helping me do the interview with Ian." She appreciated that Graham wanted to protect Ian as much as she did.

He pressed his shoulder against hers. "We make a good team."

His proximity made her heart flutter. The way he was so good with Ian heightened her attraction to him. What was going to happen next? Would he be leaving her and Ian to pursue the investigation? The notion should have brought her relief but instead sadness washed over her. "If you think someone hired Lee, that means Ian and I are not safe." Her breath hitched when she spoke the words.

Ian snored softly.

"Yes, we'll have to see what the police can set up to ensure your safety." He leaned back against the wall. "I'll help transport the two of you if they come up with a secure location."

"And then what?" It sounded like his intent was to leave them there. "I imagine you're going to tackle this investigation head-on."

He didn't answer right away. "Yes, I guess that's the next step for me." His words came out haltingly as if he were still mulling over what his next move was.

There was a knock on the door. Detective Strickland, the man who was in charge of investigating Kristen's murder, popped his head in. "I've got some things to talk to you two about."

"I need to lay Ian down somewhere first," said Marielle.

The detective opened the door wider. "There's a couch in the break room."

Graham stood up and reached down toward Marielle. "Here, let me take him." She transferred the listless Ian into his arms.

They followed Detective Strickland down a hallway. Marielle watched as Graham gently laid Ian on his side on the couch and then removed his coat to cover the boy, touching his silky blond head lightly.

The picture of Graham gazing down at Ian, how tender he was toward him, pulled on her heartstrings.

They tiptoed out of the room where the detective was waiting. He was a tall man in his forties with a mustache and widow's peak. From the beginning, he'd been supportive of Marielle's need to protect Ian, even if it slowed the investigation.

"Let's talk just outside this room," Marielle whispered. "If he wakes up, I'll be able to hear him. I don't want him to be scared because he's alone."

The detective nodded and fiddled with the folder he was holding before he addressed Marielle. "First, I wanted to let you know that Kristen and David's house is no longer a crime scene. If you wanted to get some more of Ian's things to help him adjust, that would be fine."

"It's clear Lee did not act alone," said Graham. "I don't want either Marielle or Ian out in the open. We think this might connect to a case I'm working that has wider-reaching implications."

"I've been briefed on your case," said Detective Strickland.

"I have to be the one to go to the house," Marielle responded. "I understand what to get from the home to facilitate him talking again and to help him with the transition of being with me."

The detective turned toward Graham. "Maybe you can go with Marielle once we take Ian to the secure location. There will be a female officer there to help with the childcare."

Graham looked at Marielle as if waiting for an answer from her.

"I suppose that would be all right."

Graham turned toward Detective Strickland. "Was there something else? You said it affected the investigation."

"Yes, it's the reason we went ahead with the safe house setup. Lee finally admitted to not acting alone but he won't say who hired him. Honestly, I think he's scared."

She shuddered. Yet another reason to believe they were dealing with big players with lots of power.

The detective held up the folder. "Another piece of the puzzle. We pulled Lee's financials. The guy owns a knife sharpening business, and he's about to be foreclosed on."

Graham nodded. "So he had motive. He needed a big payday."

"Not only that. A day before that storm hit, he deposited five thousand dollars." He handed the folder to Graham. "Everything we know about him so far."

Marielle crossed her arms over her chest, trying not to relive the violence that had happened because of Lee. "He probably thought it would be easy to take out a woman and kidnap a child living alone in the country."

"Well, you proved him wrong." Admiration filled Graham's voice as he reached out to squeeze her arm.

"The five thousand is probably just a portion of his pay," said the detective. "He would have gotten the rest if he'd succeeded. I've got some more work to do. I'll let you both know when we're ready to transport you to the safe house."

"I'll need a vehicle to take Marielle to Ian's house."

"We can arrange that." The detective headed back down the hall and disappeared around a corner.

Graham sat down in a chair in the hallway and opened the folder.

She sat down beside him. "Anything in there that Strickland didn't already tell you?"

Graham scanned the pages as he flipped through them. "Lee has extensive firearms experience and a black belt."

Though he was not a professional hit man, Lee clearly had skills.

She and Ian had come so close to dying at Lee's hands. An outcome that could have been very different if Graham had not been at the camp. Graham returning to the place he felt close to God after Cesar's death had saved her and Ian's life.

Marielle rose and wandered farther down the hall to a window. Outside, the snow twirling down from the nighttime sky created a peaceful scene. The calm she saw outside stood in contrast to the turmoil she was experiencing on the inside.

It appeared that she and Ian were far from safe.

Graham's stomach clenched as he pulled up to the house where Ian had lived with his mom and dad. So far since Lee had been taken into custody, no additional attacks had happened. How long would it take for whoever had hired Lee to line up another assassin?

The place was in need of paint, and car parts and broken

toys half covered in snow were scattered through the yard. The house was on the outskirts of town with other older homes on large lots.

"Did his mom and dad own this house?"

"I think it belonged to a relative who let them live there for cheap," said Marielle.

Last night, he and Marielle had gotten Ian settled at the safe house and all of them had gotten a good night's sleep. In the morning in the unmarked police car he'd borrowed, he'd driven Marielle to her place to pick up some clothes and other necessities for her and Ian before coming to Ian's old house.

The more time he spent with Ian, the fonder he grew of him. "What's going to happen with Ian anyway? Are you going to adopt him?"

"Likely not if his father is found. I don't know what David's involvement with the stolen truck is. It takes a lot to sever parental rights. Of course I'm open to adopting him. I'd have the family I always wanted." Her words were tinged with sadness.

"No matter what, I just hope the little guy has a shot at a decent life."

"Me too." Marielle unbuckled her seat belt. "I'll try not to take too long."

"I'm coming with you," he said.

"I should be okay, don't you think?" She glanced nervously toward the house.

He pushed open his door. "Let's not take any chances."

A chill settled over his skin as they made their way through the yard. Marielle used the key the police had given her. Once inside, the scent of ammonia reached him. Crime scene clean-up had done their job. Even though there was no visible sign of what had taken place, stepping into the house gave him an unsettled feeling the way visiting a crime scene always did.

"What are you looking for, anyway? You got the clothes he needs from your place."

She moved through the living room, reaching for a photograph of a woman on a shelf. "Anything that might help unlock Ian's ability to speak. Anything that might comfort him and create a sense of familiarity and safety." She put the photograph in the bag she'd brought with her.

The picture must be of Ian's mother. He stepped toward the shelf, noticing a photo of Ian being held by Kristen, both of them smiling. "Take this one too."

She placed the second photo in her bag. "I'm going to check in Ian's room. Let me know if you find anything that you think might be helpful."

He wandered toward the kitchen where the strong ammonia smell was coming from.

The photos hanging on the living room wall caught his attention. Several of them were of Charlie and David dressed in camo gear and holding bows, their arms wrapped around each other. More evidence that the brothers were close. Still, where an addict was involved, brother could turn against brother.

When he stepped into the kitchen, the floor gleamed in contrast to the dusty, uninhabited feel of the rest of the place. The murder must have happened in this room. He glanced around trying to picture what had happened. Ian could have hidden behind the wall in the living room and then run to hide under the bed where he'd been found.

Cups and bowls still sat in the dishrack, and a loaf of bread and some canned goods had been left on the counter. A sadness washed over him. No one would be returning to straighten up anytime soon. The sight of a child's wooden puzzle on the kitchen table with pieces scattered around it only added to the sense that something had been irrevocably broken.

A muffled banging noise caught his attention. He straightened his spine as his heart beat a little faster. The sound was coming from the backyard. Could be a door caught in the wind.

He went through the kitchen to the back porch. Outside, the doors of a metal shed were open, and someone was throwing items out onto the snow-covered lawn.

His first thought was that an enterprising neighbor had decided to take advantage of the house being abandoned to find things of value.

"Hey, what are you doing?"

The noise stopped. A man stuck his head out.

Graham froze as he looked into the face of Charlie Roane.

"This is my brother's place. I have the right to be here."

"Charlie Roane. I think you better come with me. The police have some questions to ask you." Graham's gun was hidden in a shoulder holster.

The man stepped out of the shed with his hands up. He was a tall, thin man with almond-shaped eyes and stringy brown hair. He was dressed in camouflage gear. "Am I in trouble? I told ya. This is my brother's place. Are you with children's services? Where is Ian at?"

Graham advanced toward Charlie. He pulled his badge and showed it. "We just need to talk to you about your brother." So far, Charlie seemed to want to cooperate. Drawing his weapon might scare Charlie off. No need to say anything about the truck from Mexico. He didn't want to clue the guy in that the police knew what he was guilty of.

"So you're with the police?" Charlie kept his hands up but shuffled his feet, growing more agitated. His gaze bounced all over the place.

"We just have some questions to ask you."

Charlie dropped his hands and took off running. Graham raced after him across a field toward a dirt road.

He ran faster when he saw Charlie approaching a car. Charlie jumped into the vehicle. Graham could hear the engine sputter to life just as he got to the car and reached for the driver's side door handle. It was locked.

The car sped out onto the road.

Graham spun around when he heard another car behind him. Marielle was behind the wheel of the borrowed car. He jumped into the passenger seat.

Even before he had time to close the door, she was rolling forward. He clicked into his seat belt. A bulging bag sat on the console between them.

"I saw from the bedroom window what was going on. I figured he had a car close by and would try to get away."

"Good thinking." He pulled his phone out and dialed the police department to let them know what was going on and maybe get some backup.

"I'll talk to dispatch," said the police officer who answered. "See if we have any officers in the area that could intercept him."

"Might want to send an officer over to the house. The guy was looking for something in the shed in the backyard. I don't think he found it before fleeing."

Graham stared out the windshield where Charlie's car had taken a turn that led into a forested area. He advised the officer of where they were going and disconnected.

Marielle navigated the rutted dirt road with skill. Because of all the curves, the other car was no longer visible. She gripped the wheel and kept a steady speed. They couldn't be far behind.

He wasn't familiar with this area. The sign as they had turned in had said they were on National Forest land and that there was a campground up ahead.

"Where do you suppose he's going?"

She shook her head. "He must have an escape route in mind."

She kept driving. Even when the road straightened out, they saw no sign of the other car. They passed the campground, which was empty.

She slowed down. "I think we lost him. He must've turned off somewhere."

The road appeared to end at the campground.

She turned the car around and headed back down the mountain. Graham scanned both sides of the road looking for any sign of where Charlie might have turned off the road. He saw only forest and rugged hills, no side roads.

Marielle drove even slower. "He couldn't just vanish into thin air."

Graham caught a flash of color in his peripheral vision. "Stop. Back up."

She shifted into Reverse. The car Charlie had been driving was a shade of gray that would blend into the surroundings so it would be hard to spot.

Graham scanned the forest where he thought he'd seen something out of place. Except where the evergreens provided canopy, snow covered much of the ground. "Pull over." He pointed to where he wanted her to park.

She backed up onto the shoulder.

Other than some flattened grass, he didn't see anything that would clearly indicate that Charlie had gone down into this part of the forest.

When she moved to unbuckle her seat belt, he put a protective hand on her leg. "Stay here."

"Are you sure? If he tries to jump you, it will be two against one if I go."

Maybe she was right. If Charlie had had a gun, he would have used it when he first saw Graham at the house. At least they would not be confronting an armed man. "All right. Let's go."

He pulled his gun from the holster. They exited the car and walked down the hill toward the forest. Just inside the tree line, Graham saw more clearly what had caught his eye. There was a sort of makeshift winter camp, a tent covered by a lean-to made of evergreen branches that not only protected it from the elements but concealed it as well. Only patches of the tent, which was blue, were visible. That must have been what had caught his eye from the road.

A ring of rocks surrounding coals indicated a fire had been built at some point. After signaling for Marielle to step back,

Graham stood off to one side of the tent and pulled back the flap, revealing a sleeping bag on a bed of boughs along with some canned goods and a cooking pot. He straightened and walked around to the back of the camp, peering deeper into the woods. No sign of Charlie or his car. The guy had to have parked somewhere.

A high-speed whizzing sound filled the air and then Marielle screamed.

Fearing the worst, he sprinted around to the front of the tent as his heart pounded in his chest.

Chapter Thirteen

Marielle barely had time to react to the arrow that had whizzed past her face and embedded in a tree trunk, before a second arrow came at her. Graham pushed her to the ground before the arrow could find its target. She hit the earth hard, landing on her stomach. Pine needles poked at her palms and belly.

He rolled off her and pushed himself up, glancing back and forth. "Stay low. Get to the car." He held his gun in one hand.

She sprinted in the direction of the car, staying in the cover of the forest. Graham was right behind her. Another arrow shot out in front of them. They both zigzagged, stepping behind the thick trunk of an evergreen. She leaned against the tree, trying to catch her breath and slow her raging heart.

Graham angled around the tree, probably trying to locate where the archer was. "I don't see him, but we have to assume he's still stalking us."

Charlie had been dressed in winter camo clothes. It would be easy enough to conceal himself.

The final sprint to the car would be out in the open. As though they were about to plunge into a deep pool, they nodded at each other and burst out into the snow-covered grassy area below the road.

Her feet pounded the earth as she ran. Graham came up beside her, creating a barrier between her and where the archer probably was. When they got to the car, she flung open the passenger side door just as an arrow hit the window and bounced off.

Graham shot his gun in the direction the arrow had come from before running around to the other side of the car.

Gasping for breath, she crawled in and slammed the door.

He got behind the wheel. Before she even had her seat belt on, he'd pulled the car forward and performed a three-point turn in the small space the shoulder provided so the car faced downhill, the direction they'd come from.

As the tires started rolling, she glanced behind her and then down the hill to the campsite. The archer kept himself well hidden.

"Call the police. They must be on this road, somewhere close by. This whole area needs to be searched. He's hidden his car somewhere."

She pulled out her phone but stopped when she looked through the windshield and saw the police car coming toward him. "Guess you can tell him in person."

Both Graham and the officer rolled down their windows when the two vehicles pulled up side by side. Graham explained the situation.

"We can get forest service involved in the search as well," said the officer before grabbing his radio.

"We need to take him into custody. He's an important player in a case I'm working on," Graham added.

The officer had turned his attention to talking on the radio to get more help.

"I'm not taking any more chances." Graham rolled up his window and edged around the other car on the narrow road. "I'm taking you back to the safe house."

By the time they got down to the main road, her heartbeat had slowed, and she could catch her breath. No matter where she turned, someone wanted her dead. Fear prickled over her skin and she shuddered when she thought about how close the arrow had come to piercing her. "I wonder if Charlie knows that I'm the one taking care of Ian. Why would he want to kill me?"

Graham slowed down on the icy road. "I think he was just trying to protect himself from being taken in by the police. He figured out I was law enforcement. He probably thought you were too."

Graham settled his focus on the road, which was bordered by forest on both sides. The chase had taken them at least five miles outside of town.

A car from a side road pulled in front of them, appearing suddenly from behind some trees. Graham braked and then kept his foot off the gas, going slow until the other vehicle was able to speed up.

As distance grew between the two cars, it took a moment for it to register that she'd seen the car before. "Graham, that car looks like—" Everything had happened so fast when they'd first encountered Charlie. She'd only glimpsed the car he was driving.

Graham had seen the car when he was on foot and for longer. "I think you're right."

The other car disappeared around a curve.

"There must be more than one way off that mountain that leads back to the highway," she said.

Her hand gripped the sides of her seat as the other car came back into view again only much farther ahead of them now. Several cars going in the opposite direction whizzed by them. "We have to go after him." The police were probably still searching the mountain and the camp where Charlie had last been seen.

Graham kept his eyes on the road. "Call the police and let them know where we are."

Graham hung back but kept the other car within view. Charlie's car sped past the exit that would lead back into Clarksville.

She held the phone in her hand. "Where do you suppose he's headed if he's not going back to town?"

"Not sure. He doesn't seem to be aware that he's being followed so far."

She pressed in the number for Detective Strickland and asked him to relay the message to the officer they'd encountered headed up the mountain and let him know what was going on.

The officer called them a few minutes later. "It's going to take me a while to get back down to the main road. I got some forest service people up here helping me search. I'll radio and see if there is anyone closer. Highway patrol might be able to help. You don't know where he's going?"

"No, he passed the exit that would have taken him back into Clarksville."

"Keep us apprised of the situation. Tell Graham not to try to take him in on his own."

When she glanced in his direction, Graham had a laser-like focus on the road and the other car. "Will do." She ended the call.

She had a feeling Graham was not going to wait for backup.

They passed a road sign that listed the next three towns they would encounter. Two of them were less than a thousand people, but the third was Bozeman, which was a city of more than fifty thousand, and fifteen miles away.

"Do you think maybe he's trying to get to the airport in Bozeman?"

Graham flexed his hands on the steering wheel. "Could be. After encountering us, things just got too hot for him and he's looking to escape."

"Funny he didn't leave sooner though. If he was able to sell the drugs, why not get out of town fast?"

"Maybe he wasn't able to sell the drugs." Graham shrugged. "Or something else kept him here."

As the road straightened out, the distance between the two cars shrank.

Marielle tensed. They'd gotten close enough to the other car for her to see that Charlie was not alone in the car. He had a passenger. Earlier when Graham had been trying to avoid an accident when he'd first pulled out on the road, she'd only been paying attention to the car and hadn't noticed the other person.

Graham slowed down. "I don't want him to figure out he's being tailed."

There were enough other cars headed toward Bozeman so they would not stand out.

Graham slowed so that there was a car between him and the one he was tailing.

The gray car took the exit that would lead to the airport without signaling first, as did the car that was between them, a dark blue SUV. Graham turned as well.

They went through a series of three roundabouts with traffic merging from four different directions.

She scanned the lanes of traffic. "I don't see him anymore."

"He's got to be here somewhere." Once at the airport, Graham found parking close to the departure doors. "If they aren't already inside, they will be shortly. Let's see if we can catch them."

She pushed open her car door. As they walked toward the building, she noticed the dark blue SUV parking. A tall blond man and a shorter bald man got out.

There was something vaguely familiar about the short man.

Graham came up beside her as the doors slid open. "I'll look for Charlie and his passenger. You try and find a security officer."

The departure lines for several of the carriers were quite long. She did not see Charlie anywhere. She hurried across the carpet in search of a security officer. When she glanced over her shoulder, Graham had been eaten up by the crowd.

Again, she spotted the tall blond man and his shorter colleague. The short man made eye contact with her for just a second.

Her heart thumped. Now she knew where she'd seen him. He was the man from the hospital who had set the trap for Lee to get at her, the man whose arm had been in a sling. Only now, his injury was miraculously healed.

Recognition spread across his face as well. He tugged on the tall blond man's sleeve to get his attention.

Marielle turned to run back to where she'd last seen Graham. When she looked over her shoulder, the short man was running after her.

The number of people in line to talk to agents and check luggage at departures had increased even more. Graham squeezed through clusters of people as he studied the faces of each person he passed. Charlie had been dressed in a camouflage coat with no bright colors on to distinguish him.

Graham continued to search, taking only a few steps at a time. He slowed down even more when a large man bumped his shoulder and then apologized. The collision had caused him to draw his focus away from the lines of people waiting to talk to agents. He turned in a half circle.

A man at a kiosk drew his attention because of his nervous gestures, shifting from foot to foot with his head lowered at an extreme angle as if he was trying to conceal his face. But unless Charlie had changed his clothes, it wasn't him. This man wore jeans, a denim shirt and a gray winter jacket. When Graham noticed that the man didn't appear to have any luggage, he moved in closer.

The man must have sensed someone staring because he looked up suddenly. Graham slipped behind a pillar but not before he saw the man's face. He had only seen photographs of David Roane at his home. He looked a lot like his brother. David must have been the passenger in the car with Charlie. Had they both been hiding out in the woods?

When he stepped out from the cover of the pillar, David was no longer at the kiosk. Graham's adrenaline surged as he glanced around. Where had he gone? It was clear the two men were trying to escape together.

Graham's heart rammed against his rib cage. He couldn't let them get on a flight. He scanned the entire area, face after face, but didn't see them. Then his gaze caught on two men waiting by the elevator. From the back, one looked like Charlie. He pushed through the crowd as the doors opened and the men stepped in. He arrived at the elevator just as the doors closed. The airport only had two floors, so he dashed to the nearby escalator, taking the steps two at a time to reach the concourse.

The second floor consisted of seating areas and offices on one side. The TSA line took up most of the floor. Restaurants, shops and gates were on the other side of the TSA line but visible through windows.

He searched the crowd waiting in line. His targets would have to be toward the end of the line. Though he could not see every person clearly, none of them looked like David or Charlie. He wandered away, still scanning for the two men. Through the windows, he could see people who had cleared TSA and were headed toward gates. No way could they have already gotten through that line.

When he moved to go back to the TSA line, he noticed a tall blond man. Something stood out about him, the way he was swiveling his head around slowly. He also seemed to be searching for someone.

Adrenaline pumped through his body as he walked briskly, surveying the open office doors and the sitting areas. When he moved past the huge open stairway that led back down to the first floor, he caught sight of Charlie just as the man reached the bottom and turned left.

Graham bolted down the stairs. He arrived at the bottom in time to see Charlie and David across the airport. They opened a door and an alarm split the air. They slipped through it as Graham raced past baggage claim, slowed down by a throng of people who had just disembarked and were milling by the carousels. The alarm intensified as he got closer, and he saw they'd made use of an emergency exit.

He glanced around. He had not seen or heard from Marielle for at least ten minutes. There was no time to try to contact her by phone.

He pushed open the door. The cold wind hit him as he stared out at the tarmac filled with planes and personnel loading, unloading and hauling luggage, along with men and women in reflective clothing directing airplane traffic. The intense rumble of a plane about to take off filled the air. There was a barrier that the two men would have had to jump in order to get out on the tarmac. They must have gone in some other direction.

On his other side looked to be a number of smaller, private planes, and he saw two men disappearing around a private hangar. Graham took off running, following the route around the hangar the men had gone. He ran past a second building that butted up against a scraggly field of low shrubs.

He glanced around. Several men were standing outside an open hangar working on a small plane. Tools were scattered across the concrete. He looked in the other direction. A group of maybe ten people stood beside a small plane while they loaded their own luggage. No sign of David or Charlie anywhere, though there were a couple of places they could've hidden.

The wind and the noise of an airplane lifting into the sky just fifty feet above him drowned out all other noise.

His attention was drawn back to the field. He saw a makeshift path where enough people had trod to create a way through the shrubs. All the same, the field looked like a tangled maze of plant life.

The control tower for the private planes would provide him with a view of most of this area. He ran toward it, finding the door marked *Authorized Personnel Only* unlocked, and he rushed up the stairs where a man and woman sat in front of monitors.

The man whirled his chair around. "Hey, you're not supposed to be up here."

Graham pulled his badge. "DEA. I need to have a look at this area through your windows."

The man nodded. "We've got twenty minutes before another plane takes off. Go ahead."

The windows of the tower provided him with a 360-degree view of the area. He was able to see most of the possible hiding places. No sign of David or Charlie anywhere, but by the edge of the field, he spotted that same tall blond man he'd seen before. The man looked like he was headed back toward the commercial airport. His breath caught. What was going on with that guy?

His eyes came to rest on an open area in the field. He leaned closer to the window, trying to see better. "Do you have binoculars?"

The woman opened a drawer and handed a pair to him. Graham peered through the lenses that magnified what he was seeing. There on the ground in the field lay Charlie and David. Charlie was motionless and prone, a crimson stain evident on his back. Partially sitting up, David clutched his stomach and then collapsed.

Graham's chest squeezed tight. "Call 911. I think we have a possible homicide and attempted murder over in that field." And the tall blond man was the number one suspect. Fear gripped his heart as he realized the blond man was headed back to the commercial part of the airport—and Marielle.

Chapter Fourteen

"I have a gun. I think you better come with me."

Marielle's heart pounded as the short bald man gripped her arm and pressed something against her back.

The short man spoke his threatening words with his mouth close to her ear. Minutes before, while she'd searched for Graham, she'd managed to initially elude the man, but he'd caught her by surprise by flanking around a crowd. Thinking she was getting away, she'd almost run into him, and he'd grabbed her.

Squeezing even tighter, he yanked on her arm. "Come on."

Her breath came out in shallow gasps as her gaze darted everywhere and she tried to come up with a plan of escape. People milled around her—some waited at baggage claim while others went into shops or stood in line to talk to airline agents.

Marielle didn't think he would shoot her in front of witnesses. She needed to stay where there were people. Once the short man led her to someplace secluded, he probably intended to kill her.

She was sure the pair of men had been tailing Charlie, just like she and Graham had. She also knew the short man was the same person who'd set her up so Lee could get at Ian at the hospital. Did these two men work for the cartel?

Still trying to come up with a plan, she spoke softly to him. "Did Charlie Roane betray you and take drugs that belonged to you?"

"Look, lady, I just follow orders." He yanked her arm, leading her toward an exit.

She planted her feet. Going outside would make her more vulnerable. "Is the tall blond guy your partner or your boss?"

"My boss. You ask too many questions. Let's go." He pushed the gun into her spine, though she barely felt it through the thickness of her winter coat. His chest pressed close to her back to conceal the gun from other people. "Where's the kid at anyway?" His grip on her arm tightened. He shoved her toward the door that led outside.

They were still trying to get to Ian. "He's safe."

Marielle knew she had to get away and fast. Pulling herself free of his grip, she whirled around. While he fumbled to conceal the gun, she pushed him and shouted, "I told you to stay away from me. After all you put me through, I don't love you anymore. I'm going to Vegas with Phil."

The groups of people close to them all looked in her direction. The short man had managed to stuff the gun in a pocket before anyone saw it. His face was flushed with rage, or was it embarrassment? She couldn't tell.

The short man reached to grab her coat sleeve.

Another man stepped between them. "Hey, man, leave the lady alone. She made it clear she doesn't want to be with you."

"Yeah, listen to him," said a woman.

She took a step back.

While everyone was still watching their interaction and the short man was prevented from getting at her, she thanked the man who had intervened and stalked away. She still did not know what had happened to Graham, or to Charlie and his passenger.

Pushing down the rising sense of panic, she scanned the area, hoping to see a security guard or Graham. When she saw neither, she pulled out her phone to call Graham. She was about to slip into the safety of a crowded gift shop when the tall blond man, the one who was apparently the boss, entered the airport from outside.

He spotted her right away.

As if a weight was placed on her chest, fear made it hard to breathe. She darted into the gift shop and worked her way toward the back of the store. When she lifted her head, she had a partial view of the blond man standing at the threshold of the store searching for her. He towered above the other people. Her heart pounded as she slipped behind a display of paperback books.

Her phone vibrated in her pocket. Graham.

"Hello." She spoke in a low voice.

The blond man had entered the store.

"Where are you?" Graham sounded out of breath.

She moved away from the paperback display toward a group of people reading greeting cards. The blond man was tracking her with his gaze edging in her direction. She hurried to get away from him.

"I just stepped out of the first floor gift shop." She kept walking, knowing that the blond man would be behind her. "A tall blond man is after me."

"I'm familiar with him. I'm coming toward you as fast as I can," said Graham.

Her head was down as she talked on the phone. She bumped a man's shoulder. "Oh, sorry."

"I bet you are," came a voice filled with intense sarcasm.

When she looked up, it was the short man. Her breath caught and she tensed up. She turned in the opposite direction. The blond man was closing in on her. Her heart skipped into overdrive.

Outside there was a cacophony of noise as several police cars with sirens blaring whizzed past. Had Graham called the police? Why? The blond man fixated on the police cars outside, shaking his head. He backed away, disappearing into the crowd. When she looked around, she did not see the short man either.

Graham's voice came across the line. "I see you."

She looked up. A cluster of people cleared a path. Graham was standing not more than twenty feet from her. She rushed over to him, and he gathered her into his arms.

"I'm so glad to see you." Her hand brushed over his flannel shirt. "Two men were after me."

"I know." He took her hand. "Did you see where they went?"

"They disappeared when the police cars went by."

"The sirens must have scared them away. We need to go talk to the police. Maybe they can be caught before they leave the airport." He took her hand and directed her toward the exit.

"I don't understand. What's going on?"

The sliding doors opened, and they stepped outside. "I have some bad news."

Flashing lights drew her attention to the private airport, where two ambulances and a fire truck had joined the two police cars.

"David was the passenger with Charlie. They both have been shot. We better hurry. Last I saw, David was still alive."

The shock of the news made her light-headed as a numbness set in. The questions reeling through her mind were interrupted when Graham tugged on her sleeve, and they took off running toward the flashing lights. She wondered if the blond man or the short man had had anything to do with Charlie and David being shot. If David died, what would happen to Ian?

She sprinted alongside Graham who directed her around several hangars to a field.

A small crowd had gathered just outside where the police tape had been strung.

Graham showed his badge to the police officer who was making sure the crowd did not encroach on the crime scene.

"I'm the guy who called this in. It may connect with a case I'm working."

The officer nodded, and he stepped under the tape. Graham walked over to one of the other officers who was standing at the edge of the field. She couldn't hear what he was saying, but he pointed toward the commercial airport. The officer spoke into the radio on his shoulder, and a second later, two of the officers on the periphery of the crime scene jumped into one of the police cars and drove toward the larger airport.

The EMTs brought a stretcher out of the shrubbery, carrying a body entirely covered in a sheet. Charlie. Her heart sank. The loss of life was always a tragedy, especially when it wasn't clear if the dead man had been able to repent of his choices. She said a prayer for Charlie's soul.

She watched the EMTs load the body into an ambulance. A moment later, a second stretcher carrying David appeared out of the tangle of shrubbery. He was still alive.

She ran toward the stretcher. "David, I'm the woman taking care of Ian."

David's skin looked translucent. Though his eyes were open, he stared at the sky in a listless, unfocused way. "My boy." A brief smile lit up his face.

She grabbed his hand. "He's all right. He's safe."

"Didn't want to leave town without him. Had to hide, stayed…camped near home…"

Graham had come up behind her. "David, was Charlie working for the cartel?"

"No." David gave a tiny shake of his head. "It was supposed to be his big payday. I got a cut for hiding it." He wheezed in a labored breath of air. "Big mistake, cost me everything."

"Did you see the man who killed Kristen?"

David's head jerked as he drew his eyes into a squint that communicated his pain.

The EMT at the head of the stretcher put his hand on Graham's arm. "Agent Flynn, we need to get his man to the hospital."

David closed his eyes. Marielle squeezed his hand before letting go. They got moving, and Graham followed, walking alongside the stretcher. "I have permission to question him."

"I'm sorry. He's critical. We need to go." The EMT looked over his shoulder as they moved past Graham and Marielle. "You can talk to him when he recovers."

"The second he's able to talk, I need to know," said Graham.

Marielle slipped her hand into his. "We need to pray for him."

Graham nodded. "Yes. I want answers about this case, but even more for Ian's sake, I want David to make it."

They stood for a long moment holding hands while they each prayed silently. Both ambulances drove away.

Graham squeezed her hand. "Give me a second to talk to the officer, and then I'll take you back to the safe house."

A cold wind ruffled her hair while she waited. She could see the ambulances in the distance as they wove through the airport toward the exit.

Graham returned after a few minutes. "The police didn't apprehend either of those two men yet."

The news caused her to tense up as she fought to keep the rising fear at bay. "That means they could still come after us."

Marielle's statement had a chilling effect on Graham. "Maybe, but the police think they may have left the airport. They couldn't locate the car I described."

"The parking lot is full, and it's a generic-looking car. They might still be here hiding somewhere."

He'd do anything to ease the concern on her face, the tight jaw and the creased forehead. He pressed his hand against her cheek. "The police will do as much as they can to take those guys in." He wrapped his arm through hers. "Let's get you back to that safe house."

She pressed closer to him as they walked. Snow swirled out

of the sky in soft lazy patterns. "Do you suppose those men killed Kristen, or were sent by whoever did?"

"Don't know exactly what their role was."

"The tall blond one seemed to be the one giving orders."

He let out a breath, recalling what he'd seen earlier. "I think the blond guy probably shot David and Charlie. It's clear now from what David said that Charlie stole from the cartel, so it was probably a revenge killing. Maybe they gave up the location of the drugs or the money from the drugs before they were shot."

"Those men came after me too. They know about my connection to Ian," she said. "The short man is the one who tried to trick me at the hospital, and he wanted to know where he was."

"It's Ian they want," said Graham. "They probably know I'm investigating the case and would want me out of the way."

"For sure, the cases are connected now," she said.

"Yes, David implied as much," he said. "My evidence against the blond man is circumstantial. I saw him close to where David and Charlie were gunned down. It's a good enough reason for the police to want to take him in for questioning."

They came to the edge of the larger airport building, moved up the sidewalk and then veered into the parking lot. Graham found himself in a state of hyperawareness as he watched the people around him and the cars pulling out. Those two men were still at large.

She pulled free of his grasp as they drew nearer to their car. "I hope David makes it." She stopped by the front bumper. "He delayed leaving town because he wanted to take his son with him." Her voice grew soft as she shook her head. "The whole thing is so sad. Regardless of what David has done in his life, he loves his son."

"We don't know David's level of involvement with all of this. What he said to me implied that he was aware of what Charlie had planned and that he stood to benefit by *hiding it*. That could mean the drugs or the money gotten from the drugs."

She nodded. "He might end up going to prison if he does survive the shooting."

"A lot of unknowns right now," he said.

Assuming that the Roane brothers had already sold the drugs, they now knew why they had not gotten out of town right away. The decision had cost Charlie his life.

Marielle and Graham climbed into the borrowed car.

Graham pulled out of the parking space and drove toward the airport exit. Fully aware that they might be followed, he kept his eye on the traffic behind them taking the road that led back out to the highway.

His phone rang. He lifted it from his pocket and glanced at it. One of the police officers he'd been in contact with. He needed to focus on driving, so he handed the phone to Marielle. "Put it on speaker."

She took the phone and pushed the connect button. "This is Marielle. Graham is with me in the car. We have you on speaker."

"Great, just wanted to let you know that we figured out what Charlie was looking for in that shed. It seems he had stashed some money and gold jewelry back there."

"Probably what he made from the sale of the drugs," said Graham. And he was probably coming to get it so he could get out of town. After Graham had found his camp, Charlie must have convinced David that things were too hot to stay in Clarksville anymore. They needed to leave without Ian.

"One other thing," said the officer. "It looks like there was another camp not too far from the one you and Marielle came upon."

Graham hit his turn signal as he came up to the exit that would lead back to the safe house in Clarksville. "Probably where David was hiding out." Separate camps meant that if one of them got caught or killed, the other might still be able to take the money and escape. "Thanks for the info. Keep me in the loop."

Marielle pressed a button on the phone and handed it back to Graham. He was on one of the main thoroughfares of the city, two lanes of traffic in each direction. Though he'd never gotten a close look at it, a dark-colored SUV behind him held his attention for some time. He hit his blinker and turned into a gas station.

"Why are we stopping?"

"Need gas."

She leaned to peer at the dashboard. "You have a quarter tank. That's enough to get back to the safe house." She straightened her back, still watching him. Her eyes held a question, waiting for an explanation.

When he looked around the gas station, he didn't see the suspicious car anywhere. He put his hand on hers. "I just don't want to take any chances that we might lead those men to Ian."

She reached up to brush her fingers over his face. "Thank you for caring as much about him as I do."

He smiled. "The kid grows on ya."

"Indeed, he does." She laughed and leaned toward him even more so that their foreheads were almost touching. Their eyes met as a charge of electricity zinged through him. He wanted to kiss her.

She pulled her hand away from his face and sat up but not before he caught that same warmth in her expression that he'd experienced.

Perhaps it was best that she'd ended the moment. What sort of mixed message would that give her anyway? Once this investigation was over, his job would take him to some other part of the world. From the beginning, his stay in Montana was meant to be temporary.

He shifted into Drive, feeling the flush on his face from the moment of connection between them. "We should get going, huh?"

"Yes, for sure." Her voice was flat, as if she was trying to purge it of any intense emotion.

He waited a few minutes at the gas station before pulling back out on the road. As a precaution, he took a circuitous route to the safe house once he got to Clarksville. Ian was the ultimate target in this dangerous situation, and they had to do everything to protect him.

Chapter Fifteen

As Graham drove through the subdivision where the safe house was located, Marielle lifted the bag of things she'd gotten from Ian's house and put it on her lap. It felt like a lifetime ago that she'd gathered the items from Ian's house. She hoped something she'd collected would aid in ending Ian's muteness, and she was glad she'd had the presence of mind to hold on to the bag when she'd run out to the car so she and Graham could pursue Charlie.

Graham parked in the car on the driveway by the garage, pulled his phone out and called to let the officers inside know that they were back. A second later, the garage door on the double garage opened up, and he parked the car beside a patrol vehicle.

From the back seat where it'd been tossed, Marielle retrieved the bag of clothes for her and Ian that she'd gotten from her own home.

"It feels like we collected these things a very long time ago," he said, echoing her own earlier thoughts.

"Yes, it does." So much had changed since then. Charlie was dead and David was in critical condition.

Graham cupped his hand on her shoulder.

His touch brought back the memory of the moment of connection they'd shared in the car earlier. She turned to face him. He reached out toward her, indicating he could carry one of the bags. She handed him the bigger, heavier bag of clothes.

When they headed toward the door that connected to the house, he placed his hand on the middle of her back. The gesture may have risen from his instinct to protect her, but still it seemed as though something had shifted between them. He'd almost kissed her in the car earlier.

When Graham opened the door, a police officer, an older man with gray sideburns, was standing several feet from the window that looked out on the street. The gun belt he wore was a reminder of the danger they faced.

Graham stepped aside so Marielle could go in first. She wondered how long it would be before Graham chose to leave her and Ian to become an active part of the investigation. The truth was that she felt safest when she was with him.

She glanced around the room before addressing the older man. "Officer Phelps, where's Ian?"

"He's in the downstairs bedroom with Officer O'Brian." The older man studied Graham for a moment. "Heard you two had a bit of an encounter. Sorry to hear about the shooting. You look like you could use a cup of coffee."

"You go on ahead," Graham told her.

Before stepping into the hallway, she looked over her shoulder at Graham. He was probably anxious to get back out and help with the investigation. She had the protection of two police officers now.

As she stepped toward the bedroom, she heard him say, "I could use a cup, thanks."

She took in a breath that eased the tension in her muscles. He'd be staying for a while anyway.

She entered the downstairs bedroom where Officer O'Brian sat on the floor with Ian while they stacked building blocks.

She was a young woman, probably in her early twenties. Her blond hair was pulled up into a tight bun.

Ian gazed up at Marielle and then lifted his hands toward her. She put the bag on the floor and reached for him. "I missed you, little man."

"I'm glad you're back." Officer O'Brian pushed herself to her feet. "I'm going to get a nap upstairs. Officer Phelps and I will be switching off on guard duty, and it would be good if I were rested."

Marielle held Ian and swayed while Ian played with her hair. "That sounds good."

Officer O'Brian left the room.

Marielle put Ian on the bed and reached for the bag of items she'd brought from his home. "Ian, I got you some things you might like. Maybe you can tell me about them."

She drew out the photographs first and pointed at the picture of Kristen. "Who is that? Can you tell me?"

Ian's fingers touched Kristen's smiling face. His lips pressed together as if he was trying to make the "m" sound.

She squeezed his shoulder and patted his back. "Take your time."

He emitted a small abrupt noise then shook his head and flopped down on the bed.

She rubbed his back. "It's all right, Ian. I know this is hard." She touched the picture again. "It that your mama?"

Ian blinked and then reached out to touch the photograph too before nodding. She couldn't begin to fathom what was going on behind those eyes. His reaction had been calm enough that she guessed he wasn't remembering the violence connected to his mother. Maybe the love and safety he'd known with her was foremost in his developing brain.

Developmentally at his age, he would not necessarily understand that his mom was not coming back.

She pulled out a blanket she'd found in his room. The home-made quilt with squares that featured farm animals looked well loved, with thinning fabric and worn edges. Ian grabbed it and drew it to his chest, resting one cheek against the bed.

"Is that your special blankie?"

He nodded and rubbed a corner of it. She pointed to one of the quilt squares that showed a chicken. Maybe she could get him to talk about something that was less emotionally charged. "Can you tell me what that is?"

He looked at her but did not speak.

"Is it a chicken? What kind of noise does a chicken make?" She had to keep trying to get him to talk.

Ian pressed his lips together as if to make a chicken noise, but no sound came out of his mouth. She tried several other animals on the quilt with the same result, praising him each time he was able to at least mime the noise.

Next she pulled out a stuffed lion and put it behind her back, thinking she would play a game that might help him talk. It too had looked to be in the much-loved and handled category. She'd found it on Ian's bed with the quilt.

"Can you guess who's behind my back? I think he's a friend of yours." She brought the lion out, shook it and made a soft roaring sound.

Ian's countenance changed from relaxed to terrified. He sat bolt upright as his eyes grew round. He shook his head, making a frantic and frightened noise. She dropped the lion and reached for him.

"Ian, it's all right."

He rolled away, crawled to the end of the bed and jumped off. He pulled on his hair.

She got up too, but when she advanced toward him, he made a sound that indicated distress.

Marielle clutched her roiling stomach. Seeing Ian so upset was hard to deal with. This was so unexpected and didn't make any sense.

Graham stood in the doorway holding a coffee cup. "I heard a cry. Everything all right in here?"

"I'm not sure." She slipped the lion back in the bag. "I showed him a toy, a stuffed lion, that I thought would bring him comfort and maybe get him talking. It had the opposite effect."

Graham put his coffee cup on the dresser by the door and rushed over to where Ian crouched in a corner. He dropped down on his knees to be close to the boy but did not reach out toward him. "Hey, buddy, how's it going?" Instead, he waited until Ian moved toward him. After a moment's hesitation, the boy fell into his arms.

Marielle watched as Graham spoke soothing words to him. After a few minutes, Graham rose to his feet and placed a half-asleep Ian on the bed. He sat on the bed and rubbed Ian's back until he fell entirely asleep.

Still shaken by Ian's reaction to the lion, Marielle reached for the quilt and covered Ian with it. She tiptoed toward the door.

After he grabbed his coffee from the dresser, Graham delicately closed the door.

Graham leaned toward her. "How are you doing?" His features filled with concern.

She rubbed her arms, wishing her heart wasn't still beating so fast. "That was pretty upsetting. I never meant to cause him more pain."

"Why don't you come to the kitchen and we can talk?" He patted her shoulder. "My coffee is cold anyway. I gotta get a fresh cup."

As they walked through the living room, she caught sight of Officer Phelps sitting in an overstuffed chair watching the activity on the street outside.

Graham poured out his now cold coffee into the sink and got a fresh cup from the coffeepot. "You want some?"

"I'm fine. I'll probably catch a nap in a little while." She took a seat at the table, still trying to sort through what had happened. "That is the most agitated I've ever seen Ian. It just doesn't make any sense. That toy was as worn out as the stuffed giraffe he treasures. I found it on his bed along with that quilt I covered him with. He had a positive response to that."

Graham sat down beside her. "He sounded afraid when I heard him cry out from the living room."

"The word I would use to describe his reaction is *terrified*," she said. "Thanks for your help getting him calmed down."

"No problem." He stirred two teaspoons of sugar into his coffee.

"No really, I mean it." She rested her hands on the table and twisted them together. "When I reached out to him, he didn't want me to hold him because he associated me with causing fear. I'm going to have to rebuild trust with him."

"He'll come back around. I'm sure he sees you as a safe person." He placed his hand on hers. "Why do you think that toy scared him?"

The warmth of his touch calmed her. "I'm not sure what's going on. Maybe it's the toy. He associates it with something bad. Maybe it's lions in general. Until he can tell us, we won't know for sure. Showing him a picture of a lion might upset him, and I don't want to put him through that again."

Graham took a sip of his coffee.

"You did so good with him, Graham. You would've been a great dad. You still could be." In the ten years they'd been apart, it seemed that neither of them had moved on into a new relationship and marriage. She wanted him to find a measure of happiness and wondered why he was just as stuck as she was. He was the one who hurt her after all.

His face grew grim as the mood in the room shifted. "I don't know about that." He pushed his chair back and rose to his feet. "I hardly had a good role model for a father."

His words held an intensity she had not heard before. She'd hit a nerve without intending to. "Just because your dad walked out on you and your mom doesn't mean you'd do the same thing."

"He did way worse than that before he left." He turned away from her and gripped the counter. "I just couldn't take a chance having kids. The acorn doesn't fall far from the tree and all that."

When they'd been engaged, they'd talked about having a family. Though Graham had agreed with her about wanting to have children, she remembered that he would often seem sullen and distant after their conversations. Maybe he'd just been agreeable about plans to have a family to make her happy. "Just because your dad wasn't a good father doesn't mean you wouldn't be."

She stared at his back, waiting for him to respond. Tension had descended in the space between them.

"It's not a risk I would want to take with kids of my own. End up ruining their life." He sat his coffee cup on the counter and stared out the window.

"Birth is not destiny, Graham. You could make different choices." This was the first time Graham had ever brought up his fear about repeating the patterns of his father.

"You don't get it, Marielle. You come from a family that has generations of stable parents with a strong faith. I come from the exact opposite."

He stomped out of the room.

Marielle sat at the table in a state of shock.

Graham hurried through the living room toward the front door.

Officer Phelps rose to his feet. "Where are you going?"

"I just need to get some fresh air." The conversation with Marielle had left him feeling shredded. He wanted to be alone.

"I don't think it's a good idea for you to be outside," said the police officer. "If you need some space, there's an office upstairs. Second door on the right."

Graham nodded and rushed up the stairs. The office was sparsely furnished with a desk, rolling chair and mostly empty bookshelf, staged just enough to make it look not like a safe house. He closed the door and plunked down into the chair, swinging it around so he could stare out the window.

Why had Marielle brought up the issue of children and fatherhood? She really didn't get it. She never had. Her mom and dad were great parents.

Years ago, when they'd talked about having a family, he'd had deep insecurities. He'd tried to convince himself that everything would be okay once they were married and a child was born, but the fear would not go away. He just didn't think he was up to the responsibility of fatherhood. He now realized that on an unconscious level, when the recruiter had dangled the offer of an exciting undercover career in front of him, it had allowed him not to have to face his fears.

He rose from the chair to look out the window to the street below. His hand formed a fist, and he pounded it on the windowsill as his jaw grew tight. The truth was he felt a growing connection to Ian that made him afraid on so many levels. He didn't know he could care about a kid that much. The feelings surprised him. But caring didn't mean he had the capacity to parent. The whole thing scared him more than being in a firefight.

If the boy's father recovered and the charges against him were minor, the child would most likely be returned to David. Forming an attachment was not a good idea. Ian's life was in danger. He could lose the little boy just like he'd lost Cesar.

He shook his head.

Everything was so fragile and uncertain.

The conversation with Marielle had been like a collision with his past choices. He'd always thought that a man like him could best serve God by remaining single and focusing on his job. But now, because of his feelings for Marielle and Ian and his disillusionment about his job since Cesar's death, he was beginning to wonder.

He stopped beating his fist on the windowsill and placed his palm on the pane. The bottom line was that no matter what he felt for a child, it didn't mean he'd be a good father. The realization created a chasm inside him.

His job had been so fulfilling for so many years, but now he felt hollow. Maybe if he could focus his energy on closing this investigation, he could get back the solid feeling he got from doing his job as an undercover agent. Time to get some work done.

He made a quick call to Detective Strickland. Police had not been able to locate the two men from the airport. "Look, Marielle and I got a look at both guys. If we can get access to the database of known cartel associates, we might be able to identify them. I can get my boss to help me with that."

"The police officers watching you should have a laptop. It wouldn't hurt to also go through local criminals as well, since that's where Lee Masters was recruited from," said Detective Strickland.

"Agreed." Graham held the phone tighter. "Any news on David Roane?"

"No update there. The last I heard was that doctors rushed him into surgery to remove the bullet."

"Interviewing him could give me a lot of answers," said Graham.

"I'll let you know as soon as I hear anything."

Graham said goodbye and rushed downstairs.

If he couldn't interview David, maybe he could figure out who the two men from the airport were.

It took only a few minutes to set up the laptop and get authorization to access the federal database. He invited Marielle to sit beside him while they shuffled through the photographs.

Marielle sat close enough to see the screen they shared. Her shoulder brushed against his when she leaned forward.

Her proximity still made his heart beat faster. He narrowed the parameters of the search to blond men over six feet tall.

They combed through dozens of photographs. Each time they shook their heads. After nearly an hour of looking at photographs, his eyes were blurry. He rose to his feet and stretched his arms behind his neck.

Marielle stared at the screen where the last man they'd dismissed was still visible. There were photos of the man's face from the front and the side along with a separate photo showing the distinct tattoo of a dragon on his chest. "Why do they show these pictures of the tattoos?"

"Tattoos and scars are another way to identify a person because they're unique. Tattoos can give a history, as well, if a man has been in prison or part of a gang."

"So the smart thing to do if you were a criminal would be not to get a tattoo," she said.

He laughed and sat back down. "Never thought of it that way, but I suppose you're right. It's part of the criminal culture to put your history and identity on your skin."

Marielle continued to stare at the screen.

His voice filled with concern. "Are you tired? Do you want to take a break?"

She shook her head. "I was just thinking about something. Can you do a keyword search for *lion tattoo*?"

He scooted his chair forward as he processed what she was indicating. "Do you think the man who killed Ian's mom had a lion tattoo and that's why he had such a strong reaction to the toy?"

"It's just a theory."

He pressed the enter button. "Looks like we have twenty-five matches for men and women with lion tattoos."

He filed through the photographs. At the tenth photo in, she stopped him. "There."

The man they were looking at was not blond and his hair was short. But his facial features resembled that of the tall blond man from the airport and he had a lion tattoo on his arm that would have been covered by his winter coat when they saw him.

He studied the photograph for a long moment. "It could be the same guy. He's just changed his hair color and let it grow out."

Her words held an icy chill. "This might be the man who killed Kristen."

A moan behind him caused him to turn in his seat. Ian had awakened and was holding his blanket.

Marielle shut the laptop and rushed toward Ian to scoop him up. "Hey." She brushed her hand over his hair. "Did you have a good nap?"

Ian nodded.

"Bet you're hungry. Why don't we get you something to eat?"

Graham waited until Marielle disappeared into the kitchen before opening the laptop back up. The man he was looking at had several known aliases, most that were a variation on Georgio Franks. By cross-referencing known associates, he also found a photo of the short bald man who went by the name Eric Smith.

Georgio had lived in different locations throughout the western US. He had some minor drug distribution convictions from years ago. The DEA had connected him to several known cartel members in Mexico. Such a profile suggested he was likely one of the distributors for drugs in the northwest.

He wrote down both names with a brief description by each.

His heartbeat thrummed in his ears as he stared at the photograph. Arched eyebrows and narrowed eyes looked back at him.

Was he looking at Kristen's killer?

Chapter Sixteen

After seating Ian at the table, Marielle found some wheat crackers in a cupboard. She searched the refrigerator for some more snack possibilities. Grapes caught her eye. She prepared a plate for Ian and placed it on the table in front of him.

After she poured him a cup of milk, she sat down beside him.

He offered her a cracker.

She took it and nibbled. "Thanks, kiddo."

Graham came and stood on the threshold leading into the kitchen. He handed her a piece of paper.

Georgio Franks—tall, blond. Kristen's killer?

Eric Smith—short, bald.

Words did not need to pass between them. He was probably thinking the same thing as she was. Could they get confirmation from Ian that a man with a lion tattoo had killed his mother?

Ian lifted a grape toward Graham.

Graham sat down in the chair on the other side of the boy and took the grape. "Hey, that looks pretty good." He popped the grape in his mouth and chewed in an exaggerated way, making loud noises.

Ian laughed.

"Are you filling your belly up?" He poked the boy's stomach which made him laugh even louder.

She leaned toward Ian. "We should maybe just make our own snack plate and quit stealing your food."

Ian picked up another cracker and set it in front of her on the table. His sweet nature never ceased to amaze her.

She locked gazes with Graham, lifting her chin slightly to signal that he could ask the questions that needed to be asked. He had a special bond with Ian that might facilitate the boy staying calm when talking about what he'd witnessed. She was still concerned that he might associate her with the lion that had frightened him so much.

Ian placed a cracker and a small bunch of grapes in front of Graham.

"Can I ask you something, buddy?"

Ian nodded and took a bite of his cracker.

"Do you remember the...stuffed animal Marielle showed you?"

Ian stopped chewing for a second. He looked at Marielle, wide brown eyes searching her face.

She put her hand on his back and leaned close to his face. "I didn't mean to make you afraid." Tears rimmed her eyes. "I didn't know it would upset you."

Ian reached up and put his finger close to her eye.

"It's okay." She touched his cheek. "I just don't want you to be afraid. That makes me sad."

He turned his attention back to eating. She listened to the crunching sound of crackers being chewed.

Graham cleared his throat and scooted his chair closer to Ian's. "Would it be okay if we talked about the lion?"

Ian stopped eating, holding his cracker in midair. It took a long moment before he nodded.

"Did the man who hurt your mom have a lion on his skin?"

Ian nodded as he pressed his quivering lips together. Marielle's throat went tight. "It's okay. Graham and I are both here with you. No one is going to hurt you or scare you."

Please, Lord, protect this child's heart and mind.

Graham's words were soft, almost a whisper. "Can you show me where the lion was on the man?"

Ian studied Graham's face for a long moment.

Graham nodded and rested a hand on Ian's shoulder. "It's okay, little buddy. You can tell me."

Ian touched his upper arm.

The tension eased from her body, and she took in a breath. That confirmed her theory. They most likely knew now who Kristen's killer was, the tall blond man named Georgio.

Ian wiggled in his seat and said, "He was a bad man." He picked up a cracker and took a bite.

Graham looked over Ian's head at Marielle as his mouth dropped open.

Joy burst through her as she drew Ian into a sideways hug. "Indeed." Ian was talking again, and they had a name and face to connect to his mother's killer.

"Come on, how about I read you a story?" said Graham.

Marielle scooted back her chair and rose to her feet. "I'll go get one from the bedroom." She went down the hall and grabbed two books from the top of the stack.

When she came back into the living room, Graham and Ian were sitting on the couch. Officer Phelps had moved to a chair closer to the door. She handed Graham one of the books and then sat on the other side of Ian.

Graham showed Ian the book. "You like this one?"

Ian nodded.

Graham read several pages of the book and then his phone rang. He looked at his phone, his expression growing serious. "I have to take this."

Marielle lifted the book from his hands. "I'll take over."

Graham went into the kitchen to take the call while she read several pages to Ian. He leaned his head against her shoulder.

Graham stepped back into the living room and ushered her over. She got up and walked over to him. After glancing in Ian's direction, he whispered, "David Roane is out of surgery. I have to go see if I can interview him."

She nodded. "I hope it goes well."

She returned to sit with Ian picking up the book.

Her throat grew tight. It was inevitable that he would have to leave to do his job. They'd shared something deep and bonding in working together to care for Ian and to see him talk again.

Ian slipped off the couch and ran over to hug Graham's leg.

"Thanks, little buddy." Graham's eyes glazed, and his voice was thick with emotion. He kneeled and gave Ian a hug.

She rose from the couch. He stood up from hugging Ian and opened his arms to embrace her. "Take care of yourself, Graham." She relished the warmth of his arms before he pulled away.

His eyes were still glazed as he touched her chin, offering her a faint quick smile before walking across the room and opening the door that led to the garage.

His leaving was a reminder that the bond she felt toward him was temporary. Wrestling with a sense of loss, she stared out the window from across the room. She didn't want him to go.

She stepped a little closer to the window, watching Graham backing the car out of the garage. Then she frowned. Something was wrong.

Graham had stopped the car halfway down the driveway with the engine still running.

From where he sat behind the wheel, Graham didn't like the looks of the blue compact car that eased down the street, slowing even more as it passed the house where Marielle and Ian were. The car turned a corner at the end of the block.

He waited for a moment while his car idled, half expecting to see the other vehicle coming back the way it had gone.

Though she was standing a safe distance away from the window, he could see Marielle staring out at him with questioning look on her face. Seeing her stabbed at his heart. Going back to his job had never been so hard.

Officer Phelps had risen to look out the window as well.

Satisfied that his suspicions had been unwarranted, he shifted into Reverse. He waved at Officer Phelps and then checked his rearview mirror. He'd backed up only a few feet when he saw the blue car again. It had circled the block and was coming up the street again.

Still halfway down the driveway, he killed the engine and jumped out. The blue car sped up. Adrenaline surged through his body as he ran toward the house.

Officer Phelps swung the door open just as Graham reached for the knob.

"I saw," said Phelps.

Two gunshots shattered the front window. Graham caught a glimpse of the blue car whizzing by just before he stepped across the threshold, dropped to the floor and kicked the door shut with his foot.

Marielle gathered Ian up and retreated toward the first-floor bedroom. Officer O'Brian swooped down the stairs with her gun drawn.

More shots, this time aimed at the side of the house, resounded through the air. Marielle emerged from the bedroom still holding Ian. She dropped down to the floor.

"They shot through the bedroom window." Her voice was frantic.

There had to be at least two shooters. To take the shot at the side of the house, one must have gotten out of the car. They were surrounded.

Officer Phelps addressed the policewoman. "I'll take care of these guys. You get them out of here."

O'Brian signaled to Marielle and Graham. "The patrol car in the garage. Come on, let's go."

As they retreated toward the door that led to the attached garage, Graham heard Officer Phelps calling for backup. Graham wrapped his arm around Marielle and guided her into the garage. He opened the back door of the car for her and Ian to get in while Officer O'Brian slipped behind the wheel.

Marielle lay across the back seat, drawing Ian close to her. Graham got into the front passenger seat with his gun drawn. Officer O'Brian held the garage door remote in her hand. She pressed the button and the door began to rise.

It was halfway up when she pressed it again. A quick glance over his shoulder told him that the blue car was going by. More shots filled the air. A bullet pinged when it hit the metal of the garage door just as it closed.

Craning his neck, he stared at the garage door. The threat of danger seemed to electrify the air around him. Resting on her side, Marielle stirred in the back seat. Her coat made a rustling noise as she drew Ian closer to her stomach.

He turned his attention to the front seat.

The hand O'Brian held the remote in was shaking.

"Here." Graham reached for the remote. "You focus on driving. I'll let you know when the coast is clear."

Graham pushed the remote. The door eased up. Because it was a double garage with a wide driveway, she'd be able to get around the car he'd left halfway up the driveway. While still looking over his shoulder, he crouched in his seat, trying to get a view of the street. "It's clear."

This time, she backed out even before the door was completely open.

As soon as O'Brian had the vehicle clear of the garage door, he pressed the remote to close it.

Officer O'Brian backed up out onto the street, twisting the wheel as she gained speed.

Graham continued to scan the area around him and behind him as their vehicle zoomed up the street. Two police cars whizzed past them. The cars split off in different directions as they got close to the safe house. Phelps must have called for more officers.

"I'm going to head toward the highway for now," said Officer O'Brian. "It'll be easier to spot a tail and lose them if we need to."

Marielle's voice floated up from the back seat. "Isn't there someplace we can take Ian so he's safe?"

His throat grew tight at the vision of Marielle holding Ian close. They both looked so vulnerable.

His voice came out as a soft whisper. "It kind of depends on if they catch these guys or not." Graham turned fully around in the seat, so he was looking through the windshield. He addressed his comment to O'Brian. "Don't you think?"

"Yes, we'll have to wait to hear." Officer O'Brian reached the edge of town and took an exit for the highway. "Once we're sure that we're not being followed, we can go back to the police station, maybe, as a temporary measure. Phelps is in charge of protection duty. He'll let me know our next move."

Both Graham and Officer O'Brian watched the cars around them. Hopefully, the arrival of the police cars scared the men in the blue compact into getting away rather than coming after them. No doubt, it was Georgio and Eric who had come for them once again.

The car radio crackled. She lifted it from the receiver. "O'Brian here."

Phelps's voice came through. "Perpetrators still at large. They abandoned the blue compact. No sign of them fleeing on foot. We think they must have had a backup car close by."

Graham tensed. That meant they no longer knew what the shooters were driving. They could be in any of the cars on this highway.

"Got it," said O'Brian. "What's our next step?"

"You can't bring them back to the safe house," said Phelps. "This place is compromised."

"Should we head toward the police station?"

"I'm concerned that it is too obvious a choice and that the suspects might be waiting and watching for your arrival."

"So what are you suggesting?" O'Brian let up on the talk button.

"My brother is a manager at the Big Sky Hotel," said Phelps. "I can make a call."

"I know which one you're talking about," said O'Brian.

"He'll let you in the back and escort you up the service elevator until we can figure out something more permanent. His name is Dane Phelps. I'll text you his cell phone number. I'll get to the hotel as fast as I can to provide the additional protection needed."

"Ten-four," said O'Brian. She placed the radio back in its slot and stared out at the road. "I got to get turned around here."

While O'Brian concentrated on getting to the hotel, Graham remained alert to the traffic around them. Being in the police vehicle made it too easy for them to be tracked, but they had no choice at this point.

When Officer O'Brian took the exit that led back into town, several other cars followed them.

Graham couldn't shake the tension that had wrapped around his chest, making it hard to get a deep breath.

Once on city streets again, O'Brian slowed down.

"How far away are we?"

"It's the other side of town," said O'Brian.

"Why don't I make the call to the hotel, so the guy is waiting for us when we get there?"

O'Brian pulled her cell phone from her shirt pocket and unlocked it. "That would be great. Check my text messages for Officer Phelps's text."

City businesses in buildings close together opened up to fields and warehouses farther apart. The hotel must be at the edge of town.

Looking down as he focused on the phone, he pressed in the

number and waited while the phone rang. He lifted his head just in time to see a car fill his field of vision as it crashed into the passenger side door.

Chapter Seventeen

Upon impact, the whole car shook, causing Marielle to mash her teeth together as her heart raced. She wrapped her arms even tighter around Ian. Though she wanted to see what was going on, her instinct told her to stay hidden.

O'Brian shifted into Reverse and backed the police car up. Graham had grabbed the radio calling for backup. He held his gun in his other hand.

A bullet hit the car as O'Brian backed up at a high speed.

She let go of Ian. "Get down on the floor. Stay flat."

The boy rolled away from her onto the carpeted floor of the back seat.

Graham lifted his gun and shot several times through the rolled-down window, ducking low after each shot.

There was another crash and the crunch of metal, this time toward the front of the car. O'Brian shifted as the car made a grinding noise but did not move. Graham jumped out.

She winced at the volley of gunfire she heard.

Oh God, let him not get shot.

She placed her hand on Ian's back.

The next few seconds went by in a blur. Glass shattered above her, spraying over her. She heard the clicks of the door locks opening. The driver's side door opened, as did the back passenger door close to her feet.

Hands like iron clamped around her ankles and dragged her out. She heard the sound of men punching each other and had only a flashing image of Ian's blond head as he was gathered into someone's arms.

She gasped and reached out toward him.

Ian cried out, "Mari."

A hood was put over her head, and she was dragged a short distance. Her captor had wrapped his arm around her.

She heard a voice say, "Come closer and I'll kill her."

Something hard pressed against her skull. A gun?

She was shoved onto a hard surface. She heard the squeal of tires. The car started to move. In the distance, sirens wailed.

She could feel the car rolling, gaining speed.

What had happened to Ian?

She reached to pull the hood off her head.

Hands wrapped around her wrists, drawing them together and binding them with what felt like rope behind her back. She could hear the man's heavy breathing as he secured the rope.

Her stomach pressed against the hard surface of the car.

The car seemed to go even faster, jostling her, and it sounded like the surface of the road had changed from smooth concrete to gravel.

She could hear voices.

"She's not going anywhere," said the first voice. That sounded like Eric Smith.

"Make the call," said the second man, and she guessed that must be Georgio Franks.

A few seconds passed, and then Eric said, "This is a message for the cops holding Ian Roane. I think we have something you want. We'll trade her for the boy. You have one hour."

As her cheek pressed against the floor, Marielle's breaths were shallow and rapid, causing the hood to move in and out against her face. She feared she would hyperventilate.

Come on, Marielle, hold it together.

The call must have gone into the police department unless the men had somehow figured out Graham's number.

At least this meant that Ian was safe. Graham must have been able to grab him before the men did. They did not know that Ian had already identified Georgio as Kristen's killer, and they must have thought they could still prevent it from happening.

She knew Graham would not put Ian at risk. It was up to her to figure out how to escape.

The two men were playing a desperate game. She was pretty sure they would shoot her if they didn't get what they wanted and fast. The whole thing might be a ruse, to buy them time to flee the country. They had to know that the police wouldn't hand a child over to them. How smart were they? Was it possible this was a plot to distract the police while they plotted a way to get at Ian?

She didn't know what they were up to. She only knew she had to get away.

She tried to draw her hands apart. She'd been bound with something that had a little give to it. A bungee cord maybe.

The back end of the car slanted downward. They were going up a hill then down the other side. The car continued for a few more minutes and then came to a stop. She heard doors opening and being slammed. The air around her grew quiet. Her heart raced. Both men must have gotten out of the car. She lifted her head, trying to push herself up.

The hood was not secured. She worked her way up to her knees and bent her head while shaking it to get the hood to come off. The car was in a lot of what looked like and defunct business surrounded by open fields. There was another metal building not too far away that looked like it was not in use either, judging from the pileup of snow and overgrown vegetation.

She was in the cargo area of an SUV. The back hatch swung open. The short bald man, Eric, shook his head.

He grinned in a sinister way. Only one side of his mouth curled up. "Trying to get smart with me, huh?"

He grabbed her arm painfully at the elbow, forcing her to move toward him. The hood went back over her head.

"Put your feet on the ground," said Eric.

When she hesitated, he jerked her arm so it hurt. She complied. He controlled her by clamping his hand around her elbow and squeezing if she moved the wrong way. Her boots stepped across the hard surface. Out of the bottom of the hood, she could see cracked concrete.

A door slid open and she was pushed inside. It grew even darker, though she could still feel a slight breeze. She was shoved to the ground. Her bound hands touched cold concrete. The odor of oil and dirt hung in the air.

The men shuffled around for several minutes. Then she felt her feet being lifted and something being wound around her ankles.

"This ought to keep them busy while we get out of here," Eric said.

Georgio laughed.

Eric pulled the hood off her head and shoved a gag into her mouth. It tasted like dirt.

Eric patted her cheek. "Now no one can hear you scream for help."

Georgio waited a few feet away. Eric moved to join him.

Her view was partially obstructed by a piece of farm equipment. She could hear the men's footfalls on the concrete. A door creaked shut and a few minutes later a car engine started up.

As the noise of the car faded, she focused on her surroundings. She was inside a metal building with broken, rusty-looking farm equipment, wood pallets and some barrels. The metal exterior of the building had holes in it where the wind blew through and light got in.

If she could get her hands free, she could reach her phone in her coat pocket to tell Graham where she was. The men hadn't thought to take it from her. She twisted her wrists in and out, trying to create more give in the bungee cord. The icky-tasting gag pressed against her tongue.

She was able to move one hand an inch or so though it remained restrained.

As she struggled, her breath came out in rapid shallow bursts. Then another sound became apparent. She stopped struggling and sat up straight. Where was the noise coming from? She recognized it as the rhythmic tick of a clock.

Her hands stilled. She looked to one side and then the other. It took her a second to process what she was seeing. When she did, blood froze in her veins. Off to one side was a clock attached to a bomb set to go off in less than ten minutes.

Graham looked at the GPS map on his phone while Officer Zetler drove the patrol car. There were three possible directions the men could have gone after taking Marielle. He'd made sure Ian was with Officer O'Brian, who would take him to the hotel where he'd be safe, and then Graham had jumped in the police car with one of the other officers. Though all had headed in the direction they'd seen the culprits' car go, each one of the three police cars had taken off in a different direction once the road forked.

The GPS showed no structures in the area. Through the windshield, he saw fields of snow-covered grass and gravel roads with a few clusters of trees.

"Doesn't look like there's anything out this way," said Officer Zetler.

Graham's heart sank. "You're probably right. No one else had radioed that they've seen anything either. We might as well keep looking."

They passed a concrete pad that must have had a building on it at one time.

The police officer pressed the gas as they climbed a hill. When they came down on the other side of it, he saw two metal buildings not too far apart. Neither looked like they were in use.

The first building had large garage doors. This might be a good hiding place for a car.

"Let's stop and search here," said Graham.

The officer nodded and grabbed his radio. "Be advised. We have stopped at an abandoned warehouse on Old Fork Road. Will execute a search."

The two men got out with their weapons drawn and made their way toward the door. Graham reached for the knob. It creaked as he opened it. The men slipped inside and pressed against opposite walls.

Graham scanned the room. Disappointment washed over him. There was no car inside.

"I guess that's a wash." He moved back toward the door.

A noise emanated from the other side of a piece of farm equipment, a sort of strange groaning.

Both men lifted their guns and moved in from opposite sides.

Graham traversed the concrete floor and swung around the old combine. He holstered his gun as a cavalcade of emotions whirled through him at what he saw. He was overjoyed to find Marielle alive but angry at the two men for having so obviously mistreated her. His relief at seeing Marielle was washed away by how frantic she appeared as she tried to say something despite being gagged. Her eyes were wide with fear as she shook her head back and forth.

He kneeled and reached up to remove the gag.

"Bomb." She tilted her head off to the side.

He followed the direction she indicated and froze in disbelief as reality sank in. They had seconds to get out of here before it went off.

He scooped her up in his arms as he yelled at the other officer. "Bomb. Go now." Slowed by carrying Marielle, he lagged behind Officer Zetler as he opened the door that led outside. The other officer stood holding the door open for them.

Graham had just reached the threshold when a blast of heat and a force like a weight being thrown at his back hit him. The explosion pushed them the remaining distance through the door and out onto the gravel.

He kept his arms around Marielle as they fell to the ground. Debris rained down on their heads. It had not been a powerful bomb, though if they had remained inside, they would not have survived.

The other officer shook Graham's shoulder. His mouth moved, forming the words, *Are you okay?*

He'd temporarily lost his hearing. Graham nodded.

Graham turned to face Marielle, touching his hand to her cheek. "You okay?" His voice sounded strange through his hearing loss. His ears felt like they were plugged, as if he'd been on a long plane flight. He reached to untie her hands.

She nodded. "They were just here ten minutes ago."

His hearing was coming back. Though she must be experiencing it too because she shouted when she spoke.

He undid the bungee cord that secured her hands.

Officer Zetler spoke up. "I'll radio the other patrol cars, so they know where to search." He ran back to the police car.

Once her hands were free, Marielle helped Graham get the rope off her ankles.

"We can still catch them. We're the closest." Her voice was hoarse.

"We need to get you to a hospital. Both of us should be checked out," he said. He didn't have any broken bones. He'd be fine. He'd been through worse. At least his head hadn't been injured this time. It was Marielle he was worried about. Not just her physical well-being concerned him. He wasn't sure what she'd been through with the kidnappers.

"That can wait. I'm just a little shaken is all." She leaned closer to him. "We can get these guys."

"You need to be checked out. That has to be my priority."

She gripped his coat. "The man who killed Ian's mother is going to try to get away, to leave the country."

He looked around. There was only one road that led away from the property. Only one direction the men could have gone unless they doubled back the way they'd come, which he doubted they would do. Too much chance of running into the police.

Officer Zetler had jumped into the patrol car and was rolling toward them. Graham helped Marielle get to her feet. His arms were still around her as he assisted her into the back seat of the police vehicle. She was still weak and shaken from what she'd been through.

He slipped into the passenger seat.

"The other two cars are on route to the intersection where this road meets the main road," said the officer.

"They're probably going to try to go to the nearest airport." Marielle spoke from the back seat. Her voice still sounded weak.

Graham glanced back at her and she offered him a soft smile. "The both of us should probably be checked out by a doctor."

"Got it," said Officer Zetler. They were headed in the same direction that the men must have escaped in. "There's an urgent care on the edge of town."

They drove for several miles down the gravel road. A few houses came into view along with a barn and a field full of cows. He could see the outskirts of town in the distance.

The radio crackled.

Officer Zetler picked up the radio. "Go ahead."

"We were waiting for him at the crossroad where the pavement starts. Thought I had hidden the patrol car well enough, but the suspect must have seen us. He did an unexpected U-turn. I'm in pursuit."

Officer Zetler adjusted the radio in his hand. "You mean the car turned back the way he came?"

"Yes." The voice of the other officer came through the radio.

That meant the car was coming toward them. He scanned the road and the area around them, not seeing the car anywhere.

Marielle sat up and leaned forward, gripping the headrest of the front passenger seat.

Graham kept searching as his heart pounded. He glanced at his GPS map. While there were side roads the men could have taken to access the farms and houses in the area, those roads didn't lead anywhere.

Officer Zetler increased his speed. He too was scanning the entire countryside.

"There, over by that red house." Marielle pointed through the windshield.

The car was traveling at a high rate of speed. It looked like the dark-colored SUV that had rammed them.

"I see it." Officer Zetler zoomed ahead and then took a tight turn to get on the side road.

Graham noticed the name of the road as the sign whizzed by.

Graham got on the radio and let the other policeman know where they were going. "We just turned onto Heebs Road. It looks like they're headed toward the forest."

"10-4. I'll get there as fast as I can."

Once the SUV turned into the trees, Graham lost sight of it.

They traveled up the dirt road that was surrounded by snow-covered trees on both sides. Graham leaned forward, hoping to see the SUV.

The road grew rougher and harder to navigate as they came

to a hill. Down below was the SUV, pulled off to one side. He could not tell if the men were inside.

They radioed the other car to let the officer know what they'd found.

A voice came through the radio. "I just turned on the mountain road. Should be there soon."

Officer Zetler rolled the car forward until he was a few yards behind the dark SUV.

Graham unclicked his seat belt. "Marielle, you stay in the car."

The two men got out and approached the car with their weapons drawn.

Chapter Eighteen

Marielle rose from the back seat and reached into the front driver's side so she could lock the doors.

After sitting back down, she watched as Graham and Officer Zetler peered inside the car and then opened the two front doors and the back hatch, shaking their heads.

Another patrol car joined them.

Officer Zetler leaned into the driver's side of the SUV and then spoke over his shoulder radio. She heard him through the radio in the car. "Looks like they ran out of gas."

A voice from the other patrol car answered, "They couldn't have gotten far. I'll drive up ahead and search on foot."

Then Officer Zetler radioed the third patrol car to come aid in the search and signed off.

The second patrol car circled around the vehicle she was in and then parked ahead of the SUV. With their weapons drawn, Graham and Officer Zetler had already headed into the forest close to where the SUV had been abandoned.

While she watched the dark forest, Marielle waited and listened. The radio crackled again when one of the officers called for another patrol car and a helicopter to help with the search.

The silence seemed to hold an unnamed tension. She studied the trees on one side of the car and then cast her attention to the view out the back window.

Glass shattered around her. Her hands jerked up to protect her face.

The driver's side window had been shot out.

Georgio was at the door, reaching his hand in to unlock the car. Eric got into the passenger seat.

Marielle's heart pounded as she moved to open the back door. The cold barrel of a gun pressed against her temple.

"Oh no you don't, you're collateral." Eric grinned. "Sit down, sweetie."

Georgio had already started the car and was rolling forward. Graham emerged from the forest and raised his gun as the blond man sped up. He fired a shot, but the stolen police car just went faster. It must not have hit anything.

She could see the other patrol car pulled off the road but no sign of the other officer, who was probably deep in the forest.

Eric still held his gun pointed in her direction, though he had half turned around in his seat. She glanced over her shoulder to see Officer Zetler emerging from the trees.

A conversation came through the radio. The voice was Officer Zetler's. "Suspects have taken patrol car. Headed in your direction."

"Got it, I'll head back to the road," came the response from the officer still hidden in the forest.

"That's sweet," Georgio spoke as he tapped the radio. "We get to know exactly what their plans are."

Eric didn't seem as relaxed as the blond man. He glanced ahead and then peered through the back window. "Maybe get turned around, huh? Those two cops behind us can't catch us on foot. We don't know where this road ends up. It might be a dead end."

Fear skittered across her nerves as Marielle studied the forest. No one else emerged through the trees. Where were the other police officers?

Georgio stopped the car and backed up, trying to get turned around on the narrow road. It took three times of backing up and pulling forward before the car was pointed back the way the men had come.

The car had just started to gain speed when three shots were fired from outside the vehicle.

Before ducking down, Marielle caught a glimpse of Graham moving through the trees. How fast must he have been running to get into place to make the shots?

The car jerked and lurched before stopping. Georgio pressed the gas but the car moved only a few feet.

"Shot the tires out." Eric pushed open the door and took off running toward the trees.

Marielle reached for the door handle on the side where she'd seen Graham.

Georgio exited from the driver's seat, flung open her door and grabbed her by her hair. The pain forced her to crawl out toward him and stand up. The blond man held a gun to her temple while still pulling her hair with his other hand.

Graham's voice came through the trees, though she couldn't see where he was hidden. "Let her go."

Georgio jerked the back of her head. He stood behind her, using her body as a shield. He remained close to the dead patrol car to shield his back. "Let me go and she's all yours."

The wind blew through the treetops, but Graham remained silent and hidden. What was he planning? Where was Officer Zetler?

Off to the side, she heard gunshots. Eric stood at the edge of the forest holding a gun. The other patrol car had stopped. The windshield was shattered. She could not see the officer behind the wheel. Had he been killed by the gunfire?

Eric advanced on the car with his gun held up.

Georgio pulled her toward the working patrol car but stopped so the defunct patrol car still provided his back with cover. She knew if she tried to get away, he would shoot her.

She watched in horror as the short man opened the driver's side door and pulled the police officer out. The officer clutched his chest where a patch of red was spreading. He fell on the ground. Eric kicked him and took his gun when the officer reached for it. He got behind the wheel and drove toward Georgio.

Her stomach roiled, and it felt like she might throw up. She had to do something. Graham must be watching and waiting for a chance to get at Georgio without killing her. This was the man who had killed Kristen and Charlie and tried to kill David. He was not going to get away, not if she could help it.

The working patrol car edged close to where Georgio stood.

She elbowed the blond man in the stomach. His back slammed against the car. He still held her hair, but the hard butt of the gun no longer pressed against her head.

Eric was feet away from them in the stolen patrol car. She could hear the engine humming.

She twisted to get away, putting a few inches between herself and Georgio even though he still held her by the hair. A gunshot was fired, not close to her.

She couldn't see what had happened.

Georgio let go of her and ran toward the working patrol car.

Graham burst from behind a tree. He held her in his arms for only a second. "Get down."

She slipped behind him, dropped to her stomach and crawled toward the cover of a nearby tree. The trunk shielded her as she kneeled.

Three gunshots spaced a few seconds apart filled the air. She squeezed her eyes shut and prayed that Graham and Officer Zetler had not been hit.

Chapter Nineteen

While Graham had been trying to free Marielle, Officer Zetler had been advancing on the working patrol car, looking for his chance to get at Eric who sat behind the wheel. He'd fired a shot but had been too far away to hit with any accuracy.

Georgio, who was feet away from getting into the passenger side of the patrol car with Eric at the wheel, lifted his gun and fired at Graham, who ducked behind the vehicle with the blown tires. His heart pounded. A door slammed and the patrol car rolled forward.

He had to stop these men before they got away.

Officer Zetler chased the car as it gained speed.

Graham stepped free from the shelter of the disabled car as the other car rolled by. He could see Eric in the driver's seat. He lifted his gun and aimed at the tires.

He ran out in pursuit of the car as it continued to roll forward. Georgio leaned out the window of the front passenger side shooting at Officer Zetler, forcing him to hang back and take cover.

Graham kept running, staying closer to the driver's side. Through the windows, he saw that Officer Zetler was still advancing with his weapon aimed in one hand while he held a bloody arm close to his body. A bullet had hit him.

Graham shot again at the tires. The car slowed but kept rolling. He caught up to the car, reaching for the driver's side door handle. He flung the door open with one hand and lifted his gun in the other. Eric leaned out of the car and grabbed Graham's wrist, bending it back so the gun was pointed upward. The short man reached with the other hand and knocked the gun free of Graham's grip.

Graham lunged to grab Eric with both hands. The car had stopped altogether. Graham pulled the driver from behind the wheel.

The man punched him across the jaw. Pain vibrated through his head. Wherever his gun had fallen, Eric had not had time to grab it. A shot was fired from within the cab of the vehicle. Georgio was trying to shoot Graham. It sounded like the bullet had ricocheted inside the car.

He wrestled the short man out of his seat as Eric hit him several times several times in the stomach and head. When he reached to get Eric in a chokehold, he was struck hard across the jaw, leaving him momentarily stunned.

Eric took off running. Graham sprinted after him and tackled him. He continued to fight even as he lay on his stomach.

Graham shouted, "DEA. You're under arrest."

The man finally stopped fighting and grew still. Holding the man in place, Graham lifted his head in time to see Marielle burst out from her hiding place and run to the other side of the car.

He called out her name.

What was she doing putting herself in danger like that?

When Marielle saw that Officer Zetler was injured, she knew she had to do something. Georgio was not getting away. She wanted him in jail. She wanted justice for all the pain he'd caused.

Officer Zetler was bent over but still holding his gun. Georgio had been preoccupied with trying to stop Graham but now had slipped into the driver's seat. She heard gears shift as she took Officer Zetler's gun and ran up to the passenger side window.

Georgio pressed the gas but on two flat tires he couldn't get much traction on the dirt road. She came to the passenger side window and held the gun up.

"Stop right there." She lifted the gun with trembling hands.

Georgio sneered at her and reached for the gun he'd set on the console.

Adrenaline surged through her. "Don't even try it." She fired a shot directly into the seat cushion.

Georgio winced at the noise and held up his hands. "You got me."

She relaxed a little, but the gun still shook.

Georgio pushed open the driver's side door and tumbled out. He dropped to his knees. She couldn't see him anymore from the passenger side.

She heard a voice on the other side of the car. "I don't think so. Not today." It was Graham.

When she circled around to the other side of the car, she saw Officer Zetler leaning over Eric, handcuffing him. Graham held a muddy gun on Georgio.

She heard the sound of a helicopter. The other injured police officer still lay on the ground up the road.

"We need to tell that chopper to land so it can transport these two injured officers," she said.

Still clutching his arm, Officer Zetler rose to his feet and reached into the patrol car to use the radio.

Graham kept his gun on Georgio.

When she peered down the road, she saw that the third patrol car was on its way. Within minutes, the chopper found a place to land and the two injured police officers were secured inside. The patrol officer in the third car handcuffed Georgio, placing him and Eric in the back of his car.

Marielle and Graham stood beside the patrol car she'd been held captive in. The officer approached them. "I radioed for three tow trucks. You can catch a ride with one of the drivers."

Graham raised his hand in acknowledgment as she murmured a thank-you.

The patrol car with the perpetrators in the back drove past them, turning around when the road got wide enough to do so without slipping off.

The officer at the wheel waved to them as the car went by headed down the mountain road.

Georgio sneered at her from the back seat, sending shivers down her spine.

Unrepentant. How could a person get to that level of evil?

Snow began to fall as she let out a heavy breath. "I guess it's over. It doesn't quite feel real to me."

Graham stood close enough to her that their shoulders touched. "I understand the feeling." He reached for her hand and held it for a long moment. "You were brave back there. I know that was scary holding the gun on a criminal and firing it."

"I just didn't want him to get away after all the evil he was responsible for." A heaviness fell around her. She wouldn't be seeing Graham much longer now that Kristen's killer had been caught. "Do you think Ian is safe now?"

"Yes, this was personal to Georgio. He didn't want Ian to identify him. I doubt other cartel members would want to expend resources on coming after the boy," said Graham. "As a distributor, Georgio is not high ranking and easy to replace."

"Thank you for helping Ian have a shot at a decent life." Marielle took in a deep breath. "Guess you'll be going wherever your job takes you next?"

"There's a few things I need to do to wrap this case up first."

He had not yet let go of her hand. She relished the warmth

and strength of his touch, feeling like there was something more she wanted to say but not knowing how to say it. The same feelings from ten years ago bombarded her. Her life would seem emptier without him. Just as it had in the past, it would take time to adjust to the loss.

The first tow truck appeared on the road below.

Graham squeezed her fingers before letting go.

They waited while the driver got the first car hooked up and then climbed into the cab with him. Marielle sat in the middle between the two men.

"Where am I dropping you folks off at?"

"I need to go to the Big Sky Hotel. There's a little boy I want to give a hug to." Ian's life would no longer be under threat, though his future was unsure. They still didn't know how David was doing or what he would be charged with. Whatever the outcome, she vowed to remain in the boy's life in whatever capacity she could. "He and I will be able to go back to my home...for now."

"I'll go with you to the hotel," said Graham. "I'd like to see the little guy one more time."

One more time. His words echoed through her head and filled her with sadness.

As the snow hit the windshield and the two men engaged in small talk, she realized that she'd fallen in love with Graham all over again. But she wasn't about to say anything. The pain of him leaving would be even worse this time. They'd both been immature when they were first engaged. She'd fallen even deeper in love with the courageous and compassionate man Graham had become.

When the tow truck driver pulled into the parking lot of the hotel and let Graham and Marielle out, Graham felt a tightening in his chest he didn't understand.

They stepped into the lobby where Officer O'Brian waited holding Ian's hand.

Marielle held her arms out and bent down. "There's my guy." Ian ran to her.

"Suspects in custody. A good day's work, huh?" said O'Brian to Graham.

"Yes, it's good, but two officers were injured in the process." Graham's attention was on Marielle as she held Ian and pressed her head close to his.

Ian pointed down a hallway. "They have ice cream here."

There was something stunning about hearing Ian speak a complete sentence. Marielle raised her eyebrows, and her face glowed when she looked in Graham's direction. Together, they had given Ian back his voice.

"Why don't you show me?" Marielle put Ian down and took his hand. She headed up the hallway with a backward glance at Graham.

The look on her face warmed his heart.

The tightness in his chest increased when he could no longer see them. What was that about?

O'Brian grabbed his arm. "David didn't make it. He died about an hour ago."

Feeling numb, he let the news sink in. "Ian's an orphan. Marielle doesn't know?"

"I sent her a text when it happened. I didn't want to say anything in front of Ian."

To his knowledge, she had not checked her phone in the last hour. "I think I'll go join them. Thank you for watching over Ian."

Officer O'Brian stood with her hands on her hips. "When you're ready, I can give you all a ride to wherever you need to go?"

"Sounds good."

He hurried down the hallway and into the restaurant. Marielle and Ian were sitting opposite each other in a corner booth. Only a few other people were eating at this hour.

A smile spread across Ian's face, and he put his arms up in the air. "Graham's here."

He still couldn't get used to the sound of that sweet voice. Ian scooted over and patted the seat by him.

He sat down.

"We've already ordered." He saw a sort of darkness in her eyes despite the lilt in her voice. Her phone sat on the table. She knew David had not made it.

"I'll give you bites of mine." Ian spoke as he tugged on Graham's sleeve.

"That's awfully nice of you to share, little buddy." His gaze rested on Marielle. "You checked your texts?"

She nodded. He wanted to ask her more. Would she be adopting Ian and raising him as a single mother? But that wasn't a conversation to have in front of the boy.

The bowls of ice cream were placed on the table. Marielle asked for an extra spoon for Graham. Ian laughed while they ate the ice cream together. Marielle scooted her bowl across the table too so he could taste her blueberry ice cream.

The waiter brought the check for them when they'd finished. He stood for a moment with his hands at his side. "Did you enjoy your ice cream?"

All three of them nodded.

"You three have a great day. You have a very nice little family here."

Marielle locked Graham in her gaze for an intense moment. Is that what they looked like to the world, a family?

They found Officer O'Brian and got into her car. Graham sat in the front seat with Marielle and Ian in the back.

"Where to?"

Where was he going? He had a report to write and he needed to check in with his handler, but where was he going? Where did he belong?

"Ian and I get to go home. Eighteen Eleven Maverick Lane."

"Okay. And then, Graham, do you want to go back to the police station with me?"

"I guess so." His things were still back at Bridger Bible Camp. He'd have to go up there eventually.

O'Brian drove out of town and up a country road to the two-story house with trees on one side of it.

"This is it. My place." Marielle unbuckled her seat belt.

Ian's soft voice floated up to his ear from the back seat. "Is Graham coming with us?"

Graham turned to look at the blond boy as he stuck his fingers in his mouth. The request made the tightness in his chest return.

"Marielle, do you want me to help you and Ian get settled in?"

"Sure." Her voice was faint, and she had said the word almost as if it was a question.

"I can send a car around to get you in a bit," said O'Brian.

"Sounds good," said Graham.

The three of them walked toward the door with Ian in the middle. Ian took Graham's hand. He was already holding Marielle's.

Once inside, Marielle spoke to Ian. "Why don't you go to your room and find a toy that Graham might want to see?"

"Or we can do a puzzle." He scrambled up the stairs and disappeared.

Graham spoke up. "With David gone, are you going to adopt Ian?"

"I'm going to do everything I can to try to make that happen." She stepped toward him, eyes fixed on him. "What's going on? Why didn't you just go to the police station?"

His mouth had gone dry. "I'm having a hard time saying goodbye...to Ian."

"I think he will be confused when you go. I'm glad you're being sensitive to that. But you shouldn't drag it out too long."

"I care about that kid."

"That makes it hard, doesn't it...to leave again." She looked off to the side and ran her fingers through her hair. "Maybe you can come back for visits."

"I'm not sure I want to leave. I'm just so confused." He massaged his chest where the muscles were taut.

"What are you talking about?"

"When I left last time, I thought I was doing you a favor. I was the only Christian in my family, and you had this long heritage of faith. I had a terrible father and no male role models. You had strong, loving parents. You deserved someone who was more solid."

She stepped toward him and grabbed his arms above the elbow. "Why should any of that matter? I never looked at you and thought that. What I was drawn to was *your* faith. There are no grandchildren in God's kingdom."

"I never thought of it that way." He looked into her eyes. "When we started talking about having children, I was afraid that I would be just like my father. You deserved better."

"I wanted to marry you, Graham." Her eyes searched his as she shook her head. "Something's changed though. You said you were confused."

"It's not just that I care about Ian. I love him. I didn't think I could ever feel that for a kid. I don't just want to visit. I want to be a part of his life and I want to be with you." He took a step back and put his hand over his heart. He knew then what the tightness in his chest was about. "I love Ian and I love you and I want us to be a family together."

Once he'd spoken the words, the tension eased from his chest and he knew that what he said was true.

"But your job. The travel and excitement, the sense of purpose."

"I used to love what I did, but losing Cesar made me think about doing something less stressful and not as heartbreaking. I want to be here in Montana with you and Ian. Marielle, will you marry me?"

Light came into her eyes as her face filled with joy. "Oh, Graham, yes."

He gathered her into his arms. "I will never leave you again. I promise." He bent his head and kissed her.

He felt pressure against his leg and looked down to find Ian holding a stuffed animal and hugging his thigh.

Marielle laughed.

Graham reached down and took Ian into his arms. Marielle wrapped her arm around his back and pressed close to him.

Joy burst through him. He kissed Marielle again, realizing he was with the two people he wanted to spend the rest of his life with.

Epilogue

As Graham took her hand and turned toward the minister, Marielle glanced around at the crowd gathered to watch them be married. All the people she loved were here with her today.

Her mom and dad and sisters smiled. Her whole family had extended such love and acceptance to both Ian and Graham. Graham's new co-workers, the other officers of the Clarksville police force, had shown up in uniform. His job with the city police would be a lot less stressful and keep him close to home.

She glanced out the window of the sanctuary of Bridger Bible Camp at the expanse of blue sky. What a perfect summer day.

"Please turn to face each other," said the minister.

Graham took both her hands in his as they said their vows. With each promise they repeated to each other she saw the light of love shining in his eyes.

She was so lost in Graham's eyes she barely heard the minister speak. "You may present each other with your ring."

Graham turned and crouched next to Ian, who held the pillow with the rings on it. The boy offered Marielle a mischievous smile. They had a long road ahead with Ian, but he was smiling...and talking much more these days.

Graham took the rings, leaning to whisper in Ian's ear. "Thanks, little buddy."

Ian swayed back and forth, his face glowing.

After they placed the rings on each other's fingers, the minister announced, "Ladies and gentlemen, may I present to you Mr. and Mrs. Flynn."

Music played as people applauded, and they headed down the aisle. The doors burst open. They stepped outside surrounded by the mountains she loved in the place that meant so much to both her and Graham.

She couldn't wait to start her life together with Graham as her husband and Ian as their son.

It truly was a beautiful day.

* * * * *

Lethal Wilderness Trap

Susan Furlong

MILLS & BOON

Susan Furlong grew up in North Dakota, where she spent long winters at her local library scouring the shelves for mysteries to read. Now she lives in Illinois with her husband and children and writes mysteries of all types. She has over a dozen published novels and her work has earned a spot in the *New York Times* list of top crime fiction books of the year. When not writing, she volunteers at her church and spends time hiking and fishing.

Books by Susan Furlong

Lethal Wilderness Trap

Visit the Author Profile page at millsandboon.com.au.

The Lord is nigh unto them that are of a broken heart; and saveth such as be of a contrite spirit.
—*Psalm* 34:18

For my son, Patrick, who continues to inspire me.

Chapter One

Ava Burke sat cross-legged on the crest of the hill, propped against the trunk of a sugar maple amid the tombstones of generations of Burkes and the freshly placed sod of her own husband's grave. Behind her loomed Burke House, three stories of red brick and white columns with rows of mullioned windows gaping over the churning waters of Lake Superior and what she knew to be the dark island beyond.

Long fingerlike clouds drifted overhead, carried on a cold breeze. Ava shivered and pulled the hood of her sweatshirt tight, tucking in a few long brown curls beneath the fabric as her gaze settled on the cross etched in Kevin's gravestone.

Kevin had passed in late January, when the ground in the Upper Peninsula of Michigan had been frozen and piled with snow and burial on the family land impossible. The past few months, while she'd waited to lay her husband to rest, had been dark and still. The only light in that gloom had been Rose, their six-year-old daughter. But since Kevin's death, Rose had slipped into sullenness, turning inward, rarely speaking and never smiling.

"How will I raise her without Kevin?" But even as she whispered the words, she knew that God had already given her part of that answer. Not long after Kevin's death, her father-in-law, Mac, had reached out and invited her and Rosie to live with him here in Sculpin Bay. She was grateful for Mac's generosity. He had a special way with Rose, and even though the lakeside village of Sculpin Bay seemed a million miles from their old home in Detroit, Ava had welcomed the change.

She stood and headed back to the house, her mind wandering to supper and what she might fix. As she neared the barn, she opted for a shortcut and ducked under the pasture fence. A promise Mac had made to Rose earlier popped into her mind: a pony. What was he thinking? She was too young.

Ava waded through the pasture's knee-high weeds toward the barn. It was a small, tired stable with only two stalls, weathered clapboard siding and a leftward list, but the stone foundation looked solid. Could it be fixed up for a pony? She pictured Rose sitting in the swayed back of a sturdy pony, her hands entangled in its shaggy main, her face all smiles. Maybe Mac was right. Maybe a pony was just what Rose needed—a friend, something to bring her out of her shell. Ava would do anything to see her little girl's smile again.

Another breeze kicked up, and Ava's gaze was drawn to the barn's patchy roof where a rusty iron weather vane creaked as it spun on top of the cupola. Out of nowhere, a large black bird appeared, paused on the roof's pitch and slipped through a jagged opening in the patchy shingles. Another bird followed and did the same thing. From inside the barn came the hollow knocking of their beating wings.

A shadow swung over Ava's head: a vulture. It, too, landed on the roof, likely attracted by the commotion of the other birds' raucous calls inside. But it spied her and lifted off to the sky as she moved forward. She sighed. Likely another dead mouse inside the barn—something common here. But if a pony was in their future, she might as well see what they'd need to repair or replace.

Ava headed into the barn, passing through the narrow opening between the doorjamb and the boarded door, careful not to catch her shirt on the splintered wood.

She blinked against the dim light, her eyes adjusting as she spied the two birds hunched on a pile of fallen timbers. They'd caught sight of her, cocked their heads and, in a flurry, careened into each other, feathers flying, before taking flight. Her gaze traced their ascent through a large hole in the roof. Well, roof and timbers could be fixed, though keeping out vermin would always be an issue, she supposed.

Then her gaze fell back to the wood pile, and she caught sight of a snatch of brightly colored fabric under one of the timbers. She stepped closer, suddenly wary.

As she neared, dank air crept up her nostrils, coating her throat and making her stomach gurgle. There, lodged between the boards, a woman's body lay, whitish blond hair splayed out around her head like a halo, arms outstretched, her body twisted and contorted, and her milky eyes fixed in a rheumy stare.

Seconds ticked by as Ava's shocked mind absorbed the scene. Then her skin prickled. Her eyes swept the shadows as fear washed over her, and she turned and bolted to the house, bursting inside the back door. Mac stood in the kitchen stirring something on the stove. Her panic-filled gaze searched the room, landing on the table and her purse.

"There you are," Mac said. "Decided to make spaghetti tonight—it's Jane's favorite. Forgot to tell you she's coming over to... What's wrong?"

"Where's Rose?" Ava gasped, her breath ragged as she tore through her bag, searching for her phone.

Mac nodded toward the other room. "In there, watching a show. Why—what's going on?" He set down the spoon, his brow furrowed.

Ava pulled out her phone and peeked on Rose, relieved at the sight of her daughter's small body hunched in front of the television.

Mac turned off the stove. "What happened? Are you okay?"

Ava shook her head, her shaky fingers pushing 911. A dispatcher answered, and Ava recited the address over the line. "Please send the police. A woman's been hurt... She's...she's dead."

Mac came to her side. "A dead woman?" he hissed. "Are you sure? Where?"

Ava's voice wavered, and her mind flashed back to the scene. "It's horrible... She was..." She couldn't finish. Didn't need to. Mac enveloped her in his arms and pulled her close while she relayed what she knew to the dispatcher. She disconnected, exhaled and leaned into him, her body trembling from the aftershock.

He pulled back and held her at arm's length. "The barn, you said?"

Ava nodded.

"Stay here with Rose while I go take a look."

"No. Don't. Wait for the police."

"I have to make sure she's not just hurt and in need of medical attention."

Ava grabbed his arm. "She's dead, Mac. I'm sure of it." But there was no convincing him. She knew Mac took care of things himself, handled pressure well and would need to check if there was any chance the woman was alive. Much like Kevin, caring and capable and... Mac gently shook off her grip and headed outside.

She watched him go, clasping her arms around her midsection to hold herself together. "Stay calm," she told herself, for Rose's sake.

"Rosie," she called out gently to keep the tremor from her voice, turning to the family room. "What are you watching, bug? Can Mommy—"

Rose was gone.

A small gasp escaped her lips. *Rosie?*

"Rosie? Rosie!"

Ava rushed to the small bathroom off the kitchen; had she slipped past them? But she wasn't there. Back through the kitchen to the dining room, where Rose and Mac had started a puzzle. But no Rose.

"Rosie? Rosie!"

A chill stillness stung the house, a silence filled with pure panic. Ava turned toward the stairs and took the steps two at a time to the second floor, murmuring her child's name— *Rosie, Rosie, Rosie*—telling herself not to frighten her daughter with her own anxiety. At the top of the stairs, she called out for Rose again and threw open the door to her bedroom. A pink bedspread, play kitchen, crayons and books strewed over a floral print rug, but no Rose. And she wasn't in Ava's room or Mac's room or the spare room at the end of the hall.

Ava stopped and spun in all directions. *She was just here. Just here! Where could she have... The attic!* Ava turned her attention to a narrow set of rickety stairs and noticed the attic door was ajar.

"Rosie? Are you in here?" Ava mounted the steps and pushed through stacked boxes and years of discarded household items. The attic was empty.

Fear pounded in her chest. *My baby. Where's my—* Her breath caught and she strode toward the window and pressed her face against the dirty pane.

"Oh no!" Rose was climbing through the fence, heading for the barn. She must have seen Mac going that way and decided to follow. Ava shuddered. The woman's body and...the birds! She'd be scarred forever.

Ava flew down the attic steps, through the house and launched herself outside, calling after Rose. Halfway across the yard, she bent over, relieved at the sight; Mac had heard her calls and come out of the barn and found Rose.

Sirens wailed as Ava made her way, composed as she could, to where Mac was crouched down, speaking gently to Rose. They both looked up as Ava approached.

"Look who followed me," Mac said, his voice calm, although Ava saw the tightness in his features.

The sirens sounded close. "I see that. Rosie, you know better than to go outside without telling me."

Rose's eyes grew wide.

"Easy now," Mac said. "No need to get upset with her. Bet she was coming out to look for that pony we've been talking about. Was that it, Rosie girl?"

Rose shook her head.

Mac looked surprised. "No? Well, she's my little shadow, this one is."

They turned as the first of the police vehicles made it up the drive. Next to her, Rose stiffened. This wasn't good—not at all. The last time Rose had seen police officers was when one came to the door to give them the bad news about Kevin.

"Come with me," Ava said, tugging at her arm. "We can color for a while or play cards, or... I know, we could cook something special for Grandpa. Cookies, maybe? Do you want to help me make sugar cookies?"

The first of the officers was out of his car and coming their way, Rosie's wide eyes on him, not hearing anything her mother had said.

Ava plucked at the girl's arm. "Rose, please. Come inside with Mommy."

Mac gave her a gentle nudge. "Go on now, pumpkin. Do as your mother says." But Rose remained still, her eyes fixated on the approaching officer.

"Rose." Mac's voice was stern. "Go with your mother now."

"But what about the lady?"

Mac and Ava exchanged a look. Rose rarely spoke anymore, and her voice was so faint, Ava wasn't sure she'd heard her correctly. She stooped down and looked her daughter in the eye. "What was that, bug?"

Rose pointed a finger toward the barn. "The lady that got shot?"

Chapter Two

The petite brunette who stepped out from behind the office counter at the Copper Jack Motel barely glanced at Agent Nolan Shea as she handed him the motel room key. "Room 129. Midway on the left." But she smiled his partner's way, tipping her head and batting her lashes. She even went as far as to stroke her hand down his back.

"Don't let it go to your head, buddy," Nolan told him as they exited the motel office and maneuvered through the parking lot to their room. "She's cute, but she's not for you."

Creed ignored him and kept his head high, his intense Belgian Malinois gaze focused on their surroundings. It had recently rained, and even with the security light gleaming off the wet asphalt, the lot was exceptionally dark. Nolan's own gaze traced the shadows, checking for anything out of the ordinary.

He still didn't know why he and his canine partner had been called to this location. It was Tuesday, almost eleven o'clock at night. Less than ten hours ago, Director Reynold had pulled them from an ongoing evidence collection in preparation for an important trial. A man was accused of murdering his girlfriend's lover and burying him in California's Joshua Tree National Park. Reynold's orders were to report to Sculpin Bay, Michigan, instructions pending.

Nolan keyed into the room, basic and dated with painted wood paneling, a floral bedspread and older carpeting, but clean. Very clean. "And don't think that I didn't see the way she looked at you, making those moony eyes. Bet you liked that, huh?"

Creed ignored the accusation and made a low and guttural noise, forceful but not quite aggressive, as he circled the room, checking under the bed, the bathroom, the closet. Creed was always on task and thorough. And while Nolan's partner got all the attention, Nolan knew he deserved it. As federal agents for the Investigative Service Branch (ISB) of the National Park Service, he and Creed investigated any crime committed on federal land, from murder to drug trafficking. And his dog had never disappointed. Creed was the best canine police officer in the ISB.

Nolan moved to a small desk, opened his laptop and signed into a secure connection. Convinced that their environment was safe, Creed jumped onto the bed and sprawled out, head down but eyes open and ears upright, as if still on alert.

A few minutes later a teleconference prompt popped up, and Reynold's face appeared on the screen. "Agent Shea. You've arrived at your destination."

"Yes, Creed and I are here."

"Good. I anticipate that you'll only be in Sculpin Bay for a few days. I received a call from the local sheriff's office regarding a recent homicide. It may be connected to one of our cold cases. The Richter case. Do you remember it?"

Nolan searched his brain. "Richter? I don't think so."

"Hannah Richter. A decade-old Jane Doe that was finally identified last year."

Nolan remembered the case now. It was tragic—a young woman, seventeen, her life over before it even got started, a Jane Doe when her body had been discovered. Her mother left wondering about her missing daughter for almost ten years. "I do remember. She was ID'd through a recent DNA connection just last year. Beckett worked that case, didn't she?"

"That's right."

"But Richter was found off the coast on Isle Royale—dead from exposure, right? What's the connection to the current homicide victim and Sculpin Bay?"

"Both female runaways, same age and from the same Detroit high school."

Nolan leaned closer to the screen. "The same high school? Detroit's what? Ten, eleven hours from here?" *And both ended up dead in this same area?*

"Yeah, about six hundred miles. And apparently neither one of them had ever traveled outside of Detroit before." Reynold cleared his throat. "I'll forward the file on the Richter case, and you can follow up with Beckett."

"Will do. What do we have on the recent victim?"

"Name's Lindsey Webber. Her body was found less than twenty-four hours ago in a barn on private property outside Sculpin Bay. Possible bleed out from a gunshot wound. Preliminaries are pending from the medical examiner."

A photo of Lindsey appeared on the screen. It looked like a school picture. Nolan studied her face. Long blond hair and a pretty smile, but there was an intelligent look in her gaze. A bit of defiance, too, as if she'd seen too much, known too much and had been ready to take on the world. This girl would have fought to survive.

Reynold continued, "Her background is almost identical to Richter's. She was seventeen and going into her senior year. Raised by a single mother, known by friends as someone who liked to party. She'd been in trouble at school and with the law. She had a record. The ID was made through a print match on the AFIS database."

Nolan nodded. The Automated Fingerprint Identification System, or AFIS, had, once again, served law enforcement well. But as Nolan stared at the screen, waiting, something wasn't adding up. They had more pressing cases, and while the connections were there, this could easily be handled by local authorities. Yet Reynold had tasked him and Creed to fly in for a reason. "There's more, I take it."

"Afraid so." Reynold blew out a long sigh. "Beckett ran a detailed search yesterday through the missing persons database. Over the past ten years there have been more girls missing, all presumed runaways, but—"

"You mean from the same high school?"

"No. But the same neighborhood."

"That's too much of a coincidence. Who's working the Detroit angle?"

"Agent West. He's flying in tomorrow."

Nolan sat back. Two dead girls with a solid connection, maybe others, too, but all of them gone missing over the last decade. "Do you think there are others who were overlooked, lost in the system? Victims that we missed?"

"I have faith that you will figure that out."

Although he appreciated Reynold's reassurance, Nolan had given up on faith and gut feelings. He'd always hated presumptions, preferred hard facts. Reynold's words echoed in his mind—*more girls missing, all presumed runaways*—and spun with the obvious implications: Serial abduction. Maybe trafficking? He shook off his conjectures. Until he had a definite explanation in hand, he knew it could be something else altogether. But what?

Nolan arrived at the crime scene early the next morning, entered the barn and crouched near the timbers. Blood had seeped between the wood and soaked into the dirt below. Even though the body had been removed, he got a whiff of leftover stench and swallowed the bile rising in the back of his throat. He rocked back on his heels and cranked his neck upward to where Sheriff Penn stood, arms crossed over his barrel chest, double chins stacked under a round jaw as he stared down at Nolan with probing eyes.

"There's a lot of dried blood," Nolan said.

"Bullet hit an artery. It wouldn't have taken long for her to bleed out."

Nolan nodded and studied the dried-blood pool, noting the darker blood in the center, which would have been the contact point, to the lighter outer rim of the stain. Despite the absorbability of the dirt the blood collected on, it had still spread quite a bit, meaning that it had evacuated her body quickly. "But she wasn't shot here in the barn?"

"There's no indication that she was shot in here," Penn said. "No blood spatter or casings—nothing."

"Blood trail?"

"Can't find one. Rain must've washed it away."

"But in here? I don't see anything."

Nolan scrutinized the barn floor and saw no blood trail. Sheriff Penn offered, "Victim had a scarf wrapped around her arm when we found her. Must have tried to stem the bleeding, but with it being an artery..."

The smell made Nolan's eyes water. He began breathing through his mouth. "Do we know what caliber was used?"

"It was a .223, hollow point. Tore up the shoulder pretty good."

"Remington?"

"I'll get you the report."

"I'll need to see the body, too."

"I'll arrange it."

Nolan rubbed a gloved hand over one of the timbers. He imagined her fear as she'd wedged herself behind the pile of wood, already shot, in pain and growing weaker as her assailant had closed in on her. And she'd been seventeen, only a few years older than his own niece. Just a kid. How had a young woman ended up shot and dying alone in a barn out in the middle of nowhere?

He slowly stood so that he was face-to-face with Penn. "It's not tourist season yet. What do you think brought her here?"

Penn shrugged. "We asked ourselves the same thing. She doesn't have any family or friends in the area—at least according to her mother. It's not the best time of year to find employment in these parts. And we haven't found anyone yet 'round here who has ever seen her before. It's like she fell out of the sky and showed up here for no reason."

Nolan shook his head. "There's always a reason."

They stared at the bloodstain in silence for a while. Finally Penn said, "Appreciate that you're with us. I called when the connection to the Richter case came up in the system. Didn't expect an agent to come out this way to investigate."

"It's good that you notified us."

Penn cocked his head, assessing the agent's presence. "You must think there's more to it than just two girls from the same high school."

"We do. And I'll get you up to speed soon. Right now, I'm heading out with my partner to see if we can pick up on anything in the woods. I'll also need to interview the woman who lives here, the one who discovered the body."

"Ava Burke. Strange thing about that woman."

Nolan crossed to where Creed was tethered to a post. "Oh yeah? What's that?"

"She just moved here, and already she's connected to a homicide."

"You suspect her of something?"

"No. Just don't like those type of coincidences."

Nolan wondered if there was something to the sheriff's gut feeling or if it was just a small-town attitude toward strangers. He respected the instincts in others but relied on facts in his own efforts. He also knew that small towns bred their own troubles all too often. He decided to let the sheriff's comment go for now and form his own opinion.

Chapter Three

It was only a little after ten in the morning, but Ava was already exhausted. Her usual Wednesday-morning trip to the grocery store had turned into a nightmare as people had stopped to ask her about the body in the barn. News traveled fast in small towns—Ava knew that—but their questions had brought the trauma of finding the body back to the forefront of her mind and Rose's. Unfortunately, these people hadn't hesitated to express their morbid curiosities in front of her daughter. She'd cut her shopping short just to evade yet another wide-eyed local hungry for information.

She pulled into her drive, parked and turned to the back seat. "All right, bug. Let's get these groceries in and put away, then we can watch a movie together, okay?" But Rose's attention was already on the police vehicles parked near the barn.

Ava stared at her child's profile, drinking in every detail of her pudgy cheeks, upturned nose and solemn gaze. She'd shut down again, withdrawing further into herself. A shiver threatened Ava as she recalled her daughter's words. What had she meant when she'd asked about the woman who had been shot? Had she witnessed the shooting? Had she seen the body in the barn? Gentle prodding had resulted in no answers.

Ava got out and opened Rosie's door. "So, what's it going to be? A Barbie princess movie, or something else?"

Rose pointed toward the barn, and Ava turned to see a man with a dog approaching.

She hurried and unbuckled Rose. "Go on inside—I'll be right in." She lifted her out and nudged her toward the house. Opening the back of the Acura, she grabbed an armful of grocery bags.

"Good morning. Can I help you with your bags?" The man moved confidently, with dark buzzed hair and an authoritative demeanor, his dog in sync with his every step.

Ava swallowed hard. "No, thanks. We can manage." She glanced up toward the house, expecting to see Rose at the door, only to find her still by the car, now reaching out to pet the dog.

Ava shoved the bags back into the car and snatched Rose's arm. "No! We don't pet dogs we don't know."

"It's okay," the man said, squatting down to Rose's level. He gazed up at Ava with a sincere expression. "He's well trained and always good with kids. Can she pet him?"

Rose shot her a pleading look. The dog did, too, and Ava nodded, watching closely as Rose reached out shyly at first, then with more confidence. The man told them, "This is Creed, and he loves making new friends." At that, Rose petted Creed enthusiastically, even smiling when he gave her a doggy kiss.

Ava's heart melted to see her daughter's smile—the first today. "She loves him."

"Most people do. Except the bad guys." He stood, keeping a tight grip on the dog's leash and pointing to one of the grocery bags. "Ice cream's melting."

Ava frowned. "Say goodbye to the doggy, Rose, and help me with these bags. Nice to meet you, Officer…?" She'd already forgotten his name. Or had he introduced himself? She couldn't recall and only wanted to get Rose away.

"Agent, and Nolan is fine. I'm with the National Park Service."

"You're a park ranger?"

"No, I'm with their investigative branch. I'm more law enforcement than park ranger, like the FBI for federal parks and
lands." He grabbed a couple of the bags with his free hand.
"Lead the way."

"No, really—we can handle it." But the agent was already
headed for the house with the dog and an armful of groceries,
Rose trailing beside the dog.

"This is a beautiful home," he said, setting the bags on the
kitchen counter. "And your view is amazing." He'd moved to
the door that separated the kitchen and living room and stared
out the back bay windows that overlooked Lake Superior just
beyond a steep embankment of rocks.

"Yeah, well…thanks for helping. It was good to meet you."

Rose was back to petting the dog, her tiny fingers digging
into his fur. Irritation washed over Ava now. As much as she
ached to have Rose happy, Ava feared that her little girl would
shut down permanently if the subject of the murdered woman
came up one more time. Even Jane Adair, a friend of Mac's
and a counselor specializing in trauma, hadn't broken through
Rose's malaise. First, Kevin's death, and now this? Her baby
didn't need any more.

"Have you always lived here?" the agent asked.

Why won't this guy leave and take his dog with him? "No.
We moved here from Detroit."

He tensed and squinted her way. His gaze felt suddenly
intimidating, and Ava went on high alert. "Rosie, let the dog
go. He has to get back to work." Then to the agent, "Thanks
again."

Rose shook her head and clung to Creed, while the dog
stood still, watching his partner for direction.

"It's okay, ma'am. I'd like to talk to you anyway. I have a
few questions I need to ask, if that's okay."

No, not really. Ava's heartbeat kicked up a notch. She'd
made Mac promise that he wouldn't tell anyone what Rose
had said about the woman in the barn—for Rose's sake. And

Mac understood. But what if she said something to this agent? "Rose, please go upstairs while I talk to Agent Nolan."

Rose ignored her, quietly petting the dog and staying put. Ava stared her down. "Rose! Do as I say."

She wheeled and ran upstairs, the sound of her feet pounding on each step, followed by the slamming of her bedroom door.

Heat flushed over Ava's cheeks. "I'm sorry. She isn't usually so misbehaved." *And I'm not usually such a crabby mother.*

The dog returned to the man's side. "It's not her fault. It's my partner," he said. "He's known to be a bad influence on women."

The dog suddenly looked up to her with soulful brown eyes, as if proving the point, and Ava laughed despite herself. She took a breath and explained, "The sheriff already asked me about finding the body. I discovered it by mistake, because of the birds…" She shivered at the memory. "After I saw her… I didn't touch anything… I ran to the house and told Mac and called the police."

"Mac Burke, your father-in-law?"

"Right."

"What did Mac do?"

She looked away. "He went out to see if she was really dead."

"He didn't believe you?"

"No, it's not that… He thought maybe if she was still alive, he could help her."

"Did you call the police before he went out to check on the woman or after?"

"Before. I think. Yes, I called them first. They were on their way when…"

"When?"

"When he was out there."

The agent leaned against the counter and folded his arms, growing quiet. She'd almost let it slip that Rose had run after

Mac. Had he picked up on that? Had she said too much? What was he thinking? Suddenly she didn't know what to do with herself. She got busy putting away a few cold items in the fridge.

"You said you were from Detroit."

"Yes. We just moved here a month ago."

"To live with your father-in-law?"

Ava nodded. "My family's mostly in Florida. I'm close to them, but Rose has always loved it here."

He glanced at her wedding ring. "What does your husband do?"

"He worked in medical equipment sales."

"Worked?"

"My husband recently passed away. A plane accident—a small plane. He and the pilot..."

His eyes widened. "I'm sorry."

Ava must have heard those two words a thousand times since Kevin's death. Everyone was sorry. She'd tried to accept the reaction of others as a blessing that people cared. But it still tasted sour whenever she heard it.

"Thank you."

He asked several more questions, and she answered the best she could. No, she hadn't seen anyone strange hanging around the property. No, she hadn't heard any gunshots. No, she hadn't disturbed anything inside the barn. No, she'd never seen the victim before or ever heard of her. And then came a question that caught her off guard: "Did Mac visit you often in Detroit?"

She hesitated. The unexpected question made her uncomfortable. She rushed to fill the silence. "Yes. Sometimes. Well, not a lot. But why wouldn't he? We're family. And he adores Rose." She stopped. She was babbling. Uneasiness churned in her stomach, her tongue dry and sticky. She felt sick.

"Are you okay, Mrs. Burke?"

Mrs. Burke? She hadn't heard those words for a while.

"Fine." She coughed a little. Felt shaky. Why was he watching her so intently? Only her faith and Mac anchored her life now, and a spotlight on her father-in-law undercut her sense of security.

Ava reached for a glass and filled it from the tap, started to take a drink but her hand wobbled. She set it down on the counter and took a deep breath.

"Is Mac here now?" he asked.

"No. He's…" Where had he said he'd been going? "He's out."

"Out where?"

"I can't remember."

Another long silence. "Does Mac have any guns in the house?"

She knew that Mac had a couple rifles he used for hunting, knew they were locked up and secure. She'd made sure of it.

"Mrs. Burke?"

"Ava." Her voice sounded small.

"Ava—sorry." He cleared his throat. "Are there any guns in the house?"

"Yes." Why was he asking this?

"Will you show me?"

Her pulse raced. "I don't know if I should. Don't you need a warrant for that?"

He pinned her with a dark gaze. He didn't seem so nice now. Neither did the dog. It looked like it could take a bite out of her at any moment. "That's up to you," he said.

She didn't know what to do. What would Mac think? Would it make him look guilty of something if she didn't? This was crazy. Mac didn't have anything to hide. She walked the agent through the family room to the back of the house and Mac's den. She pointed to the gun case with a couple of hunting rifles. "This is all he has. He keeps them locked up because of Rose."

The agent stepped closer and squinted at one of the guns, then pulled out his cell phone and snapped a photo.

"They're just hunting rifles," she added. "A lot of people in this area like to hunt."

But the agent wasn't listening to her. Instead, he'd moved away from the gun case and was focused on several photographs that hung on the wall. Photos of Mac in uniform at the helm of his ferry, Mac fishing, Mac and Kevin camping. He pointed to that one. "Is this your husband?"

"Yes. Kevin."

"Where are they?"

"On the island. Isle Royale."

He leaned in and looked closer. "Any idea when this was taken?"

Kevin had his beard in the photo. She'd never cared for it and made him shave it before they'd been married. Her face burned at the memory of the fit she'd pitched. Too scratchy, too wild-looking... Now she'd give anything to feel that beard rub against her face again.

"Ma'am?"

"It must've been before we were married. So maybe ten years ago."

"They look like quite the outdoorsmen."

She shrugged. "Most people around here are."

"That's the trouble with tourists."

She looked at him. "What?"

"Oh, I was just thinking. A hiker—Hannah Richter. Did you ever hear the name?" The question seemed innocuous, but his eyes scrutinized her face.

"No, I don't think so. Why? Who is she?"

"A visitor from the big city who was found dead on the island years ago. She died from exposure. It was all over the papers back then." He kept his gaze on her.

"That's horrible. No, I never heard mention of her." She

shifted and faced him square on, ready for this to be over. "If there aren't any more questions, I need to check on my daughter."

"Something was off about that woman. Don't tell me you didn't sense it, buddy." Creed's ears twitched in response, and Nolan kept thinking out loud as they headed back to the barn. "But she *was* willing to show me the rifle—which, by the way, takes a .223 load. But lots of folks have hunting rifles, and most of them shoot .223. Right?"

Creed kept his nose to the ground while Nolan continued puzzling through the particulars. Mac had lived here all his life, was familiar with the island, ran a ferry back and forth, and had frequented Detroit over the years. But the red flag for Nolan was the fact that Mac had gone to the barn after the body had been discovered and before the police had arrived. Why? Most people wouldn't do that—they tended to hunker down, a normal fear of more violence holding them in place. They'd wait on the police. Unless he'd had something to cover at the crime scene.

Inside the barn, Nolan touched base with Penn again before leading Creed to the dried blood. "Take a good sniff, boy." Creed inhaled the scent, his nostrils flaring and his head twisting with excitement. Nolan rubbed his hand over Creed's back. "You ready, boy? Ready?" He unclipped the lead. "Search!"

Creed spun a couple of times, then lowered his snout, pressing his nose to the ground, and zipped outside the barn and went directly to the tree line. He zigzagged back and forth, sniffing and sniffing more. Nolan watched his partner work. Creed lived for this. So did he.

A loud snort and sneezing happened as something lodged itself into his dog's nostrils. Nolan chuckled, then grew serious as he watched Creed's pacing pick up, his ears twitching, eyes blazing, movements exaggerated as he struggled to pinpoint the scent. Then he stopped, raised his snout and drew deep breaths of air before letting out a series of small barks and pouncing into the woods. He'd hit on the scent and was tracking.

Nolan followed, pushing back branches and stepping over rocks and roots and struggling to keep pace with his dog. Finally they came into a small clearing at the base of a hill, where Creed looped around a few times and sat down, his gaze riveted on Nolan.

The end of the trail, Nolan thought. He knelt, placing his nose against Creed's snout. "Good boy, good boy!"

Nolan ripped off his jacket, swiped the sweat beaded along his hairline as he circled the area, looking closely, checking for prints or blood spots or any sign that the victim, Lindsey Webber, or anyone else had been here. But the rain had washed any hope of evidence away.

He started to give up, when he heard the faint hum of a vehicle in motion. His head snapped in the direction of the noise. It seemed to come from the opposite side of the hill.

"Come on, boy, let's check it out." They climbed to the top and overlooked a sharp bend in a small, paved road. He turned and looked back to the clearing. From here it would be an easy, straight shot downhill to the spot where Creed had pinpointed the start of the blood trail.

Nolan scanned the ground, then bent and used his fingertips to prod behind rocks and under roots, searching for spent casings. Had Lindsey been dumped from a vehicle? Or had she jumped and escaped into the woods, only to be shot and pursued? He sighed. Finding something out here would be next to impossible. He stood and marked the location, planning to come back with extra manpower and metal detectors for a systematic search.

He was about to turn back when Creed let out a sharp bark that quickly shifted into a long, deep growl. Nolan wheeled and reached for his weapon, but he was too late. The man was already upon them.

Chapter Four

Nolan clenched the grip of his weapon with one hand and Creed's collar with the other. "Are you Mac Burke?" he asked. This man was much older than the one in the picture he'd seen earlier. Larger than most, in fact, with a heavy brow.

"Yeah, and this is my property." Mac clenched his hands, his features tight. "Ava said you were asking about the dead woman in my barn and that you looked at my guns. You suspect me of shooting that woman?"

"At this point, I suspect everyone. That's my job."

"You got questions for me, then?"

Mac didn't appear to have any weapons, but Nolan still didn't feel comfortable being in a secluded area with this guy. A steadfast something in Mac's posture—defiance, maybe—seemed to hold him in place. "I do, but they can wait until later."

"I see. Well, you're wasting your time with me. Didn't know the woman, and certainly didn't shoot her. I have no idea why she was in my barn. My guess is that she was on the run from someone."

"What makes you say that?"

"She was shot, wasn't she? Probably drug related. Been a lot of that going on 'round these parts."

"Could have been an accident. Someone hunting out of season and mistook her for a deer."

Mac scowled. "I don't hunt out of season."

"Didn't say you did." Nolan reclipped Creed's lead and stood. "I'm heading back to my vehicle. I'll be in touch with those—"

"Look." Mac stepped in front of him. On alert now, Nolan faced him, and so did Creed. "I get it that you have a job to do, and I don't mind answering your questions—all I'm asking is that you stay clear of my granddaughter."

His granddaughter? Nolan pictured the quiet little red-haired girl as she hugged on Creed.

"See, she's…she's been struggling with a lot, and she's fragile right now." Mac's previously clenched hands now relaxed.

Nolan's posture loosened. Had he misjudged Mac? Or was he using his granddaughter as a sympathy shield to hide something? It wasn't uncommon. He'd seen cases where children became an excuse for avoiding questions, too upsetting for the kid—or so they claimed. But the facts couldn't be ignored here. Mac had access to a weapon and connections to Detroit and Isle Royale.

"I'll take that into consideration," Nolan said. "For now, Mr. Burke, you need to go back to your house. We can continue this conversation later."

Something shifted in Mac's expression, and it made Nolan uneasy. Creed now, too. He paced back and forth, whining and pulling the lead taut until it cut into the fleshy part of Nolan's palm. Despite the pain, he held firm, his unblinking gaze locked on Mac until the man gave up and turned back for home.

Nolan watched Mac until he was out of sight, then followed. The forest had grown darker and colder, the thick tree trunks and vegetation squeezing out the sunlight and numbing his sense of direction. Every sound, every slightest snap of a twig set Nolan's nerves on edge. He was disoriented, and he thought of Lindsey Webber being pursued in these woods. Scared and bleeding and being chased down by a monster. He turned several times, homing in on the trees in the distance. It was impossible to see the barn from here. Was it dumb luck that she'd happened upon Mac's barn, or had she already known it was there?

Finally, Nolan eased his hold on the leash, and Creed quickly headed slightly left. Nolan followed, and the barn came into focus soon after. When they made their way out and back to the car, Nolan glanced up at the house. A second-floor curtain parted, and Rose peered through the window, her red hair frizzed around her face.

Creed noticed her as well and sat up on his haunches, striking a pose.

Nolan shook his head. "You're such a flirt."

Rose waved and smiled, her face radiating joy, and Nolan's heart melted. He tried to imagine what it had been like for this little girl, losing her father and moving away from her home all in such a short period of time. And Ava, so strong and composed, but she must've been torn up on the inside. He hated to bring more heartache to this family, but he knew what was ahead: he'd need to question Mac and get access to that gun.

Clearly the old man was close to Ava and Rose. How would they react? Burke had called his granddaughter fragile. Ava, on the other hand, appeared to Nolan as capable, and yes, the word *steadfast* came to mind for her as well. Not to do with defiance, but as a nurturing, loving mother type. Just what a fragile little girl needed. What neither of them needed was this kind of trauma in their lives.

He loaded Creed into the Explorer and glanced back at the window once more. Rose was still there, but she was now fixated on the barn and her expression somber. Nolan traced her gaze and didn't see anything but the barn, the field, the... Then it dawned on him. From the second-story window, Rose had a bird's-eye view of both the barn and the woods. Mac's words came back to him. *Stay clear of my granddaughter.*

Had anyone questioned the girl?

Agent Campbell Beckett was on speakerphone as Nolan navigated Highway M-26 toward nearby Eagle Harbor and the county coroner's office. "Reynold said you need the Richter cold-case file," she said. "I'm working on a secure transfer now."

Creed heard her voice and let out a series of excited barks from the back seat.

"Hello, Creed! I miss you, too," she yelled over the phone. Agent Campbell Beckett, Cam, trained both in analytic investigations and cybersecurity and was the brains of their unit. Plus, a friend. She'd been the first to welcome him when he'd arrived in DC.

She continued, "I pulled two boxes of physical evidence for this case. You want those, too?"

"Yeah, you better send them. I don't know what I'm looking at yet. I might need access to everything. Have the carrier deliver to the county sheriff's office here. Also, could you look into the owner of the property where Lindsey Webber's body was found? Mac Burke."

"Will do. This is a tough case. I hate the young ones."

Nolan gazed out the window. Highway M-26 wound alongside Lake Superior for about fifteen miles from Sculpin Bay to Eagle Harbor, where the county morgue was located. The beautiful scenery contrasted with the ugliness pervading his mind. People who preyed on children were a particularly bad breed. He used to pray about this, but during his years in the Marines and then in civilian police work, he'd seen so much evil that he'd come to believe that his prayers were powerless to change anything. No matter how hard he prayed, evil still happened. *Even to the most innocent among us.*

"Reynold told me there might have been others," Nolan said.

"So far we're looking into three other girls with similar victim profiles. No definite connection yet, but I'll keep you posted on our progress."

"Send me what you have on them, would you?" he asked.

"Sure will. How are you doing?"

"Hard to know yet. Nothing's surfaced. I've got a few hunches to track down. On my way now to meet the sheriff at the morgue to examine Webber's remains."

"I meant personally."

He knew what she'd meant. He sighed. "I'm fine."

"Really? It's only been a few weeks, and you two were together for almost three years."

"I know how long we dated." His words came out harsher than he intended. He took a deep breath. "Sorry. I don't mean to snap at you."

"You snap at me all the time."

"I do?"

"Yeah. Especially lately. I don't take it personally."

"Sorry. How's the weather in DC?"

"Crummy, but don't try to change the topic. She took a job transfer."

"What?" He resented the sinking feeling in his heart. Why did he still care? She'd cheated on him, betrayed him. He'd never forget the day he'd seen Rena with that other man... "Where's she going? No, don't tell me. It doesn't matter. I don't need to—"

"Dallas."

That far? "Dallas?"

"Yeah. The guy she...well, she's getting married to him."

He had no response to that.

"I'm sorry. I didn't want you to hear it from someone else."

He didn't want to hear it at all.

"Nolan?"

"Yeah."

"Talk to me." Cam's voice was soft but stern.

"Thanks for the info, Beckett. And don't worry—I'm fine." He turned off the highway and into a small lot outside the morgue, a squat brick building with few windows. "I gotta go, but I'll be in touch later. I'll watch for the files."

He disconnected before she could ask any more questions.

Dr. Curt Carlson was a short, rounded man with a bow tie and wire-rimmed glasses perched on the lower bridge of his nose. He met Nolan inside the front door of the morgue and led him to a small room where they both slipped protective coverings over their clothing.

"Most everything's already in the autopsy report. Is there something specific you're looking for?" Carlson asked.

Anything you might have missed. But Nolan didn't say that. He could leave no stone unturned. That was part of what made him a good investigator. It was also what annoyed almost everyone in his life. Rena included. *You're always questioning my every move*, she'd said once. *You make me nervous.* And he'd backed off, given her the benefit of the doubt, right up until he'd found her in that guy's arms...

Nolan quickly dismissed thoughts of her and focused on the task at hand. "I'm looking for any special markings on the body."

Carlson slipped off his glasses and attached a magnifying loupe to his safety goggles. "I assume you mean tattoos or scars," he said. "If there were, I would have noted it in my report. Of course, there was tissue loss from the wound."

The doctor opened the door and led Nolan down a short hall to a door marked Examination Room. The air inside felt like a cold slap in the face. Nolan's muscles stiffened, and his stomach churned—whether from nerves or hunger, he wasn't sure. Maybe both. He would never get used to this part of his job.

Carlson seemed in his element, though, moving about the room with ease. "She's over there. I brought her out before you got here. You think this will take long? I have a meeting at three."

"Shouldn't." Nolan stared at the covered body on the stain-less-steel exam table across the room and wished for the comfort of his dog. He thought of Creed in the Explorer with the windows cracked and a bowl of water. Probably napping. His partner was getting off easy, that was for sure.

Nolan approached slowly, reverently, and snapped on gloves. Her head was visible, with lots of blond hair. And her eyes were slightly open, yellowish with a crystalline appearance. The rest of her body was covered in a paper-like sheet that crinkled as the doctor lowered it. Nolan took in the sight of her damaged body and pushed his emotions—sadness, anger, regret—aside and went to work examining her skin, searching for any sort of marking. Arms, legs, feet…nothing.

Carlson sighed. "You're not going to find anything."

Nolan ignored the doctor and kept his focus, parting and separating patches of blond hair and checking her scalp. Next he looked behind the ears and in her mouth. "Here," he said, turning out the bottom lip. "It's here. See this?"

Carlson reached under his visor and adjusted his special lenses. He leaned forward carefully but said nothing.

"I'll need a photograph of this on file," Nolan said.

"I can't believe I missed it. I…"

Nolan studied the tattoo—two black-ink dollar signs on the inside of her lower lip. "It's her trafficker's mark. For the record." Nolan pulled the covering over her body. "This woman was a victim of human trafficking."

Chapter Five

Ava hurried across the parking lot of the Green Larch Inn, a small beige A-frame structure styled to look like a Swiss mountain chalet with dark brown gingerbread lattice. Heads turned as she entered. She wished she'd taken the time to change into something different, anything better than her dust-covered jeans and a flannel, but she'd already been running behind schedule.

She spied Yvette seated at the restaurant's corner table, her head lowered over a menu. Ava took the chair across from her. "Sorry I'm late."

"You're fine. We'll just say I'm early." Yvette looked her over. "What have you been doing? You're…"

"Dusty?" Ava tugged at her flannel. Yvette was petite and pretty in a bright blue sweater that accented her eye color, whereas Ava felt like a shapeless, dumpy, untidy blob. *When was the last time I had my hair done?* "I was cleaning out the attic. Mac said I can use it for homeschooling Rose this fall. There's so much stuff in there—you wouldn't believe it. Old clothes, Little League stuff, school papers… Kevin's whole life, basically. Time got away from me. Sorry."

"That can't be an easy job."

"No. It's not." Tears pricked the edges of Ava's eyes. "But it's got to be done. I'll need the space."

"You know, it is only April, Ava. You've got lots of time to do this."

Yes, but that room full of Kevin's things felt like a sink-hole to her spirit, something she needed to clean out now. She glanced at Yvette, who nodded slightly. It was good to have a friend who understood. Although Yvette was more than that. She was family, Kevin's cousin. And she understood heart-ache—the tragic loss of her own parents—which was why she and Ava got along so well. *God puts the right people in your life at the right time*, Ava thought.

They both looked up as a wiry waitress with short gray hair and bleeding lipstick slid two glasses of water onto the table, filled their coffee mugs and asked for their orders, her pen hovering over her pad as she eyed Ava with curiosity or disdain. Ava wasn't sure which.

"I shouldn't," Yvette was saying, but then went ahead and ordered the inn's specialty dessert—white-chocolate cake lay-ered with thimbleberry jam, topped with slivers of shaved white chocolate. Ava went for a cup of chicken rice soup, hop-ing it would warm her insides. She'd felt chilled ever since talking to the agent earlier. His questions had unnerved her, but he'd treated Rose kindly. Ava was grateful for that.

The waitress shuffled off to the next table, topping off cof-fee for two women, both in quilted jackets and yoga pants tucked into fur-topped boots. It was that time of year, mid-April, that shoulder season here in the UP, when one day could blow in a winter chill and the next blind you with spring's sun-shine and warmth. Who knew what to wear? Boots? Sneakers? Sandals? The waitress glanced her way and bent over the yoga-pants table, whispering earnestly. Their heads suddenly turned her way, then snapped back, followed by a round of giggles.

Ava straightened her flannel a little, leaned forward and

lowered her voice. "Those women in that booth over there... I think they're talking about me."

"Yeah. Just ignore them. Tell me, how are you holding up since finding that poor woman in the barn?"

"I keep seeing her body over and over. I can't shake it."

Yvette frowned. "I'm so sorry. Are you scared being out there now? Mac's place is so isolated."

"It's a lot different than Detroit, that's for sure." She'd moved to Sculpin Bay because Mac was here and she'd thought it would be a safe place to raise Rose. No noisy traffic, street gangs or drive-bys, just fresh, open air. Now she wasn't so sure. "What was that poor woman doing there in the first place, do you think? They didn't find a car or anyone who even saw. It's like she showed up out of nowhere."

The waitress delivered their order, topped off their coffees and left the check. Ava looked around. People seemed to be involved in their own conversations; still, she lowered her voice and continued, "There was a federal agent at the house this morning."

"Federal agent—like the FBI?"

"Yeah, sort of. An investigator with the National Park Service. He asked a lot of questions. Some of them seemed more like accusations."

"Against you? That's crazy."

"No, Mac."

"Mac?" Yvette let out a long sigh. "That's ridiculous. Like he doesn't have enough going on already." She scooped up a forkful of cake. "How is Rose doing with all this? I'm sorry— I keep meaning to stop and see her. Business has just been... well, you know. Is Mac's friend still trying to help her?"

She said *friend* like it was a bad word. "Jane? Yeah, she's coming back this afternoon. You should try to get to know her. She's nice."

"Because she wants something."

"She seems to really care for Mac."

"You're so naive."

"Hey, I…uh…well, she's trying to help Rose. We all are, but Rose…" Her voice cracked. She exhaled and snatched a napkin, dabbing at her eyes.

"She's what, Ava? Talk to me. What's going on?"

Should she even say this? Yes, she could trust Yvette. She was family, and since she'd moved back to town, they'd become a lot closer. "I don't know for sure, but I think Rose may have seen something."

Yvette put her fork down. "You mean to do with the murder? What makes you think that?"

"She seemed to know the woman's body was in the barn and that she had been shot."

"Oh no! But how would Rose… Do you think she saw it happen? Or found the body before you did?"

"I don't know. She won't talk about it."

"Did you tell the sheriff?"

"No! Not until I'm sure that she saw something. I'm not going to put her through the trauma of being questioned if it's unnecessary. It'll be too much for her. Already she's…she's so shut up inside herself. I'm worried about her. Really worried."

"I'm sure you are. And you're right to wait." Yvette reached forward and clasped her hand. "This is a mess. I'm so sorry. What can I do to help?"

"You're doing it. I feel better talking about it. Thank you."

"You know I'm here for…" Yvette's gaze locked on something over Ava's shoulder. "He's got the worst timing."

Ava turned and saw a man in pressed khakis and a heavy wool sweater coming their way. "Who is he?"

"Someone I wanted to avoid today. Every day, actually." Yvette took a gulp of coffee and reached for the check. "I need to go anyway. I've got a showing in a half hour."

"Here, let me pay for mine." Ava reached for her purse.

"No worries. You treat next time." She stood, bent down and hugged Ava, whispering into her ear, "I'm sorry for everything that's happening right now. I'm here for you. Anything you need. You know that, right?"

Ava nodded into her shoulder.

"Yvette," the man said, reaching their table. "Glad I ran into you. I left you a couple voicemails."

Yvette straightened, tucked a blond strand behind her ear and smiled sweetly. "Oh hey, Derek. I'm sorry. I planned to call you this afternoon. Things have been nonstop on my end. Ava, this is Derek Williams. He's the broker with Dunbar and Williams Realty. Derek, this is my friend, Ava Burke."

"Burke?" He looked down at her, staring a couple beats too long. "Kevin's wife?"

Ava shrank lower into her chair. "Yes, but my husband has passed away."

Derek nodded. "Yes, I know. Kevin and I went to school together. We…we were friends. I'm so very sorry."

She forced a smile. It was inevitable that she'd run into Kevin's old friends, but why today? "Thank you."

Yvette reached down and patted her arm. "Stay and finish your soup. I'll call you a little later." She dug a couple bills out of her bag and headed for the cash register.

Ava expected Derek to follow, but he turned and stared at her. She pushed away the barely touched soup and stood. "It was good to meet you."

"Wait," he said. "Could you give me five minutes?"

She hesitated.

"Please." He gestured for her to sit back down. "I won't keep you long. I just wondered if we could talk briefly about Kevin."

Ava gathered her bag and keys. "Maybe another time. I need to get home." She wasn't up to a walk down memory lane.

She was barely out the door when she heard him call, "Wait." He caught up to her on the sidewalk, placing his hand on her arm. She bristled at the too-familiar touch from someone she didn't know. "I just want you to understand that Kevin and I were close," he said. "And I—"

"I never heard him mention your name. I'm sorry." She shook off his hand and turned away.

He double-stepped and got in front of her, blocking her path. "He never mentioned me, really? I can't believe that. We go way back. We should get together and talk. I've got stories about him. Funny stories. Memories that you might want to tell your daughter one day."

Ava grew cold. Mentioning her daughter felt even more invasive than touching her shoulder. "If you'll excuse me, I'm running late for something." She started forward.

He shuffle-stepped and walked backward, keeping a few feet in front of her. "Kevin was wild back then, let me tell you. He ever mention camping trips with a friend back in high school? That was me. He was big into the outdoors, but you know that. And big into having a good time. 'Course, weren't we all back then?" He chuckled. "You should have seen how he used to—"

"I don't want to know," she blurted out. Kevin had had a past; she already knew that. She didn't need the details, whether sordid or innocent. She didn't need any memories other than those she had shared with Kevin. "I'm sorry, but I'm not ready to hear stories yet. Maybe some other time."

He leaned in closer. "I'd like that."

It was almost three in the afternoon when Nolan parked in front of the Green Larch Inn. He was starving and cranky, and this town only had a couple eating establishments. He noticed Ava right away. She was on the sidewalk talking to a man. And by the looks of her body language, she was not happy. The man, on the other hand, was smiling too much, leaning too close, flirting.

Nolan's stomach clenched. "Stay here, boy," he told Creed. He cracked the window and got out, beeped the doors locked and beelined for the two of them. "Everything okay here?"

"Yeah, fine," the guy said.

But Ava's eyes pleaded with Nolan, clearly showing it wasn't. "Excuse me," she said to neither man in particular. "I need to get home."

"I'll walk you to your car." Nolan gave the guy a hard stare and turned to follow Ava. As soon as they were out of earshot, he asked, "Who was that guy?"

"Derek Williams. He's a real estate agent, I guess. This is the first time I've met him. He said he was an old friend of my husband's."

"Had your husband ever mentioned him?"

"No. Not that I remember."

Nolan glanced back. The guy was still on the sidewalk, watching them. "What did he want?"

They'd reached her car. She unlocked it with two beeps of her key fob. "He asked if I would get together with him. To talk about Kevin. Said he had a lot of old stories to tell me."

Yeah right, old stories! He was asking her out. The thought niggled at Nolan's gut for some reason. But it was none of his business, really. Maybe she even liked the guy or was playing the field. His jaw clenched as emotions about his ex suddenly muddled his thoughts. "But you...?" He left the question open, needing to know if he'd overstepped here—if his conversation with Cam had caused him to confront a situation he should have ignored.

She stopped, her hand on the door handle, and shot a quick frown toward Derek. "I just wanted to get away." She paused as if deciding what to say next. "Thanks. For your help." She moved her attention onto him, her frown melting as she gave him a grateful nod and held his gaze a long moment.

Something inside Nolan warmed at that singular word, that little gesture. He tried to shake it off. What man didn't want to feel like a protector? He'd simply noticed what could have been a confrontation between two people and acted on it.

He wanted to give himself credit for just being observant, acting nobly, yet a bad feeling still churned inside him. Was it that the guy had asked Ava out? Why should he care? His conversation about his ex was still too recent, too raw. He needed to push those emotions aside and refocus.

He held Ava's car door open as she slipped into the driver's seat and put the key into the ignition. The auxiliary kicked in, and the car filled with the sound of seventies soul music. She shook her head and cranked down the volume with a guilty look. "I don't know how that got so loud." She secured her seat belt and looked up. "Thanks again." He still held the door open, and she cocked her head at him. "Is there something else?"

"Uh…no, not really. I mean, I'll be reaching out soon with more questions regarding the case," he started and stopped and stumbled over his words. His cheeks burned hot. "Just… be careful of who you trust," he said, shutting the door and stepping back.

She stared at him through the window, a slight crease between her brows, before she drove off.

Chapter Six

Woodland Road wound through thick, towering pines to Mac's house, which was at the tip of a peninsula point on the east end of the harbor. Ava maneuvered the twists and turns on autopilot, her mind replaying snippets of her afternoon: Yvette at the diner, so confident and pretty; the rude waitress and the gawking women at the next table; Derek, well dressed and slick, talking about Kevin's wild days—the part of her husband she didn't know, didn't want to know; and then Agent Nolan Shea. On the one side an odd guy, serious and a little intimidating, but she'd also glimpsed his caring and protective side. *Be careful of who you trust*, he'd said. Meaning what? Or who? She'd only come to know a few people in town—who *could* she trust?

As she turned a corner, an errant sunbeam flashed in front of her eyes. Although the sun wouldn't set for another couple hours, the tall pines usually shielded the light, making it seem dusk-like. She glanced at the dashboard clock, almost five o'clock, and her thoughts jumped to Rose. Jane was probably already at the house, and Ava had wanted to be there when she arrived. Since Rose couldn't or wouldn't express herself verbally, Jane had planned to start art therapy tonight.

Ava pushed her speed a little higher, staying alert and watching for deer. Suddenly her gaze caught on a streak of chrome reflected in her rearview mirror. A black car was right on her tail, its bumper coming closer. *What in the world?* She gripped the wheel tighter, pressed the accelerator, whipped around the next curve and gained more speed on a straight path of road that led up a small hill.

Her quick glance in the rearview mirror had her breathing a sigh of relief. The other driver must have finally noticed her and had backed off. *Stupid driver!* She looked ahead again just as she sped over the crest of the hill, going too fast for the sharp curve in the road. She slammed on the brakes; the seat belt cinched her chest as she cranked the wheel and stuttered to an abrupt stop on the edge of the pavement.

Collapsing forward against the steering wheel, she sucked in air, trying to calm herself. When she looked up again, the black car had stopped next to her, partially blocking her way. Derek burst out of the driver's-side door and approached her window.

You okay? he mouthed, his face wrinkled in concern. She cracked it slightly to hear him speak. "I didn't think you were going to make that curve," he said.

"You almost ran me off the road," she snapped, anger edging out her anxiety.

"I'm sorry. I was trying to catch up to you, that's all. I didn't expect you to panic like that. As soon as I saw you speed up, I backed off. Figured you were heading out to Mac's place anyway and I could find you there."

"Why were you following me?"

He held out a bracelet—her bracelet. The one Kevin had given her when Rose had been born. She frowned, looked at her bare wrist.

She rolled the window down the rest of the way and reached through.

"Found it on the sidewalk after you left," he said, his hand grazing her palm. "I knew it was yours. Noticed it on your wrist in the restaurant. Looks like the clasp broke."

She fingered the simple gold bracelet with a small emerald, Rose's birthstone, and felt a strange mix of gratitude and resentment. It had probably fallen off when he'd grabbed her arm outside the restaurant.

"Thank you," she managed, but couldn't bring any gratitude into her tone.

"Of course. Glad I saw it." He shoved his hands into his pockets and looked down the road. "You and Rose living out at Mac's place?"

She stared at him. "How do you know my daughter's name?"

"Kevin mentioned it last time I saw him."

"You kept in touch? Thought you were just friends back in high school."

"We didn't have a lot of contact. Not really. But I ran into him from time to time when he came to town. I saw him right before he died. The *day* he died, actually."

Dread seemed to overtake her. "I don't understand. What do you mean? You were in Green Bay?"

"Green Bay?"

"Kevin died in a plane crash on his way home from a business trip in Green Bay. He was there meeting a potential client."

"No, he was here. Well, just down the road in Houghton. I ran into him at a gas station not far from the airport. I didn't ask but assumed he'd been up here visiting his dad. We didn't talk long. He was in a hurry to get home to you and Rose, he said."

Ava's stomach clenched. *No, this can't be right. He's mistaken. Or downright lying.*

Be careful of who you trust.

Derek went on, "As soon as I heard he'd died, I... I don't know. It was a horrible shock."

First he'd practically accosted her outside the diner, now he was lying to her about Kevin. But doubts were already creeping into her mind. Maybe Derek wasn't lying? Maybe Kevin had been here in Sculpin Bay, or Houghton at least, the day he'd died. But how could that be? The official report on his accident had said that his flight had originated in Green Bay, going down due to mechanical failure just prior to reaching the Detroit airport. But… "I need to get home."

"Sure. Maybe we could talk more later. How about dinner on Friday?"

"No, thanks." She jammed into Reverse and wheeled in the seat, looking behind her.

"Hey, wait!"

She ignored him and punched the accelerator. Dust and pebbles and small pieces of asphalt sprayed the air.

He jumped back, shielding his face. "Are you crazy? What's wrong with you?"

She sped away. *Crazy?* She wasn't the crazy one. But what if Kevin *had* taken another flight early that morning from Green Bay up to Houghton? He would have had time to fly back down to Green Bay and catch his other flight home. But why? A last-minute decision to come up and see Mac? No, it couldn't be. Mac would have mentioned it. Unless…unless Kevin hadn't been here to visit Mac but had come for some other reason.

Suddenly Nolan's words surfaced again: *Be careful of who you trust.* She had always trusted Kevin. Absolutely trusted him.

The last few miles sped by. She shook off the worry, refocused on getting home to her Rose.

Jane's blondish-gray hair usually pooled over her shoulders, but today it was pulled back to the nape of her neck and held in place by a large barrette. She was on the family room sofa with Rose, their heads bent together as Rose drew with crayons. Soft music played from a Bluetooth speaker, a soothing classical piece, and a fire crackled in the fireplace. It was late April, but this far north the evening temperatures often dropped into the thirties.

Ava quietly observed the two from the kitchen for a few minutes before turning back to help Mac peel potatoes. Dinner would be simple tonight—soup and crusty bread. "I hope Jane can break through to her."

"If anyone can, she can." Mac scooped a handful of diced celery and onions into the stockpot.

Ava smiled. Cancer had taken Kevin's mother, Irene, back when he'd been in high school. Mac had been devoted to her care for years and had always said that Irene was the love of his life. Recently, though, he'd struck up a friendship with Jane. Yvette was leery of Jane, but Ava hoped this was a second chance at love for Mac. She was happy for him, even though her own heart ached with grief whenever she thought of love and loss.

"People were in and out of the woods all day today," Mac said. "Searching for something, it seems."

Casings, Ava knew. They were trying to piece together the moments before Lindsey Webber's death and narrow down the ballistics on the gun that had killed her. She thought of Mac's guns stowed away in the back room, wondered if she could use one if needed. "I ran into one of Kevin's old friends today. Derek Williams."

Mac shot her a sideways glance. "Oh yeah."

"You remember him?"

"I do. He and Kevin were thick as thieves back in high school. Never quite cared for him, but maybe he's changed over the years."

Perhaps not.

"Where'd you see him at?" Mac stirred the pot. Onion smell filled the kitchen. He went to work dicing the peeled potatoes.

"At the diner. I met Yvette there for coffee. They know one another from their real-estate work."

"That's right. He sells houses now, doesn't he?"

Ava drew in a deep breath. "Mac, the day Kevin died, did he visit you?"

The knife hovered over the cutting board. Mac met her gaze. "You know he didn't. His plane went down between Green Bay and Detroit. What makes you ask that?"

"Derek said he saw him that day near Houghton."

"He was mistaken."

"No, he said he talked to him. They had a conversation. He said Kevin was filling up his rental car before returning it and heading back home."

Mac resumed chopping the potatoes. "I don't put much stock into anything that man says." He scooped the final handful of potatoes into the pot and turned toward the family room, his eyes widening with surprise. "Well, there's my princess. Did you make Grandpa a picture?"

Rose stood in the doorway with a piece of paper clenched in her fist. Jane was behind her, her face pale. "Yes, she did. You should both look at it."

Ava crossed the kitchen and knelt next to Rose. She'd drawn a red barn and the woods beside it, even some fat V-shaped birds in the sky, flying between fluffy cartoonlike clouds. But what stood out most in the picture was the crudely drawn person standing by the barn with long yellow hair and a roundish splotch of red crayon marring the center. Ava's chest tightened with anxiety. Rose had seen the injured woman running into the barn. Poor Rose!

"Oh, bug. I'm so sorry you had to see this." Ava rubbed gentle circles on her back. "It must have been so scary. You should have told me. I'm always here to listen to you. You know that, don't you?"

Rose didn't move or even make eye contact. Instead she

slid her tiny finger over the paper to the thick mass of brown tree trunks with clumpy green for leaves.

Ava leaned in closer and squinted. Rose had drawn another figure lurking by the trees.

Chapter Seven

Creed let out a series of high-pitched whines from his spot on the opposite motel bed. Nolan unwrapped a plain burger, removed the bun and tossed the patty Creed's way. He snapped it up in midair and swallowed it in two gulps.

"Good boy." Creed leaped onto the bed with Nolan and nudged his arm. "No, no more. One's enough. You've got your own food." He pointed to a pair of bowls near the bathroom. Creed ignored him and rubbed his nose against Nolan's face. He laughed and gave in, peeling off the bun on the last burger and handing it over.

He placed his hands on his dog's cheeks and leaned forward until they touched foreheads, inhaling his familiar dog smell. "I love you, buddy," he whispered, then washed down a few cold fries with the rest of his warmed soda. Living out of motels and eating fast food stunk but came with the territory.

Nolan checked the time—almost six. He moved to the desk and opened his laptop. He signed in on a secure network and sat back, waiting for his team members, Agent Campbell Beckett and Agent Tyler West, to join the conference call.

Cam popped into the virtual wait room first. Nolan clicked her in and did a double take. Cam's normal shoulder-length hair was now cut above her ears. He blinked several times, searching for something to say.

"Don't stare," she said. "It's not polite."

"Uh, it looks good. Hold on. Ty's joined us."

Ty noticed Cam's haircut right away. "Great look, Techy. I like it." Ty was clean-cut and had a thousand-watt smile, which he flashed now.

Cam smiled back. "Thanks."

Nolan had to admire Ty's ability to charm Cam. She didn't even mind his nickname for her.

Ty went on, "Hope you two are having better luck than me on this case. I've got nothing here in Detroit."

Nolan gave an update on his end, relaying his findings from the victim's lower lip.

Cam nodded on screen. "Trafficking mark."

"I agree," Ty said. "And that pretty much confirms our theory. Did the tat look like a home job?"

Nolan shrugged. "Couldn't tell. Cam, you recall anything in the cold-case file about a tattoo on Hannah Richter?"

"No, but I'll run it through the system."

"You think we're looking at a new corridor?" Ty asked.

Nolan nodded. "Possible. Most traffickers use the 401 Corridor from Detroit or Buffalo up to Ontario. I'll talk to Reynold, though. If it turns out that we're heading in that direction, we'll widen our scope, get other agencies involved."

Both nodded, and Cam spoke up. "Checked into Mac Burke like you asked. On the first pass, everything seemed good. Returned from Vietnam in seventy-three, married several years later, widowed about ten years ago, one child—Kevin. Retired as the captain on the *Northern Light* ferry with an exemplary record." She took a deep breath. "But that was the first pass. Second pass, I found an expunged felony. Michigan allows law enforcement access to expunged records, so I've got a request in. Shouldn't take long for me to get the particulars."

"Let me know as soon as possible," Nolan said. "Penn's

people are still searching the woods behind the barn. Nothing yet. I'll question Mac again first thing tomorrow."

They wrapped up the meeting, and Creed gave a quick woof, jumped off the bed and trotted toward the door. A few minutes later Nolan made his way down to the beach with Creed on his lead for an evening run. He let Creed loose and watched him romp up and down the shore, dipping his nose between rocks, inhaling scents, bounding through the water as it lapped against the sand.

The hollow sound of a boat horn sliced the air. The *Northern Light* entered the harbor and was nearing the dock, bringing passengers back from the island.

So, Mac has a felony of some kind from the past, Nolan thought. This small town seemed so innocent, the kind of idyllic lakeside village he'd dreamed of living in someday. There'd been a time when he would have believed that God wanted him to find such a place of peace. But lately he was convinced that, in his life, peace was an illusion.

He called Creed in and reattached his lead. "Come on, boy, we're going to talk to the captain."

"She saw something that day, maybe even the shooter," Jane said. They'd finished dinner and were working on the dishes. Mac had taken Rose into town for hot chocolate and to watch the ferry come in to dock. "You need to talk to the sheriff about this. I can be there if he questions Rose. I'll make sure they don't push her too far."

"I don't know."

"Lindsey Webber is someone's daughter, Ava. Think of that girl's poor parents. And what if it happens again? How would you feel then, knowing that Rose might know something that could have prevented another death?"

Ava nodded. "You're right. I'll go see the sheriff tomorrow. But you have to promise to be there when they question her."

Her hands shook as she wiped down the counter and glanced

through the window. The trees bordering the land spread dark shadows across the yard. For two days now, deputies and other strangers had traipsed through those woods and her life. They were still out there now, using the last hours of daylight to search for evidence. She wondered if Nolan was supervising the search. She hoped so. Judging by the way he'd questioned her earlier, he was determined and thorough. No doubt he was good at his job, but...there was something else, too.

When she'd told him about Kevin's death, he'd looked sad, genuinely sad, and he'd treated Rose gently, speaking softly to her and allowing her to pet his dog. He seemed thoughtful and compassionate and as if he cared, more than just wanting to do a good job. Or was it wishful thinking that... A twinge of guilt shot through her.

She frowned and turned away from the window. This wasn't the first time she'd caught herself thinking of Nolan. If felt disloyal. Yet at the same time every fiber of her missed Kevin. How was it possible to feel so many conflicting feelings at once? Alone, empty, wishful, longing...

Jane finished filling the dishwasher and added a dish-detergent pellet. "It's going to be okay. I promise."

Ava bit her lip, stemming the tears that threatened to flow. "It doesn't feel that way."

Jane wiped her hands and pulled her close. "Oh, honey. I know. And I'm so sorry."

"It still hurts every day. How do you do it? You seem so strong."

Jane sighed. "It's been ten years since my Ben died, and it still hurts. Not as bad, though. Be patient with yourself. Time passes differently when we're grieving, and your loss is still so fresh." She stepped back, shook her head and smiled. "And don't confuse *strong* with *prideful*."

"Prideful...what do you mean?"

"When Ben first died, I didn't let anyone see how much I was suffering inside. But it wasn't strength that kept me from showing my grief. It was pride. And the more I soldiered on, the more bitter I became. There were people who tried to help me, but I wouldn't let them in. I isolated myself because it was easier to cry in private than have anyone see how weak I was."

Jane picked up her jacket from the back of the dining chair and slipped it on. "I wasted a lot of time keeping it all inside myself like that. There's no shame in being honest with your feelings."

Jane stood on the front porch and turned back, the golden sunset light softening the lines on her face, and Ava caught a glimpse of what she must have looked like as a younger woman. "Have you ever let Rose see you cry?" Jane asked.

Ava's stomach twisted. "No... I... I thought... I've been afraid of upsetting her more."

"I know. That's only natural. But let your daughter see how strong you really are, Ava, by *not* hiding your feelings. Let her see you cry. Show her how to show emotion." She waved and started down the porch steps. "I'll see you soon."

"Wait!"

Jane turned back.

"How did you finally learn to cope with losing Ben? I mean, how did you learn to open up and..."

"And feel peace again?"

Yes. Peace.

"God put Mac in my life and made me want to open my heart again. Your father-in-law is truly special."

"Truly special," Ava whispered as she shut the door, and her mind flashed to Agent Nolan Shea again. She'd come to like the man, his soft side, his kindness. Part of her felt comforted by his very presence, but... She cringed thinking of Nolan's reactions to Mac. Could she trust Nolan, whose only real involvement with her and her family stemmed from his job as an agent? She had to protect Rose, yes, but Mac could equally be at risk from the agent's probing. Not that Mac had anything to hide.

Her heart sank. She hadn't thought Kevin had hid anything from her, either. But now she felt the itch of uncertainty about Kevin's whereabouts the day he'd died...

She paused and wondered. Kevin, Mac, Rose and now Nolan. *Be careful of who you trust.*

The house suddenly seemed too quiet, and Mac and Rose wouldn't be home for a while. Ava fidgeted a bit before overcoming her procrastination and heading upstairs to the attic. At first glance she felt overwhelmed. Had she accomplished anything this morning? It looked worse than before she'd started.

She took a deep breath and tackled a box of clothing first, sorting and designating each item to one of three piles: donate, keep and pitch. She cruised through the first box: a collection of baseball trophies—keep, an old baseball bat—donate, well-worn pair of football cleats—pitch, and she stopped. Kevin's favorite sweatshirt, gray and frayed at the edges, crumpled in the corner of the box as if it'd been ripped off and tossed in on a whim. She lifted it to her face, inhaling the faint smell of hard work... Kevin. Tears burned her eyes. She slipped it over her head and for a second imagined his arms around her again. She'd keep this sweatshirt forever. Tears flowed freely now. She allowed herself to cry and it felt good, and she knew Jane was right: she'd held in her feelings too much.

Finally she swiped her face with her sleeve, took a breath and bent again to her task. She uncovered a shoebox, worn and faded red. She lifted it, and the lid shifted. Several newspaper clippings fell to the floor. She looked closer, reading the headlines: *Unidentified Body Found in Wilderness Area, Isle Royale Claims Life of Young Woman, Exposure Likely Killed Isle Royale Hiker, Identity of Dead Hiker a Mystery.*

Dead Hiker... Hannah Richter. It had to be. She hadn't yet been identified when these articles were written, but this was the hiker Nolan had asked about.

The realization turned her stomach. The clippings were yellowed and crumpled, so it was impossible to tell which newspaper they'd come from, but one had the year, 2013, still visible. Ten years ago, and a couple years before she and Kevin had been married.

She leaned back. He'd talked freely about his early child-hood, but...what was it he'd said? The few years before they'd married had been his "dark period." So, they'd never discussed that. But why would he keep these unless he'd known the girl?

Her fingers trembled as she carefully gathered the clippings, set them on her lap and started to read.

Wind whipped at Nolan's face as he and Creed stood port-side on the *Northern Light* ferry and held his phone out to one of the crew members. The man scrolled through the pictures of the missing women and stopped on Lindsey Webber's photo. "Isn't this the girl who was found dead?"

"Yes, that's her. Lindsey Webber. Have you seen her before?"

The man swiped at his beard. "Just her picture in the papers."

"How about the rest of them?"

"No. Sorry. I haven't seen any of them."

Nolan thanked him, and he and Creed moved to the front of the boat. The other two crew members hadn't seen any of the women before, either.

Frustrated, Nolan led Creed to the narrow metal stairs and they climbed to the wheelhouse. Creed immediately moved in circles, sniffing the ground. A man around thirty was bent over a panel of instruments, jotting down information in a record book.

"You're NPS Investigative Services," he said without look-ing up.

Creed raised his head, ears pricked, as he studied the man.

"That's right. Agent Nolan Shea. You're Captain...?"

"Koberski." He straightened and pinned Creed with a steely

gaze, his lips pressed thin under a crooked nose. "Deck officer told me you were asking questions. What can I help you with?"

Nolan shifted Creed's leash to the other hand and showed him the pictures.

"Never seen any of them. Are they all dead?"

"Why do you ask that?"

"I was told you're asking about that dead girl found in Mac Burke's barn."

"How well do you know Mac?"

"Worked for him since I was seventeen. Bought the boat from him when he retired."

"When was that?"

"About five years ago."

"Ever known him to lose his temper or…?"

"Mac?" He shook his head. "He didn't kill that girl, if that's what you're thinking."

"Her body was found in his barn."

"Don't know how she got there, but it doesn't mean anything. He's not your guy—trust me."

Nolan shifted direction. "His son ever work the boat?"

"Yeah, when he was younger."

"He didn't have an interest in taking it over when Mac retired?"

"Kevin?" He chuckled. "No. Kevin couldn't get out of Sculpin Bay fast enough. The summer after graduation he picked up and left town, didn't even tell anyone. Never came back much either—maybe a quick visit here and there. Guess Sculpin Bay wasn't good enough for him."

"When was that?"

"When was what?"

"When did he graduate—you know?"

"Ten years ago. We were classmates. Never much hung out together. He was in with a different crowd back then."

Nolan asked a few more questions and then let the captain get back to work, but his words lingered in Nolan's mind. He was stuck on the time line. Ten years ago, Kevin Burke had picked up and left town. In a hurry.

Nolan stepped onto the dock and was headed up the pier, Creed close to his side, when his phone rang. It was Sheriff Penn.

"Had deputies out in those woods all day and half this evening. There's nothing out there. The shooter must have taken the casings with him."

Another dead end. Frustration mounted. "I sent a file with photos of the other missing girls to you earlier."

"Yeah. I've got a couple deputies canvassing with the pictures. Nothing so far."

"How would someone cross over to Isle Royale unnoticed?" The lead went taut as Creed pulled toward a group of seagulls picking at a garbage can next to Jensen's Bakery.

"Wouldn't be that hard. Private boat or seaplane. You're talking over two hundred square miles on the main island, most of it remote and secluded with plenty of places to land or dock without anyone seeing you."

The ultimate hiding place, Nolan thought. Creed let out a loud woof, his back straight and tail rigid. Nolan traced the line of his focus and saw Ava's little girl skipping their way, tendrils of red hair bouncing out from under the hood of her pink jacket. "I gotta go," he told Penn, and made plans to meet him first thing in the morning at the Burkes' place to question Mac.

Nolan bent down as Rose approached. "Hello again. Are you here with your mom?"

She ignored him, instead clasped her hands around Creed's snout and smiled. Dog and girl reunited, both sporting silly grins. Nolan glanced up and saw Mac coming their way, carrying two foam to-go cups.

He turned back to Rose. "Creed really likes you. He doesn't like everyone, you know. Just special people, like you."

Mac towered over them. "Rose, you know better than to

walk away without telling me." His voice was stern, but Nolan didn't see anger, just concern in his eyes.

Rose barely glanced his way before turning her attention back to Creed.

Nolan stood face-to-face with Mac and tried to keep things light. "She likes my dog."

"I see that. What were you talking to her about?"

"Nothing. I only asked if she was alone. I didn't see you, so I thought maybe she was lost."

Mac glared at him. "She's fine. Just got away from me for a second. Come on now, Rose. Let's go."

Rose clenched Creed's collar and stared up at Nolan.

"Right now," Mac reiterated.

Nolan bent down to her eye level. "Go with your grandfather. I'll bring Creed to your house tomorrow, and you two can play some more then."

Rose gave him a quick smile before leaving Creed and grasping Mac's outstretched hand. Mac glowered at Nolan a moment. He glanced worriedly at Rose before turning away— a "tell" to Nolan's practiced eye.

As the two of them crossed the parking lot, Nolan redirected his gaze and looked out over the churning water, his mind reeling. *Rose knows something.*

Ava was still in the attic reading through the newspaper clippings when she heard Mac drive up. She crammed them back into the shoebox, replaced the lid and hesitated. These clippings had been stored away in Kevin's belongings. Why had he taken so much interest in the missing hiker? Had she been a school friend, maybe even a girlfriend? But Nolan had said she'd been a visitor from the big city.

A heavy shadow of dread overcame Ava. Her instinct was to destroy the clippings and pretend she'd never seen them. Instead, she stood and tucked the box under her arm.

She reached the bottom of the stairs as the front door popped open. "Hey, you two. How was...oh."

Rose was sound asleep, her cheek pressed against Mac's shoulder, her arms hanging limp and a mop of red hair covering her face. Mac held his finger to his lips and carried her into the family room, gently lowering her onto the sofa. He tucked a throw blanket around her little body and headed into the kitchen.

He began riffling through the cabinet. "Where's the tea?"

"Tea? Thought you had hot chocolate by the dock. Was Jensen's closed?"

"No, we had hot cocoa. It didn't settle so great on my stomach, though. Thought I'd have some chamomile tea. Irene used to make it for me. It always did the trick."

Ava was surprised to hear him say Irene's name. He rarely spoke of her. Or Kevin. Mac kept everything bottled up inside himself. She thought of the clippings and realized Kevin had done the same. Like father, like son.

"Sit down, and I'll get it." She put the shoebox on the table and retrieved the tea from the pantry. She glanced his way as she set the kettle to boil. "You thinking of Irene tonight?"

"Guess I am."

"And Kevin?"

"Every day."

"You never talk about it...his death, I mean."

"Don't want to upset you. Or Rose." He rubbed at his stomach. "Talking about it's not going to change anything."

She took down a couple mugs and set out the box of tea bags. Steam billowed from the kettle. "Jane and I talked today. She told me that I should express my feelings more."

"Counselors always say that type of thing."

"I think she may be right. She says that I need to let Rose see me mourn."

The shrill whistle of the kettle filled the room. Ava poured the boiling water and carried the mugs to the table. Mac was shuffling through the tea box. She sat next to him. "I've been thinking about what Jane told us, that Rose may have seen the shooter. She said I should take her in to talk to the sheriff, but maybe Rose should talk to that agent instead. She seems to like him."

"We saw him down on the dock tonight."

"You did? What did...?"

"We hardly talked. He mentioned coming by in the morning. To question me, I assume."

"Maybe I'll tell him about Rose's picture when he's here."

Mac frowned. "He'll want to question her. I don't like the idea of that."

"They can't just question her on the spot. They'd have to set something up officially. Jane said she'd be there with Rose if it came to that. But I probably need to let them know about the picture at least. It's a murder investigation."

"We'll see. Let me think on it tonight."

She tapped the lid of the shoebox. "Is this yours?" she asked.

"No. Never seen it before." He opened it, saw the newspaper articles and pulled reading glasses from his front pocket. His eyes grew wide. "Where'd you find this?"

"In Kevin's things. All the articles are about a hiker that went missing ten years ago."

Mac took a shaky sip of tea. "Looks that way."

Ava sipped her own tea and waited for him to say more. He shuffled through the articles, his face growing ashen. "Mac, what is it? You don't look well. Do you know why Kevin would—"

A gunshot and shattering glass exploded from the other room. Ava ducked, screamed, then leaped up again. *Rose!* She launched herself toward the living room. Rose sat on the sofa, her face a mask of horror; shards of glass from the living room window littered the room. "Get down, get down!" Ava screamed.

Another shot. Pieces of drywall pelted them, white dust

filling the air. She lunged toward Rose, then felt herself being pushed forward as Mac fell on top of them both.

Another shot and the sound of drywall pieces crumbling onto the floor. Ava buried her head against Rose, crying and praying. *Help us, Father. Please help us.*

The room grew still. They huddled on the floor; Ava's heart pounded in her chest. She clung to Rose, felt her baby girl trembling and heard Mac's heavy breath near her ear.

Mac suddenly bolted upward and snatched them off the floor, half dragging, half leading them to his den. He pushed them toward the desk. "Get down between the desk and wall."

"My phone," she said. "It's in my purse, in the kitchen."

He tossed his cell onto the desktop for her and punched numbers into the gun cabinet lock. He took out two guns, loading one with large red shells. He handed it to her. "This is a shotgun. It's ready to go. Just point and pull the trigger. Understood?"

She swallowed and nodded, the gun heavy and cold in her hands.

Mac shoved a full magazine into the other rifle and snapped back a lever. The gun was long and black and had a scope on the top. "I'm locking you in here," he said. "If that door opens, look first but don't hesitate to shoot."

Could she pull the trigger? Shoot someone? "Stay with us," she pleaded.

"I can't. I've got to stop this evil before it comes in here. Before it hurts you or Rose."

Ava understood. Mac was going to confront the shooter outside, not in here where either one of them could be hurt.

At the door, he turned back, his gaze landing on Rose, who hunched on the floor and silently clenched her knees, her pupils large dark pools of panic against her pale face.

The love Ava saw in Mac's eyes as he looked at Rose penetrated the fear in her own heart. She gripped the shotgun tighter. *I can do this. I can protect my child. Whatever it takes.*

Chapter Eight

"Help is on the way, ma'am." The emergency dispatcher's voice was calm and reassuring. "Who's in the house with you?"

"Me and my daughter. My father-in-law is outside looking for the shooter."

"What's your daughter's name?"

"Rose."

"And how old is Rose?"

"Six. Please tell them to hurry."

"They're on their way. Is Rose right there with you?"

"Yes, she's next to me. We're in the back room, and I... I have a gun. A shotgun."

"Is your father-in-law armed?"

"Yes."

The phone, lying on the desk inches from where she rested the barrel of the shotgun, went silent as the dispatcher switched over to relay information. The stock of the gun slipped in Ava's sweat-slicked palms and blood pulsated in her ears. Next to her, Rose's breath came in ragged spurts, her body trembling. Ava wanted to hold her but didn't dare let go of the gun. She kept it pointed at the door, her finger on the cold metal next to the trigger. Sirens faintly wailed in the distance, giving her hope.

"It's okay, sweetie. Don't be scared. Mommy's here." Yet her own pulse pounded. She listened for any sign of activity from outside or movement inside the house and prayed. *Oh, God, make them hurry.*

"Hang in there, ma'am. A unit is five minutes out."

Five minutes. Relief warred with anxiety. They were so close, but Mac was out there with a shooter. A lot could happen in five minutes. "Please tell them to hurry."

Her gaze slid to a clock on the far wall. *Tick, tock, tick, tock…*the long pendulum swung back and forth, like a heartbeat. The clock should've comforted her, shaped like a little Swiss chalet, topped with a carved bird above a half dozen oak leaves, long pendulum and weights, and a tiny door that held a colorful cuckoo that popped out on the hour. The gaudiest thing ever, a wedding gift from Irene to Mac, and it'd hung here in the den ever since Ava had known Kevin. Mac cherished it. Rose was fascinated by it. And now it mocked Ava as its second hand ticked off each moment in slow motion. *Tick, tock, tick, tock—*

A blast of three quick shots rang out, and Ava screamed, shifted, snapped the shotgun barrel toward the window across the room. Rose clung to her. Her body trembled against Ava's back.

"Ma'am, what is it? What's happening?" came the now anxious voice from the phone.

Her throat constricted with terror. Saliva pooled in her cheeks. She swallowed hard. "Gunfire," she managed to answer. "Outside the window."

"Are they firing at you?"

Ava kept the shotgun pointed at the window, staring at her own pale reflection in the black square of glass. "No. No, but Mac—"

A sound came from the front of the house.

Ava strained her ears, struggling to hear over her thundering heartbeat. *Footsteps!* Someone was inside the house and coming toward the den. Mac or...? She swung the shotgun back to the door and slid her hand over the desktop, her fingers finally connecting with the phone. The dispatcher was still talking when she disconnected and silenced the ringer.

"Rose, listen to me," she hissed. "I want you to crawl under the desk and stay there. Do you hear me? Do it now."

Rose squirreled past her and burrowed herself under the heavy oak desk, its front panel hiding her little legs and feet.

The footsteps came closer. And a low, guttural sound, like a wounded animal.

Terror thundered down on Ava, twisting in her gut. Her hands turned icy and sweaty as she slid her finger closer to the trigger, her gaze locked on the door. "Mac? Is that you, Mac?" But her voice was nothing more than a dry breath.

The doorknob turned.

Ava moved her finger onto the trigger.

A crack appeared as the door opened, and a low moaning sound reached her ears. Then the door swung completely open and Mac stood there, his hand over his shoulder, his skin ashen, his features frozen in pain.

Ava let go of the gun and watched in horror as Mac tottered, then collapsed forward onto the floor.

Nolan gripped the steering wheel and pushed down on the accelerator. Dark trees blurred by the window. Creed hunkered on the back-seat floorboard, panting, echoing Nolan's anxiety. Penn had called ten minutes ago reporting that shots had been fired at the Burke place. Nolan couldn't get there fast enough.

He thought of Ava and Rose. Ava's face overlaid the face of the dead woman in the barn, and he felt heartsick and pressed the accelerator harder. He tried to shake off the image, but thoughts of Rose's little arms around Creed didn't help. What would he find at the scene? He'd only just met them, but the silent Rose tugged at his heartstrings. If he was honest with himself, so did Ava. His mind raced over every word Ava had said to him—had there been any clue that she'd known she was in danger? Something he should have picked up on? Any way he could have prevented this? The thought of either one of them being harmed cut him to the core.

Four county units and an ambulance were already on the scene when he arrived. Lights pulsated the night air, casting an eerie glow over the property. He parked behind a cruiser, the frigid lake wind hitting his face and seeping through his jacket as he scanned the scene for Penn and instead spied Ava and Rose huddled together in the back of a cruiser. He took in a long breath and headed toward them, Creed at his side sniffing the air and snorting.

Nolan showed his ID to the female deputy who hovered nearby and popped open the back door, kneeling next to Ava and Rose. "Are you two okay?" Creed pushed beside Nolan and placed his front paws on the floorboard and nudged his nose against Rose.

The girl didn't respond to Creed, only stared at Nolan with eyes round and dark like two black wells of despair.

Ava's lips were drawn tight, her voice weak. "It's Mac… something's happened to Mac. They won't let me back in the house to check on him."

"Was he shot?"

"No. I don't think so. I didn't see any blood. He was upset earlier, and he didn't look good, and…and…maybe it was his heart." She trembled and pulled Rose closer.

Nolan reached in and touched Ava's shoulder. He half expected her to pull away, but instead her free hand reached up to graze his fingertips, her glistening eyes pleading with him for help. He nodded. "I'll go see what I can find out. I'll be right back."

Seeing a flash of fear in the little girl's eyes, he said, "Creed will be right here with you." He led Creed to the opposite side of the cruiser, opened the door and watched as the dog scurried inside and perched on the seat next to Ava and Rose, his back rigid, ears high and his muscles rippling with alertness. *Like a watchman in the night*, Nolan thought. *Scripture.* When was the last time he'd thought of Scripture?

He went to find Penn inside the family room. A young deputy was with him, listening intently to directives. Shattered glass and plaster peppered the hardwood floor, a blanket was crumpled on the sofa and a small side table overturned, its contents spilled over the floor.

"Someone shot at them," Penn said as Nolan approached. "Three, maybe more, shots initially. We're assessing the scene."

Nolan looked about at the damage as he asked, "Mac?"

Penn thumbed toward the back room. "Looks like a heart attack. He's stable now, but they're almost ready to transport him. I'll get a statement later at the hospital. He couldn't tell me anything."

"What did you get from Ms. Burke?" He thought *Ava* but kept it professional. It was one thing to call Mr. Burke "Mac," but...

"She's shell-shocked at this point, so not a whole lot. Just basics. Seems the kid was sleeping in here and she and Mac were in the kitchen when the first shot was fired." The sheriff clapped his hands to emphasize the shot. "Then both she and Mac ran for the girl, got her down before two more shots penetrated the room. Somehow they got back there," Pen added, pointing down the hall to the room Nolan had been in before. "That's Mac's den. There's a gun case back there."

Nolan nodded, and Penn continued, "Seems Mac loaded a shotgun for the woman and took an automatic rifle outside with him, scouting the property. The woman stayed in the den with the kid and called 911. While on the call, three more shots were fired. It's not clear who fired those. And it's too dark to see much outside at this point."

The sound of moving wheels and jingling equipment filled

the room. The first responders pushed Mac on a stretcher through the house and out the front door.

Penn sighed. "Ten to one, these people know more than they've told us and this was an effort to try to silence them. They're lucky they weren't killed. All of them."

Nolan pointed at the ceiling where three bullet holes were visible, three small holes disbursed in a tight pattern. If all three shots had hit at the same point, high and grouped together, then... "The shooter wasn't trying to kill anyone, just scare them."

Penn glanced up and nodded. But the sheriff was right about one thing: someone in this house knew more than they were saying. The question was who? And how far was the shooter willing to go to keep them quiet?

Nolan left Penn and his team and went outside to retrieve his dog and check on Ava and Rose.

Ava's eyes were red and her lips tight. Everything about her spoke of the tension that kept her tears at bay, at least for now. He understood. He'd seen it before, felt it as well. You toughened up, stayed strong, got things in order, and then, only then, it hit, and other emotions took over.

"He's going to be okay, but it'll take a few minutes to get him hooked up to transport." She released a long breath and muttered a prayer of thanksgiving. He glanced at Rose, sitting with her head resting against Creed's fur. "I need to borrow my buddy. He's got some work to do. Then I'll get him back to you, I promise."

Rose nodded and kissed Creed's snout before Nolan called him out of the cruiser. Most of the scene investigation would be put off until daybreak, when evidence could more easily be found and marked. But Creed's nose didn't require light, and any scents left behind from the shooter would be fresh now.

Nolan retrieved a heavy-duty flashlight from the cruiser and attached Creed's lead. Instantly his dog snapped to attention, lifted his black snout to fill his lungs with air and pranced excitedly.

The cord of the lead was taut in Nolan's hands as his dog maneuvered over the ground, taking in scents. Back and forth, Creed pulled, his fur rippling under the flashlight's beam, before he suddenly stopped near the house, turned around several times with his nose still to the ground, tail flat and rigid. He was onto something. Nolan knelt and released the lead, letting his dog work freely.

Creed was trained for tracking but also sniffing out drugs, gunpowder residue and blood, among other things. And he was good at his job.

Nolan stayed still, maintaining his distance and watching as Creed worked his way around the yard. From his vintage point, Nolan couldn't tell where the scent was leading him. He lost sight of him in the shadows of a tall pine, when Creed let loose with a low, mournful whine.

Nolan scrambled to catch up with him, focusing his beam on the area. "Good boy!" He leaned down and gave him a pat. Creed shook with excited anticipation of a successful find.

"Over here," Nolan called out to one of the deputies. "He's hit on casings."

The deputy jogged over and looked—three casings nestled together on the grass. "I'll be danged." He shot Creed an admiring look. "We'll get it marked. Looks like this might have been where the first round of shots was fired."

Nolan nodded, then turned to the sound of heavy doors slamming shut. He clipped on Creed's lead and hustled back to the driveway to where Ava sat in her own car now, eyeing the ambulance, hands tight on the wheel, ready to follow it. Rose was in the back seat, her face still pale and her gaze glued to Creed.

"Are you okay to drive?" Nolan asked when Ava looked up at him through the open window.

She nodded, sighed and forced her left hand off the wheel, let it rest on the window's edge. "I just feel…"

"What?" he prompted, and stepped closer, hoping she'd reveal something she'd been holding back.

"So angry and helpless." Her voice rang with the determination of someone willing to do anything to help. And with the frustration of knowing sometimes nothing helped. Instinctively he covered her hand with his and instantly felt a tremble. In his hand? Hers?

She pulled her hand away quickly and snapped her eyes to him. But the look she gave him didn't reprimand his touch. It questioned.

The ambulance started to move, and she took the wheel, her focus again on Mac.

"Creed and I need to finish here," Nolan told her. "Then we'll meet you at the hospital."

He started to back away but stopped when she glanced at him. He saw her rubbing her left fingers gently on the wheel. "Thank you."

She'd whispered the words, but he heard them clearly, and they echoed in his mind as she drove away.

Ava thought she'd climb out of her own skin if she had to wait another second for news about Mac. He'd been rushed forty-five minutes south to the hospital in Larium and taken directly for an emergency angioplasty. It was Thursday already and almost two in the morning. Nolan and Creed had eventually caught up to them, and they'd been in a waiting room together for a couple of hours, desperate for news of Mac's surgery.

Nolan handed her a paper cup of hot coffee. "Drink this. It'll help."

She smiled gratefully, her fingers brushing against his as she reached for the cup. The same tingle she'd felt when he'd covered her hand at the car flustered her again. Her cheeks warmed, and she glanced at Rose, asleep next to her on a bench. She'd called Jane and told her everything. Their friend was on her way, but Ava was grateful for Nolan's presence. And Creed's. The dog was curled on the floor near Rose. He hadn't left her side this whole time.

Ava sipped the hot liquid. Her muscles began to relax, but the tenseness was quickly replaced with overwhelming sadness. Mac was Rose's world. What would happen if he didn't pull through this? She reached over and placed her hand on Rose's shoulder, felt her body rise and fall with each breath. Squeezing her eyes shut, she whispered another prayer, ending with a mouthed *Amen.* She opened her eyes again to see Nolan look away quickly from her lips, his gaze avoiding hers, followed by a self-conscious clearing of his throat as if her praying had somehow caught in his windpipe.

The silent awkwardness that followed was interrupted by "Family of Mac Burke?" A middle-aged woman in green scrubs had come into the room.

Ava stood. "Yes."

"He's in recovery. You can go back and see him now."

"How is he?"

"He's doing well. The doctor will be in to talk to you in a few minutes. Follow me."

Ava looked to Nolan. He nodded. "We'll keep her safe."

They passed several doors with a few left ajar, exposing rooms with patients in beds and loved ones in chairs, watching and waiting, maybe praying—little vignettes of suffering and hope, people in different stages of illness, all of it life-threatening to some degree. How did this happen to Mac? He was the healthiest, strongest person she knew.

The woman stopped and opened the door to a room. Inside, a nurse was seeing to an IV bag.

And suddenly the rug of security was snatched out from underneath Ava, and a sense of vulnerability overwhelmed her. She crossed the room and looked down on his weathered face, touched his cold hand. Tubes and beeping machines, oxygen hissing and clicking. He was so still, a ghost of the Mac she knew.

"Oh, Mac." Ava pulled a chair next to his bed and took his hand.

"He's a fighter, that's for sure," the nurse said.

Ava nodded and squinted at her name badge.

The nurse flipped it forward. "I'm Selma." She moved to the other side of Mac's bed and checked the monitor. "Are you Mr. Burke's daughter?"

"Daughter-in-law. My…" She stopped herself from telling her about Kevin's passing. She used to speak confidently about herself, but since Kevin had died, she didn't know who she was anymore. Ava, Kevin's wife? Ava, Kevin's widow? Lately she put everything into just being Ava, Rose's mom, and avoided thinking too much about anything else.

Mac stirred and opened his eyes. Ava squeezed his hand. "There you are. How are you?"

"Gonna be fine," he said, his breath shallow.

"You scared me." She fought the tears forming on the edges of her eyes.

The nurse patted her shoulder. "The doctor will be right in," she said, and asked Ava if she needed anything before popping out to take care of another patient.

"I'm here for you, Mac. Don't worry. We'll get through this together." But even as she said the words, her mind turned over obstacles. Someone had shot at them. They couldn't go back to Mac's house. Where could they go to be safe? And how would she care for him and Rose?

"Where is Rose?"

"She's safe. Don't worry. You just had a heart attack. You need—"

"Where is Rose?" he bit out.

"In the waiting room with Agent Shea."

He seemed to relax a little. "You and Rose are in danger.

The killer must know that Rose saw something. That's the only reason I can figure that someone would shoot at us. He must have been watching for me to return with her."

"I've been thinking of going back to Detroit, staying with friends. But I won't leave you here. So, maybe we should—"

"You can't outrun this. They'll follow you, watching and waiting for the right time to…to take another shot."

Ava picked at the edge of the blanket. "I heard three more shots after you went outside. I was so afraid."

"Shooter was there lurking around the window. I fired high, and he took off for the woods. Wish now I would have aimed to kill. Just couldn't without a good visual on my target."

His hand shook inside hers. Ava was sure Mac had killed before. In Vietnam. He'd alluded to it but never elaborated about his wartime experiences.

"I thought you'd been killed," she said. "And I—"

"I can take care of myself. Don't worry about me. I need you to focus on you and Rose. This guy isn't going to stop."

Her mind reeled. "I don't know what to do."

"Go to the sheriff. Tell him about Rose, what she may have seen. Ask for protection. But promise me you won't go back to the house. It's not safe."

Ava nodded. "Mac…is there a chance that Kevin was involved in all of this somehow? With those clippings and what Derek Williams said about him being here that day when—"

"Stay away from Williams. That man's no good. Never was. He was a horrible influence on Kevin."

"What do you mean?"

Mac shook his head, wincing from the pain. "Nothing. Never mind."

Ava lurched forward. "You're hurting. Let me call the nurse."

"No." He clenched her hand. "I'm fine. Please, listen to me. Nothing good comes from digging up the past. My son was a good man. He loved you and Rose, did right by you two. That's all that matters."

"But..."

"Let it go, Ava."

She stayed with Mac until he fell asleep and then returned to the waiting room. Jane had just joined them. Ava went straight to her, and the two embraced. Jane pulled back and studied Ava's face. "Mac is the strongest man I know. He's going to be fine—don't you worry."

Ava swiped at her cheek and introduced Jane to Nolan and Creed, just saying that she was a close family friend.

"What are you going to do to keep Ava and Rose safe?" Jane demanded of the agent. "Someone shot at them in their own home. They can't go back there." For the first time since she'd known Jane, Ava saw the calm counselor losing her composure.

"I agree, ma'am."

His instant agreement allowed Jane to take a calming breath, then she turned to Ava. "Come stay with me. Just until they catch this guy. I can help you with Rose. And Mac, too. He'll need some extra care after they discharge him."

Ava squeezed her hand. "Thank you. I can't tell you how blessed we are to have you in our lives. But I... Why don't you go see Mac? He'd love to see you, and there are a few things that I need to talk to Nolan about."

Jane paused briefly, then gave her another hug and glanced at the sleeping Rose with concern before heading to see Mac. Ava pulled Nolan aside and kept her voice low. "Jane is a counselor. Rose's counselor. And..." She rubbed the sore muscles in her neck, suddenly aware of how awful she must've looked. And smelled. She'd give anything to go home, take a long hot shower, slip into her comfy pj's and snuggle on the sofa with Rose. But that was impossible now. "I think I know why someone was shooting at us."

"Did Rose see something the day Lindsey Webber was killed?"

Ava blinked. *He already suspected it?* She pulled out her cell phone and scrolled to the photo she'd taken of Rose's drawing. "She drew this picture. This is the barn and Lindsey, I assume. And here…" She tapped the photo and widened the view. "This is what scares me. It looks like she's drawn someone in the woods. She won't talk about it. She won't talk about anything."

Nolan took the phone. His features hardened. "When did she draw this?"

"Yesterday." Sweat pricked along Ava's hairline. The truth. She had to tell the truth. "But I suspected that she'd seen something before that."

His jaw twitched. "What do you mean?"

Ava glanced worriedly at Rose, still asleep on the bench. "The day we found Lindsey, Rose seemed to already know Lindsey was in the barn. Like she'd seen her go in there, or…" She shuddered. "Or she'd already found her body."

"And you didn't tell the sheriff this?" His voice was calm but with an undercurrent of suspicion or maybe disappointment.

Ava's palms began to sweat. Was she going to be in trouble? She'd done what any good mother would do, right? Tried to protect her child.

She scrambled to explain her actions: "I didn't know what she'd seen, and I was worried that the sheriff's questions would add to her trauma. But yesterday when she drew this, well, I planned to tell you first thing this morning, but then…" She clutched her midsection, her stomach rolling with nausea. Maybe if she'd gone to the sheriff right away none of this would have happened. She hadn't protected Rose at all, in fact—if anything, she'd put her in more danger.

He handed back the phone. "Is there anything else you haven't told me?" All professional now, but still an annoyed undertone tinged his words.

"No. Nothing." She'd answered a little too quickly, covered

with a tiny cough, reached for her coffee and took a long sip. Anything to avoid Nolan's probing stare.

"Nothing," she repeated. Hiding Rose's words about "the lady that got shot" in the barn earlier had endangered them— nearly gotten them killed. But the fact that her late husband had collected newspaper clippings about a hiker who'd gone missing ten years ago had nothing to do with Lindsey Webber's recent murder or the shooter bent on hurting them. Did it?

Nolan left Creed with Ava and Rose and went outside to his vehicle to make a couple calls. Ten minutes later, he had a plan in place for keeping Ava and Rose safe over the next few days while Mac recovered in the hospital. He locked the rental and leaned against the bumper, staring at the hospital entrance lit up like a porch light against the dark night. Ava wasn't telling him everything. She didn't fully trust him, and that bothered him, but the question was what was she holding back? And was it something that would put her and Rose in even more danger?

Back in the waiting room, he explained his plan to Ava. "Logistically, Mac's isn't a safe place for you to stay. It's too remote and, with the woods, impossible to secure. I'd like for you and Rose to stay in a hotel room adjoining my room. Just temporarily. I've called for another agent, a female agent, to aid with the investigation and to help protect Rose."

"Thank you, but I think we'd be better off at Jane's place. Rose has been there before, and she trusts Jane. So do I."

And you don't trust me. But he understood. She barely knew him. "I'll need to see if that is safe enough. But either way, I'll need to talk to Rose," he said. "I'll need to question her about what she saw that night."

She lifted her chin. "Both Jane and I will be present when that happens."

"Sure. Right now, we need to get moving. It's only a couple more hours until sunrise, and I'd prefer to get her settled under the cover of dark. Make a list of things you need from your house. I'll have a deputy pick them up and bring them over later."

Thirty minutes passed, and the three of them were now traveling Highway 41 back to Sculpin Bay. He'd snuck Ava and Rose into the car from a side door of the hospital and had taken evasive maneuvers for the first few streets to ensure they had no tail. Now they rode an empty highway. The pitch blackness had given way to deep blue, the stars were gone and the moon hovered low and silver near the horizon. So much promise in the start of a new day.

He glanced at Ava in the seat next to him, light from her screen illuminating her profile as she searched something on her phone. Her features showed strength and resolve and, to his relief, more calmness. In the back seat Creed sat upright next to Rose, her arm swung over his neck, her head resting on his back. Creed seemed happy. Nolan got it. Something about having Ava and Rose in the car made him feel content, too. Maybe *complete* was a better word.

They entered the village, and Ava looked up from her phone. "Turn up here," she said. "Jane's house is on the left."

The cottage was small but tidy, with a wide white trim, grilled windows and a postage stamp–sized front yard encompassed by a white wooden fence. Cute, Nolan thought, but *secure* was another question. When he'd talked to Jane, she'd explained about the neighborhood and its safety, but he knew all neighborhoods could be vulnerable. He scanned the entrance points, the surrounding homes, a clump of pines on the right side of the house.

As planned, Jane had left the hospital before them and had the garage door raised. She was waiting inside, and as soon as Nolan pulled in, she pushed a button to lower the door behind them. Nolan followed Jane into the home with Rose slumped on his shoulder. They moved silently through the front room, with its oversize floral prints and handwoven rugs over a rich but aged hardwood floor, to one of the upstairs bedrooms. Ava and Creed followed. Nolan lowered Rose gently onto the bed, and Ava removed her little girl's shoes and rolled her under the comforter. He checked the window and made sure it was latched securely and said good-night to both women.

The motel was just a few blocks away, but instead of going back to his room, Nolan parked his car on the curb in front of Jane's house, Creed curled on the passenger seat, already making his usual sleep sounds. Nolan checked messages, found one from Cam.

ETA: 2 p.m.

Then a second message—this one Cam had sent earlier, but he'd missed it.

Mac Burke has an expunged felony for aggravated assault and battery.

He glanced back at the house, saw an upstairs window with the shadow of someone passing by before the light flickered off. And he wondered what other shadows he would discover in the lives of this family.

Chapter Nine

Before the first footsteps or the snap of a twig, a hint of heavy breathing made her sense him. Run, she told herself. And she did. Her legs were like mower blades, circular steel tines rotating and chopping through the forest brush, while branches reached out and snatched her hair with their angry fingers, tearing it from her scalp until she was completely bald, her head a misshaped bowling ball, too heavy for her body, for her legs. The tines slowed, the breathing coming closer until the earth slipped out from under her and she realized she'd run right off a cliff, her body plummeting into the cold lake water—only it wasn't cold but hot and...

Ava woke with a start and startled again at Rose's blue eyes inches from her face, her little fingers tangled in her mother's hair.

She bolted up in bed. "You know I hate it when you do that. How long have you been staring at me?"

Rose answered with a quick shrug and pointed to the bed.

Ava swung her legs over the side and stared down at the wet spot on the sheet. "Oh no. You had an accident?"

Her daughter shrunk back, her chin quivering.

Ava reached out to her. "No, it's okay, sweetie. It's not your fault. It just happens." Though this was anything but okay. The bed-wetting had started a little after Kevin died but had subsided over the past month. Ava thought they'd worked through it, and now...*this.*

She picked up Rose and headed into the bathroom. A short time later, after both were cleaned and dressed, she stripped the sheets from the bed and checked her phone. Just a little after nine and no messages from the hospital, but several from Yvette. The first had been sent around eight this morning.

Sorry to miss your messages. Went to bed early. Had my phone off. Heard what happened. Is everyone okay? Call me.

Not surprising that Yvette had heard what had happened. News of a shooting would send shock waves through a small village like Sculpin Bay. Yvette's second text had been sent a half hour ago.

Drove out to check on you. Cops everywhere. Where are you? I'm worried.

Cops everywhere. Something niggled at Ava's mind, but she wrote it off as mental goose bumps that came with knowing bullet holes riddled Mac's house. And of course the cops would be there—it was a crime scene. She started typing a reply.

Rose tugged at her arm. "Hold on a sec, honey." Ava finished the text and turned her full attention to her daughter. "Bet you're starving. Come on—let's see what Jane has in her fridge."

They made their way downstairs, Rose's hand sweaty against her palm. She gave it a squeeze. "Everything's going to be okay. You're safe here with Mommy and Ms. Jane."

The smell of coffee and bacon drifted from the kitchen. *Thank You, God.* Ava's brain was a foggy mess, and her stomach raw with hunger. When had she last eaten? Oh, poor

Rose—when had she last fed her daughter? Hot chocolate and a candy bar at the hospital? She shook her head, details of the last day evading her.

They passed by the front window, and Ava peeked through the curtains. Nolan had parked out front the night before, but a sheriff's car with a male deputy had taken his place. She wondered when the female agent Nolan had mentioned would arrive.

"There's my girl." Jane's voice was exceptionally cheery as they entered the kitchen. She helped Rose onto a bar stool, where bacon and juice were waiting. "Do you like pancakes or waffles?" she asked Rose, then turned around to get something from the fridge.

"Pancakes," Rose whispered to Jane's back.

Ava's heart soared, but Jane had warned her about overreacting when Rose spoke, so she kept quiet and gave her a quick hug before heading to the coffee maker. Cream, sugar and several gulps later, her head began to clear.

"I already talked to Mac this morning," Jane said from the pantry. "He's doing well. Tired. But that's to be expected. Officers boarded that window last night, but he wants the glass fixed. You know how he is. I can call if you want."

"Thanks, Jane. I appreciate it. Glad he's doing okay. I'll give him a call soon."

The local paper was folded on the counter. Ava caught a glimpse of the headlines. *Shots Fired at Prior Murder Scene.* She carefully slipped the paper under her arm and migrated to the kitchen table with her coffee and a couple slices of bacon. The article was brief, without a photo.

On Wednesday, at approximately 9:30 p.m., the sheriff's department responded to a report of shots fired at a rural residence on Woodland Road. Upon arrival, they discovered one adult male who had sustained a non–gun related injury. Officers also discovered an adult female and a minor barricaded inside the home.

The initial investigation reports that the residents were inside the home when an unknown shooter fired three shots through the window, nearly missing the minor resident. Three more shots were subsequently fired. The shooter then fled the scene.

One adult male was transported to the hospital in a life-threatening state and is currently reported to be in stable condition.

Investigators have not stated if this crime is connected to the murder that occurred on the same property last week. The victims' names will not be released at this time.

If you have any information that could assist in the investigation of this case, please contact the County Sheriff's Department.

Ava almost laughed out loud. Like the whole village didn't know in whose barn a dead body had been found and when.

She set the article aside and listened to the happy noises coming from where Jane and Rose were mixing pancake batter. *Thank You, God, for Jane and her willingness to help us in our time of need.*

The doorbell rang, startling the house into silence.

Jane turned off the stove and snatched up Rose and stepped back against the cabinet. "Who would that be?"

"I don't know." Ava rose and glanced out the front window. A sheriff's deputy was on the front step, and next to him was... "Yvette!"

Ava's mood instantly lifted as she headed for the door. "It's okay," she told the deputy. "She's family." She kicked herself for not informing the deputy that she'd texted Yvette to stop by. Too many things to remember.

He nodded and backed up. Yvette passed by, shooting him

a sideways look. "Didn't know you would have a bodyguard. I just came by to check on you and give this to Rose." She held up a pink gift bag. "I've been so worried about her—and you. Both of you."

"We're okay. I'm so happy you're here. I need to talk to you." Ava thanked the deputy and shut the door. She led Yvette to the kitchen.

Yvette gave Jane a curt "Hello" and bent down to Rose's eye level. "Got you a little something." She held out the bag.

Rose tore into it, pulling out a stuffed pony—white with big blue eyes and a pink mane. She smiled at Yvette and skipped into the family room, cradling the pony like a baby.

"What a perfect gift," Ava said. "Thank you."

Jane chitchatted a little before excusing herself. "I'll finish making these pancakes when you're done visiting. Rose is too excited to eat now anyway. Nice to see you again, Yvette."

As soon as she left, Yvette did a small circuit around the room. "Never been in her house before. Cute... I guess, about twenty years ago."

"Be nice," Ava warned, but she couldn't help smiling.

Yvette sighed. "I was worried about Rose. But she seems okay." The two of them had settled at the kitchen table, Rose playing with the pony in the family room. "Is Mac okay? Your text said a heart attack, but the newspaper article made it sound like he was hurt."

"He's fine. They did an angioplasty late last night. He'll be in for a couple more days. It's Rose I'm really worried about. In some ways she's regressing again, but..." Ava told her about Rose speaking earlier. "Jane is so good with her."

"I'm sure she is." Yvette fussed with a set of bangles on her wrist. "It's all over town that you were the ones shot at, and guess who called me this morning? Derek."

Ava set her coffee down. "What did he want?"

"Information, but I didn't give him any. He'd heard what had happened and had all sorts of questions, like how you were doing and if you were sticking around now or planning to go back to Detroit. He said you two had some road incident the other day. He even asked if you'd talked about him. I felt like I was talking to a high school guy with a crush, but then he told me that you'd acted strangely out on the road and he was concerned about you. What's that about?"

"Me? He's the one... Oh, maybe... I mean, it probably did seem like I was acting weird, but for good reason, in my opinion." Ava rubbed her temples. "After you left the diner the other day, he sort of asked me out."

"What?"

"He wanted to get together to 'talk about Kevin.' Old stories, he said."

"He moves fast. What did you say?"

She rolled her eyes. "Seriously?"

Yvette scoffed. "You're not ready to date—I get it."

"Not to mention he gives me the creeps. He didn't want to take no for an answer, then he followed me home."

Yvette's eyes bugged.

"And that incident on the road he mentioned, it was his fault." Ava filled her in on what had happened that day, her cheeks burning hot. "Maybe I overreacted. Turns out he was just trying to return a bracelet that I'd lost back at the diner. But chasing me down like that? It was..."

"Aggressive." Yvette crossed her legs. "That's Derek. He's always been that way. He's that way in business, too—that's why we don't always get along." She shook her head. "Still can't believe he asked you out after just meeting you."

"Maybe I misunderstood him. But it doesn't matter. I'm not dating anyone. And there's no chance I would ever be alone with him. He scares me."

"Nah, he's harmless. Trust me. I've known Derek since... forever. He's just a good ol' boy who thinks too much of himself. Lived around here his whole life." She smiled mischievously. "He is sort of good-looking, though."

"Sounds like you want to go out with him."

"That'd be a disaster. I can't stand being with him long enough to work through a house deal, let alone a relationship."

They laughed, then Ava grew serious again. "He said something..." Mac's words rang in her mind: *Nothing good comes from digging up the past.* But she needed Yvette's opinion. "Derek said that he saw Kevin here, in this area, the day he went down in the plane crash. But that can't be possible. His business meeting was in Green Bay. But I can't figure out why Derek would lie about it."

"Maybe he's not?"

Ava tensed. "Mac said he didn't see Kevin that day. There's no other reason why Kevin would come this far and not see his father. They were close."

Yvette nodded, but the look on her face told Ava all she needed to know. There were only a few reasons a husband lied to his wife, one of them being an affair. Her friend knew about that firsthand. She'd gotten married young, but her husband had cheated on her, then taken all their money and left. Yvette didn't let her troubles define her life, though. She'd rebounded, studied for her real-estate license and built a successful business. Ava admired her resilience.

She picked at one of the place mats, her fingers working the fringe along the edges.

"What is it?" Yvette asked. "What aren't you telling me?"

Ava hesitated, then let it spill about the newspaper clippings and the uneasy feeling she had about them. "It was before we'd met. Kevin never talked much about that time. His mother had just died, and he went a little wild. Rebelling and drinking, I don't know what else."

"I sort of remember that story about the missing hiker," Yvette said. "But it was so long ago. Kevin would have been... what?"

"Eighteen."

She offered a weak smile. "I wouldn't worry about it. He

was just a kid. Hard telling what he was thinking when he clipped those articles. Where are they now?"

"Where are...?" Ava grew silent. Panic gripped her as Yvette's earlier words churned in her mind. *Drove out to check on you. Cops everywhere.* She and Mac had been looking at the articles when the shooting had started, and she'd left them on the kitchen table.

In plain sight.

Facts were Nolan's thing, and he knew that while this drab, windowless hospital room looked clean, it was in fact a hotbed of roving microbes. Staph living on the faucet, fungus breeding on the floor, bacteria hanging on the bed rail... Creed, out in the car, was getting off easy. Nolan stood in place and kept his hands to himself as he questioned Mac. "Assault is a serious charge, Mr. Burke. Want to tell me about it?"

"Assault?" Mac's ears turned red. "If you mean that episode back in my twenties, that was nothing more than a bar fight that got carried away."

"Is that a habit, getting carried away?"

"Look, I'd just got back from Vietnam. I was messed up at the time. Things weren't easy over there. Ever fought in a war?"

Nolan frowned and took a deep breath.

"Figures," Mac said, not waiting for a reply. "I was long-range recon patrol. We risked everything to be the eyes and ears of the war. Sacrificed, too. I lost two good buddies out there. Civilians like you don't understand the sacrifices we make for our country."

Mac didn't realize it, but Nolan had been a marine, had served in Afghanistan and sacrificed more than most people knew. But right now, Nolan wanted to stay on topic and get the answers he needed. "The report says that you fired several shots last night."

"I got the right to defend my family. The shooter was out

back, near the window to the room where my girls were. You would've done the same thing."

Nolan nodded. "Did you get a good look at him?"

"No. It was dark, and his clothing was dark. But I could make out the gun in his hand."

"Can you describe it?"

Nolan jotted down a couple notes about Mac's description, then shifted his stance and the direction of his questions. "Do you remember the report of the hiker found dead on the island about ten years ago?"

Mac blinked, then answered, "Yeah, I remember. What about it?"

"Her name was Hannah Richter. Did you know her?"

"No."

"Did your son, Kevin, know her?"

"Never mentioned her. Why?"

The hospital bed did nothing to diminish Mac's hulking stature, but right now, he seemed to shrink into the sheets, his face flushed, and tiny beads of perspiration pricked the edges of his upper lip. Proven signs of stress. Or guilt.

"We found a box of newspaper clippings on your kitchen table."

Mac set his jaw and glanced away.

Nolan pushed him. "What made you want to clip out all those articles about Hannah? There must have been twenty or more, from all different sources. That seems like something an obsessed man would do. Is that it, Mac? Were you obsessed with Hannah Richter?"

Mac shook his head.

"We're looking into a connection between the deaths of Hannah Richter and Lindsey Webber, the girl found murdered in your barn."

Mac turned back and glared at him. "No, that's not even possible."

"And why's that?"

"The Richter girl was over ten years ago. What possible connection could there be?"

"Your barn, Mr. Burke. Your box of clippings. I'd say the connection is *you.*"

Nolan's phone buzzed. The old man's jaw relaxed at the interruption, and Nolan winced. Lousy timing. He could ignore it, but it had already broken the power of his accusation. He glanced down; it was Penn. He stepped out to the hallway.

"There's been a development," Penn said. "Island rangers called, wanted us to be on the lookout for an armed man and a possible abduction victim. Seems a hiker ran into what he thought was a dad and his teenage daughter out on the trail, but when the girl saw him, she called out for help and tried to break away. The guy pulled a gun on the hiker. They're searching the area now."

"The hiker give a description of the girl?"

"Young, late teens or early twenties, long brown hair, light skin, jeans, sweatshirt."

Nolan started for the parking lot. "Same age as our other missing girls. Send me everything you have. I've got to pick up a few supplies, then I'm heading over there."

Inside the Explorer, Creed greeted him excitedly, scurrying into the front seat, breathing his doggy breath, sour and meaty, in his face. Nolan gently nudged his snout away. "Give me some space, okay, buddy?" He reached for the hand sanitizer, squirted and rubbed before opening the earlier email from Cam. He checked the pictures of the missing women while Creed peered over his shoulder.

Several had brown hair and all of them were young, but only two had gone missing as recently as the past few months. His heart ached for these young girls and their families who had endured so much. *God help them.*

He blinked. How long had it been since he'd thought words like that? And why now? But he knew that answer: Seeing Ava praying earlier in the hospital waiting room had reignited an old conflict within him. Something about how she'd looked with her head bowed, eyes closed and her lips moving softly. Beautiful, yes, but something more. Peaceful.

If only peace could find him. Maybe he was supposed to find it, but... He stared at the women's faces again. Where was peace for girls like this? Girls who the world chewed up and spit out? His stomach clenched. He already knew the answer to that question. There would always be hate and ugliness in the world, people would continue to hurt one another, even those they were supposed to love the most. He'd been a believer, grown up in faith. But he'd learned over and over that peace wasn't going to come from a few words muttered under breath to a God who wasn't listening anyway. Nolan needed to make his own peace. And it would only come once the facts lined up, the case was solved, the bad people brought to justice.

Creed nudged his wet nose against Nolan's cheek as if he sensed the darkness of his handler's mood. Nolan set his phone aside and looked at his partner. "We've got work to do."

Nolan had driven directly to the motel and picked up his gear, then met with Penn and several deputies at the harbor dock. Penn had spoken to the witness over the phone, and a search strategy was underway. Nolan and Creed were now leaving the harbor aboard an NPS seaplane piloted by Aaron Reid, a ranger with the local park division.

A thick cloud of fog hung just feet above the choppy waters of Lake Superior. The engine's roar filled the cabin.

"Flew up from Houghton soon as I got the call," Aaron said.

They taxied across the water, the lake breaking on either side of the plane's pontoons, spray misting the windows. Nolan adjusted his headset to hear the pilot better. Creed was buckled in next to him, sitting up straight on his haunches, his long tongue hanging limp as he panted nervously. Nolan stroked his back, trying to calm him. "How long you been flying?" he asked the pilot.

"Don't worry. You're in good hands, sir." He pointed at the instrument panel. "Twenty percent on the flaps, and lifting the rudders now. See the nose rise? I'll release the yoke, and we'll work up to about forty to fifty knots soon."

The plane accelerated. Nolan sat back and adjusted his seat belt. Creed whined and panted harder, slobber dripping from the side of his mouth. Creed had trained on helicopters, but this was his first seaplane ride. It wasn't going well. Nolan used the sleeve of his shirt to wipe a pool of doggy saliva from the seat. "You're okay, boy."

"Forty, forty-one, forty-two..." The pilot counted off the knots and grinned his way. "We're approaching the sweet spot."

The plane went airborne. All traces of land disappeared as the craft slipped into the cloud bank. They were surrounded by white, misty fluff broken up by long blue-gray stretches of Lake Superior. It was beautiful, tranquil, and Nolan exhaled. The tension seemed to be easing from Creed's muscles. "Smooth takeoff."

"Thank you. We'll cruise along at one hundred twenty-five miles per hour. Should arrive in approximately thirty minutes." He pointed out a couple instruments on the panel as he spoke.

Nolan noticed the pilot's wedding ring. "Been married long?"

"Long enough to have a baby on the way."

"Congratulations." But Nolan felt a stab of envy. It seemed like the whole world was happily married and starting on a family. His dream, too. Wasn't meant to be, though. At least not with Rena. Thoughts of Ava flashed through his mind, but he quickly dismissed them. *Forget it*, he told himself. Under any other circumstances, yes, but Ava's father-in-law was a suspect in Lindsey Webber's murder, and Ava was prone to hide crucial facts in the case, although likely that was just misplaced loyalty. Hard to condemn that motive, but it didn't help him trust her.

He shifted the conversation back to the case and quickly briefed Aaron, filling in with an overview of the possible connection between the current homicide and the cold-case victim. "We believe we're looking at a human-trafficking operation. We're not sure of the scope yet. We've connected two girls to the island, and one was found deceased in Sculpin Bay. We don't know the *who* or the *how*, but I believe they use the island because of its proximity to the Canadian border."

Aaron nodded. "Easier to slip someone into the country on the open waters than on land. Border Patrol tries, but there's too much territory to cover and not enough officers."

"If we're right and the deceased in our original cold case was a trafficking victim, then this route has been used as a corridor for over a decade." He rolled open the map and studied the area where the hiker had reported seeing the gunman and girl. "Lane Cove Trail is only an hour's hike from the docking area in Rock Harbor."

"Makes sense," Aaron said. "Rock Harbor is one of the island's main ports—accessible by seaplane, ferry or private boat. Easy in, easy out. And enough traffic that no one would seem suspicious."

"You know this trail? Lane Cove?"

"Yeah. It merges with Greenstone Ridge Trail, which dissects the entire island. So your target could be anywhere by now. And ground search is the only viable option. The tree canopy is so thick, you wouldn't be able to see much from the air."

"The witness is waiting to take us to where he spotted her," Nolan said. "We'll start there, setting a perimeter and mapping out a search strategy. More searchers are on their way."

"Yes, sir." Aaron adjusted the headset fully onto his ears, turned on the radio and spoke to someone about wind direction. Then he pushed the yoke forward, and the plane descended through the fog. Isle Royale appeared, hovering on the horizon. "There it is," Aaron said. "The legend goes that the waters surrounding the island were the home of an evil, red-eyed creature, with a snakelike body and horns, that moved through the water, claiming unsuspecting victims." He chuckled. "Sounds like something out of a horror flick, right?"

Nolan didn't laugh; instead his breath grew shallow. He stared over the water as they descended. A cold chill crept over him as the plane banked left. This island, this green dot on the waters of Lake Superior, looked so serene, yet in the depths of the thick woods, there was a reason for fear. What he faced, what Ava and Rose faced, wasn't a mythical creature, but a real live evil force that had to be stopped.

Chapter Ten

Ava checked the door locks after Yvette left. Then checked them again. Ever since the shots, she had been consumed by paranoia. Thankfully Jane lived in a crowded neighborhood—no woods and no place for a killer to hide. Of course, homicides weren't limited to rural areas. *Are we really safe anywhere?*

Goose bumps popped up on her arms. She rubbed them down and busied herself with some light housekeeping. Jane started to object but then smiled, left her alone, understanding her need to keep busy. Ava wiped the counters, swept the floors, but no matter how she tried, she couldn't clean away the thoughts that cluttered her mind. Finally giving up, she borrowed Jane's laptop and sat at the kitchen table. A few answers might put her mind at ease. Who was Hannah Richter? And what was her connection to Kevin?

Ava spent the next hour scouring the internet while Rose played nearby in the family room with the new stuffed pony, feeding it pretend hay and using the sofa as a mountain. Best of all, occasionally, Rose forgot herself and let out a small horsey high-pitched *neeeeigh.*

Ava smiled. One good thing anyway—more sounds were

coming from Rose. Before Rose could talk, Kevin would sing silly nonsense to her and Rose would light up, babble shrill little sounds to join in, making them all laugh. Such priceless memories.

Ava sighed and looked again at the photo of Hannah Richter on her screen. What kind of family memories had such a young and pretty girl like this had? Memories so painful that they would make her run away? Or something else entirely? And why had she been in this area? The internet search was bringing more questions than answers. She snapped the laptop shut and leaned forward, running her fingers through her tangled hair. *I could tell you stories*, Derek had said.

Up till now, Ava hadn't wanted to know her husband's former life, those difficult days before he'd become the man she knew and loved—a good man, a faithful man and a loving husband and father. But now…could she live with the unknowns? The idea that he might have returned to this area to meet another woman was ridiculous. Kevin hadn't been the type. But he also hadn't been the type to keep anything from her. Or lie.

The sound of her phone startled her. Not recognizing the number, she considered not answering, then snatched it up at the last second. "Hello?"

The man's voice was low toned and efficient. "This is Craig from Hospital Administration. Is this the family of Mac Burke?"

"Yes, yes, it is."

"Are you his daughter-in-law, Ava Burke?"

"Yes. What's going on?"

"Mac had a fall this morning. Are you able to come into the hospital?"

"Did he break anything?"

"I'm not able to discuss the particulars. The nursing staff will give you more information."

"I understand. I can be there in about an hour." Ava hung

up and found Jane in the laundry room. "It's Mac," she said. "The hospital called. He's had a fall."

"Oh no! Poor Mac. Is he going to be okay?"

"They weren't specific. Can you watch Rose?"

"Of course." Jane threw the unfolded shirt into the basket and followed Ava into the family room. Ava spoke calmly, not wanting to upset Rose. "Honey, Mommy is going to run down to the hospital to see Grandpa. Jane will be here with you. Is that okay?"

Rose kept playing but smiled just a tiny bit, which Ava took as a yes. She snatched up her coat and purse. "Thank you, Jane. I'll let the officer outside know, and I'll call as soon as I get there."

Ava made the usual forty-five-minute drive to Larium in a half hour. It was a little after noon when she whipped into the parking lot and practically ran to the second floor of the hospital. She burst into the room to find Mac sitting up in bed doing a word search puzzle.

"Thank goodness you're here," he said, setting the word search aside. "I'm bored out of my mind. When are they going to let me out of this place? Have you heard? How's my Rosie? I miss that little—"

"You're okay?"

"Right as rain. Except that agent came by earlier and—"

"I thought you'd fallen and hurt yourself."

His brows furrowed. "No."

"But I got a call and… Hold on a sec. I've got to go check something. Be right back."

She exited the room and made a beeline for the nurses' station. "Excuse me," she said, leaning over the counter.

The nurse's head popped up.

"I'm Mac Burke's daughter-in-law. I had a call from Administration that he'd taken a bad fall."

"Uh…from Administration? Let me check into this." She ducked into an alcove behind the desk and came back a minute later, her expression clouded with confusion. "Your father-in-law hasn't had a fall that we're aware of, and no one from here called. Are you sure…?"

The nurse's voice faded to the background of Ava's suddenly muddled brain. Fumbling as if her limbs were detached, she extracted her phone and scrolled through her recent calls. The number she'd thought had come from the hospital could have belonged to anyone.

The blood drained from her veins. She wheeled and ran through the hallway, not waiting for the elevator, almost knocking over a woman in blue scrubs in the stairwell. Five minutes later, she was speeding up US 41.

She pushed a button on the steering wheel to activate the voice-control system. "Call Jane," she commanded. The phone rang. And rang. There was no answer. She disconnected, punched the button again. "Call Jane!" With each unanswered ring, fear built inside her until her very soul ached. "No! No! No!" She banged her palm against the steering wheel and then pushed the button again. "Call 911."

How could I have been so stupid? Someone had lured her away from Rose. She'd never forgive herself if something happened to her daughter.

The dispatcher answered, and she relayed the emergency and added, "There's a deputy parked outside my home. Tell him to hurry!"

Please, God, please, please…

Ava sped toward town, muttering a thousand prayers, pleading with God. First Kevin and now… Rose had to be okay. She had to be, or…

"Please, God, please don't take my child. I couldn't bear it."

Nolan stopped along the trail and pulled a collapsible bowl and water bottle from his pack. Creed lapped greedily. They'd hiked about two miles so far, and the midday temps were only in the fifties, average for late April, but the terrain was steep and their packs heavy. A Glock 22 was holstered at his hip and a semiautomatic tactical rifle slung over his back. Creed pranced at his side in a law enforcement vest, camo green with large white block letters *LAW ENFORCEMENT K9*. As soon as Nolan had buckled the vest, Creed snapped into police mode. His body had gone rigid, every muscle rippling in anticipation, ready for whatever command Nolan would issue.

There were four of them on Lane Cove Trail. Him and Aaron and a noncommissioned ranger, Steve Moore, who'd met them on the seaplane dock with the witness, Jason White, a college student from Michigan Tech who'd come over for a day hike.

"We're close. Maybe another half mile," Jason said.

Nolan slid the bowl and bottle back into his pack, and they continued to pick their way along the narrow trail, kicking up pine needles and stumbling on rocks and roots. Some trees were budding, even though snow still patched the shadowed areas of the woods. Creed followed at his own pace, often distracted by a scurrying rodent or an unknown scent. He wandered away, pushing his snout first into the dirt and snow, then lifting it into the air, snapping his jaws as he gulped in scents. Nolan loved watching his partner out in the wilds but kept a close eye on him, knowing that the island was home to a pack of wolves, descendants from wolves that had crossed an ice bridge between the island and Canada back in the forties.

"Here," Jason said. "I marked it." He pointed to a rock cairn—three rocks piled in a small haphazard tower along the trail. "It was barely daybreak, and they came from that way. Heading north. The man walked behind her. Close."

The kid couldn't provide a description of the man, who'd worn a gator covering most of his face, but he'd gotten a good look at the woman.

"I took one look at her and knew something wasn't right," Jason continued. "She looked scared, and her clothing was torn. As soon as she saw me, she screamed for help and tried to make a run for it. I was shocked, you know. And the guy, he whipped out a gun and pointed it at me. I took off, didn't know what else to do."

"You did the right thing," Nolan said, surveying the surrounding ground while Creed sniffed a nearby patch of early spring weeds. He turned this way and that and finally did his doggy thing before returning to Nolan's side.

"We might have a few partial footprints here," Nolan observed, glancing at the spongy ground layered with leaves. "Hard to tell how many people have been through since the call. Mark these, and we'll photograph all of them." Better to be thorough. He stood and glanced at Creed. "Doubt there's any scent lines for my dog to follow."

A light breeze kicked up, a bird's whistle pierced the air. The men remained still, scanning the area. "Seems impossible," Aaron finally said. "They could be anywhere."

Nolan opened a handheld GPS device and traced his finger along the screen. "If they're on the move, it probably means they're getting ready to transport off island to Canada. My bet is that they're heading there." He looked up at Moore. "What's your best guess?"

"North is the Five Fingers area," Moore said. "Long narrow bays and coves. It's mainly a paddling, portage destination. Lots of shallows. But small boats could navigate parts fairly easily. There are also a few campgrounds up there and shelter sites, too."

Nolan considered this. "We'll need to concentrate our search. We only have so much manpower. Moore, you got any men up north that could search the shelters? And we'll need boat patrol on the north shore. Whatever you've got."

Moore nodded and spoke into his mobile radio on a secure channel. "402 to Ranger 301."

A response came right away. "402, this is 301."

"I need a search of campsites Duncan, Belle Isle, Lane Cove and Pickerel. Put all boat units on the north shore." He relayed their physical descriptions. "The male is armed. Call for backup if you spot them."

"Copy. I'll advise."

Moore disconnected and said, "It's in motion. What now?"

Nolan checked his watch. The sun wouldn't go down until nine thirty, so there was still a lot of daylight left. "Mostly we wait. Reinforcements should arrive via boat within the hour. Moore, you and—"

"Excuse me, sir. You need to see this." Aaron approached with a satellite phone. "We've got an SMS message from the base station."

Nolan read the screen: Inform Agent Nolan Shea that Rose Burke is missing. Probable abduction.

He couldn't believe what he'd read. Rose? Abducted?

He handed back the phone and turned to Moore. "There's been..." His words trailed off, his mind tormented by the idea of Rose in the hands of these criminals. And Ava... She must've been terrified. He needed to get back to her. "Listen, reinforcements are on the way. Continue the search, focus on the north shore as a possible exit point. I've got to get back to the mainland."

If something happened to Rose, he would never forgive himself. *Or God.*

Chapter Eleven

Sheriff's vehicles were packed into the street. Ava parked at the end of the line and ran the rest of the way to the house. The front door was wide open. An officer stopped her before she got across the threshold. "Hey. What do you think you're doing? Stop right there."

"Is my daughter okay? Rose? Is she okay?"

The deputy did a double take. "You're the girl's mom?"

"Yes!" She started to push past him. "Where is she? Rose! Rosie!"

He spoke into his radio, and another deputy came forward. He held his hands in the air. "Wait here, ma'am. Agent Beckett wants to talk to you."

Ava ignored them and pushed her way inside the door. "Where's my daughter? Where is she?" Her voice was thin and shrill, her throat constricted with fear.

Deputies were in the kitchen and family room, all of them staring at her now. Their expressions filled with pity. And she knew. Rose was dead.

She fell to her knees. A chilling silence consumed her entire body, then a pain rolled up from her core until she arched her back, her mouth gaping open as a noise like no other escaped.

Jane appeared next to her on the floor and enveloped her, rocking her gently. "Ava, I'm sorry. I'm so sorry."

"How...how can I live without my Rose, too?"

Jane stopped the rocking, pushed back, holding Ava at arm's length, staring at her tearstained face. "What?"

"Mrs. Burke." A blonde woman stood above her. "Your daughter has been abducted."

Ava's mind was struggling to process the woman's words. All her eyes and mind registered was an officer with short, cropped hair, a pretty face and deep brown eyes that seemed insistent on telling her... *Abducted?*

"She's shivering. Help me get her to the chair."

Jane. Always there for her, always helpful.

Ava was helped to the chair, a blanket placed over her body. Someone flipped a switch, and the gas fireplace burst into flame. Someone else brought her a cup of hot tea. Several minutes later, she was still shaking. *Rose. Rose. Rose.*

The blonde woman cocked her head in an assessing look before pulling a chair over and introducing herself as Agent Campbell Beckett. "Mrs. Burke, we're doing everything we can to find your daughter, but I need you to answer a few questions. Do you understand?"

"I'll do anything..."

"You left the house this morning. Where did you go?"

I shouldn't have left. This is my fault. A wave of blame, of remorse, threatened to take her again, but she held firm against any emotions. She couldn't afford that. Not now. Not when Rose was still out there somewhere.

"Mrs. Burke?"

Ava took a breath. "I got a call from the hospital saying that my father-in-law had fallen and that I needed to come to the hospital right away. But when I got there...he was fine... It was a way to lure me away from Rose."

And I fell for it.

"Male or female caller?"

"Male."

"You went to the hospital. Then what?"

Ava explained how the nurse had told her that no one had called. "I was confused, but then I realized…and I got back here as fast as I could."

"We'll need your phone."

Her phone. Where was her phone? "It's still in my car. In my bag."

Agent Beckett nodded and glanced at one of the deputies before continuing, "Rose was wearing jeans and a white shirt, with a pink jacket, is that correct?"

"Yes, but how did…?" Anger hummed inside her, and she turned her focus to Jane.

"I'd just checked on her, I swear." Jane wrung her hands. "She was in the family room playing. Everything was fine."

"You were supposed to be watching her."

"I was. I mean… I didn't think—"

The agent quickly stood and stepped in front of Ava, redirecting her attention away from Jane. "This isn't her fault, Mrs. Burke. And it's not your fault, either. No one here is to blame, understand? Let's keep our focus on finding the person who did this and bringing Rose back safely."

Ava's anger slid into guilt. Why was she accusing Jane? She'd been the fool to go along with the call. She should be the one to find Rose. She glanced about at the milling officers. "Why are all these deputies here? Why aren't they out looking for Rose?" She stood. The room spun. She gripped the back of the chair to steady herself. "I need to find her."

"We will find her. Please, sit down, Mrs. Burke. We need your help. Okay?"

Jane gently took her by the shoulders. Ava hesitated, wanted to shake off the gesture, go find her Rose, but finally she sat down.

The agent sighed and raked her fingers through her hair

until it stood out in every direction. "Let's go back to the call. You said it was a male voice."

"Yes."

"Did either of you see anyone around the area yesterday or today that...that gave you a weird feeling or seemed strange in any way? Don't second-guess yourself. Anything, no matter how small, might mean something."

Ava opened and closed her mouth twice before she found her voice. "There's this man, he was my husband's friend back in high school. And he..." He'd what? Sort of asked her out? Gone out of his way to bring her a lost bracelet?

"What's his name?"

"Derek Williams." Ava took in a deep breath and told her everything about Derek, how he had asked her out, then followed her. "My bracelet had fallen off, and he chased me down to return it."

"When was that again?"

"Yesterday afternoon."

"And you were shot at last night."

Ava nodded and wrapped her arms around her midsection. *Whoever did this already killed one woman. What would they do to Rose? Rose. Where is she right now? Is she scared? Hurt? Is she crying?*

That was when Ava spotted the stuffed pony on the floor. "Her pony," she said, pointing at the toy by the table. Then she burst into a fresh round of tears.

The flight back to the mainland took too long. Then Nolan drove too fast, his mind consumed with anger and panic and feelings he couldn't identify until he skidded to a stop outside Jane's house. It was a little after six o'clock, and Cam had already briefed him over the phone, so he knew the basic details of Rose's abduction.

He wove his way through emergency vehicles, showed his ID to the scene officer and entered the house with Creed on his heels. He stopped short in the family room, his world slowing as his gaze locked on Ava pacing near the fireplace, a phone to her ear. She noticed him and disconnected. She appeared rigidly determined, but when she looked his way, the pain in her eyes tore at his very soul.

Every part of him wanted to go to her, hold her, comfort her. Seconds ticked away before he realized that everyone was watching him as he looked at her. He collected himself and crossed the room. "Ava. I'm sorry."

"I've looked everywhere. She's just gone. I'm calling everyone I know." She held out the phone in her hand, her gaze resolute. "This is Jane's phone. They took mine. I need it back in case someone calls about Rose."

Cam cleared her throat. "An unidentified male called on Ava's phone, lured her away by claiming that something had happened to Mac at the hospital. Jane offered to watch the girl while Ava went to check on Mac. We're trying to trace—"

"Rose was right here." Jane waved her hands around the room. "Happily playing. She was fine, and I only went into the laundry room for a second, just long enough to change over a load of clothes. When I came out, she was gone."

Ava drew in a shaky breath, her fist clenched.

"He entered through the sliding glass door," Cam added. "It's been processed for prints. I'm waiting to hear back on that." Nolan nodded, and Cam continued, "An Amber Alert was issued, and we've reached out to news outlets." Creed circled the family room, whimpering, and whining, repeatedly stopping to sniff at the stuffed pony still lying on the rug.

Jane came closer and wrapped Ava in a hug. "Someone needs to let Mac know what's going on."

She stiffened and stepped away. "I called earlier and couldn't reach him. I plan to call back soon. Leave that to me, okay? This will…" Her unspoken words hung in the air: *This will kill Mac.*

Cam brought the conversation back to the investigation:

"We've canvassed the neighborhood. And Penn and his deputies are interviewing people on this street, checking for doorbell cameras or any other cameras, but most people here don't have security systems."

Not in a village as small as this, Nolan thought. People knew each other, and in a place where the elements on any given day could be deadly, they relied on one another and trusted their neighbor.

Ava asked urgently, "What about my phone? How long does it take to trace a number?"

"We're working on it," Cam said. "The call was made from a disposable phone. It's going to take time."

"Then how will we find Rose?" she asked. "And what if we don't get to her in time and he...?"

Nolan stopped her next words. "Don't go there, Ava. We will find her. I..." He glanced away, stopping short of a promise. "Creed and I need to take a look around outside."

Creed heard his name and raised his head.

"I'm going with you," Ava said.

Jane frowned. "Mac wouldn't want you to put yourself in danger."

"Danger? The danger was in leaving my baby with..." She stopped and took a deep breath. "I can't just sit here. Rose is out there. She needs me."

"Yes, she does need you, but not out there, not now." Nolan stepped close to her, wanted to hold her but couldn't. So many eyes stared at them both. "Creed has to do his job to the best of his ability. That means no distractions."

"But I have to—"

This time he reached for her hand, held it tight, wishing she could see what was in his heart. She quickly dropped her hand and met his gaze, her blue eyes pleading with his.

"Please trust me," he whispered.

She nodded, ever so slightly, and his heart soared, then fell. The first two hours after a child abduction were the most crucial. Cam's search had come up empty, no leads, and time was still ticking away.

"I need something with Rose's smell on it." Nolan scooped up the toy and motioned for Cam to follow him toward the door. Now, out of earshot of the others, he asked her what she'd discovered since her call. She explained that Ava had pointed at Derek Williams as a person of interest. His fists clenched at the mere thought of the guy and the fact that anyone could hurt Ava so deeply.

"A team went to his home, but there was no answer, no sign of him or Rose. They're waiting there to see if he turns up. The others know to be on the lookout for him," she finished.

"Good. Because when we do catch up with him, I want to be the one to question him." He looked Ava's way and felt his hands start to clench.

"Right," Cam answered slowly.

"Something else," Nolan said, lowering his voice. "Run a full search on Kevin Burke, Ava's deceased husband. I should have asked for it earlier. I think he's somehow connected to all this. If we can find that connection it might point us to Rose's abductor."

"Can I ask what's prompted this?"

"Several things—I'll fill you in later." He avoided looking at Ava again, attached Creed's lead and gave him a long sniff of the toy.

Cam stopped him before he headed out the door. "This has become personal for you, hasn't it?"

"What do you mean?"

"Ava. You like her. The way you look at her, and avoid looking at her as well. It's obvious."

He didn't deny it.

She continued to push the issue. "It's so soon after Rena and—"

"This has nothing to do with Rena." He instantly regretted his tone. Too late. Cam's expression hardened. He'd put her on the defensive. "I'm sorry," he said. "I know you're only trying—"

"It's fine. Just remember that this case needs your full focus. A little girl's life is at stake."

"You think I don't know—" He stopped himself. Cam was right. It was personal. And that wasn't a good thing; he needed to stay objective. That was how good—effective—police work functioned best.

His mind turned to Rose, the silent little girl already traumatized by cops from her father's death, yet she'd looked at him with trust. His heart had opened when her blue eyes had looked up at him as her fingers ruffled Creed's coat. Innocent, young. Ava, too, had trusted him, and he had felt that in his heart as well. And what had it gotten them? Only one thing mattered to him now: that little girl was out there in the hands of an evil person. And he needed to find her at any cost.

"I am fully focused. Believe me."

Ava took Jane's phone and retreated upstairs to the guest bedroom where she and Rose were sleeping and where she could make the rest of her calls in private. Tension had been strong between her and Jane all morning, ever since Ava's earlier outburst. Why was she so angry at Jane? *I'm being irrational. None of this is her fault.*

She reached out to a few more people, messaging them with a current photo of Rose. Earlier she'd called her mother in Florida, who was both devastated and stoic and assured her that the whole family would be arriving within the next twenty-four hours to join in the search. She texted a few of her prayer-group friends whose numbers she remembered. She asked for both prayers and help searching, and then the phone rang.

It was Yvette. "Just got your voicemail. I saw the call, but I didn't... Whose number is this?"

"I'm using Jane's phone."

"I can't believe this. I just can't." She broke into small sobs, followed by a long sniff and nose blow. "I'm sorry. I told myself that I was going to be strong for you. Tell me what I can do."

"I need you to help me get the word out. Jane and I are doing our best, but the more people who know, the better."

"I'm on it."

"We'll need help searching. People can meet here and organize. There's plenty of room. I'll text you with photos of Rose for social media."

"Everyone wants her home safely. It won't take much to get the word out."

Get the word out. She needed to try Mac again and soon, before he heard it from someone else.

Rose's crumpled top sat at the end of the bed as if mocking her. Ava noticed the smear of pink on the sleeve, her lipstick. Expensive lipstick. Rose had gotten into her makeup, playing grown-up, and Ava had been cross with her. *That's Mommy's makeup. It's too expensive to play with.* Rose had dipped her head, confused and chastened. Now regret settled heavy in the pit of Ava's stomach. Why had she been so upset? It was just makeup, and now Rose was gone, in the hands of...

"Ava, are you still there?"

"Yes." Salty tears rolled over her lips. She swiped them away. *I've got to get my head in the game. Think clearly. Rose is depending on me.* "If only Jane had... I should never have left Rose. Never."

"Jane? What do you mean that you 'left Rose'?"

She remembered Agent Beckett's warning. "Nothing. I shouldn't have said that. I... I'm not supposed to talk about the details with anyone." She looked toward the window. Creed and Nolan weren't back yet. That was a good sign, wasn't it? Maybe they found a lead.

She heard Yvette sigh on the other end of the line. "I understand. You must be so worried and exhausted. Your mind is playing tricks on you. Just keep your focus on the real enemy and on getting Rose back."

Playing tricks... "Yes, you're...right."

"Oh, sweetie. This is such a horrible thing. I'm so sorry. She'll be home soon. Just trust that, okay?"

Ava disconnected and rested her head on Rose's pillow, inhaled the sweet fruity smell and released her emotions. Prayers mixed with deep wrenching sobs until her whole body felt turned inside out. She reached for a tissue just as a notification dinged on the phone. She glanced at the screen—

We're praying for you. We'll be over to help.

She was so grateful for her friends. And then she did a double take. A text had come in from someone listed only as *Derek* from Jane's contact list.

I need to see you. The sooner the better.

Derek? Derek Williams? The phone shook in her trembling hand. She opened the text thread—there were no other texts from Derek. Yet he was in Jane's contact list. Had she deleted them?

It could be a different Derek. Or not. But how would Derek know Jane? And why would he need to see her? Was this real?

Your mind is playing tricks on you.

What did she really know about Jane? Mac cared for Jane deeply, but the heart could cloud judgment, even Mac's. The floodgate of mistrust burst open, and now she saw a dozen small things as giant red flags. Jane working alone with Rose. Jane's offer to let them stay at her house. She'd been such a help from the outset that Ava had only appreciated her offer of advice. But...had Jane been helping her or leading her? And something else became clearer in her mind. The intruder had entered through the sliding patio door, but Ava had locked that door. Double-checked it, even. Had Jane opened the door to Rose's kidnapper?

Be careful of who you trust.

Chapter Twelve

Ava was waiting for him in the living room when he returned from his search, her face flushed and her eyes wide and a bit wild-looking, as if she were about to crawl out of her own skin. Shock, stress, surging adrenaline... Her child was missing. There couldn't be anything more horrific for a parent.

"Did you find anything?" she asked.

He glanced over her shoulder at Cam, who tipped her head toward the corner of the room where she'd set up a table and several monitors. She had an update for him, but it would wait. He turned his focus back to Ava. "I'm sorry. Creed lost the scent trail."

Ava's shoulders slumped. She opened her mouth to say something, closed it again and glanced toward the kitchen table where Jane was on her cell phone. "I got a hold of Mac and told him about Rose. He's devastated. I don't know what this is going to do to him."

I'm not sure what it's going to do to you. But Nolan didn't express his worries out loud.

"Jane is going to the hospital later to be with him," she continued. "She and some others are still working to get the word out. I'm going to drive around the village and look for Rose. It doesn't sound like much, I realize, but I'm not sure what else to do. I was just waiting for you to come back with..." She looked up at him, and his heart ached that he hadn't brought back the news she'd hoped for. She finished, "But I won't just sit here. She's out there, and I've got to do something."

"I understand." Nolan pulled his keys from his pocket. "We've only got a couple hours of sunlight left. Give me one second to talk to Cam, and then I'll go with you."

She nodded and went to retrieve her coat and bag. A couple of minutes later, he unlocked the Explorer and opened the back door for Creed. Ava settled into the passenger seat. As soon as he started the engine, she cranked up the heat and adjusted the air vents. Then she adjusted them again, and he saw her jaw clench and unclench as her fingers and face and mind worked over something. Something she had yet to tell him? About Kevin?

"I think Jane is involved," she said.

He frowned, pulled onto the street. "Jane?"

"The patio door was locked," she said. "I know it was. I checked it twice before I left. There was no sign of forced entry, right? Jane must have let the kidnapper in. What other explanation is there?"

"You're sure it was locked?"

"You don't believe me?"

"No, it's...you have a lot going on right now. It would be easy to forget something like that."

"I didn't forget, okay? There's something else, too. I borrowed her phone, and a text came in from Derek. They could be in on it together. I don't know why or how, but you have to do something. I bet she knows where Rose is."

"The contact was listed as Derek Williams?"

"No, just Derek. He wanted to see her. That's what he said. That he needs to see her soon."

"When was this?"

"While you were out searching with your dog."

Penn's men hadn't been able to locate Derek yet. And time was slipping away. "It could be a different Derek texting her."

Ava looked at him. "I need you to believe me… He has Rose—I know he does. We've got to get her back before he kills her."

Suddenly Creed pushed his head into the front seat, his paws on the armrest, and gently nudged Ava with his snout. Nolan felt the same as his canine partner—witnessing her concern, he wished he could console her.

Cam had just told him, *She's about to crack.* Understandably so, but Nolan had seen strength in Ava earlier. He believed in her, but he also needed to trust her.

He pulled into a nearby parking lot and put the gear into Park.

Ava sat straighter and looked around. "Why are we here?"

"We need to talk."

"The shoreline. I think that's where we should start."

"Not about that. This is important."

She shook her head. "Not more important than finding Rose."

She was right, but roadblocks had been set up. The Coast Guard had joined the efforts and were patrolling the waters. Penn and his deputies were searching for every possibility. Everyone was looking for Rose. He'd gotten Ava out of the house for another reason.

Truth was that the world seemed huge when you were searching for a tiny girl. But finding the participants in the trafficking ring would shrink the playing field, give them an edge on finding her. His gut told him that Ava knew something she hadn't revealed. Not yet. And that could point him in the right direction to save Rose.

"We have evidence that the dead girl that you discovered in your barn is tied into a bigger crime."

"A bigger crime?"

"Human trafficking."

She paled even more.

"There's a possible corridor into Canada through Isle Royale. And it's been in existence for a long time. We now know that a woman found dead on the island ten years ago was an early victim."

"The...hiker?"

He sat back. "Yes, Hannah Richter. What do you know about her?"

"I... I'm not sure."

He kept his gaze steady, letting his question hang in the air.

"When I called Mac about Rose, he told me that you found the newspaper clippings. I know that you suspect him, but you're wrong. Mac would never hurt anyone. Besides, he's in the hospital and couldn't have—"

"I'm not talking about Mac."

A dark shadow crossed her features.

Nolan leaned forward, his voice soft but direct. "Sometimes we sense things about someone we love, but we deny them in our mind. We bury it deep or excuse it or convince ourselves that we're crazy for even thinking something so absurd about the person. Love really is blind."

"I don't know what you're getting at."

"Don't you? Mac didn't clip out the articles about the lost hiker all those years ago, did he? Kevin did."

"My husband and I had a good relationship, built on respect and trust and, most of all, faith. Kevin was a good man, honest and loyal."

"But you knew he had saved those articles. Doesn't that seem strange to you? And I'd asked you about Hannah Richter, if you'd heard of her—"

"Yes, but... You didn't say there was a connection between the hiker and the dead woman in our barn."

"Now you know."

"Kevin never would have participated in something so evil."

"If there's anything else, no matter how small, you need to

tell me. There has been another possible trafficking victim spotted, and there are other women missing, and now Rose... I need to know everything, Ava."

She squeezed her eyes shut. Human trafficking. It was something she'd always heard of but had never thought would touch her life. If these people had Rose, she could be in Canada by now. Lost forever, being bought and sold... Ava shivered. Horror stories ran through her mind. *Don't go there*, she told herself.

She opened her eyes and touched the bracelet Derek had brought back to her the day he'd followed her home. The bracelet Kevin had given her. "There is more," she told Nolan. "Derek told me that he'd seen Kevin the day he died."

"Where, exactly?"

"At a gas station outside Houghton. He said Kevin was driving a rental car. They spoke to one another, and Kevin told him that he was going home to Detroit to see us."

"You didn't know that Kevin had come up to Houghton?"

"No. He told me he was going to be in Green Bay on business."

"Maybe he got done early with business and drove up to see Mac."

"That's what I thought. But Mac didn't see him or even hear from him. He had no idea he was in the area."

"What other reason would he have for coming up here?"

Ava struggled for an answer. "My friend Yvette thinks he might have another woman in the area, but Kevin would never have had an affair. He wasn't the cheating type." She saw a pained expression cross Nolan's face. "What is it?" she asked. "Do you know something?"

"No. It's nothing." He put the vehicle in gear and pulled out of the lot and turned toward the lake. "How long were you and Kevin married?"

"Seven years."

"And you never once doubted him?"

"Not since the day we were married." She didn't mention the doubts that lingered about the time when she hadn't known him. When he'd been buddies with Derek Williams.

They searched the rental areas on the south side of the village, the campground out by Fort Wilkins and the east-side boat launches, talking to people and showing them Rose's photo. So far no one had seen her. Hunter's Point Park was their last place to check.

By the time they turned onto Harbor Coast Lane, the sun was dipping low on the horizon and Ava's earlier adrenaline-fueled energy waned. She'd barely slept the night before, and every muscle in her body ached, her heart laden with despair.

"Pull into the main lot," she said. Hunter's Point Park, with its pristine trails and almost five thousand feet of shoreline, ripe with agates, was always crowded, but the growing darkness was sending the visitors home. Before the beach completely emptied, they parked, walked over and spoke to a half dozen people who scurried to pack up their things. No one had seen any sign of Rose.

Frustrated, Ava was about to turn back to the parking lot when a flash of color caught her eye. About ten feet offshore, a long base of protruding rocks rose out of the water, their jagged edges like dark arthritic fingers. There, snagged and floating on the surface, was something…pink. Sick dread settled in her gut and pulled her closer to the edge of the lake, her brain registering the cruel reality of what bobbed in the waves. Pink nylon, just like Rose's jacket.

Rose!

She ran full speed into the water, so focused on the pink floater that her body barely registered the shock of freezing water that quickly reached her knees then waist. She pushed forward, her feet struggling to keep traction on the slippery rocks under the surface, each step more difficult as her clothes soaked up the lake. *Rose!* Waves pelted her, the water tasted muddy and murky and fishy, her eyes stung as she reached out her arm. *Almost there.*

She heard her name floating over the water, but she ignored it and leaned forward against the cold waves…she was almost there. She lurched forward, swiping at the material, her fingers catching on the pink nylon… Not Rose's jacket but a large, tattered Mylar balloon.

She leaned back, off balance, and a wave pushed her sideways, the lake bottom dropping off from under her. She bicycled her feet, struggling to reconnect to secure her footing, but the hole beneath her now was too deep. She flailed her arms, trying to tread water, stay afloat, but her clothing felt like anchors, and she began to sink. A wave pulled her back, then propelled her forward, pressing her body against the rocks. Fear seized her.

The next wave dragged her down. Darkness surrounded her, but she fought toward the shattered light, out of the deep, lunging for the murky surface water, and finally she burst through and gulped for air. Pressure built behind her eyes, her movements slowed, and she thought of Rose and blissful sleep. Her body exhausted, she let herself go, sinking down, down…up. Up? Her collar stretched out above her as a hand snatched her by the back of the neck and yanked her upward. She broke the surface, coughing and sputtering freezing cold water. She flailed her arms, kicked out as she was pulled back and against another body, against Nolan, his voice strong in her ear: "I've got you. You're safe now. Let me help you."

Chapter Thirteen

Nolan got her back onto the beach, and she collapsed onto all fours, her body heaving as she sucked in air and began to vomit. And vomit. He kept his hand on her back, speaking calmly. "It's okay. You're okay. I've got you." But he was worried. Lake Superior's water was maybe thirty-five degrees this time of April, the evening air temp dropping into the midforties or lower. They were both in danger of hypothermia.

Ava rocked back on her heels, trying to take in more air. "I thought… It looked like…"

"I know what you thought." He slid his hand under her arm. "Come on—we need to get warm. Can you walk?"

They started across the rocky beach. Several times she stumbled, and he caught her, steadying her, and then held her close enough for her to lean against him. And as she did, he held her even closer.

"I'm sorry," she said over and over as he helped her into the Explorer. He managed to climb into his seat, wet jeans making his leg heavier to lift. He started the engine and blasted the heater, wishing that the air would hurry up and turn warm.

She reached across the seat and placed her hand on his arm. "You saved my life. Thank you."

He covered her hand with his free hand and kept it there, watching for her reaction. She didn't pull back; instead she stared at their combined hands with an expression of wonder, and then a raw emotion, so full of pain and sorrow, made her chin tremble.

He moved his hand, gently cupped her face and traced his thumb over her cheek. "Let's get you warm. We'll head over to Jane's to change. We're out of daylight, and you need to rest. We start again first thing in the morning. Okay?"

She looked up into his eyes, gave his hands a squeeze and they set off.

They arrived at Jane's house ten minutes later. Cars clogged the road out front, and when they walked inside, everyone stopped and stared. Jane came forward. "What happened?"

"We're okay. Ava needs dry clothing and something warm to drink."

Ava turned and looked over her shoulder at him as Jane led her through the crowd to the back room. The gesture wasn't lost on Cam. "Hmm," he heard her say under her breath.

He shook his head and said, "That wasn't about me. I'll tell you in a minute." Cam looked down the hall as Jane took Ava into the bathroom.

Nolan focused on the nearly twenty people who were scattered throughout the kitchen and family room. Small meetings had convened, and a large map was thumbtacked to the family room wall. Kevin's cousin, Yvette, seemed to be running the show.

"Anything on Rose?" Cam asked.

"No. Nothing. This is wonderful, everyone pitching in to help. Anything yet?"

"Just a half dozen well-meaning types mistaking Rose for every kid in town. Sheriff's forensics couldn't trace the call from the hospital. They returned her phone. Anything turn up on your end?"

He kept his voice low and told her what had happened at the lake, the text on Jane's phone and the supposedly locked doors. "She swore she locked them before she left for the hospital."

"I'll see what I can find out about it, but Ava's under major stress—maybe she's confused. You know she's not thinking too clearly if she ran into Lake Superior after a piece of trash."

He looked down at the floor. "It's her daughter. Any parent would be half crazy with fear and worry." He'd left two giant wet footprints on the carpeting. "The newspaper clippings belonged to Kevin, not Mac."

"How do you know that?"

"Ava told me. There's more. The day Kevin died, he was supposed to be in Green Bay on business, but Derek Williams claims he saw him in Houghton in a rental car. Ava didn't know he was in this area, and she indicated that Mac didn't know, either."

"Clandestine trips between here and Detroit." Cam folded her arms and rocked back on her heels. "Interesting. If she found the newspaper clippings, there might be more to find. I'll see what we need to get a warrant for the Burke residence."

Nolan felt like he'd just betrayed Ava. He had. But he had a job to do. People's lives depended on it. Rose's life depended on it. It was his sworn duty to get Rose home safely and back to her mother. Nothing else mattered.

He left Creed with Cam, stopped by the motel for a quick shower and change, and got a call from Penn. They'd brought Williams in for questioning.

Nolan took the M-26, which wound along every curve of Lake Superior to Eagle Harbor and the sheriff's headquarters. Moore called while he was en route with a report from the search for the girl and gunman on the island. Rangers had canvassed the northern campgrounds and searched all shelter areas, still coming up empty. They were calling it a day and would resume first thing in the morning.

The sheriff's office was located on the west side of the inlet village, housed in an historic three-story white clapboard, red-roofed house—a stark contrast to the cold, utilitarian government buildings he was used to in DC. He identified himself to the night desk officer and was directed to where Penn waited for him outside a conference room. "His attorney's on the way. Should be here soon."

"Right. Where are the case records?"

Penn pointed down the hall. "Last room on the left."

The boxes Cam had shipped were stacked in a storage room. It didn't take Nolan long to locate the items he was looking for: the hard copy of the case file and Hannah Richter's personal effects.

He carried both to a small table and skimmed over the documents in the case file. There wasn't anything he hadn't seen in the electronic copy. He reread the witness account from the person who'd discovered Hannah's body, a researcher with the Isle Royale Wolf-Moose Project who'd been documenting the migration of a dwindling wolf pack when he'd come upon Hannah's body, curled in the fetal position under the bough of a pine tree. Nolan used a map to pinpoint the location and drew a line to the location where the unidentified girl and gunman had been sighted earlier. He drew a circle encompassing both areas and gauged the distance to be about two miles. Two miles of nothing but wilderness. What was he missing?

He snapped on gloves and opened the box of Hannah's personal effects. A large paper bag held the clothing she'd died in, leggings and a large gray sweatshirt, both scissored in half during the autopsy. Next, her socks and tennis shoes, size seven. An outfit she would have worn in Detroit to go to school or out with friends to the mall but not substantial enough to survive the bitter temperatures of late April on the island.

Nolan went back to the leggings and looked closer, then double-checked the autopsy report, skimming for specific information. He found it just as the door opened behind him.

He turned to see Penn. "They're here. Not that it matters.

A waste of time—that's what this is. The attorney's not going to let him say squat." He raked his hands through his hair. "Doesn't look good for the kid, you know."

Nolan nodded. Rose was a witness to a crime connected to a major trafficking ring. There was no benefit to letting her live. He just didn't allow himself to go there, didn't want to give up hope of finding her alive.

Penn let out a long sigh and echoed his thoughts. "We're not giving up, though. I've got all my people dedicated to nothing but looking for her. Tell the mom that, won't you?"

Nolan carefully folded Hannah's shirt and reached for the evidence bag when the description Ava had given of Rose's outfit flashed through his mind: blue jeans, a white T-shirt, pink nylon jacket... He clenched his fist at the thought of her clothes ending up in an evidence bag like this one. "Yeah, I'll do that," he said.

"Thank you for coming in to talk to us, Mr. Williams," Nolan said. He slid a couple of bottled waters to Williams and his attorney, Mr. Braun. "Is there anything else I can get you two?" He glanced at Penn, who stood behind him. "Do you have a vending machine around here or—"

"We're fine," Braun said. "It's after nine. Let's get on with this."

Nolan ignored the lawyer and spoke directly to Williams. "I am sorry that we have to meet so late, but since a child is missing, I'm sure you can understand that time is of the essence."

"Is my client a suspect in Rose Burke's disappearance?" the lawyer asked.

"We're hoping that he might know something that will help us find her." Nolan kept his gaze on Williams, who stared at the table and sniffed. His eyes were hard, his posture stiff—not the nervous type of stiff but more rigid, defiant. "I believe you know Mrs. Burke?"

Williams nodded. "Yes. We've met."

"You can imagine how distraught she is, then. Any mother would be."

"It's tragic," Braun said. "But it doesn't have anything to do with my client."

Williams sniffed again, a short little intake through his nose followed by a finger swipe under the nostrils. A tell. Only thirty seconds into the interview and Nolan had already picked up on it.

Nolan shuffled a few papers and rubbed a kink in his neck. "Where were you today, Mr. Williams?"

Derek shot a glance at his lawyer, who nodded ever so slightly. "I went to Houghton around eight this morning and spent the day meeting with investors. All day."

Penn spoke up. "Before you leave, we'll need you to write down the address and the people you met with."

"When did you return?" Nolan asked.

"You should know the answer to that. Your people were waiting for me at my house."

"What time?"

"Just a little before nine p.m."

"You were in Houghton the entire time between eight a.m. and nine p.m."

"Yes."

"Have you ever met Rose Burke?"

"No."

"But you know Ava, her mother?"

"Like I said, I've met her. I don't know her well."

"You met her at a restaurant, correct?"

He sniffed and glanced at his attorney. "Yes. A mutual friend introduced us."

"And you followed her home that day, is that right?"

"She'd dropped her bracelet outside the restaurant. I wanted to return it to her."

"So, you followed her home."

"Okay, maybe I was a little interested, you know? You've

seen her, right?" The slightest twitch to his lips put the ugly into his words.

Nolan gritted his teeth. He didn't like anything about this man. His instinct, sharpened after a decade spent in investigations, wasn't something he would ignore.

Williams continued, "Call it whatever you want, but I wasn't stalking her, if that's what she said. I already knew she was living at Mac's place. I was going to run the bracelet out there, but then I saw her on the road and thought I'd try to pull her over. She overreacted."

"How did you know that she had been staying with her father-in-law?"

"Really? You must be from a city. Well, Sculpin Bay is a small town, and everyone knows everything about everyone here."

"So, you also must have heard that there was a woman found dead in the Burkes' barn?"

His attorney sat a little straighter.

"Yeah." Williams shrugged. "Everyone's talking about that, too."

"Did you know that victim?"

"No."

"Are you sure? Like you said, this is a small town. Maybe you saw her around?"

Braun made a scoffing sound in his throat. "My client has already answered that question. Move on."

Nolan sighed. "Okay, let me back up here a little. You don't know Ava well, but did you know her husband, Kevin?"

"We went to high school together, so yeah."

"You were buddies, then?"

"Yeah, we were. He was a fun guy."

"So, you did typical things that friends do like movies, camping, stuff like that?"

"Guess so."

"Ever camp on Isle Royale?"

"Not with Kevin."

"Did he go there a lot?"

"I can't remember. Maybe. I think he went over there with his dad."

"You and Kevin do a lot of partying together?"

Williams smiled, looking squarely at Nolan. "Oh yeah. Sure did. We were young and kind of wild."

"Pick up a lot of girls, that type of thing?"

"Sometimes. Sure," Williams said. Another sniff and swipe.

Nolan pulled out a photo of Hannah Richter. "Ever party with this girl?"

Williams picked up the photo, held it for a few seconds and swallowed hard. "No."

The attorney clicked his pen. "Doesn't seem like these questions are going anywhere. Are we about done?"

Nolan ignored the attorney, knew his window of opportunity was closing. He tapped the photo but kept his gaze on Williams. "Do you want to look at her again? Make sure you haven't seen her before?"

Williams avoided the picture and looked at his attorney. "I've never partied with this woman."

Braun leaned forward. "He's said no already. Twice now." He grabbed the handle of his briefcase. "Okay, we're—"

"Have you talked to Ms. Adair lately?" Nolan interrupted. He leaned in and fixed on Williams's expression.

Williams's eyes widened. "Jane?" Sweat slicked his upper lip. He glanced at the door. "No. Why? Did she say we'd talked?"

Braun did a double take, his brow wrinkling at the direction the questioning had taken. He pushed back from the table and abruptly stood. "We're done. Let's go, Derek."

"Oh, I don't think so," Nolan said.

"Listen, my client has answered your questions about an active case, will leave the information about where he was today, so unless Ms. Adair is missing or claiming some charge, my client has no reason to be here. Right, Penn?" Braun gave the sheriff a glare.

"For now," Penn answered slowly, avoiding Nolan's frustrated look. After Williams and Braun left the room, Penn shrugged. "Best to let them stew a bit. We can always get them back."

It was almost one in the morning when Nolan pulled in front of Jane's house, defeat heavy in his steps as he worked his way down the walk. The house was dark except for a small glow coming from the center window. He called Cam's cell, and she let him inside. Her hair was matted and her face creased with sleep. They spoke quietly and sparingly in the entryway about the case, mostly about Derek Williams's interview, before she headed down the hall and back to bed.

Nolan made his way to the living room, where Ava was asleep on the sofa by the fireplace. Creed was curled on the floor next to her, his head down but his eyes open and on Nolan. The light from the flames cast a glow over Ava as she slept. Nolan stared at her. Dark lashes fanned over her cheeks, her arms wrapped around Rose's stuffed pony. He was caught off guard by the emotion that unfurled in him. On impulse, he bent over to pick up the blanket that had slipped onto the floor and adjusted it to cover her.

She startled, reached up, grabbing for the blanket and dropping the pony in the process. "Oh!" Her eyes popped open, and she swung herself down to reach for the toy.

Nolan reached down at the same time, and their heads bumped, arms tangled. The pony tumbled farther from their reach. They both leaned back, laughing at the slapstick comedy of it.

"Ah, sorry I woke you," Nolan finally offered. "May I?" He motioned to the toy.

"Yes." She laughed again, rubbing her head theatrically.

He grinned and picked up the pony. When he went to hand

it to her, he saw she'd brought up her knees and wrapped her arms around them. She patted the sofa, and Nolan sat and handed back the toy.

She looked the toy over as if searching for an answer somewhere in its patchy fur. Finding none, she glanced at him. "Ever wonder what life would be like in a different setting, different world, maybe a different time?"

Nolan considered whether he should read anything into her question but instead just answered truthfully. "No, not really."

"So you are happy with your life just as it is?"

He laughed at that. "No. I just don't think about other scenarios for myself. Maybe I'm not that much of a thinker or wishful or whatever. And you? Ever imagine another life for yourself?"

She sighed. "I never did. Never had to. Things were…fine. Good." She shrugged. "But now everything is…" She let the words linger, a frown starting, and he put a hand on her knees.

"We'll find Rose. Your life will go forward." He knew then he would do anything to make sure Ava found happiness again, that everything would work out. "Gotta get some sleep. We both need to be ready for tomorrow." He gave her knee a single pat and rose to settle into the chair across from her. She laid back, pulling the blanket up to her chin.

Nolan took one last look at Ava and Creed, the two of them together as if they belonged that way, and he felt Rose's absence even more. The four of them would make a good family. But without Rose, Ava would be shattered into a thousand pieces. And no one would be able to put her together again.

Finally he closed his eyes, just to be jolted from sleep by a loud noise. He grabbed his pistol, blinked against the fog of sleep. *Bam, bam, bam!* Someone pounding on the door, Nolan realized. Creed stood in the center of the room, back straight, tail rigid, growling.

Ava was on her feet, confused and still half asleep. "What's going on?"

Cam appeared, weapon in hand. "Ava, come with me." She quickly escorted Ava to the back of the house.

The knocking persisted. Creed snarled and snapped at the air. In the background, Nolan heard Cam yell at Jane to stay in her room.

Nolan parted the drapes over the front window and craned his neck. The porch light cast a dim glow over the deputy sheriff standing there. He relaxed and let the gun fall to his side, but his heart seized with fear of what was coming. A deputy at three in the morning couldn't be good.

He commanded Creed to stand down and opened the door slowly. "Deputy…" He glanced at his name tag, vaguely remembering seeing the guy before at Lindsey Webber's crime scene at the barn.

"Sir. Deputy Turner."

He opened the door for him to step inside. "What's going on, Deputy?"

"We have a development."

Nolan sensed movement behind him and turned to see Cam, Ava and Jane. Ava stepped forward. "Is it Rose? Is she…?"

The deputy noticed her. "You're the mom?"

Ava nodded.

The deputy removed his hat and scratched the back of his head. "Sorry. I was sent over to tell you that a witness saw a young girl fitting Rose's description being loaded onto a boat on the west-side docks."

"Thank You, God. Thank You," Ava whispered from the hallway.

"When?" Nolan asked.

"A little before two a.m. We just got the information ourselves."

"That was over an hour ago." Nolan's mind was a firestorm of thoughts. "He's taking her to the island. Have the rangers been notified?"

"Yes."

"Coast Guard?"

"Dispatched from Houghton fifteen minutes ago."

Nolan looked at Cam. "Get me in touch with Isle Royale Ranger Division in Houghton now. Tell them I need immediate air transport."

Ava came to his side. "I'm going with you."

"He's taking her to the island. You're not equipped to handle that type of search. It'll be brutal."

"You're underestimating me. Don't try to stop me. I'm going." She turned on her heel and disappeared down the hall.

Nolan followed and found her in the guest room, riffling through a large duffle bag. "What are you doing?"

She looked up from the bag. "Getting some clothes together."

What was she thinking? *She's not*, he realized. "I know you want to go, but this is a criminal pursuit. It's too dangerous."

"But I can help you and Cam by—"

"Cam isn't going. She's an analyst, not trained for field work. Neither are you. I'm sorry, Ava. Your daughter's already in danger—we can't take the chance of that happening to you."

"Please just take me to the island with you. I'll stay at one of the ranger stations. I won't go any farther. But I want to be there as soon as you find her." She pushed past him with a backpack and an armful of clothes and other items. Back in the family room, she tossed everything onto the floor and began organizing it in the pack. Creed circled around her, nervously sniffing.

"How can I help?" Jane asked.

Ava ignored her.

Cam finished on her call. "It's arranged. A helicopter is on the way. They'll touch down in the field at Fanny Hooe Lake campground in an hour."

"I'll be ready," Ava said.

Cam looked between the two of them. "I checked. It's a Bell 505 Jet Ranger. Seats four passengers."

Ava craned her head upward, her blue eyes pleading with him. Logic and reason told him to say no. But how could he? "Meet me at the parking lot in one hour."

Chapter Fourteen

Helicopters, Ava decided, don't fly, they just beat the air into submission. She gripped the seat belt over her chest and stared at Creed, who sat on the floor, his gaze steady. The dog must have done this before. He seemed to be a natural. She, on the other hand, had never been in a helicopter. Never cared to go in one again, either.

The humming and buzzing of machines inside the chopper combined with the thrumming of the blade permeated her entire body. The noise was deafening, and her life was now in the hands of the pilot and the rows and rows of illuminated buttons and instruments in front of him. Unwanted thoughts about Kevin and his final moments pervaded her mind, quickly overcome by the thought of her child somewhere on the island, alone and scared. Fear and vulnerability were quickly replaced by determination. She closed her eyes, praying that Rose would be returning home with her.

The craft began its ascent, and every organ in her body pulled downward, then without warning thrust forward, pressing her tight against the seat belt. Chatter came over her headset. "Doing okay?" Nolan asked her.

She nodded and opened her eyes, her gaze landing on Nolan.

He had a bulletproof vest and carried both a pistol and automatic rifle. He looked like he was getting ready to do battle. Maybe he was. And she felt a twinge of fear for him mixed with overwhelming gratitude. He was risking his life for Rose. And without a doubt, she knew it wasn't just because it was his job. He cared, deeply, about the little girl who meant the world to her. And every touch, every look they'd shared these few days had been sparked with emotion that spoke more than words.

Even now as she caught his eye, he gave her a gentle nod. If they'd met in normal times and she'd felt these flutters when she saw him, felt the warmth of his presence, she wouldn't question her feelings for him. But these weren't normal times. So it was only natural for her to feel affection for him. That was all this was.

Still, she'd sensed his developing feelings for her over the last couple days. She could only hope it was true, since she felt the same way. But she couldn't be sure.

The only thing she could be sure of was her faith. And already she knew her prayers had been answered: Rose was still alive. Now it was up to Ava to help find her.

She looked over at Nolan again, his square-set jaw as he peered through the dark night outside. She'd seen that look in his eyes, his determination to uncover the truth, and she understood that. And maybe it made sense to him that Mac or Kevin was somehow involved in those past heinous crimes. Part of her couldn't get past her fear of what Nolan might find—and then do. But for now, all she needed to do was trust that Nolan would find Rose. She closed her eyes and offered a prayer for Rose…and for Nolan.

Nolan's voice came into her headset. "We're nearing the island. The plan is to drop you at the Malone Bay Station. A ranger will meet you there. I'll go on farther north, where I'll meet up with other law enforcement. I'll try to radio in updates, but communication can be sketchy out here."

She kept her eyes on the horizon, which had transformed from light blue to surreal hues of orange and yellow. The island came into sight, so dense with foliage that it appeared to be an inky oil spot floating on the gray lake waters. She'd been here before, years ago while visiting with Kevin. He'd called it one of his favorite places on Earth, but Ava had never shared that enthusiasm. Despite the breathtaking scenery and the tranquility of its remote trails, she'd always sensed a hidden danger lurking in its forests.

She leaned forward and pressed her forehead against the cold glass, knowing that Rose was out there now. Her whole body ached to hold her child.

The helicopter slowed and hovered over a clear spot not far from the water's edge and slowly descended. As soon as it came to rest, Nolan unbuckled and opened the door, reaching inside for her hand. They jogged to where a ranger stood. Nolan introduced the man as Leroy Karr.

"Leroy will take good care of you," Nolan said before turning back to the helicopter.

He'd only taken a step before she reached out and stopped him with a hand to his shoulder.

He turned, and she shouted over the chopper's deafening roar, "Be safe. I need... I need you to find her and—"

He nodded quickly, lifted her hand, giving it a tight squeeze before releasing it and rushing back to the chopper. Ava folded her arms and stood strong against the whirling wind of the giant blade and watched the helicopter ascend without her. Staying behind was one of the most difficult things she'd ever done.

"I've got radio communications from ground search," the pilot told Nolan. "There's no place to land—we'll have to insert." The man looked down at Creed. "Is your K9 capable?"

"Yes."

"There's a rappel kit in the under-seat storage in the back.

Should be rope gloves, too. Prepare the seat and hookup. I'll get you as close as possible."

Nolan unbuckled and found the kit. He double-checked Creed's vest first, then connected a rappel ring and hooked him to a cable that would secure the two of them together. He attached the seat harness to the descent control device. Pressure built in his ears as the chopper descended. He took off his headset and secured head and eye protection. They were not equipped with canine head and eye gear, so he'd do his best to keep Creed's head tucked close to him.

"About ready?"

Nolan double-checked the system's hookup before securing Creed's hook to his vest. "Ready."

"Listen for my command. We'll drop the bag first," the pilot yelled.

The force of air from the blades shook the trees and sent small pieces of debris whirling in the air. A handful of rangers were huddled together, shielding their eyes and watching.

"Drop the bag!"

He did and watched it fall through the tree canopy. Next he threw the rope, making sure it hung properly.

"Ready. On my count." The pilot clutched the control stick and studied his instruments. "Okay, five, four, three…"

With one hand on the rope, Nolan slipped the other around Creed, pulling him close. Creed was calm, stoic even. He'd done this maneuver a hundred times and lived for this type of adventure. Truthfully, so did Nolan.

"Two, one…go."

Nolan slipped from the deck and descended, legs tight and extended, Creed hanging limply from the rope attached. They reached the ground, unhooked and signaled the pilot.

Ranger Moore and the others caught up to him immediately. "You're not going to like my report," Moore said. "We've got nothing. No evidence of recent foot traffic in this area, no witness sightings, nothing. And I've had two rangers positioned near the last sighting this whole time, but there's been no additional activity in that area. If they've brought her here to the island, they're not transporting her along the same path."

"They must know we're looking for them," Nolan said. "Or maybe they changed their route in anticipation of taking Rose and already had another escape route planned."

"If that's the case, we've been wasting time." Moore looked stricken. "Valuable time."

"We've got water patrol all along the north shore," one of the other rangers said. "We'll spot them as soon as they depart the island for Canadian waters."

"No," Nolan answered. "They evaded us in the water once already. We're not taking that chance. Let's find her before they get her off the island."

If they connected with their transport and got Rose across the border, she'd be gone forever. A sense of helplessness overcame him, and the surrounding woods suddenly ensnared him in a suffocating gloom. The small prayer he'd muttered the other day seemed stupid now, like praying to thin air. No God—no good God—would let an innocent child go through what Rose had been through and then fall into the hands of such evil.

Ava tried to focus her attention on the ranger station, her stomach roiling from both the leftover motion of the helicopter and anxiety over Rose. A woman's voice came out of nowhere: "Is this our guest?"

Ava straightened, facing a middle-aged woman with short blond hair. "This is my wife, Ruth," the ranger explained. "We live here at Malone."

Ruth smiled and pointed toward the simple wood structure, a wood duplex-like cabin partially hidden from view by thick brush and towering trees. As they neared, she saw it was painted brown with a large moose rack over the door bearing the sign Malone Bay Ranger Station.

"Leroy has manned this station for as many seasons as I can remember," Ruth was saying. "I know it doesn't look like much, but he's responsible for the entire south shore from Chippewa Harbor to McCormick Reef, which is about forty miles of coastline. Raised our daughter, Lisa, here during the park season, in Houghton offseason. Homeschooled her in the wilds, I did—the woods were our classroom, the wildlife her classmates."

Ava did her best to take it all in. *Homeschool. My dream for Rose, too.*

"Oh, sweetie, I'm saying all the wrong things, aren't I? Come into our cabin, and let me get you some tea. Peppermint, to settle your nerves. Leroy needs to make a short trip to the docks to fill the propane tanks—everything here runs on propane, our water heater, stove, everything—so it'll just be you and me for most of the afternoon. But don't worry—we'll wait this out together, okay?"

Ruth and Leroy's cabin was modest: two bedrooms, a kitchen, living room, a couple closets and a bathroom. Ava settled at a small wood table in the kitchen, and over tea she listened while Ruth tried to reassure her that Rose would be found. Ava was grateful for someone to pass the time with her, even though every fiber of her being wanted to be on the search with Nolan.

Her frustration and fear must have shown. Ruth reached across the table and touched her hand. "I know they'll find your Rose," she said again. "I have a sense about it. Tell me about her, will ya?"

She's precious and beautiful, loves dolls and horses, has the cutest freckle between her pinky and ring finger, is as sweet as sugar but can be precocious—or at least that's how she used to be. Mostly now she's just so, so sad... Ava wanted to tell Ruth all these things, but the words were stuck inside her. Instead, she asked to use the restroom.

"If there's no toilet paper, let me know, hon."

Ava excused herself and exited through a creaky wood door to the back of the cabin. On her way back to the kitchen, she noticed how little they had here. Was this how all rangers lived? She thought of Leroy and Ruth and their little Lisa living like this summer after summer and how happy they seemed together, living a simple life... *Oh, God, I've lost so much. Please, don't let me lose my child, too.*

She took her seat at the table again and was about to sip her tea when there was a loud knock on the door and someone called out. Both she and Ruth jumped up.

"Are you the ranger?" a man asked after Ruth had opened the door. "We have an emergency. A woman and girl in trouble."

"A woman and..."

"We were about three miles in on Ishpeming Trail when we heard a kid scream and—"

"It was coming from the woods," the woman next to him finished. "So, we walked toward it and found an abandoned shack tucked in the forest. We ran to see if we could help, but when we got close, we heard a man's voice. He was yelling and saying awful things, so we hesitated and hid in the trees. Then we saw him. He was outside the shack, and he was berating a young woman, telling her she better never try to run away again. And then he pulled a gun and pointed it at her head, told her to get back inside. I thought he was going to kill her."

"I should have done something," the man said.

The woman shook her head. "What were you going to do? He had a gun. There was nothing..."

A high-pitched buzz in Ava's ears drowned out the rest of their words. A man with a gun, berating a woman, a child. A child...

"The child who screamed," Ava managed to say. "Did you see her?"

"Yeah, poor thing. She looked so scared."

"Did she have red hair?"

"Yes. But how do you know that?"

* * *

"They said he was armed," Ava said. Ruth had radioed for help, but there was no way Ava could wait. She had to go to Rose. Now.

"You need to wait until help comes."

"I can't. That's my daughter. You would do the same for your daughter—don't tell me that you wouldn't." Ava shouldered her pack and crossed to the kitchen. She riffled through the drawers and found a few sharp knives. She slid one into her pack.

"What are you doing with that? A knife is no match for a gun. Can't you wait until Leroy and the others get here?"

Ruth was pleading now, but Ava couldn't help that. She had to get to Rose before he hurt her. Or worse.

She pushed past Ruth and grabbed every map and brochure about the island she could from a rack by the door and ran outside. She kept running in the direction that the couple had said they'd come from, her feet catching on rocks and roots along the trail. She ran until her lungs ached and her legs burned and sweat poured from her body.

When she couldn't go one more step, she stopped, caught her breath and gulped some water. The world spun like a blue-and-green kaleidoscope, and mosquitoes swarmed and pricked her skin as she checked the map. The couple had told her that they'd left the trail just a little way up from here, hoping to catch photos of the wildlife on the island. They'd marked on the map where they'd seen the shack, although they'd disagreed as to its exact location. They'd each ticked a slightly different spot. Over the next mile, she'd have to decide on which direction to take. If she made the wrong choice, it could cost Rose her life.

She shoved her water bottle back into her pack, her fingers brushing against the handle of the knife she'd brought. Before, in her former life, before Kevin had died, before Rose had been stolen from her, she never would have considered harming someone. Now she had no doubt that she would do anything to save her daughter.

Ava started down the trail again, still fearful but determined. Forty minutes later, she saw the outline of a roof through the trees. She'd chosen correctly and thanked God for guiding her to the right spot. She worked closer, trying to get a better view of the shack, which was buried by weeds and vines and listed to one side. It was barely visible from her vantage point. She shed her pack and removed the knife, tucking it into her waistband, and crept forward. The woods seemed eerily quiet. Too quiet. She feared they'd moved on already.

She crouched in the brush and watched the shack. Her skin crawled, either from sweat or insects, she didn't care. She continued to watch for what seemed like forever, her ears straining over the buzzing flies. Ava was about to come out from cover when she heard a man's voice. He popped out from the weedy hovel, a radio in hand, and headed toward the woods on the other side.

Now or never. She stayed crouched and moved toward the shack, pushing through the briars until she found the door—nothing more than a piece of nylon tarp nailed over an opening. She slipped around the tarp.

Inside her eyes adjusted to the scarce light bleeding in from the cracks between the boards, and what she saw sent waves of horror through her. Rose, slumped on the dirt floor, next to a bucket of dirty water, an old kerosene lamp and empty candy bar wrappers. *No, no, no...* Ava went to Rose, scooping her into her lap. She flopped like a rag doll, red hair falling in front of her face. She wasn't dead, but she wouldn't wake, either. She'd been drugged. Ava pushed Rose's hair back and, out of the corner of her eye, caught a glimpse of another woman in the shadows against the wall, her body upright but limp and her head lolled to one side. Ava would check on her, but for the moment she stayed with Rose, patted her cheeks that were crusted with dirt and swollen with insect bites.

Finally, her baby's eyes fluttered open, but not her normal beautiful eyes—instead tiny slits of blue with hazy pupils. "Rosie, I'm here," she whispered. "Mommy's here."

Rose's eyes rolled closed; her head slumped to the side. Ava had to get her out of here. She stood and bent, about to pick her up when a sliver of light crept into the room and footsteps sounded behind her. She turned and faced the barrel of a gun.

"Back away from her, lady."

Ava raised her hands. "Don't shoot—please, don't shoot."

His sharp features twisted with hate, and his gaze pierced her with stark, cold evil. "Who are… No, I know who you are. You're the girl's mother."

Ava slowly moved aside, trying to draw him away from Rose. She'd never seen this man before. How did he know she was Rose's mother?

"Who else is with you?" he snarled.

"No one."

"Don't lie to me!" In two quick steps he towered directly in front of her, the barrel pressed against her forehead.

"I'm not lying. I swear it's just me, but others are coming. They'll be here soon." She inched backward, her hands behind her now, her fingers grasping for the knife tucked in her waistband.

"Put your hands where I can see them!"

Ava obeyed.

"Turn around." She slowly rotated, the barrel tracing a circular path along her skull. He ripped the knife from her waistband. She turned her head in time to catch a flash of steel as the gun came down on her temple. A sickening *crack* exploded in her head, dots broke out in her peripheral vision, her knees buckled, and she felt her body crumple as blackness overtook her.

The sound of a faraway voice. Throbbing pain in her head. Slowly, fuzzy details became clearer as Ava remembered where she was and the man who'd hit her and... Rose! She opened her eyes only enough to see that Rose was on the ground just inches from her. The other woman, too, and now she realized that the kidnapper's voice came from outside the shack, his tone low and angry, his words indistinguishable. Her gaze circumvented the room, looking for a weapon, a way out.

The words stopped, the tarp moved, and she snapped her eyes shut again. Footsteps echoed on the floor, coming closer and then next to her. *Be still, be still.* She sensed his stare on her face and willed her breathing to stay steady, even, calm.

A heavy weight pressed against her ribs, and her breath started to catch. *Breathe normal, breathe normal.* The pressure on her ribs turned into a nudge, then a push, and she was forced onto her back. *He's going to kill me.* She willed her expression to remain motionless, but on her back, she felt vulnerable. *This is it*, she thought. But she didn't care about losing her own life. She was ready, but... *God, please protect my daughter, please save her.*

Seconds ticked by, and she felt the man watching her, his gaze heavy and impenetrable. Could he see her heart pounding in her chest? Did he know she was awake? Was he pointing the gun at her head that very moment, his finger squeezing the trigger?

"Faster. Come on, go faster!" Nolan called out to the boat pilot through his headset. They'd searched on foot for several hours, finally changing their strategy and meeting with water patrol in the Five Fingers area. They'd been patrolling the northeast shore and just rounded Blake Point when a radio call had come through. Hikers had reached the Malone Bay Station with a report that they'd seen Rose and another woman, matching the description of the girl seen by the hiker, being held in a shack off the Ishpeming Trail.

And another report: Ava had left on her own to rescue Rose. His heart had sunk when he'd heard that—both Rose and Ava now in jeopardy, and he was miles away. The helicopter was already restationed at Houghton, so they continued in the *Eagle*, a twenty-foot rigid inflatable patrol boat with a 150-horsepower engine when pushed to the max, which still wasn't fast enough for Nolan.

It was just the pilot, Moore and Creed with him in the small craft. Creed stood rigid at the bow, his ears flat against his head, his gaze steady as they bumped over waves, the boat's stainless-steel reinforced nose cutting the surface, wind and frigid spray pelting them and chilling Nolan through, but he barely noticed. Ava and Rose were his focus, and the threat of losing them terrified him. He should never have brought her onto the island.

They entered Siskiwit Bay and neared the Malone Bay Station. The plan was to dock near the station and go the rest of the way on foot. The two witnesses had disagreed on the exact locale but pinned a general location.

Leroy and his wife were waiting for them on the dock with supplies. "I tried to stop her," Ruth said. "But I also can't blame her. I'd do the same for my daughter." She handed them water canteens and a fresh mobile radio.

"Did she leave anything behind that would have her scent on it? A sweater? Jacket?"

"Nothing. It was chilly in the cabin. She did use a blanket. Would that work?"

"I can try."

After a quick update from the witnesses, Nolan and Moore hit the trail, hiking at a good pace, Nolan in the lead, Creed at his side. They made minimal stops to rehydrate and give Creed the water he needed. Nolan watched the map, and within the hour, they neared the area the couple had marked.

Other rangers converged on the area, and Moore's radio crackled with the first report. "907 to Ranger 101, come in."

"907, this is 101."

"Approaching from the Greenstone. Approximately one mile from marked location. Please advise."

The ranger looked to Nolan, who said, "Tell him to continue with caution and radio if he sees anything."

Moore relayed the message. More messages came over his radio as rangers coordinated with him. They located the cairn mentioned by the witnesses and left the main trail, pushing through the forest, Creed's nose working off Ava's scent on the blanket. They wandered for a while, Nolan quickly losing heart. He felt desperation like never before. Miles and miles of thick forest and Creed hadn't picked up on anything. Precious time was ticking away.

Ava waited, but no gunshot came, and the man moved away from her. She remained still, eyes closed, not knowing where he was or if he was watching her. It dawned on her that he didn't want to draw attention to their location by firing a gun, and her mind raced with other possibilities. Was he going to keep her alive? If so, what for? Would she be moved with Rose and the other woman across the border to be…what? To become another trafficking victim? Or to be taken off somewhere far away and then shot and killed? She imagined the other victims before her, Hannah and Lindsey, and now knew the same terror they'd felt in their final moments. The terror Rose would feel if she weren't drugged. And for the moment, Ava felt that her baby being drugged was an unbidden blessing.

Thoughts and images swirled in her mind, vying to be her final thought before dying… The thought of death made her heart break for Kevin. What must have been in his mind when his plane had spiraled from the sky, sending him to his death? Had his last moments been filled with prayers, a plea to God for mercy, memories of her and Rose? Or guilt and remorse? Had he regretted the lie he'd told her? Or something else in his past? Had he wished for time to set things straight?

And then her thoughts turned to Nolan, and deep inside her

stirred an aching mix of guilt and regret. Guilt because ever since that moment on the beach, where he'd rescued her from drowning, then comforted her, she'd felt herself drawn to him. Truthfully, even before that moment. How could she have feelings for anyone other than Kevin? But she did, didn't she? And suddenly she regretted that she'd never have a chance to tell Nolan how she felt. The tumult of regret mixed with sorrow and fear and an overwhelming desire to embrace her daughter, to tell her how much she loved her, and in the din of it all an ache welled inside her, consuming her until her mind and heart cried out to the Lord. *Please help me.*

What little peace that came with her prayer was shattered a second later by the sound of splashing liquid and a pungent smell. She dared crack her eyes open and saw the man, his back to her as he moved about the shack with a can of kerosene. He was abandoning his mission. Better to sacrifice three lives than lose his own. And a fire would be a perfect way to kill his witnesses, destroy evidence and distract the rangers while he escaped.

She watched in horror as he pulled a lighter from his pocket and bent, holding the flame to where the oil had pooled. Flames hissed, then licked higher into the air. The man backed up and retreated through the tarp.

Ava sprung to her feet, unsure what to do first. She blinked and tried to take a deep breath, only sucking in heat and smoke. Neither the woman nor Rose stirred. The dry wood of the shack crackled and popped. She had minutes, maybe less, to react.

She grabbed her pack, found a bottle of water and doused the woman, hoping to wake her or at least saturate her body against the flames. She scooped Rose and pulled her close, running through the tarp, sunlight burning her eyes. She trudged about fifty yards away, set her on the ground and, against every instinct to not leave her daughter alone, she ran back.

The tarp was melting as she approached, smoke billowing from every gap and crevice, one whole wall engulfed in fire, and from behind her came the terrified voice of her child: "Mommy, nooo!"

Ava ran into the burning shack.

Chapter Fifteen

Nolan kept one eye on Creed as he picked his way through the woods, working the scent back and forth along the forest floor, digging his snout into the ground and then lifting his head in the air for deep sniffs.

Moore brought up the rear. "Nothing out here but trees and more trees," he said. "Maybe we need to go with the direction the guy gave us."

"Give it a little longer." But Nolan had doubts, too. It was easy to see why the couple was divided on the location of the shack. It was a late spring, and even without full foliage, the trees were dense and packed together, and every part of the woods looked the same as the next.

"Hey," Nolan called out. "Look over there, along the east side of that ridge."

Moore shielded his eyes and spotted the stream of dark smoke rising in the air. "That can't be good. Let's go."

Branches scraped at their faces and snatched their clothing as they cut through the dense woods toward the smoke. While he ran, Moore radioed their location and reported the smoke. Creed ran in front of Nolan, his agile body dodging trunks and weaving between obstacles. As they drew closer, Rose's voice pierced the air and echoed through the trees.

Creed burst ahead, running full speed, while Nolan and Moore struggled to keep up. A minute later, Creed let out a series of sharp barks. Nolan ran toward the sound. Creed had found Rose, who was sitting on the ground with her arm around his neck. He ran to her, shed his pack and looked her over. She was fine. *Thank You, God. Ava?* "Where's your mommy? Where is she?"

She pointed to a shack. Ava stood near it, her back to him, hunched over as one whole side became engulfed in flames, the roof close to collapse. *What is she doing?* "Stay!" he ordered Creed, then cupped his hands to his mouth and hollered as he ran toward her, "Move back, Ava! It's going to collapse!"

Heat intensified as he rushed to her, wood smoke clinging to his sweaty skin and coating the back of his throat. A loud pop startled him, then a creaking sound. The burning wall had shifted.

"Help me!" she called over the roar of the flames. She was struggling to drag a woman away from the burning structure.

He stepped in front of her, taking her place. "I've got her. Get back. Now!"

He bent and grasped the woman's arms, putting his full weight into it, and pulled her limp body over the ground, five feet, ten feet... Moore caught up to him through the now billowing smoke, grabbed her feet, and they hoisted her like a hammock and sprinted as best as they could, finally nearing Ava and Rose where they huddled with Creed... All at once, the shack fell in on itself, flames crackling and hissing, and a million tiny embers floating into the air like fireflies on a dark summer night.

They placed the unconscious young woman on the ground. She had long brown hair.

Moore stood nearby, speaking into a satellite phone. "INDU Dispatch, ISRO 402."

The call dropped, and he tried again to reach the Indiana Dunes National Lakeshore dispatcher for the Great Lakes national parks. "INDU Dispatch, ISRO 402."

Nolan had already focused on assessing the girl's injuries. Ava and Rose appeared next to him—Creed, too. "Her leg," Ava choked out. "It's been burned."

Nolan nodded and used his knife to gently cut away part of her jeans, revealing angry red, blistering skin. She began moaning, then thrashing. Ava turned Rose away from the girl and placed her with Creed several feet farther off. Then Ava moved back and spoke gently to the girl, trying to calm her.

Moore stood a few feet away, staring now at the open burn wound, his voice more agitated as he tried the call again: "INDU Dispatch, ISRO 402."

Nolan motioned to Ava. "Run to my pack—it's over there—and get my canteen."

She returned a second later with the supplies, handing him the canteen. The girl was screaming in pain now. Nolan flushed the burn with cool water and glanced up at Moore. "We'll need air transport." Then to the girl. "Can you tell me your name?"

"Sadie. Sadie Reece."

"We're here to help you, Sadie. You're going to be okay."

The phone crackled as dispatch finally answered. Moore transmitted their location. "We have an uncontained fire and a burn victim who requires immediate air transport."

Nolan relayed the victim's name and vitals to Moore. "Sadie Reece. Female. Approximately one hundred thirty pounds." He felt her wrist. "Pulse elevated—one hundred twenty bpm." He glanced again at the blistering, raw burns and estimated the total body surface area effected. "TBSA affected five percent."

Moore received instructions and finished the call. He knelt to assist. There wasn't much else to do for her other than keep her calm and comfort her.

Until three shots sounded.

Moore flinched. "Gunfire!"

Nolan moved to shield Ava and Rose with his body, his eyes scanning the area off to the left where Creed stood, barking at the sound. But where was it coming from?

The sound of more shots carried through the air, then a staticky message came over Moore's radio. "405 to 402."

"405, this is 402," he said. "We heard gunfire."

"We encountered the suspect, and he opened fire on us. We returned fire. The suspect is dead. I repeat, the suspect is dead."

Nolan relaxed and gave Ava and Rose some space. "He's gone," he said.

Ava squeezed her eyes shut. She lowered her head slightly, her lips silently moving. Nolan, too, felt like uttering a prayer of thanks that these two were safe, when he caught a couple of her words. Her prayer wasn't of thanks. Her words asked for forgiveness for the man who'd just tried to kill both her and Rose. He sat back, in both amazement and admiration.

When she opened her eyes again, he locked gazes with her. Part of him wanted to be angry at her for running off, for putting herself in danger, but all he could say was, "You did an incredibly brave thing here."

She took a deep breath and let it out slowly. "I had to save Rose."

"You did that and more. You saved this woman's life, too." Sadie was badly injured, but Nolan was sure she'd make it. Thanks to Ava's courage. "What made you run back in after her? You could have been killed."

"You would have done the same thing. You risk your life every day for people you don't know. You're the bravest person I've ever met." Her words, spoken with admiration, shot through to his heart. The past few hours had been the most fear-filled moments of his life. Not because of the danger or the risks but because of what he'd stood to lose.

His gaze swept over Ava, who continued to comfort Sadie

while Rose sat nearby loving on Creed, and he knew that he wanted to be in their lives forever. He didn't know what that looked like yet, but for the moment it was enough to admit it to himself. Now he just had to figure out a way to make it happen.

A few minutes later, three more rangers emerged from the forest. The shack was nothing more than a bonfire now, but the flames had spread and sprouted up in small patches over the surrounding area. Ava watched as the new rangers joined Moore in clearing dry wood from the reaches of flames and beating down flare-ups. They seemed to be losing the battle. Panic squirmed in Ava's belly. She wanted to get Rose out of here and back to safety. Wherever that was. Not Jane's house. She couldn't trust her.

Moore appeared with an update. "Just got word," he said. "There's no suitable landing spot nearby. They're doing a short-haul extraction. The chopper is at the staging area. They'll be here in five."

"Sadie," Nolan said. "You're going to be airlifted out of here to the University of Michigan burn center in Ann Arbor. You'll get good care there."

She moaned with pain and licked her dry lips. Ava held the canteen to her mouth and lifted her head slightly so she could take a sip.

Nolan continued to speak softly to the young woman. "Were there any more girls with you?"

She nodded. "Lindsey," she whispered, barely able to mutter the name through her pain.

Lindsey. The girl found dead in her barn.

Suddenly flames flashed up a nearby pine. The fire was spreading fast. "How much longer until we get some water?" one of the rangers called out to Moore. "This thing's getting too big to handle."

Ava admired how calm Nolan remained as he continued to question Sadie. "Was it just this one man?"

She shook her head. "And a woman."

"Do you know her name?"

"No."

"What did she look like?"

"She kept us blindfolded..." She winced and let out a long moan. "The pain. It hurts so much."

Ava helped her take another drink of water. The hum of a helicopter filled the sky, and she gazed up to see it approach.

Nolan spoke into her ear, pressing her for information. "Anything else at all you can remember about the woman?"

Sadie started to shake her head, then arched her back and cried out in pain. Ava caught a glimpse of a tattoo inside her lip. Its odd location niggled at her brain—was this important?

The helicopter hovered nearby, the sound deafening. "I'm scared," Sadie murmured, over and over. Ava held her hand and reassured her the best she could.

"Do you know where you were kept?" Nolan asked.

"No...no."

Moore motioned as he yelled out to another ranger, "Just got word. We need to move her. She's too close to the fire. The air from the blade will fuel the flames." The two men jogged over to them, prepared to move Sadie.

Ava turned to Nolan. "There's something that might be important." She told him about the tattoo.

He held out his hand and told the rangers to wait, then to Sadie, "You have a tattoo on the inside of your lip."

"Yes. We all did."

"You got it right away in Detroit?"

She nodded.

"Who did the tattoos?"

For a split second, the pain in Sadie's expression disappeared as her jaw clenched with a memory and a hard-won determination.

"What is it, Sadie? What do you remember?" Ava held her breath.

"I could see under my blindfold. Just his forearm. He had a tattoo, a hissing snake with two nails through it, made to look like a dollar sign."

Nolan sat back and smiled. "Good job, Sadie. You have no idea how helpful this is. You may have helped save more girls."

Sadie half smiled, then winced again in pain. Ava leaned in close and whispered into her ear, "I'll be praying for you."

Moments later, Rose and Ava watched together as the chopper hovered in the air and a man descended on a rope. The short hauler reached the ground and, without delay, unfurled a bright orange bag and laid it out. The rangers lifted Sadie into the bag, zipped and secured her, and gave a signal. The helicopter ascended, carrying Sadie high over the treetops.

Ava tucked the quilt around Rose and leaned in to kiss her cheek, inhaling the faint scent of Ruth's bath salts. She had used almost a whole bar of soap on her daughter, scrubbing the dirt and grime away.

It had been late by the time Nolan wrapped up his investigation at the scene. Instead of risking a night flight over the lake, they'd returned to Malone Bay Station to stay with Ruth and Leroy. A seaplane flight back to the mainland was scheduled for first thing in the morning.

Ruth had cooked a wonderful dinner for them—fresh fish and potatoes, wild asparagus and chocolate cake. Rose had eaten every bite and even taken seconds. A good sign, considering everything she'd been through. A female medic had come over from the Windigo medical station on the west side of the island and thoroughly checked over Rose. Other than mild dehydration and a few bruises, she was unharmed.

Ava had been able to relay via satellite phone the good news of Rose's rescue to Mac and Yvette and to her mother and sister, who had arrived in Sculpin Bay to help search for Rose. Everyone was overjoyed, and Ava was so grateful. Her daughter was okay.

The dead man had been identified as John Shreve, a Canadian citizen who had no known ties to anyone in the United States. But Cam was working her technical expertise on the man, taking a deep dive into his background, and Ava was confident that she'd come up with answers.

Now, with Rose finally asleep and a little quiet time to herself, Ava draped one of the bed blankets over her shoulders and tiptoed past Nolan, asleep on the sofa, and onto the back deck. Ruth and Leroy had offered her and Rose their second bedroom for the night, while the rest of the guys had retired in the bunkhouse next door.

Ava sat in one of the deck chairs and propped her feet on the deck rail. She burrowed into the blanket, the night sky cold on her face and the rhythmic call of tree frogs soothing her anxieties. She thought of Sadie and the other girls still missing, and Lindsey dying alone and scared in the barn, and Hannah Richter dying anonymously in the woods without even her name known for a decade, and the man shot today by rangers, and her dear Kevin, missed every second of every day.

Ava drew in a deep breath and let it out slowly, turning her gaze upward. The sky was pitch-black, and without any light interference, the stars were the most brilliant she'd ever seen. Proof that God's beauty would always prevail over the ugliness, sorrow and evil in the world. And she chose to focus on that and the good things she'd experienced: Mac and Yvette, who loved and supported both her and Rose, and her own family and new friends, and especially Nolan.

A rustle in the darkness momentarily alarmed her, but then she heard Nolan's voice, barely a whisper. "It doesn't get much more peaceful than this, does it?"

He joined her on the deck and settled into the chair next to her. Creed sat between them, brushing his head against Ava's arm. She indulged him by petting him from his ears down his back over and over, taking solace in the warmth of his fur until he let out a huge yawn and lay down on the deck floor.

"How is Rose?" Nolan asked.

"Physically, she's fine. Emotionally, though…"

"She's been through so much. And so have you." His hand found its way to her arm and slid down until he grasped her hand.

Her heart thudded in her chest, but her breath grew easy. Being with Nolan made her feel safe and happy. She never thought she'd feel those things again. "Tell me about your family."

He chuckled. "The Sheas are a wild bunch, as my mom would say. I have four siblings."

"You're kidding."

"Nope. I'm in the middle. Two older sisters and a younger brother and sister. Grew up in Ohio, but now we're scattered all over. One of my sisters lives near me in DC. She's married with twin girls, who I adore. Luckily I get to see them a lot."

"Your family sounds wonderful."

"It is."

"But you've never married?" Ava regretted the words as soon as they were out. Nolan noticeably tensed and grew silent.

"I'm sorry for asking something so personal," she said.

"No. It's just not easy for me to talk about. I was engaged not too long ago, to a woman I dated for a couple years. I thought… I really thought she was the one who God chose for me, but it turns out that I was wrong."

"What happened?"

"She cheated on me."

Ava was shocked. She hadn't expected that answer. "With someone you knew?"

"No. I couldn't imagine how painful that… We were supposed to meet for dinner, and when she didn't show up or answer my texts, I went by her apartment. Her roommate told me she'd gone to a different restaurant, so I thought there was a miscommunication. I went there to catch up with her, and that's when I saw her with this other man. They were holding hands, and they seemed…intimate with each other. I came to find out that it'd been going on for months."

Ava shook her head. "I'm so sorry. That must have been devastating."

"It's just that I never suspected. I thought things were fine between us. I must not have been in tune to her or our relationship." He drew his hand back and sat up straighter, putting his hands on his knees. "I can't blame her, really."

She'd heard him, but her focus drifted to his hand that now rubbed the denim of his jeans. The hand that had felt so warm in hers a moment earlier. She realized she'd paused too long and said, "What do you mean that you can't blame her? That's not fair. Why would you blame yourself for someone else's dishonesty?"

He shrugged. "But if I missed that, what else had I missed?"

"Oh, Nolan, when you love someone, you don't think anything but the best about them. Someone like you, trained not to miss anything…well, you must have loved her very much." Even as she said the words, she thought of Kevin and the lie he'd told her. She'd thought the best of him, still did. And yes, she'd loved him so much. And still did. But…had she, too, missed something? No, her heart told her, there had to be an explanation for that lie.

"You're a thousand miles away right now. What are you thinking, Ava?"

It was her turn to shrug. "About Kevin and the day his plane went down. The day that Derek claims to have seen him here and not in Green Bay like he told me. As far as I know, there were never lies between us, but if that's true—"

"I'm afraid it is."

A chill ran down her back at his words. "What?" She turned in her seat and faced him. "What do you mean?"

"Cam looked into it. Kevin flew into Green Bay on business like he said. He attended a meeting with a medical-supply rep for some equipment he was considering. But then he rented a vehicle and apparently drove up here. Or at least to Houghton. We have records of him purchasing gas at a Houghton gas station."

That must have been where Derek ran into him. So, Kevin lied for some unknown reason, Derek forced the issue on me and when I told Nolan... She wrapped the blanket tighter around her shoulders and tucked her hands into herself. "So, you're looking into my husband because of the things I told you the other day on the beach when...when I was so upset. I thought I could trust you."

She looked straight ahead but knew from her side vision that he'd turned to her, started to reach out but stopped himself.

"I have a job to do. It's my responsibility to get to the truth."

"Truth. What about friendship and loyalty?"

"Ava, this is bigger than that. This has to do with the lives of several young women. I'm sorry your husband is a suspect. I don't want to believe that he was involved in this."

"He wasn't." She snapped her head toward him.

His jaw hardened. "Well, if he was innocent, then there's—"

"*If* he was innocent? I have no doubt that he was innocent."

"Okay, then you wouldn't object to us going through his belongings and business files?"

Ava's mouth dropped open. She couldn't believe what she was hearing. This whole conversation had been a setup to gain access to Kevin's things without a warrant. She felt her heart shatter. How could she have been so naive? She jumped up from the chair, stared out at the black sky, its darkness a sudden blight on the landscape.

Nolan rose and stepped forward to duck his chin, trying to catch her gaze. "My number one concern is putting a stop to this trafficking ring and protecting you and Rose. Your husband knew something about our first victim, and I need to know what it was. You can help me find out, or you can fight me the whole way. But I'll eventually get to the truth."

Tears pushed to the edges of her eyes. "I'm seeing a whole

lot of truth right now. Like how you'll do anything to get the facts you need, even if it means hurting people."

"I don't ever want to hurt you, Ava. Believe me."

"Believe you? This whole time you've been using me to get information against my husband." She took a step closer, anger surging through her. "Tell me something, was holding my hand part of your act? Nice touch, Agent Shea."

"Ava, please—"

"No. That's it." She turned away and headed back into the house. She couldn't bear listening to any more of his lies. She paused at the door and turned back. "You can look at whatever you want. All you'll find about Kevin is that he was a loyal, loving husband. The one man, the only man I've ever loved."

Chapter Sixteen

The next morning, Nolan stood in the corner of Mac's living room and watched the happy reunion. He'd wanted to keep Rose's return quiet, but word was out. Outside, search volunteers, curiosity seekers and the local media gathered for a glimpse of Rose. Inside, family and friends and Mac himself, who'd been released from the hospital in the early hours, filled every inch of the place. Everyone was elated that Rose had gotten home safely. Everyone except the people responsible for her abduction in the first place, Nolan thought.

Earlier he had gently questioned Rose. With Creed nearby for reassurance, she'd opened up a little, answering with a nod or shake of her head. He'd been able to ascertain that the man in the cabin had not been the same person who'd shot Lindsey Webber. Which meant one of the captors was still at large, along with the woman Sadie had talked about. And with all this publicity, they knew exactly where Rose was. He and Cam would have to double down their efforts to keep her safe.

Ava was still leery of Jane, and maybe rightly so. Nolan kept returning in his mind to the interview with Derek Williams. He'd seemed nervous when questioned about Ms. Adair, and he'd referred to her by her first name. How well did they know each other? At least Mac's release from the hospital and the arrival of Ava's mom and sister made it easy to explain the need for them to leave Jane's house without tipping her off that she was under suspicion.

Nolan watched Ava now as she buzzed about, taking care of Mac and seeing to everyone's needs. She'd barely spoken to him since last night on the deck. He'd thought of nothing else since then, how she'd defended Kevin, even considering so many facts detracting from his innocence. He admired her loyalty to her husband, even in his death. *The only man I've ever loved*, she had said. *Past tense, not future.* Nolan wanted this to mean, or at least imply, that there might be room in her heart to love again. He'd clung to this notion and hoped for a chance to win her over.

He became lost in his thoughts until he noticed her staring at him. They locked gazes—he smiled, she didn't. She shot a quick glance toward the ceiling, then turned back to Mac.

Nolan understood. He left Creed, who was basking in Rose's affection, and wandered upstairs to the third-floor attic, where Ava knew Cam was sorting through boxes. Mac and Ava had given them permission to search Kevin's things, both insisting that there was nothing to hide.

Cam sat cross-legged on the floor, surrounded by stacks of papers, red-framed glasses low on her nose. "Good news," she said. "We got a hit in the system on that tattoo that Sadie described. Satiro Smith, goes by 'Snake.' He's got a felony warrant for assault. We've got his vehicle license plate number. The automated readers will pick it up soon."

"Just the break we need. Good." He nodded to the papers. "How's it going with this stuff?"

"Kevin kept meticulous tax records," she said. "His medical-equipment sales were profitable, too. Looks like he employed about a dozen people, his payroll seems current, everything on the surface looks clean."

"Except…?"

She held out a piece of paper. "Except this."

He scanned it and shrugged, handed it back.

"It's a numbered account," she explained. "The name of the account holder is replaced by a number. It's a way to keep the account secret."

"For tax evasion?"

"Not necessarily."

"If it's so secret, why is it with his other account papers?"

"Maybe by mistake. Or could be info he collected off someone else's account. There aren't any other papers in here for this file. And this is a printout, per the footer printed on January twenty-fourth. Maybe he printed it offline for some reason, then hadn't gotten around to destroying it yet. Kevin died January twenty-sixth, right?"

"I believe so. Yeah."

She pointed to one of the columns of numbers. "A large payout was made from this account on the twenty-fourth." She looked at the paper again. "Oh...wait a minute. Guess when this account was initiated?"

"Hmm... I'm going to guess ten years ago."

"Bingo. And every month, money has been deposited on the first and a payment transferred out on the tenth. Always the same amount of money, except for a substantially larger payment was made two days before Kevin died."

"Or a day before he traveled."

"True," Cam agreed. She handed him the paper. "I need to make a few phone calls. You ask Ava about this. See if she recognizes any of the account numbers in this document or if she knows what this is about." She stood and brushed off her jeans. "Ask me, looks like Kevin Burke was involved in all this. We just need to figure out how—and why."

Ava busied herself in the kitchen making a salad for Mac's lunch. He would've preferred a salami-and-cheese sandwich, but she was determined to give him a more heart-healthy diet.

The extra attention this morning had been overwhelming, and Ava was glad that the house had quieted down. Her mom and sister had gone back to the motel to rest, so it was only Mac and Yvette now. And the two agents, of course. They were upstairs in the attic, trying to find something that would incriminate Kevin. She gritted her teeth at the memory of her conversation the night before with Nolan. He'd taken advantage of her vulnerability to get information to use against Kevin. How could she have been so foolish as to have trusted him?

"I feel sorry for the lettuce," Yvette said.

Ava turned, the knife still in her hand. "What do you mean?"

"You're whacking it to death."

"Am I?" She sighed. "Just frustrated, I guess."

Yvette poured leftover coffee from the morning and put the mug in the microwave. "Care to tell me about it?"

Ava hesitated. The last time she'd told Yvette about Derek having seen Kevin in town the day he'd died, Yvette had practically accused him of having an affair. "I don't know if I should talk about it." She rooted in the kitchen drawer for a carrot peeler.

"I understand. It's okay. Just know I'm here for you if you need me. I'm so thankful that you two are home safely and that Mac's okay. I can't imagine how hard this is on you two, being under constant threat and having agents camped out in your home. And Mac...being a suspect..."

"I think they've cleared him."

"Well, that's good news."

"They've moved on to Kevin."

"What?" Yvette's shocked tone echoed her own feelings.

Ava shut the drawer, turned and leaned against the cabinet. She couldn't keep all this inside any longer. "They have proof that he was in Houghton the day he died. They're upstairs now searching his business files, looking for a connection between Kevin and this human-trafficking ring. Can you believe that?"

Yvette shook her head. "There's no way. That's the wildest

thing ever. They should be looking at Jane. I don't trust that woman one—"

"It's my fault."

Her friend stepped forward and touched her shoulder. "No. Nothing about this is your fault."

"Oh, but it is. They wouldn't have even known Kevin was in Houghton that day if I hadn't told Nolan. I made a mistake. I trusted him."

Yvette pulled her close. "You didn't do anything wrong. There's got to be an explanation for all this. We just don't know what it is yet."

A soft rustle came from the right. They both turned to see Nolan standing in the kitchen doorway. "Excuse me. I'm sorry. But Ava, I need to talk to you and Mac for a minute."

Yvette gave her arm an extra little squeeze. "I'll finish Mac's lunch. You go ahead."

Ava followed him into the family room, where Mac and Rose were engaged in an energetic game of checkers, Creed nearby. Rose let out a small giggle, and Ava thought again about how much Creed had helped Rose adjust since he'd come into their lives. Her daughter had smiled more this past week than she had in the months since Kevin had passed.

Creed unwound from his sleeping position next to Mac's chair and came to Nolan's side. "Rosie," Ava said. "Go to the kitchen and help Yvette with lunch. Agent Nolan needs to talk to Grandpa and me alone."

"Okay, Mommy." Rose scooted off the sofa, slipped a finger under Creed's collar as she passed by to the kitchen. The two of them had been inseparable since Rose's return.

Ava stared after them. And what was going to happen when Creed left? The realization hit her, and her heart broke for Rose. Creed was just one more thing she loved and would lose.

"Ava?" Nolan's voice was low and full of concern.

Focus on today, she told herself. *Trust tomorrow to God.* He'd always taken care of them. He would now, too. She straightened her shoulders and faced Nolan straight on. "What is it you want to discuss with us?" Her voice sounded harsher than she intended.

Mac had picked up on the tension between her and Nolan—everyone had. But Ava hadn't told him the reason. This was his first day home from the hospital, and Rose's abduction had been enough to handle, along with these suspicions surrounding Kevin possibly being involved in human trafficking.

Nolan settled on the sofa, then leaned forward with his elbows on his knees, gazing at the rug as he gathered his thoughts. Ava stared at the top of his head, bracing herself for whatever might be coming next.

"Mac, can you tell me a little about the summer after Kevin graduated?" he finally asked.

Mac drew in a long breath and exhaled slowly. "Well... Irene died that year. And it was rough on Kevin. He got a little wild. A lot of kids do at that age, but he had the added issue of grieving the loss of his mother. I'm afraid I let him get away with a lot. Irene's illness had worn me down, and I was devastated by her death." He shrugged. "I don't know. Maybe I was depressed. It's all a blur."

Ava found herself nodding. She completely understood the shock during early days of grief. The way she'd felt immediately after Kevin had died...numb to the needs of those around her. She now felt like she'd failed her own daughter during those days when she'd acutely mourned Kevin's passing. Maybe if she hadn't been so wrapped up in her own pain, she would have been able to help Rose more.

Mac continued, "I didn't see how much it had affected Kevin until it was too late. He got mixed in with a rough crowd, getting into trouble, failing school. He barely graduated. It was a difficult time."

"He left that summer, correct?"

A shadow crossed Mac's face. "Yes."

"Any reason why?"

Mac looked away and shrugged again. "Guess there wasn't anything holding him here."

"Was he running from something?"

Mac narrowed his eyes as if he was trying to make sense of Nolan's question. His face grew flush as he stammered for an answer. "I... I don't know for sure."

Ava spoke up. "Is this really necessary?"

Nolan kept his gaze on Mac, while she seethed inside.

"There was something," Mac said. "One of the ladies at church... I can't even remember her name—she was a busybody—but anyway, she cornered me one day and claimed she saw Kevin heading into a room at the motel with a woman. A pregnant woman. I asked Kevin about it, but he said that the church woman didn't know what she was talking about. I let it go at that."

Heat rose on Ava's cheeks. Reflexively, she glanced over his shoulder toward the kitchen, where Rose was helping Yvette. Dishes clanking, silverware clinking and Yvette chatting away to a smiling Rose. At least they weren't paying attention to this conversation.

"But you must have wondered," Nolan said. "When the articles came out in the paper about the hiker found on the island, didn't you put two and two together?"

"No. There was no 'two and two.' Someone claiming they saw Kevin didn't mean squat. And why would I connect that woman to the hiker anyway?" Mac answered, a scowl on his face indicating his disdain at Nolan's implied accusation. "The only thing that gossip mentioned was a woman who was pregnant. Those articles would have made a big deal of it if the girl who was killed had been pregnant."

Mac sat back. Ava sensed a shift in the conversation. He was tired, yes, but it felt as if he'd closed the subject, had no intention of saying more.

But Nolan had also shifted—or at least there was something different about the way he sat, or maybe because he now pursed his lips. As if either a wall of sorts had suddenly been erected...or maybe been breached. When he spoke, his words were clipped. "Not all facts in any case are released to the public. Like this fact—the coroner confirmed that Hannah Richter had given birth right before she died."

Chapter Seventeen

Nolan recalled the official wording of Hannah Richter's autopsy report, the part that had been kept secret from the public: *definite presence of parturition scars on pelvic bone.* Cam had translated for him. Basically, there had been small pit marks on the pelvic bones where the ligaments had popped out of place when the baby had passed through the birth canal. The idea that this murdered young girl had been a new mother had made him feel sick. That same feeling churned now as he heard Rose giggling in the kitchen with Yvette, and the question festered in his mind again: Hannah's baby. Where had her baby gone? That question had nagged at his conscience ever since he'd read the initial case file.

Now he focused on the financial report in his hand. "Other evidence has come to light that I need to discuss with you." He handed the paper to Ava. "This was found in your husband's business records. It's a special type of account that is identified by number rather than the name of a person or business. As you can see, the same amount of money is deposited and withdrawn every month."

Seconds ticked away as she pondered the report in silence, her forehead crinkling, as if unsure of what to make of the evidence in front of her. Evidence of one more lie that Kevin had told. What would she say now? Would she keep on defending him, or would this be the final straw?

"Do you recognize that account number?" he pressed.

"No, I've never seen it before."

"Let me see that paper," Mac said. He placed his reading glasses on his nose and raised his chin as he read. "I don't get what you're seeing here. This could be anything. An investment account for Rosie, maybe."

"Accounts like this are used to hide financial activity. Put money into a numbered account and transfer it to another numbered account. It's like adding pieces to a disguise. Eventually the original account holder is buried under so many layers of anonymity that they become untraceable."

"I don't understand," Ava said. "Where was this money coming from?"

"That's what I was hoping you could tell us."

Mac tossed the document onto the coffee table. "Not from anything illegal. I can tell you that. Not my son."

But a shadow of doubt briefly flashed over Ava's features. She drew in a deep breath and was about to say something, when Rosie marched into the room with a lunch plate for Mac.

"Well, look at this." His face lit up with grandfatherly pride. "I don't think I've ever seen a better lunch. The only thing that would make this lunch better is the company of a beautiful young lady."

Rose glanced at Ava and then went wide-eyed when she realized Mac was talking about her. She nodded and scurried next to him in the chair, snuggling close, her smile beaming as he took his first forkful. Creed, watching from the floor, looked a little put out.

Mac might have been done with the conversation, but Nolan sensed that Ava had more to say. He picked the report off the coffee table and motioned for her to follow him. He felt Mac's eyes on them as they headed down the hall to the back room.

"I really don't know anything about that money," Ava said once they were alone. "I'd know if it was coming from one of our personal accounts. I keep track of those things. But I'd... There's got to be a good explanation for it. A reason why he kept it from me."

Still loyal. Even now with all this evidence that pointed to her husband. "Cam is in the process of checking with his office's accounting services," Nolan told her. "My guess is that it'll be a dead end. If he went to all this trouble to cover it up, his accountant won't know about it."

She looked down and shook her head.

"You disagree? Ava, I know Kevin was a good husband to you, but people sometimes lead double lives."

"I can't accept that. Not about Kevin. You just don't know him the way I do."

This discussion wasn't going the way he wanted. "But you didn't know him back then. You hadn't even met him when Hannah Richter died on that island, alone, after giving birth to a baby. Is it possible that they...well...that they dated and that the baby might have been his?"

"He would have told me something like that."

"Why do you think that? He didn't tell you a lot of things. This financial report is proof of that."

She stared at him for a few beats, her eyes blazing. "Isn't this where you reach out and try to hold my hand? Or wrap a supportive arm around my shoulder? Be the 'good cop' to get something out of me?"

He flinched as if he'd been wounded. "That's not fair."

"Fair? What's not fair is you focusing all your time and energy on Kevin. Are you even looking into any other leads? What about Derek and the man with the tattoo? And Sadie said there was a woman involved. And that text I saw on Jane's phone. Have you even questioned Jane? Maybe she's the woman Sadie mentioned."

"We're looking into all those things," he rushed to say. "It's not just me working the case. There's Cam and my colleague working in Detroit." He held back from telling her that he had an appointment to talk to Jane this afternoon. He didn't want that information to get to Mac, then to Jane. There were too many people with too many personal connections in this case. "I can't share everything with you because in a case like this, information has to be carefully managed and—"

"Oh… I see. Managing information. Yes…well, if there's nothing else right now to manage out of me, I need to go see to my daughter."

Nolan watched her walk away and rubbed his hands over his tired eyes.

Ava found Yvette on her laptop at the kitchen table. She slid into the chair next to her. "Got a minute?"

"For you, more than one. What's up?" Ava caught a glimpse of real-estate listings on the screen right before Yvette snapped it shut.

"I'm furious."

"Oh. Did I do—"

"Not with you. Of course not. With Nolan."

"Agent Shea? Why?"

"Not just with him. With Agent Beckett, too. Both of them. This whole thing, really. They're trying their best to tie Kevin to that hiker who died over ten years ago. Now they have some sort of evidence of financial payouts that they think are connected."

"Oh? What's that about?"

"It's nothing. Something with his business. If he were here, he could easily explain it, I'm sure, but he's not, so…" She sighed and leaned in closer. "I don't know if I should… Well, Mac and I both know, so you'll hear it soon enough. The hiker was pregnant. They think she had the baby right before she was murdered."

Yvette shrunk back in her chair.

"Horrible, I know. And Nolan thinks that the baby could have been Kevin's."

Yvette's eyes bugged. "What? Oh no…and there's a part of you that believes him? Don't listen to him. He doesn't know Kevin like we do. He's just looking at the facts and trying to put them together some way that makes sense. You can't blame him—that's his job, but he's just on the wrong track. We know that."

Ava tried to set her doubts aside. "You're right. I hope."

"I am right. Don't worry. Time and evidence will prove them wrong."

"That's the thing. They're so busy looking at Kevin, they're ignoring the other evidence."

Yvette nodded. "You still think Derek had something to do with Rose's abduction, don't you?"

"No, not anymore. I mean, I did, but not since everything that happened on the island." She explained what Sadie had told them about being blindfolded the whole time but remembering the man with the tattoo on his forearm and the woman's voice she'd heard, and how Ava believed that woman could be Jane. "The man that was on the island who'd taken Rose was killed. And Rose said he wasn't the man she saw in the barn."

"She said that?"

"Not in so many words, but yeah, she made that clear." A glimmer of happiness shot through her at her brave little girl. "She's doing great. Despite all this, she's getting better. It's Creed. That dog has been a blessing. I think Mac has been right all along—animals are great therapy. A horse will help bring her out of her shell more. She's already getting there. Today with both Creed and Mac… I saw bits and pieces of my old Rosie. Kevin would be so proud of her."

"He *is* so proud of her. He's looking down on you two every moment. Don't you forget that. And Rosie getting better is all that matters. Just let the authorities do their jobs, and they'll take care of the rest."

But they're not doing their jobs. And what if they continued to make accusations against Kevin? How would that affect Rose? Before, Ava had never been interested to know about her husband's past. Part of her still wasn't. All that mattered was the loving, kind and wonderful husband and father he'd been to them. Now the hard fact was that she didn't know enough about Kevin's past to protect that image, to protect her daughter's memory of him.

Ava needed the truth. She couldn't help Rose if she remained blinded to Kevin's past—and that meant finding the truth for herself. Even if it meant walking into the devil's own lair.

"I didn't expect you to text," Derek said in an oily-sweet way that made Ava shudder inside. "What made you change your mind?"

They were sitting across from each other in a booth at the Green Larch Inn. It was a little after one o'clock, but the place was still packed with a lunch crowd. "I got curious about the stories you mentioned. You know, the things you and Kevin did 'back in the day.'"

"Ah...yeah, so many stories." He turned in his chair and waved to the server, then looked back at Ava. "What are you ordering?"

"Just a quick coffee. I have to get back soon. Rose needs me, and Mac, well, he's just home from the hospital." Yvette was with Rose and Mac, but the truth was Ava couldn't be gone long. She'd slipped out unnoticed, without telling Agent Beckett, who was still up in the attic sorting through Kevin's things.

"Oh? I thought we'd spend some time getting to know one another better." He ran his tongue over his lips and smiled.

The gesture was enough to make Ava scramble for an excuse to leave, and she eyed the exit when two glasses of water appeared on the table. She looked up to see the same server from the other day, one thinly drawn eyebrow cocked as she looked from Ava to Derek. "What can I get you two?"

"We'll both have the fish and chips," Derek said. The server marked her pad and hustled off. Ava started to protest, but he cut her off. "Don't worry, you'll love it. Trust me. Best in the area."

Ava bit back her irritation and forced a smile.

"Oh, I sold a house today. Lake property. Went for a little under a million."

"That's great. Congratulations." His achievement. His money. His food choice. This conversation wasn't going where she needed it to go. She decided to come right out with it. "Back to the stories you promised to tell me. I'm hoping there's something you can help me with."

"Sure. Tell me what you need, and I'll do what I can." He leaned forward—all too willing, it seemed, to help.

"Something's come up about Kevin's past, and I need to know the truth. It's important."

"Sounds serious."

"It is." She took a deep breath. "Back when you and Kevin were hanging out, there was a girl, a pregnant girl…" His expression changed immediately. "What is it? You remember her, don't you?"

"This is the hiker that died, right?"

"You must have met her, then. Were you with Kevin? Or did he…did they date?"

"Date? No. And I don't really know anything about her." He sat back, chin up. "Your cop friend sent you to ask me about her, didn't he?"

"No. But he's investigating Kevin for her death."

Derek blinked, then chuckled.

"You think that's funny?"

"No. Just surprised. Thought they were trying to pin it on me."

"I don't…what do you mean?"

"I've always wondered if Kevin didn't have something to do with that girl's death. I didn't say that to the cops, though." He leaned forward again. "You should be grateful for that," he added.

Ava's mouth went dry.

"Yeah," he continued. "I didn't tell any of this to the cops. For your sake. And that sweet little girl of yours. Who'd want to grow up thinking their daddy had done something bad?"

Ava swallowed the bile rising in the back of her throat. "You think Kevin did something to that girl?"

"Think? I know."

The server slid two plates onto the table, asked if they wanted anything else and plopped down the check. Derek snatched it right away with a triumphant look on his face. "My treat."

His treat? She sat in shock while she watched him dive into his lunch, first dumping his condiment container onto his food, then hacking off a piece of fish and running it back and forth through the tartar sauce. He looked up, seemingly surprised that she wasn't eating. "Take a bite. You're going to love this. What are you waiting for?"

"What do you know about Kevin and Hannah Richter?"

"Hannah? Oh yeah. I almost forgot her name."

Ava glared across the table at him.

He waved his fork in the air. "Eat. Eat up."

Ava slowly unwrapped her silverware and cut off a tiny piece and popped it into her mouth. Her gut clenched, but she had to know more. She had to swallow this bite as well as whatever she learned from this jerk if she ever wanted to be able to move forward.

"You're right—delicious." She watched him take three more bites before interrupting him. "Now tell me, how do you know that Kevin had something to do with Hannah's death?"

He swiped grease off his chin. "Okay, I'll tell you, but you're not going to like it. Here's how it went down. Kevin and me were out one night, and we were both drinking a little, but we ran out of booze and were looking for more fun, so we decided to head out to this bar on 41—it was in the middle of nowhere. Bartender was chill, never checked IDs." He popped a fry into his mouth and washed it down with a gulp of soda. "We passed this girl on the road."

"You mean Hannah."

"Yeah. I never got her name back then. She was our age, though. And cute, too, so we picked her up. I couldn't tell she was pregnant until she got in the car. She had on this oversize sweatshirt, and she was skinny. Too skinny for having a kid. And she was sick. She puked in my car. Ticked me off."

"So, did you make her get out?"

"Should have. But Kevin wanted to take her to the hospital. She wouldn't go, though. Started screaming stuff about people being after her and… I don't know. I think something was off about her. We ended up dropping her at the Copper Jack."

"The motel?"

"Yeah. That's where she wanted to go. Kevin even gave her money to get a room."

"What happened after that?"

"We started back to the bar, but Kevin got all worked up over leaving her, said we should've helped her more. Told him it was none of our business. I mean, we did our good deed. And I had a pile of puke to thank me for it." His pointed at her plate. "You using that?" She shook her head, and he snatched her tartar sauce. "Anyway, I finally got disgusted and pulled over and let him out. Told him if he was so into her, he could walk back to the motel. I went on to the bar."

"That doesn't mean he had anything to do with her death. He just wanted to help her. You don't even know if he saw her again."

Derek tipped back his head and laughed. A piece of fish fell from his lips onto the table. He picked it up and popped it back in. His outburst drew attention. The server glanced over from the bar where she was rolling silverware. A couple other people looked their way, too.

Ava took a shaky sip of water. "I don't understand why you didn't tell the police this. Nothing here implicates you or Kevin." She cocked her head at him. "If it's the truth."

Derek blew out a long breath and got serious. "It's the truth. I asked him the next day about the girl, and he got all mad at me. I'd never seen him so…so on edge. Made me promise not to tell anyone about her. So, I said I wouldn't. Then a few days after that it came out in the paper about a hiker found dead. I was pretty sure it was that girl. But I didn't say anything to anyone. And Kevin was gone by then. He'd moved out from Mac's and gone on somewhere else."

Ava didn't know what to say. It did sound bad for Kevin.

"Something wrong with your fish?"

She looked up. "What?"

"Your fish. Don't you want it?"

Ava pushed the plate his way. "I'm not hungry. Go ahead."

Derek shrugged. "Hate for it to go to waste." He snatched her fish and gestured to the waitress. "We need some more tartar sauce over here."

He turned back to Ava, his expression turning smug. "Hey, listen. I want you to know that I never did break my promise to Kevin. Not until today. You're the only person I've told so far. So, I guess it's just between you and me now." His foot brushed against hers under the table as he added with a wink, "I'm sure you want to keep it that way."

Chapter Eighteen

"She's gone."

"Gone?" Nolan gripped his phone tighter. He couldn't believe what he was hearing. "What do you mean 'gone'?"

Cam's voice held an undertone of irritation. "Apparently she's off doing her own investigation."

Nolan pressed his head to the steering wheel. He and Penn had just finished interviewing Jane, who'd had a reasonable explanation for everything and refused to even comment on the text from Williams. The whole interview had been a waste of time, and now Ava was off doing her own thing.

Cam was still talking. "Yvette said she went to meet with Williams. Thought she could get some information about hubby and our cold-case victim. Guess that account info got her thinking."

"Did Yvette say how long ago she left?"

"An hour, maybe a little longer. She was meeting him for coffee."

"Where?"

"Green Larch Inn."

Nolan peeled away from the curb. "I'm only a few blocks away from there. I'll go check it out. Let me know if she shows up at the house."

"Will do. Another thing—Ty arrested the tattoo guy, Satiro, this morning. They made him an offer, and he's ready to talk. I should get the report any minute. We're going to bust this thing open and get the guys at the top of the ring."

"Good. Forward anything that comes in my way."

He tried Ava's number. No answer. What was she thinking acting on her own? Satiro in custody and ready to talk, Sadie as a witness, they were close to resolving the case. But he should have anticipated this from her. He remembered the first time he'd seen her with Derek Williams. She'd told him that Williams had wanted to get together with her to talk about old stories, things he and Kevin had done way back when. That was what she was after—information that would prove Nolan wrong about Kevin.

He lurched to a stop in front of the restaurant and ran inside. The place was jumping. But no Ava. No Williams. The server, juggling an armful of dirty dishes, paused in front of him. "Just one? I think we can manage that."

"No, thanks. I'm looking for someone."

She gave him a curious once-over.

"A woman," he explained. "Longish dark hair and..." He tried to recall what she was wearing. Couldn't remember.

"Was she here with Derek Williams?"

"Yes. I believe so."

"They left about a half hour ago."

"A half hour ago." His mind ran wild. "Together?"

She lifted an eyebrow and said, "Oh, they were together, for sure. Should have seen them whispering and flirting with one another."

That didn't sound like the Ava he knew, yet the words stung. "Did you see them leave?"

"Don't think so. But I've been busy. We're always packed for the Saturday lunch hour. The money was with the bill on the table."

He thanked her and left, his mind reeling with possibilities.

He'd just talked to Cam, and Ava hadn't been there. Maybe she'd stopped off on the way home for something. She wouldn't have gone somewhere with Williams, would she? Her earlier repugnance about Williams...had it been a lie? He couldn't believe that. Didn't. But she was determined to protect Kevin's reputation. And that unrelenting loyalty had already put her in danger once.

He tried calling Ava. It went to voicemail, so he took a quick spin around town, looking for her car or Williams's car, found nothing. On a whim, he turned back toward Jane's place. Maybe she'd headed there to talk to Jane, but there was no sign of her there, either. He was halfway down the street when Williams passed by him.

He slammed on the brakes, craned his neck and did a double check. It was Williams, all right. What was he doing here? He flipped a U-turn and pulled in behind Williams just as he was getting out of his vehicle in front of Jane's house.

"I need to talk to you."

Williams scowled. "I see someone can't keep a secret. I'm not talking to you without my attorney."

"What are you talking about? I'm looking for Ava."

"Yeah. Sure. Call my attorney, buddy."

Nolan stepped in front of him, cutting off his path. "I asked you a question. Where's Ava?"

"Relax, man. She went home. Go look for her there."

"What are you doing here at Jane's place?"

"I don't have to answer that."

Nolan moved forward again, and Williams threw up his hands. "Okay, Jane is my counselor. That's all there is to it. I see her once a week. Have for years. So, just back off, okay?"

Of course. He should have guessed that. The way Jane had gone all tight-lipped when he and Penn had brought up Derek and the text on her phone. She wouldn't talk about him, and now he realized she *couldn't* talk about him—counselor-client privilege. "How long ago did Ava leave for home?"

"I don't know. Maybe thirty minutes ago."

Nolan was on his phone before he even got back into his car. He tried Ava again. Still no answer. Next Cam, and when she didn't answer, either, a chill crept over him. He rammed the Explorer into gear and took off for Mac's place.

Mac's house came into sight, giving Ava that small jolt of comfort she felt every time she neared Burke House, the house where Kevin had grown up, the house where she and Rose now lived with Mac. Although Kevin had chosen not to live here after he'd graduated, he had always talked with pride about his roots, his father the ferry captain and how the Upper Peninsula, land of the extremes, formed hardy, strong individuals. By marital osmosis, she'd always shared the same pride. She still did as she happily carried the Burke name, after all. But everything she'd learned over the past few days had diminished those proud feelings, and now as she approached the home, she felt deep doubts.

She hugged herself, her arms crossed tight against the cold wind as she made her way from her car to the house. A normal evening, that was what she needed—pasta, a movie, cuddle time with Rose in front of the crackling fireplace, but she stopped just inside the door. Something wasn't right. A couple deep barks pierced the air, followed by a thumping noise and scratching. The rest of the house was stone-cold silent.

Where is everyone? Mac's chair was empty, the television off and silent, no Rose playing on the floor. The wood in the fireplace had burned down, showing a single line of embers smoldering. She opened her mouth to call out for Rose, then closed it again, an inner alarm bell warning her to keep quiet as she continued through the first floor, the kitchen next. Her heart pounded as her gaze darted from the dripping faucet to the saucepan with congealed gravy to the partially open fridge door. It was as if someone had stopped midtask and walked away. Or run away. *Rosie...where's Rose?*

Another sharp bark and she was moving now. Fast. Not for the door, but through the house. Her fingers fumble-dialed Nolan's number, but she realized her phone was dead. She grabbed the portable one and dialed, muttering a thank-you to Mac for his old-fashioned ways. Her eyes flickered into every corner of each room. She had to find Rose. She had to be hiding somewhere, safe but afraid, and Ava just needed to find her. Behind the sofa, inside the coat closet, under... It rang and rang.

She dialed 911, still scanning for Rose, Mac, Yvette... *God, please don't let me be too late.*

"911. What's your emergency?"

She pushed open the door to the den. Looked under Mac's desk. Nothing.

"Hello. Are you there? What's your emergency?"

"Send the sheriff to Mac Burke's house." She whispered the address. Creed had amped up the barking, and the scratching turned frantic. Ava headed toward the noise, rushing up the stairs, and stopped. The barking—it was from the attic. She ran to the back steps, sprinted up and saw her: Agent Beckett lay sprawled, face down, one leg cocked at a ninety-degree angle as if she'd fallen midrun. Blood pooled around the crown of her head. "Agent Beckett's been hurt," she said into the phone.

"Is she breathing?" the operator asked.

Ava knelt to feel for a pulse, but her hand came up sticky with blood. The sight sent her to another level of panic. She bolted up, turned to careen back down the stairs, leaving behind the frantic scratching and muffled barks as only one thought consumed her: *Rose! Where's Rose?*

"Is she breathing?" the operator asked again.

"She needs help. Agent Beckett needs help," she hollered into the phone.

She bounded down the steps, across the second-floor hall, jumped the final steps of the stairway to the first-floor landing and found herself back in the family room, where she turned several times and clasped her hands over her head. *They're gone. They're all gone.* What if... No, she couldn't let her mind go there. She'd found Rose before. She had to remain clearheaded.

A flash of movement outside the window caught her attention, and she moved closer to investigate, her mind registering what she saw in the distance—Mac with his rifle pointed at Yvette...and Rose!

She bolted from the house toward the rocky shore. "Stop, Mac! No!" Nolan's warning ran through her mind: *Be careful of who you trust.*

"Get back," Mac called out as she approached. "I mean it, Ava. Get back."

Yvette stood with Rose in front of her, protectively clutched in her arms, their backs to the lake, its dark waters lapping violently below them. Rose's eyes widened with terror.

Wind whipped at Ava's hair, but her complete focus was on shielding her daughter. She approached slowly and came up directly behind him. Mac and Jane. It'd been them all along. How could she have missed it? She'd let her emotions get in the way of seeing the truth. Now it was too late.

"Please, Mac. Please, don't hurt them."

Nolan navigated the twisty road toward Mac's place. He couldn't drive fast enough, get there fast enough, and he hated that he had left Ava and Rose alone in the first place.

He ordered his dashboard hands-free option to call Cam again. Ava, too. No one answered. He pressed the accelerator harder, and trees whipped by his windows. A notification chimed for an incoming text message from Ty. He called out, "Read," and the app's monotone voice came over the speaker: "Satiro gave up the major players. Warrants forthcoming. Check your email for a list of names."

A mixed bag of emotions, both relief and worry, flooded through him. Relief that they were close to resolving this whole thing, making arrests, bringing justice to the families, and with the traffickers off the streets, Ava and Rose would finally be safe. Worry that the resolution had come too late, that something had happened to them. Why weren't they answering his calls?

A mile out from Mac's place, a deputy cruiser gained on him. He lit him up and then turned on the siren. Nolan ignored him; it would take too much time to stop to explain. Precious time. He kept on track, pushing the Explorer as fast as he could on the road's curves. Another deputy cruiser appeared in his mirror, and by the time he got to Mac's, several law enforcement vehicles pulled in behind him, lights and sirens blaring.

He jumped from the car, started to raise his hands, turned to them to shout an explanation...but their eyes weren't on him at all but focused on the house. Nolan's throat went dry.

Penn popped out of one of the vehicles, his gun drawn toward the front door. "Possible intruder. Officer down!" he yelled, and cautiously made for the front door.

Cam! Oh no, not Cam. Nolan drew his weapon and backed the sheriff up as they stepped inside. Other officers filed in behind them, two going up the stairs, Nolan following Penn on the first floor.

"Clear," Penn yelled out.

A series of frenzied barks sliced through the house. Nolan glanced upward to where the sound came from. Creed needed him, but he kept his position, backing up Penn.

"Clear," Penn said again. They were through the family room and kitchen, making their way down the hall toward Mac's room. His dog's cries were making Nolan lose his control. Sweat dripped over his eyebrows, but he kept his grip tight on his weapon, watching Penn's back.

"All clear." Penn relaxed his stance. "Nobody—"

"She's up here!" The call came from somewhere above them.

Nolan turned and raced up the stairs. By the top step, a pungent, coppery odor emerged and grew stronger as he made his way to the end of the hall and up to the attic where two officers knelt over a body. A shock of blond hair, soaked with blood... "Cam." He scooted in closer. "Is she...?"

"No. She's alive. Barely. Transport's coming."

"Thank You, thank You," a whispered prayer escaped his lips. He reached down and touched her shoulder. "Stay with us, Cam. Stay with us."

A small dresser had been pushed against a storage closet, just feet away, where Creed was going berserk, barking and ramming his body against the door. Nolan stood to go to him, when Cam's phone buzzed. He stooped down and loosened it from under her outstretched hand. A single line text from Ty flashed on the screen:

Verified trafficker: Duran, Yvette.

Yvette? He pulled his own phone from his pocket, opened his email app and scrolled for an email from Ty. He found it and opened a list of over a dozen people. There, halfway down the column, was Yvette's name. Nolan realized Ty had tried to warn Cam, knowing Yvette was in the house. But too late.

Penn was behind him now, and the last "Clear" sounded as the deputies on scene filed around them in the hallway. Each face told of the fear that haunted all law enforcement officers as they stared at Cam: officer down.

"Yvette," he told Penn and the other deputies. "She's one of the traffickers. She's been on the inside the whole time. She probably has Ava and Rose now. Who knows where she's taken them or if..." He couldn't finish. Despair washed over him. Yvette. This whole time and he'd missed it.

He continued to the storage closet and pushed aside the dresser. As soon as he opened the door, Creed bolted past the deputies and down the attic stairs. His claws clacked on the wood floors as he scurried through the house, then stopped and let out a series of sharp barks, followed by a low, undulated growl.

Nolan drew his weapon again. Penn and a couple other deputies followed down the steps with their weapons raised. Creed had moved to the family room, his focus fixed outside the window toward the lake. He whimpered, his ears twitching as if to hear what was going on, then turned his face to Nolan.

"What is it, boy? What do you see?" Nolan joined him at the window, looked out and shouted, "Penn! Outside, by the water!"

Nolan started running. Behind him, Penn spoke into his radio. "Suspect outside, rear of the property."

Creed zoomed forward, flying like an arrow, ears pinned, lips pulled back, teeth showing like the crazed smile of a clown. As his dog bolted farther ahead, Nolan ordered, "Stand down, stand down." Creed immediately pulled up, and he lunged for his collar, maintaining a grip on his weapon with his other hand.

Creed dragged him toward the group. "Federal agent," Nolan called. "Let go of the girl, Yvette."

Yvette yanked Rose closer with one arm and wrapped her other arm around her neck, pressing a kitchen knife to her throat. "Drop your gun and call back your dog, or I'll kill her. I swear I'll kill her."

"No!" Ava shrieked. Mac lowered his gun, and they backed away from the line of fire.

"Creed, stand down," Nolan repeated the command. Creed fought him, snapping and snarling, wrenching against his hold.

Penn was next to him, his gun trained on Yvette. "Drop your weapon, Yvette. Drop it now!"

Deputies streamed around them, in position with their weapons aimed at Yvette. "Give it up, Yvette. You're surrounded," Penn said.

She trembled, and the knife bounced against Rose's skin. "No. I... I can't go to prison."

Ava held out her arms and pleaded. "Please, Yvette. Let her go. She's just a little girl."

Yvette glared at Ava, her grip tightening on the knife. "You don't get it, do you? You've never had to work for anything in your life. Everything handed to you by that rich cousin of mine—a nice house, nice cars. He treated you right. I didn't have any of that. I had to earn my way the best I could. Earn it! You have no idea what that even means, do you, Ava? And now here you are, living in this house, Burke House, with your precious little girl. And guess what. You win again. All this will be yours one day."

Nolan had to think fast. Yvette was unpredictable. That knife was too close to Rose's lifeline. If Penn or one of the other deputies risked a shot, they might hit Rose. Even if they hit Yvette, the drop-off behind them was a good fifteen feet if not more, the deep-freezing waters waiting to snatch them both under.

Ava shook her head. "You can have whatever you want—just let her go."

"Liar! I'm not going to get anything I want. I'm going to prison. I'm going to lose it all." She lowered her gaze to the top of Rose's head, a cruel smile twisting on her face. "And so are you, Ava."

Rose's eyes no longer held fear but were fixed on Creed.

The dog went still, his gaze locked on Rose, and in that instant she drew in a deep breath and screamed out, "Creed!"

Something in his dog snapped. With a sudden jerk he twisted his powerful neck and broke free of Nolan's grip. Creed bolted and then launched into the air.

Yvette's eyes widened with terror as Creed made contact, his jaws clamping around her leg. She screamed, dropped the knife, released Rose and stumbled backward, her arms backstroking through the air. Ava snatched Rose to herself, turning her away from the violence of the attack, as Creed and Yvette continued plummeting over the edge and hitting the water with a loud splash. Nolan raced forward in time to see Creed surface and swim toward the bank.

Nolan lowered himself over the rocky edge, down the steep incline, landing on a small outcrop of slick rocks. Three other deputies entered the water—two diving under, the other treading and watching the surface. A moment later, Creed was back with him, Nolan checking to make sure his hero was all right. Seconds ticked away until one officer emerged empty-handed, gulped for air and was about to dive again when the other surfaced, Yvette in his grip. Her expression defeated, she lifted her face to the sky as she sputtered water.

Nolan pulled Creed close as they made it midway up the bank. "You did well, boy. You did well."

Creed stopped and shook from his head to his tail, water spraying everywhere.

A giggle came from above, and Nolan turned and saw Ava and Rose peering over the edge, smiles on their faces. "It's over," he told them. "You're safe."

Chapter Nineteen

Ava stood aside and watched the flurry of activity. Yvette was Mirandized and arrested, an ambulance had rushed Cam to the hospital, a deputy bagged the knife, Mac's gun had been confiscated and he was being questioned, and then Nolan was in front of her with Creed at his side. His jacket was missing and his hair and clothes were soaked. "You must be freezing."

Rose suddenly broke away from her grip and wrapped her arms around the dog's neck. "You're such a good doggy, Creed. I love you."

Ava gasped at the sound of Rose's words, and tears of joy sprung up in her eyes. She turned from her daughter and met Nolan's gaze. "We're really safe?"

He nodded, closed the distance between them and wrapped his arms around her, holding her tight. He was wet and cold, but she didn't care. She reached up and touched his cheek. "You and Creed saved us. Thank you."

He gazed into her eyes and whispered, "I don't know what I'd do if I lost you two."

She melted into the shelter of his arms, letting go of the terror that had gripped her these past days, repeating to herself, "We're safe."

He pulled back, his warm eyes searching hers. She offered him a small smile, and his lips covered hers, tentative at first, then greedy, and then gentle and...loving.

Rose's sweet giggles floated through the air. Ava tensed and tilted her head away, brought her hand to her lips and looked at Rose. She was busy with Creed, laughing at his antics, and thankfully hadn't seen the kiss. She'd only seen Ava and Kevin kiss that way. What would she think of her mother kissing another man?

What did Ava herself think about kissing someone other than Kevin? They'd been so young when they'd met. It'd only been him, and now...

Nolan dropped his arms and backed up, realizing what he'd done. "I'm sorry." He glanced at Rose. "I shouldn't have... I should go—I need to change."

Ava nodded and watched as he walked away, calling Creed to his side. His words caught up to her—*I don't know what I'd do if I lost you two.* And she realized, too, that she didn't want to lose him from her life.

It was early evening when she finally got Rose cleaned up and settled with a movie. She'd drawn all the curtains in the house to keep the press from seeing inside. They lined the road, filming news segments with Burke House in the background.

Nolan had returned and was upstairs on a virtual meeting with his director and the investigative unit, discussing updates on the case. Ava fixed Mac a light snack and took it to him in the family room. He was in his chair, fuzzy socks sticking out from under the cover of a wool blanket. A fire was roaring in the fireplace, and the heat felt wonderful.

She handed him the plate and a cup of hot tea. "It's just some cheese and crackers, a few slices of salami. I don't have the energy for making dinner."

"It's okay. It's all I need. I don't have much of an appetite."

After things had quieted down and the last of the deputies had left, she'd avoided Mac. Ashamed of the things she'd thought, of not trusting him and the accusations she'd made against Jane. Why had she so easily believed Yvette's lies? She needed to admit to her mistakes. Important things shouldn't go unsaid.

"I'm sorry... I don't know how I could have thought that you would ever hurt Rose. And the things I said about Jane. Yvette was telling me lies, and I chose to believe them. And you've been so good to Rose and me, and...can you ever forgive me?"

He set the plate aside and reached out his hands. "Come here." She knelt next to his chair. "Listen to me. There is nothing to forgive. You were doing just what I would expect you to do—protecting that precious girl of ours."

"But—"

"No, let it go. We're fine." His smile radiated love. "More than fine. And I know that Jane is, too. She understands that love you have for Rosie. Love for your child outshines everything. That's the way God made mothers. Don't apologize for something God made so right."

She laid her head on his hand, her tears spilling over his palms.

"Aw, now...don't start crying on me. You're a wonderful mother. Always reminding me of my Irene."

"I wish I'd had a chance to get to know her."

"She would have loved you. You two are a lot alike, you know." He touched her cheek, ever so lightly, and sighed. "I miss her."

Tears streamed down Ava's face now. "I know, and I miss him."

"I know you do. We all do. And nobody can give you the answers to why he had to go home so soon. Pray and trust. That's what you have to do, or you'll end up bitter like..."

"Like Yvette."

Mac nodded, and they both stayed silent a moment, lost in the image of an Yvette they'd never really known. "Yes.

She was an only child—spoiled rotten, too. I always told my brother he wasn't doing her any good by giving her everything. She was just nineteen when they died. Tragic. She blamed God, you know? Turned her away from Him, and that's when bitterness took root. I saw bits and pieces of it over the years. Anger. Envy. Greed. So much greed. It took over her life. Always trying to fill that empty spot in herself with material things."

"But what she did to those girls...how could she do something so evil?"

"I've been asking myself that all afternoon. All I can think is that when you don't feel worthy yourself, you don't see the worth in others. Those young women must've become nothing more than objects to her. Objects to be bought and sold to make more money to buy more things to fill up the hollow spot in her heart."

Ava stared into the fire, thinking about what he was saying. "That's so sad."

"Yes, child. It's so sad."

"We should pray for her."

He smiled and took her hands in his again. "I hoped you would say that."

Nolan heard voices murmuring as he descended the stairs. He stopped halfway, captivated by the scene before him. Ava and Mac, heads bent together in prayer. And as their words became clear to him, he realized that they weren't thanking God for their safety, they weren't asking for more blessings, they were praying for Yvette, the very woman who'd caused them so much pain, who'd almost robbed them of what they hold most precious, and his heart burst wide open. This was the faith that he wanted for himself, the faith he wanted for his own family one day—for him and Ava and Rose. He continued down the stairs and, as awkward as it felt, entered their space. He bowed his head and closed his eyes and joined them in prayer.

When they finished, he caught a glimpse of admiration in Ava's eyes. "I'm sorry to interrupt your prayer. I have a few things to tell you. First, Cam is doing okay. A lot of blood loss and a possible concussion, but she'll be fine." Echoes of relief filled the room. "Penn talked to her, got the scoop on what went down here today. Seems that Satiro's arrest made the other members of the ring nervous. Someone on the inside must have tipped them off that he gave up names. Yvette was alerted. But they were too late. Ty had already sent a message out with the names Satiro gave up, including Yvette's. Cam said she made some excuse about needing to run into town, but Cam knew by then and confronted her upstairs. It got ugly. They struggled. Cam broke free and tried to warn Mac and Rose, and that's when Yvette hit her over the head."

Nolan continued, "Good news, though. Satiro identified over a dozen members, including the director of a runaway home in Detroit where the girls were initiated. Also, a local guy, Jared Calle. He's a crewman on the *Northern Light* ferry. The director would target the most vulnerable girls at the shelter, and Yvette and a couple others would abduct them. They'd be held in Detroit until they had two or three, then they'd send them by vehicle to Sculpin Bay, where they'd hold them—usually at one of Yvette's vacant listings—until contact was made by their Canadian cohorts. Then Calle would transport them at night, by private motorboat, onto the island.

"Over the years, they'd mostly used campground shelters to overnight until the handoff could be made. They'd changed their route after they abducted Rose, hoping to evade us long enough to get her off the island and into Canada. Calle was the one who shot up your house, faked the hospital phone call and abducted Rose. He handed her off to his contact on the island."

Ava shuddered. The thought of her daughter...

Nolan noticed her reaction and quickly went on, "More good news is that most of the ring members have already been arrested, and we expect to have the others in custody by tomorrow afternoon. Between all of them, we should be able to start finding the remaining victims. In fact, several women were already found just across the Canadian border in Thunder Bay at a holding house. Yvette gave up their location. She's hoping for leniency, I think."

"What will happen to the girls?" Ava wanted to know.

"They'll be reunited with their families. Hopefully with counseling..." He took a deep breath. The thought of those other women and the evil they'd been subjected to was heartbreaking.

"That is good news," Mac said. "How long has Yvette been involved in this?"

Nolan hesitated, dread churning inside him. To Mac and Ava, this was over. But to his investigator's mind, there were still several unknowns. "According to Yvette, it all started right here in Sculpin Bay, ten years ago."

Mac bolted upright. "She better not have accused my son in any of this. My Kevin would never do anything so evil."

Nolan looked from him to Ava. "She didn't. And I believe you. But there are still a lot of unanswered questions, and it's my job to answer them."

That night, Nolan and Creed left Burke House and went back to the Copper Jack Motel. Over the next several days, he called and texted, but he didn't visit in person. One day he sent Cam over with Creed for a few follow-up questions. Cam said he'd sent her as her first "light duty" assignment, but Ava and Mac both knew it was less a need for any answers from them and more a way to reassure the Burkes that Cam was doing fine now. And to send Creed for a visit with Rose.

Rose was delighted. Creed brought out the best in her. As would the new pony Mac was having delivered in just a few days. Surrounded by her loving family and with Jane's help once again, Ava felt in her heart that Rose was going to be okay.

Penn's press conference the day after the final arrests had been made had opened a plethora of interest in Ava's story, and the press had been relentless. Mac assured her that it would all die down soon, and things would get back to normal. The question was what would "normal" be like going forward?

Ava used her time away from Nolan to pray about her feelings for him. Her mind kept returning to the kiss they'd shared. The way it had felt so right yet brought up feelings of guilt. Was it too soon? Was it the right thing for Rose? She also remembered the judgmental faces of the other women in the restaurant that day she'd had that disturbing encounter with Derek, and a part of her worried what others would think of her, in a relationship so soon after her husband's passing.

Now she climbed the hill toward the family graveyard and sat at the base of the sugar maple overlooking Burke House, the home she'd come to love, and the gravestone of her husband, whom she'd always love, and beyond over the vast waters of Lake Superior. The rough, choppy water mirrored her mood. But she remembered what Mac had said about prayer and trust, and she turned over all the doubts of her heart to God, praying that He'd bring her answers and peace. As she prayed, Nolan's rental Explorer pulled up the drive and parked. Ava watched as the front door of the house burst open and Rose ran out, meeting Creed in the yard.

"Hi, boy, hi. Hi, Nolan!" Rose smiled and waved.

Mac stepped out of the house, too, and talked to Nolan, shaking his hand and pointing him to where she sat.

She stayed where she was, waiting as he climbed the hill. He carried something in his hand, a piece of paper. Proof against Kevin or a written accusation from Yvette, perhaps, but for some reason, Ava didn't feel dread. She trusted that whatever news he brought, God would get her through. He always did.

She greeted him with "You're here. I didn't know when I'd see you again."

"I've been occupied."

"Oh? Wrapping up the investigation?"

"Yes. And…interviewing."

"Interviewing? Where are you going?"

He sat down in front of her. "Malone Bay. Leroy and Ruth are retiring, moving out northwest to be closer to family. I interviewed for the position and got it."

She congratulated him and meant it. Her heart warmed at the idea of Nolan being closer. And he'd be so happy in that cozy cabin on the island. She'd thought about Ruth and Leroy and how happy they'd been tucked away on Malone Bay during the summer months, homeschooling their daughter and then living on the mainland during the offseason. The best of both worlds. What a beautiful life.

He held up the paper, pulling her back to reality. "I've brought you answers," he said. "A couple saw Penn's press conference, and…well, they came to the sheriff's department with this letter that was written to their son." He handed it to her. "This is what Kevin delivered that day he detoured to Houghton. Kevin wrote it."

"Kevin?" She unfolded it and read, her husband's voice floating through her head.

Dear Samuel,

I'm writing you this letter because I need to make something right. I was there when you were born, and I promised your mother that I would never tell anyone about you or where you came from. I've kept that promise for over ten years, believing that I was doing the right thing. I was wrong.

Your mother was forced by bad people into things beyond her control. But she said you were a blessing, the only real gift she'd ever been given. And even though she feared she'd be killed by running off with you, she risked her life to save yours.

I happened upon her while she was on the run and

took her to a motel, where she had you in secret. She labored all night, and after you were born, she looked at you with so much love, it made my heart hurt. That night she told me that because of the life she was forced to live, it would be impossible to know who your father was. And her own parents, your grandparents, hadn't treated her well. It's important that you know that she wasn't angry toward anyone who had hurt her. She said she held no grudges; she was at peace. Because she'd had you.

She asked me to help pick a name for you. There was a Bible in the hotel room, and she flipped through the pages, looking for just the right name. She picked Samuel—meaning "a strong faithful man, dedicated to the Lord," a name given by his mother, Hannah. That was your mother's name—Hannah Richter.

I believe that more than anything, she wanted to keep you. But she knew she couldn't and still protect you. The next morning, she was gone. She left a note asking me to keep her secret and find a safe home for you. She'd made the ultimate sacrifice. She left you to save you.

I kept my promise and honored her wishes and drove you thirty miles away to Holy Protection Monastery. In my young mind, I thought the name—Holy Protection— was a sign that I was doing the right thing. I know now that I was wrong. Had I gone to the police and told them everything, your mother might have lived. As it was, the bad people caught up to her, and she died three days later.

The story of a newborn left secretly at the monastery hit the news and said that the child went to a family in Houghton. I was happy you'd found a home, but guilt ate at me. Over the years, I started a secret account and had money sent to you every month in hopes that you would use it for college or something else to make your life and the lives of those you love better.

It wasn't until my daughter started to grow up and I witnessed the special bond and love shared between my wife and her that I realized that it was time to break that promise to your mother. You deserve to know the truth about how desperately she loved you. And you deserve to know how you got your name, Samuel. I pray that you live up to your name and that you live a life that honors the woman who chose it for you.

Ava turned to Nolan with tear-filled eyes. "Thank you," she whispered.

"Your husband was a good man, Ava."

"He was a blessing to me. To both of us."

"And he was blessed to have you as his wife. Any man would be."

Her breath caught, and she glanced away. But he reached out and touched her face, drawing her attention to him, meeting her gaze. "You are the most amazing woman I've ever known. You don't even realize how strong you are, do you? Ava, you could be resentful or bitter, but you remain faithful and loving to everyone, and when I watch you with Rose... you're such a good mother. And a good wife. This whole time, you've remained true to Kevin's memory. Fighting for him."

"Nolan, I..."

"Wait, please, I need to finish." He took her hands in his and held on tight. "I could never take Kevin's place. I wouldn't want to. But I would like the chance to be your husband, to be a good stepfather to Rose. And I promise that I will do everything I can to make sure she knows how good of a man her father was. I will honor his memory while I strive to make new memories for both of you. A lifetime of memories for whatever time we have left on this earth. That is...if you'll marry me?"

She looked deep into his eyes and knew the answers she'd prayed for had been delivered. By a letter about the first man she'd ever loved. And by the promise of the man before her who she also loved. "Yes," she answered.

And he kissed her again, a gentle kiss, full of beauty and trust...and love.

* * * * *

Romantic Suspense

Danger. Passion. Drama.

Available Next Month

Colton At Risk Kacy Cross
Renegade Reunion Addison Fox

Canine Refuge Linda O. Johnston
A Dangerous Secret Sandra Owens

 LOVE INSPIRED

Searching For Justice Connie Queen
Trained To Protect Terri Reed

 LOVE INSPIRED

Wyoming Ranch Sabotage Kellie VanHorn
Hiding The Witness Deena Alexander

 LOVE INSPIRED

Lethal Reunion Lacey Baker
A Dangerous Past Susan Gee Heino

6 brand new stories each month

Romantic **Suspense**

Danger. Passion. Drama.

MILLS & BOON

Keep reading for an excerpt of a new title
from the Intrigue series,
FUGITIVE HARBOUR by Cassie Miles

Chapter One

A jagged shard of lightning pierced the low-hanging clouds and streaked across the night sky above the Cape Absolute lighthouse on the Oregon coast. The bolt might have struck a tall Sitka spruce, or torn a chunk off the basalt cliffs, or spent its force plunging to the depths of the roiling Pacific. Standing at the mullioned window in the dining room of the lightkeeper's cottage, Ava Donovan touched her fingertip to the cold glass and traced the path of a raindrop down the pane. She braced for the thunder. In seconds, an explosive boom rattled her eardrums.

A lightning storm was unusual for the coast. They got plenty of rain, but only a few of the storms erupted into lightning. The celestial light show mesmerized her and sent shivers marching down her spine. Not that she was cold. Her plaid, flannel pajamas and wool socks kept her plenty warm.

She turned away from the window and padded down a short hallway to the study where a desk lamp shone on a document she'd been studying—a copy of a lightkeeper's log from the 1920s, one of the few written by a woman, Elizabeth Mayes, known as the Widow of Cape Absolute.

Ava took a seat at the rolltop desk, straightened her shoulders and shook off her tension. *Nothing to be scared of.* The lightning was odd, but rain was typical for late April when the daffodils were up and rhododendrons started to bud. Night temperatures hovered in the forties. Gusting winds kicked up to thirty miles per hour. If she'd been an official lightkeeper, like Elizabeth, she would have paid attention to the tide charts and barometric readings, but she wasn't here to maintain a daily record. Her job for the next six to eight months was to renovate the buildings on this property in an accurate manner to satisfy the National Historic Landmark requirements.

Uniquely qualified, she had an MA in archeology and another in American history with a published thesis highlighting landmarks of the Pacific Northwest. In addition, she'd put herself through college working on home remodels. Happily, Ava had accepted the lighthouse project, which marked a step forward in her career, and moved into the cottage on a cliff jutting into the Pacific. The only access was an unmarked dirt road that veered off the paved route through the Siuslaw National Forest and wove through the old growth forest for 2.7 miles.

No traffic. No neighbors. No problem.

Though her family—three brothers and a sister—told her she'd be lonely, solitude didn't bother her. Still, she'd felt restless tonight, apprehensive for no particular reason. At eleven o'clock, she should have been tucked into bed. Instead, she wandered. After living here for two-and-a-half weeks, she knew her way around and left most of the lights off.

In spite of being referred to as a "cottage," the lightkeeper's residence was substantial—a two-story house that was separate from the lighthouse tower. The cottage had five bedrooms, an extra-large primary suite and three other rooms that could be converted to more bedrooms for the proposed B and B. Built in the late 1800s and refurbished several times since then, the cottage had a lot of square footage, lots of windows, lots of hallways and even a couple of secret passages, rumored to be used by ghosts of former lightkeepers.

From outside, she heard a crash.

Ava bolted to her feet and dashed back to the dining room window. Another flare of lightning illuminated the forty-eight-foot-tall tower at the edge of the headland cliff. The lighthouse stood about fifty yards away from the lightkeeper's cottage. The once proud beacon warning approaching vessels of dangerous rocks and shoals had been dark for over fifty years.

Peering into the night, she couldn't see well enough to know what caused the noise. The battery-powered light she'd installed over the lighthouse entrance wasn't very bright—just a glimmer. On a cloudy, rain-soaked night like this, moonlight provided scant illumination.

She waited for another lightning flash to give her a clearer view. An aluminum ladder had fallen outside the tower and smashed into a couple of sawhorses. Though she recalled using the ladder earlier, she couldn't imagine herself being so careless as to leave it standing unattended. A chilling thought occurred: someone else might have tampered with the ladder.

Though she didn't see a shadowy figure creeping through the night, Ava had legitimate reason for concern. Over the years, graffiti artists had literally made their mark on the whitewashed exterior of the tower. Of course, they wouldn't attempt to paint in the rain. But what about the interior? She'd purchased a lock for the door to discourage them from entering, but someone might use the cover of the storm to break inside and scrawl their mark on the walls. *Not on my watch.*

In the kitchen, she flicked on the overhead light before going out to the enclosed back porch to don a heavy-duty rain poncho over her pajamas. Rubber galoshes covered her socks. Armed with a Maglite from a shelf by the door, she turned on the back porch light and paused. Though she didn't see a vehicle parked beside her truck in the rear parking lot and hadn't heard a car approaching, intruders could have hiked through the forest.

She might be facing a vandal. An intruder. A dangerous person.

When her oldest brother—the notorious Barry Donovan—helped her move in, he warned about the dangers of a twenty-seven-year-old woman living alone in a secluded place like this. He disregarded her comment that she had practiced tai chi—which was, in fact, a martial art—for years. Moves like Cloud Hands and Grasping Bird Tail probably wouldn't stop an assailant.

Barry had taken her shopping for a gun.

Now might be the time to use it. Clumsy in galoshes, she ran through the dining room and down the hall to the desk in the study. In the lower right drawer of the old rolltop, a locked box held her brand-new Glock 48. Both Barry and the saleswoman told her it was lightweight, easy to handle and held ten rounds. To operate the weapon, she only had to aim and squeeze the trigger, unleashing the automatic safety. Just pull the trigger. *Easy enough.* Plus, the neon pink Glock gleamed with bravado.

Ava punched in the combination code to unlock the small gun safe, retrieved her weapon and checked the clip the way Barry showed her. *My phone!* She definitely needed her phone in case she had to call for backup. Taking it off the charger on the desk, she stuck the phone into the flappy pocket in her poncho and returned to the kitchen. Holding the flashlight and Glock in her left hand, she used her right to unlock the back door and pull up her hood. Glock in hand, she went down three rickety stairsteps. The wind from the northeast blew rain onto her back and shoulders, pushing her toward the lighthouse and the edge of the cliff. The crashing of waves against rock accompanied her footsteps with a primeval rhythm. The beam from her Maglite barely kept the darkness at bay.

She trudged onward. Though she'd pulled the hood over her head, rain spattered her nose and cheeks. With the hand holding the gun, she pushed her bangs off her forehead. Lightning burst across the night sky, and the trees became grasping shadows, threatening to drag her into the foreboding forest. She stumbled and fell to her knee in a puddle. Accidentally, her finger squeezed. The gun went off. An explosion rocked the air. She had fired into the dirt.

"Damn, damn, damn." She bounded to her feet and ran the last several yards, trying to ignore the twinge in her wrist from the pistol's recoil. A twenty-eight-foot aluminum extension ladder lay on its side blocking the lower portion of the closed door, but the lock remained firmly in place. Even if someone had gotten inside, they couldn't have reached out to refasten the hasp. Unless they had an accomplice. *There might be more than one of them.*

Peering through the rain at the back porch, she saw the cottage door hanging wide-open. *How could that be?* She thought she'd shut the door but had been busy juggling the gun, her phone and the flashlight. Apparently, she hadn't fastened the latch tightly enough.

Splashing through puddles, she hurried back to the cottage, climbed the three steps, entered, pulled the door closed and turned the key in the dead bolt. Off with the poncho. She hung it on a hook, kicked off her boots and returned the Maglite to its place on the shelf by the door. Still carrying her Glock, she padded into the kitchen in her damp socks. The overhead light shone on the worn green-and-yellow-patterned linoleum floor where a trail of watery footprints led into the adjoining dining room. *Trouble!* Her heart thumped heavily. While she'd been outside, an intruder must have crept into the cottage. Gaining entry might have been their plan all along.

She needed backup: 9-1-1. Her phone ought to still be in her poncho, but when she went back to the porch to look, the phone was gone. She must have dropped it when she fell or when she was running. Going outside and searching in the dark seemed futile. But calling for help seemed like the best option, even though emergency responders would take at least a half hour to get here. In the study, there was a landline and her car keys. All she needed to do was go through the kitchen to the dining room. From there, the study was down a short hallway. Place the call. Take the keys. And make a mad dash for her truck.

Cautiously, she inched toward the doorway leading to the dining room, which was dark except for faint moonlight through the windows. She reached around the corner and groped for the switch. A rustling noise crackled in her ears. She heard a shuffle, sensed his presence before he grasped her wrist and yanked hard.

Off-balance, she stumbled into the dining room. He clamped an arm around her belly and pulled her back against his chest. He easily overpowered her. Releasing her wrist, he twisted her arm and took the gun from her hand.

She inhaled and prepared to scream. Not that anyone could hear her. There were no neighbors. Just forest.

"I'm sorry, Ava."

"Who? What?"

"Let me explain."

She craned her neck and tried to see his face, but she couldn't turn her head far enough. "Who are you? How do you know me?"

"It's been a long time. Six years."

"Let me go." Her muscles tensed, but she couldn't move. He held her too tightly. His wet clothing soaked her flannel pajamas."Just relax."

"Tell me who you are?"

"You came after me with a gun. Let's make sure we're on the same page. Okay?" His tone softened, but his grasp stayed firm. "Six years ago, how old were you?"

"Twenty-one."

"Where were you?"

"Eugene." She'd been in grad school at the University of Oregon, working on her MA in archeology. She couldn't imagine why he was asking these mundane questions but figured the conversation might work in her favor. If she kept him talking, he might relax his grip, and she could escape. She asked, "Were you at U of O? Are you a Duck? Did we have a class together?"

"You wore your long, dark hair in a ponytail. You've cut it."

He knew her name, knew what she looked like. "Have you been stalking me?"

"Hell, no." He sounded offended as though he wasn't the sort of man who stooped to stalking. "I saw an article in the *Register* when you signed on for this project. And a recent photo."

She glanced toward the hallway that led to the study. If she could get there, she'd lock the door and make her call. There had to be something in that rolltop she could use as a weapon.

"I remember," he said, "you were an excellent swimmer. And diver."

His mention of her water skills was a clue. "We both must have been in the nautical archeology course that studied ship-wrecks near Coos Bay."

"You were the only woman in the class."

"Yeah, I was popular."

A chuckle rumbled in his chest, and she felt his grip loosen. *This is my chance.* She jabbed her left elbow into his gut and dodged to the right, slipping out of his clutches and falling to the floor. Though she wanted to go left, she was facing the opposite direction. On hands and knees, she crawled frantically toward the light in the kitchen.

He followed. Before she got very far, he grabbed her arms and pulled her up. Though caught, Ava didn't quit. She kept wriggling, fighting to free her arms and wildly kicking back at him. *To no avail.* He lifted her as though she weighed no more than a rag doll and carried her to a straight-back chair at the kitchen table. After he sat her in the chair, he stepped back a pace.

In the overhead light, she stared up at him. Her jaw dropped. "Professor Brody?"

"Are you okay? I didn't mean to hurt you."

"Why did you hide? You grabbed me. Why?"

"The gun." He reached behind his back and took her pink Glock from where he'd stashed it in the waistband of his jeans. Her lethal weapon looked tiny in his large hand. "When I heard gunfire, I didn't want to take the chance that you'd shoot first and ask questions later."

His response almost made sense. *Almost.* "Is there some logical reason why you couldn't come to the door—like a normal person—and ring the buzzer?"

"Would you have let me in?"

She pinched her lips in a tight, angry line and looked away from him, unwilling to be influenced by the glow emanating from his stormy gray eyes—eyes she remembered much too well. She'd spoken to him on the phone less than two weeks ago and couldn't believe she hadn't instantly recognized his voice. "I'd have slammed the door in your face."

"Haven't changed your mind."

"No."

Dr. Liam Brody placed her gun on the stained, cracked, beige tile countertop. "I need your help, Ava. But I'll understand if you refuse. You don't owe me anything."

As she stared at him, her firm resolve weakened. He had a mesmerizing effect on people, particularly on her. "If you understand that I don't want to get involved, why are you here?"

"I hope you'll give me a chance. Will you, at least, listen to me?"

Six years ago, she'd imagined herself in love with this tall, darkly handsome professor. They'd flirted and teased but kept a distance, except for one night when they were out on the dive boat, drinking beer on the deck and watching starlight dance across the waves. He embraced her. The warmth from his body raised her temperature several degrees, and she melted like chocolate in a double boiler. His kiss took her breath away.

Too quickly, he had turned away and apologized. An intimate relationship between professor and student was inappropriate. He never touched her again, much to her disappointment.

For years, his likeness had haunted her dreams. Liam Brody was educated, accomplished and looked great in his black wet suit with orange markings. Back then he was only thirty—young for a PhD—and had garnered international renown for the archeological reclamation of shipwrecks in the Strait of Juan de Fuca between Washington state and Canada. On the U of O campus, he'd been kind of a celebrity. A documentary crew had covered his accomplishments and praised him to the skies.

Recent news reports about him weren't so complimentary.

He was charged with murder.

"Is it true, Liam? Did you kill Stuart Whitcomb?"

"I don't think so. But I don't know for sure."

She'd followed the reports on his arrest and had heard that his defense centered on not remembering what happened. Certainly, that was a possible explanation. Amnesia often occurred in cases of trauma, especially when accompanied by a bout of unconsciousness. Still, selective forgetting seemed like an awfully convenient alibi for an accused murderer. "My sister is good friends with Stuart's ex-wife."

"I know. Stuart grew up in your hometown."

That coincidence was, of course, the reason he'd come to her for help. As a lifelong resident of Narcissus, she knew the ins and outs, the disasters and the triumphs of that small town on the Yaquina River. The Donovan family was an intrinsic part of the community. Her oldest brother had frequent confrontations with the local police, usually while drunk. Jerome, her youngest brother was a contractor who she'd hired to work on the lighthouse. Unlike Barry, he had a reputation as a hardworking, well-behaved pillar of the community with a wife and kids. Memories of the brother between those two, Michael, filled her mind and clenched her heart. Michael was eight years older than Ava who was the youngest. Shortly after he turned eighteen, he had been accused of murdering his girlfriend and wrongly convicted, sentenced to life in prison.

Ava had only been ten years old, too young to help her brother. All she could do was cry herself to sleep every night. It took twelve years to discover fresh DNA evidence proving his innocence. When he finally came home, she made it her mission to support him in spite of the townspeople and former friends who sneered at an ex-con even though he'd been proven innocent. When Michael decided to leave Narcissus and start over someplace new, she begged him to stay, offered to come with him and help out. She'd been twenty-four, old enough to make a difference in his life.

He refused to take her along. She'd just completed her university studies and had several relevant jobs and research studies lined up. Her life was going well, and Michael didn't want to disrupt her progress. He was proud of her. Told her how much her acceptance meant to him while he was incarcerated.

She'd always known he wasn't a murderer. Never ever stopped believing in him.

And now, there was Dr. Brody—a man in a similar predicament. If he wasn't guilty, she needed to take the risk and try to help him. If someone had stepped up and supported her brother, his life would have been different.

"I'll listen," she said, "but you'd better talk fast."

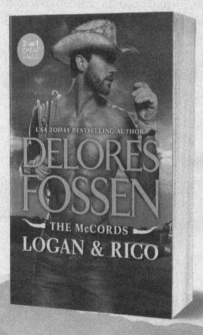